Praise for Magic Show:

When a neurologist receives a call from an archbishop, he becomes drawn into a mystery involving a Las Vegas winning streak, church politics, terrorists, magic, and the supernatural in this debut novel.

Gilbert Gilbertson, a wannabe magician, wins several once-in-a-lifetime jackpots, consecutively, at a number of Vegas casinos. He somehow manages to blur his face on security cameras and leaves a note, which, among other things, mentions neurologist Jack Madison, an amateur magician who writes books debunking myths, cons, and counterfeit miracles. When he begins to investigate the unlikely casino winner, Madison is suddenly forced to question his own beliefs about how the world works.

Michaelis' tale is not only complex on many levels, but deftly written, topical, and exhilarating. Throughout, Madison and readers are tossed back and forth between natural and paranormal explanations. Added to that, Madison must wrestle with his growing feelings for his partner in the investigation, Detective Lt. Joan Firestone. Together, they unearth information about Gilbertson and his sudden rise from a bumbling prestidigitator to an expert who baffles professionals with his proficiency. Meanwhile, a right-wing terrorist group wavers between hailing Gilbertson as a saint and condemning him as the Antichrist. Many of Madison's allies are not what they seem, and neither is the mysterious Gilbertson.

Michaelis nicely paces both the unraveling mystery and developing love affair, delivering readers an engrossing tale. At the same time, the author skillfully examines church politics and questions what exactly constitutes extrasensory perception and exceptional ability. This intricate and entertaining tale should appeal to fans of religious thrillers like The Da Vinci Code.

—Kirkus Reviews

Book design by:
Arbor Services, Inc.
www.arborservices.co/

Cover art by:
Michael Murdock
www.sabordesigns.com

Printed in the United States of America

Magic Show
Lawrence Michaelis

1. Title 2. Author 3. Fiction

Library of Congress Control Number: 2018904269
ISBN 13: 978-0-692-10357-9

LAWRENCE MICHAELIS

**with New York Times Best-selling Author
Maya Kaathryn Bohnhoff**

DEDICATED TO THE MEMORY OF:
William B.F. Hall
1905–1967 – Fort Wayne, Indiana

Bill Hall taught me that good magic is done with the head first,
then with the hands.

Acknowledgments

The author is deeply indebted to New York Times best-selling author Maya Kaathryn Bohnhoff for her extensive assistance, advice, editing, and structuring of this novel. It would have been impossible for me to complete this work without her.

My thanks to Emily Regan and Jeremy Kruse for assistance and advice on the first iterations.

I would not have completed this project without the input of my family and friends who encouraged me to complete it.

Special appreciation is extended to my daughter, Cecilia Prentice, for her wise and experienced counsel.

Contents

Preface

The Hindu rope trick is a legend in the world of magic. Stories about it—or something like it—date back to the 1300s, often told of Chinese jugglers. Far more common are performances by Indian street magicians or fakirs. The trick has allegedly been witnessed by thousands of people over the centuries; one variant was even captured on film (more on that later). I say "variant" because the trick is comprised of several elements, any one of which would be miraculous in and of itself.

All versions involve a conjurer and a length of rope. The magician throws one end of the rope into the air, where it stays as if caught by unseen hands. It mysteriously rises until the top of it disappears into thin air or darkness or clouds or perhaps another dimension. Now that's a pretty good trick right there, but as they say in the world of infomercials, "But, wait! There's more!"

The trick continues when a young boy climbs the rope until he disappears into thin air or darkness or whatever. Pretty cool, right? Ah, but wait! There's more.

Now, the fakir becomes agitated with the boy—perhaps because he refuses to reappear. He pulls out a sword or other sharp weapon and scurries up the rope after his assistant. As you might guess, he, too, disappears into thin air, and the crowd goes wild.

Great trick. But it's not over yet.

As the audience watches in horror, body parts rain from the afore-mentioned thin air onto the ground, or possibly into a large basket at the bottom of the rope. And this is where it gets truly magical. The fakir reappears, slides down the rope, and pops a lid on the big basket full of body parts. He may utter an incantation of some sort. When he takes the lid off the basket—ta-da!—the boy miraculously reappears, very much alive and with all his parts intact.

The trick of legend is alleged to have been performed in the open without benefit of modern technology. Or smoke. Or mirrors. Or proscenium arches and lofts. It was said to have been seen by countless thousands during the Raj.

What's the secret of the Hindu rope trick? Sleight of hand? Misdirection? Hypnosis?

None of the above. The secret of the Hindu rope trick, I submit, is human gullibility and suggestibility.

Peter Lamont, researcher at the University of Edinburgh and a former president of the Magic Circle in that city, maintains that the rope trick was a hoax perpetrated by the *Chicago Tribune* in 1890 for the purpose of increasing circulation. In fact, the *Tribune* admitted, months after the story ran (under the byline Fred S. Ellmore; get it?), that this had been the case.

And it worked. It worked because their audience—many of whom believed in religious miracles or folk magic—didn't find the story far-fetched. Yet, as I've explained, this trick didn't originate with the *Tribune*'s editorial staff; it was merely exploited by them. It exists as a believable legend for the same reason so many readers of the *Tribune* failed to recognize the hoax: human suggestibility. Lamont referred to it as the "exaggeration effect." Simply put, the more time elapses between seeing something and telling someone about it, the more a person exaggerates the event.

About twenty years ago, my colleague and mentor, Sam Bernstein, interviewed two British missionaries and an American physician who claimed to have seen a variant of the trick performed by an Indian holy man outdoors: the rope stood upright, the fakir climbed it, disappeared, then reappeared and climbed back down. Dr. Bernstein interviewed each man separately, and they were in complete agreement on what they had seen. All three also agreed to let Sam hypnotize them. Their recollections of the event remained identical—down to minute detail. For the record, Sam Bernstein is arguably one of the most effective medical hypnotists in the world.

"But wait, Dr. Madison!" you're thinking. "You said there was a film."

I *did* say there was a film—a 16mm home movie (not the greatest quality—but good enough) that showed the fakir standing next to a coiled rope the entire time. *According to that film, nothing the three men described in glowing detail actually happened.*

What did happen? Sam and I were convinced these three gentlemen thought they saw what they described, and after all these years, they continue to stick to their story.

Human suggestibility? Maybe. But there are other possibilities. Researchers have offered mass hypnosis, levitation, astral projection, a magic trick involving mirrors, poles, or a suspended wire so thin as to be invisible to watchers, to which the thrown rope attaches itself. Hell, maybe the cameraman screwed up the filming.

Now, you're probably thinking, "But, Dr. Madison, doesn't Ockham's razor demand that you at least consider the simplest explanation—that there really is magic in the world? That a miracle is possible?"

Not at all. William of Ockham was a Franciscan monk—a man of the Church, predisposed to believe in miracles, if not outright magic. The Hindu rope trick, if it ever existed as a legitimate act of legerdemain, is some form of hoax.

Which begs the question: what is a hoax?

—Dr. Jack Madison, MD, from a lecture given at Carnegie-Mellon University, June 18, 2001 (published in *The Inquiring Skeptic,* October 2001 issue)

Chapter 1

"This evening's final guest, Dr. Jack Madison, has been on the show many times, and tonight we will be discussing subjects from his controversial new book: Medicine, Magic, and Miracles. Jack, as you certainly know, the book has been labeled 'divisive' by a number of Church spokesmen because of your treatment of the subject of miracles—specifically the sort of miracles the Church commonly uses to justify canonization. The pot you're stirring is boiling even higher here in Chicago because of our large population of Polish Catholics and your views on the illegitimacy of the canonization of Pope John Paul II. For many devout Catholics, miracles are the truest expression of a belief system that, otherwise, must be taken on pure faith. But miracles are cited to validate sainthood. Isn't that correct?"

"Adam, that is one of the best definitions I have ever heard of the word miracle as it exists within the Catholic Church. And, of course, this is ironic since the Christ of the Gospels downplayed miracles and used them as symbols of a greater or more significant reality. There are multiple ways you can understand what it means to be lame."

Dr. Jack Madison glanced up at the sound of his own voice coming from the flat-screen TV in the neurology unit's sparsely tenanted waiting room. It was tuned to a popular local talk show for which he'd recorded a book interview. He thought he looked pretty good

1

for a fifty-year-old with twice as much mileage as that age suggested. He sometimes reminded himself of the venerable Volvo he'd given his daughter, Kate, when she'd gone off to college: still sleek, still solid, with plenty of miles left on the engine. His hair was going to a professorial silver at the temples, but he knew from the gender balance of the long lines at his book signings that he was still attractive to women. Not, he told himself, that it mattered. The thought of having a woman in his life was still painful for reasons he was eager to distract himself from.

"Adam, the canonization of John Paul II is especially troublesome to me," TV Jack said. "The so-called miracle was lame, even by Church standards, and John Paul, although he did many good things in his life, was notorious for totally ignoring the horrible plague of pedophilia in the Church—circumstances that ruined countless thousands of lives and which he might have prevented. To compound things, he then provided sanctuary from prosecution for a number of offenders, including the American bishop, Bernard Law, and a Mexican priest named Marcial Degollado—a pedophile, womanizer, embezzler, and drug addict."

Jack turned his back on the TV and joined the little bevy of residents, interns, and students he'd been herding through teaching rounds in the Neurology Department of Chicago's Midwestern School of Medicine.

"So, who's presenting on the next patient?"

A young first-year resident with dark curly hair and gray horn-rimmed glasses bobbed his head and raised his hand. "That'd be me, Dr. Madison."

Jack gestured down the hall. "Lead on, MacDuff."

The first-year—Kyle Berliner by name—turned and began walking, consulting his iPad as he went. "Uh, the patient is Billy Turner, age twenty-four, suffering from meningitis. He's responded very well to treatment but still has a mild headache and some dizziness . . ."

Kyle turned in at the door of a room on the right-hand side of the broad, bright corridor, continuing to rattle off a summary of his clinical notes to the group. Jack brought up the rear.

Behind him, in the waiting room, his onscreen self said:

"I have spent my life studying the relationship between illness and the mind. That includes spontaneous healing and remission. In the Church's eye, if someone prays for the intercession of a potential saint and obtains relief, it is assumed, res ipsa loquitur, that the remission was caused by this dead person's intercession. But it's bogus, Adam, phony—a religious flimflam worthy of an old-time tent show revival. That something like this is considered proof that John Paul II—a pope who had complete disregard for an incredible moral disaster in his Church—now has special access to God's decision-making process, is simply appalling."

Jack heard the acid in his voice. It made him cringe a little. He prided himself on being forthright and unapologetic in his views but knew he sometimes stepped over a slender line into mockery. It was hard not to, given the absurdity of the subject matter.

He shook his head and ducked into the room where Billy Turner reclined in his raised hospital bed, blinking at the teaching team, their faces glowing slightly in the light of their tablets. The TV was on, but with the volume turned down. Kyle Berliner was outlining the prognosis, which was good—miracle enough for Jack. Meningitis was nothing to trivialize.

Neither was this tour of duty in the neurology service. Even tenured professors had to take their turn, as Jack was doing today. He savored this part of his job more than nearly anything he did. It gave him two hours a day that he was free from phone calls, committee meetings, academic bureaucracy, dealing with his agent, hyping his latest book, or answering interviewers' questions. Seeing patients and teaching bright young people kept him focused . . . which was not to say he wasn't looking forward to the vacation he'd scheduled to begin tomorrow morning.

"So, Billy," he said, "do you have any questions for Team Turner?"

"Yeah, how soon can I get back to work—I mean after you let me outta here? My dad and sister are running our shop all by themselves—Mom doesn't know squat about cars—so they need me back yesterday."

"Well, we can't do yesterday, but what *can* we do . . . Kyle?"

The young resident pushed his glasses up his nose and consulted his device. "We hope to discharge him within twenty-four hours after the dizziness goes away. As early as Friday afternoon. Uh, then a light work schedule could be resumed roughly a week after that, with Dr. Thomas's approval, of course." He nodded at the chief resident, Sally Thomas, who stood in the rear of the tour.

"How light?" Billy wanted to know.

Kyle and his colleagues looked to Jack.

"You're the best judge of that, Billy," Jack said, "if you're honest with yourself. You do no one any good—least of all your family and your business—if you overdo things."

Billy smiled. "So, brake jobs, yes—engine jobs, no?"

Jack wagged his head. "Sounds fair. But, if you have any sign of a fever, or any more than a slight headache or dizziness, you get in touch with us ASAP."

After a moment more of consultation, the team filed out of the room with Jack trailing.

"Hey, that's you, isn't it, Doc?"

Jack turned back to Billy, who'd picked up the TV remote and was gesturing with it at the television. Jack followed the gesture to the screen. It was the same program that was running in the waiting room.

"Yeah, that's me. I did that interview last night."

Billy had turned the sound back up a bit. Jack could hear the interview as an underlay to their own conversation.

"I feel quite comfortable in stating that I have seen many remissions of serious diseases," TV Jack was saying, *"a few cases that I would say qualify as spontaneous cures, and more than a few misdiagnoses. Not one has related to praying to a dead pope. Take the woman from Costa Rica who was cured of a brain aneurysm. I cover her case in my book in some detail, but in a nutshell, why could it have not simply thrombosed—filled with blood and clotted so that it was no longer a threat?"*

Billy shook his head. "Praying to a pope. Man, that's just not right, is it? I mean, a pope is still just a guy, right? You pray to God. Right?"

"So, Dr. Madison," the talk show host asked, *"do you believe in miracles at all? Do you think there has ever been a legitimate one?"*

"Not in my experience. At least, not by the religious definition. And every last one is related to subjective complaints and explainable by nonmiraculous means. Now, if I saw the healing of a cleft palate or third-degree burns, then I'd be more inclined to belief, but as I see it, what the Church calls miracles are just another attempt to prove what can never be proven—the existence of God. They're in the same category as Bigfoot sightings and UFOs."

Jack could feel Billy Turner's gaze on his face. "You don't believe in God, Dr. Madison?"

The TV host echoed the question a second later: *"Do you believe in God?"*

The Jack on TV leaned forward in his chair and posed another question in return: *"Tell me, Adam, what do you mean by God?"* The host came back with something about needing to book another appearance to discuss that.

Jack gave Billy a wry smile. "I guess I'm not sure about God, Billy." "I am. And I'm sure about miracles, too. It was a miracle that I made it to this hospital in time for you to save my life. A lot of people who get meningitis don't live to tell about it."

"Yes, that's true. But that's the kind of miracle I *do* believe in—a miracle of science."

Jack heard a soft sound from the hallway and turned. Sally Thomas was in the open doorway, leaning casually against the frame. The rest of the team was clustered behind her across the hall, poring over their notes.

"Care to join us, Dr. M?"

Jack gestured at her. "Dr. Thomas here will be in to see you in the morning, Billy. She'll decide if you're ready for discharge and set up your office visits. She'll also help you decide when it's time for you to go back to work."

Sally nodded. "All true. And if you have any problems, I expect you to call me right away. If your dizziness and headaches stay gone, you probably can go back to work in about a week after discharge, but no sooner. The last thing any of us want, including yourself, is an accident at work—like a car falling on that big, thick head of yours."

Billy raised both hands in a defensive gesture. "Hey, I swear I'm feeling better already. The headache's almost gone." He gave the two doctors a pleading look. "Are you sure I can't go back to work sooner? I mean, what'm I gonna do at home for a whole week?"

Sally laughed. "From what some of the nurses have been telling me about the girl who's been visiting you, I'm sure you'll think of something."

Jack and Sally stepped out into the hall, half closing the door behind them. Jack checked his watch. Sally looked up from tapping notes into her patient-tracking app.

"What's the matter, Jack? Got an emergency talk show?"

"Actually, Jerry Springer and I are going out to cruise Rush Street tonight, scouring the neighborhood for interesting characters. He can put them on his show and I can write them into my next book." He spoke loudly enough for the rest of the team to hear; he appreciated the knowing smiles. The students especially enjoyed him poking fun at himself; he sure as hell got his share of pokes from others at MSM who thought his writings were too sensational for a major medical school. Jack was not known for his political correctness.

"Seriously, Sal, if you wouldn't mind taking over and finishing up rounds, I'd appreciate it. I've got an early flight in the morning, and I really need to get home and finish packing. I'm officially off the clock in about forty-five minutes anyway."

"No problem. Let me know if there's anything you need me to do while you're gone. I promise I'll keep close tabs on Billy. He's likely to take it into his head to go back to work without talking to me."

"Just make sure he stays on antibiotics for an entire month."

"You got it." She flipped him a jaunty salute, turned on her heel, and went off to gather the troops.

Jack had barely taken two steps in the opposite direction when he heard someone calling his name. He turned to see his longtime administrative assistant, Hillary Riles, striding purposefully down the corridor toward him. She had a troubled look on her face.

"Dr. Madison, I know I'm not supposed to interrupt you during teaching rounds, but you have an urgent call from the Office of the Archdiocese. Cardinal Archbishop O'Connor has asked if you can drop by his residence for dinner."

Jack was puzzled. "An urgent dinner?"

"A dinner *meeting*, he said. He didn't tell me what he wants to see you about, but he told me it was important."

It wasn't unusual to get a call from Tom O'Connor, but an urgent call was downright mysterious. Jack's curiosity was piqued. Thoughts of packing evaporated as he followed Hillary to the elevator and back to his office. Curiosity, Jack knew, had been the strongest motivator in his life. It could be a blessing or a curse, and he often wasn't sure which.

Back in the office, Jack grabbed his laptop and his coat and asked Hillary, for probably the twentieth time, if she had everything she needed from him to keep the office humming while he was gone. He'd worked with Hillary for over ten years in his practice. Hillary was never much for small talk and was so class conscious, she never called him by his first name. He had the absurd idea that she probably called her husband "Mr. Riles" like one of those characters in a Jane Austen novel.

Now, she gave him a reproachful yet arch look and informed him (as if he didn't already know) that he was free the rest of the evening and that she had cleared his teaching calendar for the next two weeks. Then, to put him completely in his place, she reminded him of his departure time to the Virgin Islands the next day.

Touché.

He was chuckling as he trotted down three flights of stairs, stepped outside, and grabbed a cab. It was the last day of February, the worst month in Chicago. The city had not seen the sun for at least ten days, and the streets of the Loop were filled with wet, dirty snow and disgruntled drivers. Jack was looking forward to some sun, snorkeling, bone fishing, and time alone at Caneel Bay in St. John's. At least that's what he told anyone who asked.

On the cab ride home, he texted his agent to make sure nothing was brewing on that front, then turned his mind to the urgent call from Cardinal O'Connor. The most likely catalyst was his latest book. It was undoubtedly his most controversial, at least in Catholic circles, as it spent many pages debunking religious miracles. He more than suspected that tonight's *Adam Keenan Show* had pushed the good cardinal over the edge. If that was the case, he must've called the office before the end commercials had run.

Jack had known Thomas O'Connor since he was an up-and-coming diocesan priest. He'd been a patient referred to Jack for headaches that turned out to be caused by a small, benign tumor of the covering of Tom's brain that was easily removed. During the course of the priest's treatment, the two men had become good, if unlikely, friends. They had a lot in common; both were outdoorsmen who loved to camp and fish. They managed to sneak away several times a year for four or five days with a group of buddies. Tom would fish, drink, smoke cigars, and tell off-color jokes like an ordinary man. Since he'd been named cardinal four years ago, the fishing trips had stopped, but the friendship had continued, celebrated with the occasional cozy dinner.

With the ascension of Pope Francis, Tom's cachet with the Church in Rome had increased greatly; Jack was pretty certain he'd be called to the Vatican one of these days and then there would be neither fishing trips nor dinners. He shook his head. A prince of the Church and an angry agnostic. What a pair.

The cab dropped Jack off at home—a WWI vintage brownstone that he and Carolyn had had completely remodeled when the girls were in middle school. Since her death eighteen months earlier, he'd thought about selling the place in favor of setting himself up in a smaller urban bachelor pad, but the girls still needed a place to come home to, and he knew, without having to ask, that this would always be home to them. So he stayed, living among all the reminders of what he'd had and lost.

He trotted up the front steps, steeling himself for that moment when he walked through the door to the familiar scents of wood oil and cedar that had always marked Carolyn's territory. He pretended not to anticipate the sound of her voice. That got a bit easier each day.

Except today. Today he was about to take his first-ever vacation without her to a place they had talked about going together but never had. A hit-and-run driver had made certain of that when he plowed into her in the bike lane on their quiet residential street. If Jack gazed from their second-floor bedroom window, he could see the spot where Carolyn had begun to die. He hadn't looked out that window for over a year.

He owed Tom O'Connor a huge debt for guiding him and the girls through their grief. His old friend knew how to keep the right mix of faith and reason in their grieving process. Tom had told Jack once that it was easier for men of the cloth to be friends with heathens than with apostates, but Tom had somehow gotten around that in Jack's case. Any last vestige of Jack Madison's childhood Catholicism had died with his wife on Juniper Street.

Distracting himself by mentally humming Brubeck's "Take Five," Jack vaulted up the stairs and went about changing his shirt, his tie, and his jacket without looking at anything that would bring Carolyn to mind or, like the lone suitcase on the window seat, remind him that his mind was now the only place in the universe she still lived.

Chapter 2

The cardinal archbishop of the diocese of Chicago lived in a drab, stone, post-Victorian mansion on several acres along North State Parkway south of Lincoln Park. Jack's cab dropped him at the bottom of the driveway at six o'clock p.m. It was already full-on dark, so the house was lit from within, the leaded glass in the front door and sidelights making it look as if it were vaguely hungover from Halloween.

Jack had no more than set foot on the porch when the front door was opened by a young, tall, serious-faced Franciscan priest dressed in the order's brown robe and knotted rope belt—three knots as a reminder of the vows of poverty, chastity, and obedience or, as a Franciscan had once told Jack, "No money, no honey, and I've got a Boss—for all eternity." Jack suspected this guy wouldn't get the joke.

The priest ushered Jack into the dimly lit foyer, which was decorated with oil portraits of several of the cardinal's more prominent predecessors. "Good evening, Dr. Madison," he said in a soft, throaty voice that suggested he'd gotten some woodwind instrument lodged in his throat. "I'm Father Lyons. Thank you for coming on such short notice; your secretary was most accommodating. Cardinal O'Connor is in his study and asked if you would join him and his other guests there."

Other guests? Hillary hadn't mentioned that there'd be other guests. Puzzled and curious, Jack gave Lyons his coat and scarf, then followed him down a short hallway that ran to the left of the broad central staircase. Jack opened his mouth to say that he knew the way to Tom's study, but Lyons was already tapping on the half-open study door.

"Cardinal, Dr. Madison is here."

The cardinal came to the door himself and swung it wide, greeting Jack with a handshake and a brief hug. He ushered Jack into the room, turning back to stop Lyons before he, too, could enter.

"Father Lyons, I'd like to dine at seven. Have Arthur put the food out on the sideboard. We'll serve ourselves; I want no interruptions."

Lyons's posture was suddenly more rigid. He pulled himself to his full height and looked down his nose at the cardinal. "Of course, Your Eminence."

Jack hid a smile. Cardinal Thomas O'Connor was a big guy—six-feet-four inches, two-hundred-twenty pounds of solid muscle. The fact that Lyons *could* look down at him made Jack realize that Lyons was taller than he'd first thought; he merely slumped to make himself seem smaller. Franciscans, after all, took vows intending to quell the ego through service—to attain anonymity before man so as to get noticed by God.

Tom O'Connor was not such a man. Jack would describe him as larger than life. At fifty-three, he had a full head of wavy, jet black hair and shockingly pale eyes. He was moderate, as American cardinals went, and the best natural politician Jack had ever met. Right now, he looked poised and relaxed in gray slacks and a blue turtleneck sweater, an outfit he would never be seen wearing in public and which stood in marked contrast to Lyons's uniform. Jack wondered if that offended Father Lyons's obviously formal sensibilities. He seemed the kind of guy who would like to see his cardinal dressed for Mass 24/7.

Beneath the subdued overhead lighting set in a coffered ceiling, the cardinal's large study held an uncluttered mahogany desk topped by an old-fashioned green banker's lamp, with a pair of leather upholstered armchairs in front of it. On the other side of the room, two teal leather love seats and several matching easy chairs were arranged around a hearth where a fire burned cheerfully. This was where the cardinal's other guests were seated. They rose as Jack joined them.

They were a mixed bag: a nondescript middle-aged cleric in a black suit with a Roman collar, a skinny sixtyish guy in a four-thousand-dollar Armani double-breasted silk suit with garish diamond cuff links, and a stunningly beautiful African-American woman in a charcoal gray business suit. She had *café au lait* skin with an unusual hint of copper, and calves that proclaimed her an athlete. Jack guessed she must be in her late thirties or early forties, though her complexion was ageless.

"Folks," Tom said, "I would like to introduce my dear friend, Dr. Jack Madison. Jack, this is Bishop Robert Powell of the diocese of Las Vegas, Mr. Arnie Rosen who represents the Nevada Casino Association, and Detective Lieutenant Joan Firestone of the Las Vegas Metropolitan Police—Casino Fraud Division. She has been assigned to the case we are about to discuss."

Jack pulled his gaze away from Joan Firestone long enough to shake hands with the men. When he took her hand and met her gaze, he was struck anew by her unusual features; her eyes weren't dark brown as he'd expected, but a rare shade of deep amber.

"Hello, Dr. Madison," she said in a voice like warm honey.

She smiled, and Jack found himself smiling broadly in return. "Jack, please," he said reflexively. Realizing he'd held her hand a moment too long, he released it and turned back to Tom.

"Before we begin," the cardinal said, looking Jack square in the eyes, "I want to give you my assurance that Jack is a man of absolute discretion, and he has my full confidence that this will remain a private matter."

Okay, message received. Whatever we're going to discuss is not to become fodder for a morning talk show or an exposé.

"A few days ago," the cardinal began as his guests seated themselves, "I was contacted by Cardinal Munoz of the archdiocese of Los Angeles. Cardinal Munoz is an old friend of mine. He's new to his job and asked me if I would lend a hand with a . . . situation that could be embarrassing to the Church. Cardinal Munoz was concerned about the provenance of a particularly large donation that came to a Catholic charity set up within his archdiocese for people who have been victims of child abuse by the clergy."

"The provenance of the donation?" repeated Jack.

"The gift came from a man who won it in Las Vegas, under most unusual circumstances. The man is giving it all away to this organization and has pledged three million more in the near future. As this occurred in Bishop Powell's diocese and he was made aware of it by Mr. Rosen—" the cardinal gestured at that gentleman "—he called Cardinal Munoz to consult about the matter."

Jack shook his head and shrugged. "It sounds like a very generous gift. If it was fairly won, why would the Church—and the LVMP—get involved?"

"The donor sent copies of letters to Bishop Powell that he intends to release to Las Vegas media outlets at some point in the near future. These letters promise even larger amounts of money to be sent to organizations all over the country that advocate for victims of clerical sexual abuse."

Jack stood, annoyance tickling his hindbrain. "Tom, if you're going to tell me this is about the reputation of the Church . . ."

The cardinal raised a hand. "Jack, please, hear me out. This man claims he is going to win the money legally in Las Vegas, and he's been explicit about the amounts. Certainly that's a lot of money, and yes, the bad press will open up some old wounds for the diocese. But that's not the central issue here. The way this fellow obtained the money is highly suspicious and has the powers that be in Las Vegas more than a bit concerned."

"Tom, I'm due to start my vacation first thing in the morning. I really don't see how this could possibly be—"

"Please, Jack. Sit. Mr. Rosen, if you'd be so good as to explain . . ."

Rosen leaned forward in his chair, putting the elbows of his elegant suit on his knees. Jack caught a whiff of an equally elegant—and no doubt expensive—cologne.

"Dr. Madison, I've been working in Vegas for over forty years, and what I am about to tell you is the most amazing thing that I, and my bosses at the Casino Association, have ever seen. It's no exaggeration to say that it could have a profound effect on the future of Las Vegas. I'm grateful for your promise of absolute confidentiality."

"As am I," interrupted Bishop Powell. "Please understand, Doctor, Las Vegas is not all wealth. It has a large population of the poor, indigent, and destitute that looks to the Church and Catholic charities for ongoing assistance. The Casino Association has always made generous contributions to our causes." He glanced aside at Rosen. "They have let it be known that they will have to be much less generous to balance these losses."

Rosen's lips twitched. "We're not a charity, Excellency. We're a business. We can't afford to spend more than we take in."

"Gentlemen," the cardinal said sharply, "you are wasting Dr. Madison's time. Mr. Rosen, please continue."

This was a tone Jack had never heard his old friend use before. Both Powell and Rosen seemed chastened by it.

Rosen said, "The man at the center of this brouhaha is a frequent visitor to Vegas but up until now has been an occasional and low-stakes gambler. Ten days ago, at two thirty in the afternoon, this guy won the Megabucks Progressive Wheel of Fortune Jackpot at the Tropicana for $7,100,000 and some change. These one-dollar slot machines are interconnected among a large number of our casinos, and someone wins a big jackpot like this every few years, so no big, right? We pay out, snap up the publicity and the photo ops, and go about our business."

"Just like that?" asked Jack.

Rosen shrugged. "Okay, a bit more than that. There's a protocol: take a lot of pictures, do an immediate background check, and then bring in our team of technicians to make sure the machine is absolutely straight and has not been tampered with. Everything checked out, so we wrote out a four-by-six-foot check and arranged for the money (minus the pound of flesh for the government, of course) to be transferred to a bank account set up for the winner at the Bank of Las Vegas. The money was deposited at ten the next morning. Like I said—so far, nothing all that unusual. In fact, we love this kind of publicity. News of it travels fast and brings slot players in by the busload.

"Okay, so this is where it gets weird. The next afternoon, the guy at the Tropicana calls his boss and tells him that none of the digital pictures of this guy's face are visible on the download or even in the camera. And he'd taken almost a dozen photos of the guy. Everything was clear as a bell through the viewfinder, but in the photos, where his face should have been, was nothing—it looks like a round white balloon."

Jack frowned. "Some kind of high-tech trick?"

Rosen shook his head. "Security's never seen anything like it. And the camera was never out of the photographer's possession."

"Maybe he was wearing some sort of reflective makeup?"

"I doubt that." The detective spoke for the first time since she'd greeted Jack. "Any light-refracting makeup would also distort his features if you were just looking at him."

"So . . . what?" said Jack. "A magic trick?"

"We don't know," said Tom. "Which is why when these folks explained the situation to me, you were the first person I thought of who might be able to shed some light on it."

Jack looked at Arnie Rosen. "Do I detect a 'but wait, there's more' in this scenario?"

"Oh, yeah. There's more all right. Do you know what keno is, Dr. Madison?"

"I'm not that much of a sucker, sorry."

"Keno is one of the most popular games in Vegas and one of the most lucrative for the house. Odds are over sixteen percent in our favor, and for the guest it's cheap and easy to play. Doesn't require a lot of bandwidth. You buy a one-dollar keno card and circle from one to twenty numbers on the card. A machine then randomly selects twenty numbers that are posted on large monitors throughout the casino so guests can play anywhere—even on their hotel room TV sets. The payout is determined by how many numbers you pick and how many of those turn up. With me so far?"

Jack nodded.

"Most payouts are for four or five of the twenty numbers chosen. But if you check off ten numbers on your card and all ten are among the twenty chosen, you can win up to $250,000 for a one-dollar ticket. That's the maximum payout allowed. It happens once or twice a year. Okay, so the day after Mr. Lucky Balloon Face won the Progressive Jackpot, he buys twelve one-dollar cards from four other casinos: the Monte Carlo, Mandalay Bay, MGM, and the Golden Nugget. All different games, all numbered differently. Each was a $250,000 winner." As he recited this information, Rosen's expression got grimmer and grimmer. "Do the math, Doc. That's $3,000,000 in keno payouts from four different casinos in one evening. It is unheard of in the history of gambling."

"That is . . . extraordinary," Jack admitted.

Rosen dropped the other shoe. "Our lucky winner sent photos of those twelve cards, which are redeemable for up to ninety days, to Las Vegas TV stations and newspapers, along with letters explaining that all of the winnings—slot machine and keno—will go to kids who were screwed up by pedophile priests."

Jack caught the tightening of Powell's mouth, though Tom's expression remained meticulously neutral.

"I'd've said this was impossible," Rosen went on, "but we have absolutely no evidence that there was cheating. In spite of that, we're so sure there had to be something screwy going on that we instructed the casinos to hold up on paying the keno cards. Obviously, we can only obstruct that for so long, especially given the publicity about this guy giving the money to abuse victims."

"Are you sure it's the same guy?" Jack asked.

"Positive. Same build. Same type of cheap suit. Same hair. And in all of the videos his face is blank."

"Balloon face?"

Rosen nodded.

"What about fingerprints?"

"He failed to leave any. Which could be pulled off with a number of tricks."

Jack spread his hands in bemusement. "Well, there's got to be a reasonable explanation. As you said, it's impossible. Even I understand enough about gambling to know that." He turned to Detective Firestone. "What's your take on this, Detective?"

"My take, Dr. Madison, is that I've no better idea what this is than anyone else. My team and I—with assistance from a variety of PIs hired by the casinos—have been on this case twenty-four hours a day since it happened. Most of these guys are real pros—some are ex-cheaters themselves—there's virtually nothing they haven't seen. The slot machine is clean. For sure. I'd bet my job on it. The keno cards . . ." She shook her head. Her hair—thick, black, and wavy—brushed the shoulders of her suit. "Twelve different cards, each with a different set of twenty numbers circled, for twelve different games, at four different casinos."

"I gather," Jack said, "that the numbers are chosen using some sort of random number generator."

"Uh-huh. State-of-the-art, computer-driven, and in an isolated environment that is passkey protected and offline. These are all high-end gaming establishments; they have world-class guards against cheating. And before you ask, yes, we checked the computer for signs of hacking anyway. Our experts have checked and rechecked every one of the keno games, given exhaustive interviews and polygraphs to every worker who could have possibly been involved, and we have close to a hundred different cameras that show absolutely no irregularities—except for the blank face on this guy. Which I've gotta say is really creepy."

She hesitated and made a wry face. "There's something else. The morning of the day our guy won the progressive jackpot, he came by my office at police headquarters beforehand. The desk sergeant let him in to see me. He sat down and announced that he was going to win a whole lot of money in the next few days but that it was all going to be honest and aboveboard. He sort of rambled for a few minutes and then left. Told me repeatedly that he was not a cheater. I thought he was a nut bar—we get enough of those in Vegas. I was pissed at the sergeant for letting him in. Now, of course, I wish I'd paid more attention to him, but at that point, he hadn't won a cent."

She fell silent and turned expectant eyes to Jack. So did the three men in the room. He met each gaze, then laughed.

"This is all very interesting, but I still don't know why I'm here. You've got a cheater that you can't prove has been cheating and who's causing an embarrassment to the Church and the gaming business and disrupting their profit cycle. I get that you have a plate full of shit sandwiches—if you'll pardon my French—but I'm a neurologist, not a detective."

"A neurologist who sidelines in exploring unusual mental and physical manifestations," the cardinal observed.

"I don't expose cheating gamblers, Tom. I debunk myths and miracles."

Rosen scooted to the edge of his chair. "Doctor, that's exactly why we want to talk with you. You see, we're coming to the conclusion that this guy is not a cheater. I never thought I'd say what I am about to, but we're beginning to believe he has some sort of honest-to-God psychic powers—ESP, whatever. And if he does, it could bring ruin to the whole state of Nevada. We want you to help us find out what's going on with this guy. We can't imagine anyone better qualified than you to help us out."

Tom O'Connor moved away from the hearth to put his hand on Jack's shoulder. "Jack, I know you have a vacation planned—one I'm sure you really need. But you know I wouldn't ask this of you without ample reason." He turned to the detective. "Ms. Firestone, would you show Jack the letter?"

She reached into a sleek messenger bag at her feet and pulled out an envelope. "After his big wins," she said, "we traced this guy to a room at the Tropicana. When we got there, he'd already checked out, but we found this letter on the bedside table."

She rose and crossed the carpet to hand it to Jack, who found himself distracted by the turn of her ankle and the way her hips swayed. She wore a silver charm bracelet on one wrist—a delicate chain with several tokens on it that Jack didn't recognize. Her fingernails were carefully filed ovals and buffed to a high shine. He took the envelope and caught a whiff of vanilla and spice.

Suits her, he thought.

He concentrated on the envelope. The front was blank. The note within was handwritten, in almost childish script, on Tropicana hotel room stationery. It read as follows:

To Whom It May Concern:

1. I have left Las Vegas—for the time being. I doubt you will find me if I don't want to be found.

2. You will not believe me, but nothing I have done is in any way illegal or could be proven illegal. I want the poor people who were molested by all those priests to get the money and turn up the heat on the Church to go after those guys. All of them.

 3. I need to talk to somebody, and maybe you can help me with that. His name is Dr. Jack Madison. He is a doctor in Chicago and a writer. He specializes in nerve conditions. He may not remember, but he once tried to help my mother.

 4. When you find Dr. Madison (and I am sure you will), please ask him to be in the House of Magic in Chicago at 9 PM on Sunday, March 2nd. I will be doing a show in the main dining room. Tell him not to interrupt me. I think he will see why I make that request and that all this is real.

 5. I'll be back in Vegas sometime after that and you'll know when I get here.

 6. Some very strange things have started happening with me and I have a feeling more are coming. Things that I really don't want, and I think you won't like them either.

 7. I hope that by now, Detective Firestone, you know this is not a joke. G. Gilbertson.

Fighting a strange tight chill in his chest, Jack folded up the letter and handed it back to the detective. "He . . . asked for me by name."

Tom nodded. "You can see why I contacted you."

"He mentions his mother. Gilbertson . . ."

"I think you treated her when you were Dr. Bernstein's junior associate, about twenty-five years ago. I'm sure you remember her. Ruth Gilbertson. The archdiocese asked Dr. Bernstein to evaluate her. You've since referred to her condition a number of times in your books. Her son would have been a child of four or five then."

Jack remembered the case. With the memory came a mixture of surprise and uneasiness. Ruth Gilbertson had been referred to his mentor, Dr. Sam Bernstein, because of her claim—and the archdiocese's conviction—that she manifested stigmata.

Before he could control it, the anger was back. "Tom, may I have a few moments alone with you?"

They adjourned to a small formal parlor adjacent to the study. The grate here was also laid with a cheerful fire, but Jack didn't feel particularly cheerful. Thoughts tumbled through his head faster than he could pin them down and identify them.

Tom O'Connor was perhaps the most influential American Catholic, and it was no mystery why the cardinal of Los Angeles, a pious man brand new to his job, had asked for his help. Cardinal O'Connor had shown himself to be above reproach throughout the pedophilia scandals; he had not covered up so much as a single case, nor transferred a suspected priest. And he had been ambiguous enough with his public comments to keep Rome appeased. From moments of candor over the past years, Jack knew that his friend had no use for the old guard at the Vatican—thought they spent too much time worrying about the prestige of the Church and too little considering what the vast majority of Catholics held dear. He found the new pope, Francis, to be much more aligned with what he called his "Christian values."

His Eminence Tom O'Connor, cardinal archbishop of Chicago, was a good man and no toady to authority. Still, the more Jack thought about this labyrinthine situation, the madder he got. Tom knew he needed a vacation, that he was still recovering from Carolyn's death. This was going to be nothing but a royal pain in the ass, without even the inducement of being able to write or talk about it.

He swung around from a dark study of the fire to find the cardinal watching him.

"Tom, what the hell are you trying to get me into? You know what's been going on in my life. This is the last thing I need right now. You know what I think about those loonies who claim to have the stigmata or who think they've witnessed miracles. Hell, I'm not at all sure how that even relates. You surely don't think I'm interested in some Las Vegas scam, especially since you've shamed me into a promise of silence on a topic I'm about ninety-nine percent certain will never be worth writing about anyway. You also know that, in spite of our friendship, I would never want to get involved in any sort of PR deal to help whitewash a Church scandal. I value your friendship, I really do, and I owe you for how you helped us out when Carolyn died, but Tom, this is just too much."

Tom made a T with his hands. "Time out, Jack. I don't blame you for being angry. And I'm not going to get into an argument with you over articles of faith, nor am I asking you to whitewash anything. All I can tell you is that I wouldn't have asked you to get involved unless we really needed you. Yes, it's a personal favor. You have done a lot more for me than I have for you, but in spite of all that crap you write, you're still one of my dearest friends. By the way," he added, "I didn't think you were the kind of guy to keep score."

"I'm not keeping score," Jack growled.

"The casino owners are willing to pay you whatever you ask to help them out with this. I repeat: whatever you ask." One corner of his mouth twitched, and an impish gleam sparked in his eyes. "More than that, I think you're going to find this to be a most fascinating experience—one that will engage all of your talents . . . and help you concentrate on something besides being alone with yourself. I honestly can't believe that two weeks of undirected time with no company but your own thoughts is good for a man like you."

Jack wasn't about to admit that was an uncomfortable echo of his own thoughts. "Oh, so you're a shrink now?"

Tom laughed—a big rumble of mirth that started deep in his chest. "Jack, I was a priest. A priest is part shrink, part offensive lineman, part catcher, and part Sherpa guide." He paused, fixed Jack with a gimlet eye, and said, "Besides, I didn't say you couldn't write about it—once it's all over. So get your ass off your high horse and come back and join us. There's more to hear."

Jack swallowed his ire with less effort than he expected. "Fine," he said and followed the cardinal back into the study. In the hallway, just before they reentered the room, Jack spoke again. "Didn't think you read any of that crap that I write."

Tom glanced back at him, smiling. "Always good to know what the enemy is thinking."

"Pardon, Your Eminence."

Jack jumped and turned at the sound of the soft voice. Father Lyons regarded them solemnly from the foyer.

"Dinner is laid out, Eminence." He gestured at a door on the opposite side of the staircase.

"Thank you, Father Lyons," Tom said imperturbably. He opened the study door and invited his guests to join him in the dining room.

Chapter 3

As the group of guests entered Cardinal O'Connor's dining room, Arnie Rosen pulled Jack aside. "Here's the deal, Doc. We figure we've got very little time to get our arms around this thing, so instead of getting into the hassles of haggling, I'm gonna offer you $250,000 for your services up front, and another quarter of a million once this thing is over. We pay all expenses and you go first class. We need a signed confidentiality agreement that you won't write about any of this without our okay. I have an NDA with me as well as a cashier's check for the up-front money. If for any reason this drags out longer than a month, we pay more."

Jack paused to contemplate the offer. "Two weeks," he said. "If it drags out longer than two weeks. I'm on vacation that long; after that, I'd have to start juggling my calendars. I've got a lot of calendars."

Rosen grinned. "I bet you do."

The table in the cardinal's state dining room would easily seat twenty people; five places had been set at the head of the table, two on each side of the end seat, which Tom took. Fireplaces blazed at each end of the room. Along one wall was a buffet sideboard set with salad, baked salmon, sliced beef tenderloin, and assorted vegetables. White and red wine sat in decanters on the table. Everyone served and seated themselves. Jack ended up at his friend's right hand with Joan

Firestone to his right. He wondered if he'd unconsciously engineered that . . . or if she had.

"Please, Cardinal O'Connor," said Bishop Powell, "won't you bless the meal? Surely your intercession would be most pleasing to God."

Tom's mouth tightened, and Jack had the distinct impression that he was on the verge of refusing the obsequious request. Cardinal Tom Archbishop O'Connor did not suffer flattery, something the bishop apparently had not yet learned. In the end, Tom gave a brief nonsectarian blessing, during which Jack closed his eyes and tried to look meditative.

"Dr. Jack," said Arnie Rosen as soon as the last amen had sounded, "I and my associates know a bit about you from your book covers and what Cardinal Tom has told us. But would you please spare some more detail on how you got to be such an authority on all the stuff you write about?"

Jack smiled and glanced at Cardinal Tom. "Sure, although I don't want to give the cardinal and bishop dyspepsia by going into my religious views. I think they both understand that I don't write to attack good, sincere religious people, only those who I think are phonies or hypocrites."

Bishop Powell seemed to find his fork of sudden interest. Tom's face was a map of Switzerland. Neither of them said a word.

Jack cleared his throat. "I grew up in Chicago. As a kid I was always interested in magic. I mean, who doesn't wonder where the rabbit goes when the magician shows the inside of his hat or how he always pulls the right card out of a deck? That led to me learning entry-level magic tricks and reading about Harry Houdini and his relationship to Conan Doyle and their disparate views on the occult. Then I discovered Magic, Inc.—that's a famous shop here in Chicago.

I spent my allowance on books and tricks, learned stuff from the guys who worked there, and hobnobbed with the oddball assortment of customers. By the time I was eleven, I was earning money doing kids' birthday parties instead of mowing lawns."

He shook his head and laughed at the memory of his misspent childhood. "Believe it or not, I stuck with it all through college and medical school. I bought textbooks with money I earned doing card and coin tricks, some basic mind reading, that sort of thing. I dreamed of being a professional magician for years."

"Why didn't you?" Joan asked.

He glanced over at her and found her studying him.

Why hadn't he taken up magic? "I guess . . . it didn't seem like something grown-ups did for a living. I had this image in my mind of going home for Christmas every year and having relatives ask me when I was going to get a real job. That, and I wanted to do something useful in the world."

"Yeah?" Joan met his eyes, and Jack had the profound impression he was being read cover to cover. The other people in the room might as well have been in Toronto. "So, what happened to set you on the straight and narrow?"

Jack shrugged. "When I was twenty, I spent my summer vacation at Harold's Club in Reno doing a small magic act as an opener for an established performer. Went by Mad Jack. Met some real characters, including a guy who ran the sideshow for Harris Brothers Circus and Carnival. I learned a whole lot about mentalism, fortune telling, and carny con games from him. He offered me a full-time job doing what I loved . . . and I got accepted to the medical school at Stanford."

"So I guess you turned him down."

"As they say, it was complicated. My two paths had literally crossed. So I got a one-year deferment from Stanford because I knew how much I loved all this magic stuff, and I . . . well, I wanted to throw myself into it, figuring that I was either going to get it out of my system or somehow incorporate it into my medical career. I spent a whole year with Harris Brothers doing a two-bit magic/mind-reading gig in their sideshow. That failed to get it out of my system, of course, but I could hardly turn down Stanford. So, I hung up my Mad Jack routine and went back to school. Long and short of it: I made neurology my specialty because of my involvement with magic."

Joan wrinkled her nose. "Okay, I'm not sure I see the connection."

"Magic is about tricking the mind. It's misdirection. Willful suspension of disbelief—or willful suspension of belief in reality. I was fascinated by that in both environments—how we trick ourselves into belief."

"Or nonbelief," said Tom softly.

Jack chose to ignore him, but the sense of intimacy he'd felt with Joan evaporated and the room once more had five occupants. "Anyway, one of the world's foremost authorities in the field of mind-body interactions at that time was Dr. Samuel Bernstein, chairman of neurology at the Midwestern School of Medicine in Chicago. In my interview with him we discussed my experiences in magic, the occult, and the mysterious, and it got me an extended residency. The last year of it I spent working with people involved in the scholarly study of parapsychology—mainly ESP. After I finished my fellowship, I was invited to join the faculty at MSM and worked with Dr. Bernstein for the last three years of his life."

"And you started writing books," Joan observed.

Jack nodded, with a glance at Tom O'Connor. "The first one was a book for medical professionals: *Medicine, Magic, and Myth.* To my initial dismay, medical professionals didn't pay much attention to it, but the general public did. It became a best seller. Since then I've written two more books: *Medicine, Magic, and the Paranormal*, and then, two months ago my publisher released *Medicine, Magic, and Miracles.*"

"You said the other medicos didn't pay you much attention," said Rosen. "They still ignore you?"

Jack chuckled. "Not just no, but *hell* no. They're now hyperaware of me. Ironically, I suppose, a few of my academic colleagues think I'm a flimflam, just one step up from some of the folks I write about. Some believe I'm trivializing grave illnesses. Fortunately, the dean of the school thinks I raise important issues and ask incisive questions, the things a good clinical academician ought to be doing. So, I've kept my job and even have tenure. Which doesn't mean I still don't take some flak."

"Jack," said Tom, "you're being modest. You're one of the most respected neurologists in Chicago, in spite of the oddball, heretical material you write."

Jack didn't need to look at him to know he was smiling. "So, what else do I need to know about this little research project you've wangled me into?"

Arnie Rosen had gotten up to go back to the sideboard for seconds. "We want you to work with Firestone here," he said, forking roast beef onto his plate. "She's under orders to devote one hundred percent of her time and energy to this matter until it's solved. You pursue your investigations here in Chicago, back in Las Vegas, or anywhere the two of you think is necessary. She has backup should you need it, and on paper, she's in charge, since she has the necessary credentials."

"I'm in charge. Period," Detective Firestone said. "Not just on paper." Rosen blinked at her as if she'd derailed his train of thought. "Yeah. Yeah, of course. Anyway, Cardinal Tom can pull any strings necessary here in Chicago, but my guess is that's not going to be necessary. If you'll pardon my French, I think Las Vegas is where the shit is going to hit the fan."

"No need to apologize to me for a bit of salty language, Mr. Rosen," said the cardinal. "Before I entered the seminary I was in the Marine Corps, so I'm no stranger to off-color language. To tell you the truth, I've been known to use a bit myself when it suits."

Jack raised his hand. "I'll vouch for that. You should hear him when he's fishing and has a few beers in him."

There was some easy laughter at that, and Jack felt the residual tension in the room unwind a bit.

Bishop Powell cranked it back up again. "I don't know how you can laugh with this hanging over the Vegas diocese. As far as I am concerned, we need the Casino Association's money to go to the Church here in Vegas, not these specialized charities in another archdiocese that has its own contributor base. Moreover, much of the money went to non-Church-related charities that are quite possibly bogus. Honestly, these scandals are in the past, where they should remain. No good comes of—of resurrecting them."

"Bishop Powell," said the cardinal in the same warning tone he'd used earlier, "we have no evidence that these charities are 'bogus,' as you put it. The debate over the Church's role in these cases is over. What happened was horrific, and we are struggling to recover our dignity and the trust of our congregants."

"Besides," Rosen added as he reseated himself at the table, "we're not about to give the last three million to anybody. We need to get this mess figured out and to get our stories straight. If this thing goes down the way this clown says, three mill is going to be a drop in the bucket to the Catholic Church in Las Vegas, 'cause a whole lotta people are gonna be out of jobs, and the first ones to go are the ones you and that Mexican cardinal from Los Angeles worry so much about." He pronounced it "Los Ang-hel-es."

Jack bit back a caustic comment at that display of racial bias. "What is the Casino Association doing about the situation, Mr. Rosen?"

"Call me Arnie, Jack. This Gilbertson guy has blabbed his story all over, and it's up to us to, you know, pull its teeth. So, we've spun a counternarrative about a large sum of money that was won under unusual circumstances." He made little air quotes around the word "unusual." "None of our local media outlets are gonna break the story until next Wednesday morning; they will only mention that the money was won in slots and keno and that we are in the middle of a complete investigation of said circumstances. All the details will be made fully available to them and so on and so forth. We figured that would keep this guy from coming across like freakin' Robin Hood."

"But on the whole," Jack said, "this is still great PR for your casinos, right? Gamblers are bound to think, 'Hey, if this guy can do it, so can I.' It's not as if they're likely to win anywhere near three million."

Rosen shrugged. "Off the record, we don't give a damn about the three mill. It's chicken feed in the grand scheme of things. If you solve this . . . debacle, we'll give that amount to the Vegas diocese. But—" He set his steak knife down hard enough to make his wine glass jump and stared directly at Bishop Powell. "—listen to me real careful. If we don't figure out how this jerk-off has been stealing our money before we lose as much as he's threatened, the Church can get its charity bucks somewhere else. The owners figure he's doing this because of a bunch of randy priests who couldn't keep it in their pants and the guys above 'em who covered it up. What do they call that—karma?"

Jack sat back and regarded Rosen from beneath lowered eyelids. He pegged him for a glorified messenger boy who found himself in a position to throw his weight around. But why throw it in an attack feint at Powell? Was there some personal animus there, or was Powell merely the most convenient (and least dangerous) target?

Aloud he said, "What do we know about Mr. Gilbertson? I'm assuming he paid for his hotel stay with a credit card." He looked to Detective Firestone. "I'm sure you ran a background check."

She nodded, glancing at Rosen, disdain tightening the corners of her mouth. "I ran it myself. Gilbertson is a semiprofessional magician and clown who resides in Springfield, Missouri. He's a regular attendee at the magic conventions Vegas hosts every year. Always stays in the convention hotel and has preferred accounts with most of the major chains—Hilton, Marriott, Westin."

"I have to admit," Jack said, "I've been to several of those conventions myself. Vegas is the Magic Capital of the World, after all."

"Small world," said Rosen.

"Maybe you've seen him at one of the conventions?" Joan suggested. "I know they have open mic performances during the cons. Gilbertson's stage name is Gilly the Magic Clown."

Jack shook his head. "No. Never heard of him."

"From what we can gather, he's a bit of a laughingstock among his peers. He's apparently a flop as a magician *and* a clown but seems to get a kick out of hanging around with guys who know what they're doing, trying to learn their schtick. Then he goes out and makes a fool of himself trying to copy them."

Jack had a fleeting thought of an old Russian fairy tale about the Frog Princess who put chicken bones up her sleeves at her wedding feast and shook out live doves. When her fellow brides tried to copy the trick, they pelted the other wedding guests with greasy chicken parts.

"So," he said, "the guy's a freakishly good gambler and a freakishly bad magician."

"That's the interesting thing. Just before I got on the plane, I got a call from one of the magicians we've interviewed about this case. Someone who's caught bits of Gilly's act at past conventions. He told me that he and some of his buddies saw him do some magic tricks at the most recent con that—as he put it—were 'mindblowingly good.' I didn't have time to get the details, but I've tentatively scheduled another interview with this guy and his buddies when we get back to Vegas."

Jack nodded. "Meanwhile, we visit the House of Magic and take in Gilly the Clown's act?"

Joan smiled. It lit up her face and made Jack's heart quiver in a way he hadn't felt for months and wasn't sure he should now.

With the meal at an end, the cardinal saw his guests out to two waiting limousines. One was to take Rosen and Bishop Powell to the airport for their flight back to Vegas, the other was to deliver Jack and Detective Firestone to their respective destinations.

Just before Jack slid into the gleaming white Lincoln, Tom O'Connor put a hand on his shoulder. "Jack, I want to thank you for agreeing to take this on. Keep me posted, won't you?"

"Sure thing. And thanks, Your Eminence, for a very interesting evening."

The cardinal laughed. "As in the old Chinese curse—May you live in interesting times?"

"Bingo. If I had known this was going to be this interesting, I would have left for St. Thomas straight from work."

Tom leaned in close to his ear. "Don't bullshit a bullshitter, Jack. You are going to love this."

As the limo pulled away, Jack ruminated on how much he was going to "love this." Tom tended to be a glass-half-full kind of guy who believed with all his heart that there was a better world awaiting them all. Well, if there was, maybe helping the cardinal archbishop of Chicago would earn Jack enough brownie points to at least win him a brief stint in purgatory before he went to hell.

Chapter 4

Joan was wide awake. She was still physically on Las Vegas time, and she had slept on the plane flying out—her first flight ever on a private jet. Back in her room at the Drake, she changed into jeans, sweater, and quilted parka, and headed out for a walk along Michigan Avenue. She'd expected to find the street more or less deserted and so was amazed at the number of people out strolling on a frigid Friday night. Of course, they were used to the cold; that was no novelty, but perhaps the lack of wind was.

She stood on the corner of Michigan and East Walton Place and gazed toward the lake, taking in the gleaming and glittering buildings, the subtle lights, the groups of people talking and laughing.

This is what a real downtown is like, she told herself. *No drunks and hookers on every corner, no glitzy neon promising instant riches, no pirate ships or volcanoes with burning flames, no drive-thru wedding chapels or funeral homes, no grim-faced gamblers scurrying lemming-like from one smoky den to another. Just normal people dressed appropriately for winter, enjoying a stroll and looking into the artistically lit windows of nice stores.*

Joan was jaded and knew it. Las Vegas did that to you . . . in roughly the first ten minutes you were there. Living there as long as she had,

Joan had forgotten that there were places like Chicago, where people were not at their worst nearly every waking moment.

She had arrived in Las Vegas with virtually nothing. Lacking bootstraps, she'd pulled herself up by the laces of her aging Converses, gotten a job as a police dispatcher, enrolled in night school at UNLV, and eventually joined the Las Vegas Metropolitan Police Department as part of what was then known as the Bunko Squad.

In those days, the Mob still had a great deal to say about how the city was run, and it was Bunko's job to curb their enthusiasm and influence. Being an attractive young black woman was a major reason she'd been assigned to help the casinos catch cheats. She had the ability to stand out and yet blend in; she looked like she came with the territory but was eye-catching enough to pop from the background of noise and smoke and lights to gain a potential cheater's attention and, eventually, his confidence.

Big-time cheaters, of course, were handled outside of police channels by the Boys, which sometimes resulted in crushed kneecaps . . . or worse. She was glad those days were pretty much over. The part of the Mob that hadn't been shut down or driven out had become much more sophisticated and subtle. They'd diversified.

So had Joan Firestone. She'd become very good at her job, and acknowledged it without arrogance. She could identify virtually every kind of casino cheat seemingly by instinct. She'd caught card players trying to add chips to their piles, craps players trying to swap in loaded dice, roulette players trying to bribe croupiers. Thieves and cheats were everywhere, and Joan could spot them in a heartbeat, which contributed to the fact that she now ran the Casino Fraud Division. She liked her job; she did not always like the people it brought her in contact with.

That got her thinking about tonight. Before Jack Madison had walked into the cardinal's study, she could safely say she had only liked one third of the men in the room. She had never warmed up to Arnie Rosen. When he was in the room, she half expected to step on a cockroach. She hadn't liked the bishop much better and felt vaguely guilty about it. You were supposed to like—or at least trust—clergymen, but she found herself unable to feel the same ease around Bishop Powell that she did with their host. She'd liked Tom O'Connor on sight, though he had a watchfulness about him that she recognized because she had it too.

Then there was Jack Madison. *Dr.* Madison, MD, thank you very much. "Like" was the wrong word to use with him. She was fascinated by him and, okay, attracted. His easy self-confidence was sexy.

And there, my girl, it stops.

She'd piqued his interest, she was certain; her work required her to know when she'd pinged a man's radar, but she was on a job, he was a consultant; he was white, she was black . . . and this whole line of thought was ridiculous.

She laughed at herself. Out loud. Not doubting for a moment that the normal people moving past and around her on the broad sidewalk would assume she was talking to someone through a Bluetooth device or listening to something funny . . . or was a little drunk. She walked around the entire city block, stopping to buy a bag of hot candied pecans that warmed her hands on the way back to the Drake.

Back in her hotel room, she found she was still too wide awake to sleep. She drew a hot bath and soaked for long enough to make her toes prune up, singing along with Gershwin on her iPhone. She liked the sound of her own voice—a rich contralto well-suited to the territory Leontyne Price covered in *Porgy and Bess*. No brag, just fact. She didn't compare herself to Price, of course, but it was in her to want to be as good a singer as she was a detective.

No, better.

She felt herself flush with a memory she had neglected to share with her fellow investigators. She had told them about Gilbertson coming to her office to warn her before he started winning and how she had simply dismissed him as a nut bar. What she did not tell them—what she had not even told her chief of police, Devin Spader—was that she had fallen asleep while she was talking to Gilbertson. Sound asleep—for maybe five or ten minutes. When she'd wakened, he was gone. Joan had never fallen asleep during an interview in her life. She'd tried to write it off to simply being overtired or maybe coming down with something. Now she wasn't so sure, but she was too embarrassed to tell anyone about it . . . yet.

She felt her eyelids drooping and realized she'd been in the tub too long. She put on her PJs and fell into bed, where she dreamed of music and moving through darkness into light. There was someone with her in the dream, someone she was aware of only as a presence and a hand holding hers.

That you, Lord? Or is that the new guy?

Immediately after breakfast, Joan spent forty minutes on the phone with colleagues in the LVMP, bringing them up to speed on the investigation. She then took a cab to Chicago Police Headquarters down on South Michigan. The place looked brand new and more like an upscale community college than a police station. She entered an unusually spacious lobby, stopped at the front desk, and showed the officer there her badge and a handwritten note from the cardinal directing her to see Commander Edward Mathews.

The duty officer said he wasn't in his office but was in the building. She called a young uniform over to escort Joan to the commander's office—which was impressive. While she waited for him, she took the grand tour, checking out pictures of him with a variety of dignitaries and more awards than you could shake a stick at. They decorated the walls, the bookshelves, and a credenza by the floor-to-ceiling window that overlooked the street. She'd just completed one turn about the room when Commander Mathews walked in. He was a short, muscular black man dressed in a Bulls sweatshirt and jeans. He was imposing as hell despite his lack of height and civvies. Annoyance stood out all over him like quills on a porcupine.

"I got a call last night *at home* from the chief of police," he said without preamble, "informing me that the mayor would like it very much if I met you here at eleven a.m. on a Saturday morning. You do realize it's Saturday, don't you, Detective Firestone?"

She met his gaze squarely. "Yessir. Because it's Saturday for me too."

He paused to read her for a moment, then directed her to a chair opposite the massive desk that angled across an inside corner of the office. (So he could gaze out the window and daydream, Joan suspected.) She nodded her thanks and seated herself, crossing her legs in a gesture that was as instinctive as it was tactical.

"My chief," Mathews continued, glancing obliquely at her legs, "also informed me that I'm not supposed to tell anybody I met with you. So what's a sista from Vegas got on her mind that is all so important and hush-hush to keep me away from my kids this morning?"

"Why how do you do, Commander Mathews? It's nice to meet you, too. Yes, my flight from Vegas was just fine. I *am* a bit tired, though.

A little jet lagged. Why, yes, I *would* like a cup of coffee, thanks."
She gave him her best smile.

A corner of his mouth twitched. He pressed a button on his desk
phone and said, "Danny, would you be so good as to bring a couple
of cups of coffee in to my office?"

He quirked an eyebrow at Joan, who said, "Just cream, thanks."

Mathews repeated her request for his admin's benefit, then steepled
his hands on this desk. "I apologize for my abruptness, Detective
Firestone. Please tell me your side of this . . . situation. Why are you
and I spending our Saturday morning in this outlandish fashion? And
why has the mayor seen fit to get involved?"

Joan explained the situation with as much detail as she thought
made sense, including the fact that even though they thought the
mysterious Mr. Gilbert was in Chicago at present, he was apparently
a resident of Springfield, Missouri. Mathews' only indication that
the bizarre nature of the story registered was a slight widening of his
eyes when she described the series of strange wins and the promises
or prophecies Gilbertson had made. She concluded by describing
the conversation the night before at the dinner meeting overseen by
Cardinal Archbishop O'Connor.

Now, Mathews' eyebrows scooted upward. "You had dinner with
Cardinal O'Connor last night at his residence?"

"Yes, I did."

"My guess is not many sistas dine at his place."

Joan grinned. "Oh, I don't know about that. I get the sense the
cardinal is a man whose door is open to anybody who needs to walk
through it. As for the mayor, I suspect he's a good Catholic who may
have walked through that door himself on occasion. Now it's your

turn. I assume your chief and the mayor think you have something important to tell me."

Mathews lowered his gaze in a way that told Joan he was mulling something, then he met her eyes again and said, "What I'm about to tell you about is an open case. So, please be judicious in who you share it with."

"Of course."

"I don't know if it will aid your investigation, but it involves your man, Gilbertson. Three weeks ago, we had a torch job on a women's health clinic that does abortions. Late at night, no one there, nobody hurt, just property damage. Only lead we had at the scene was an abandoned car—stolen, as it happens—and we found a slip of paper stuck in the seat with this guy Gilbertson's name on it and a St. Louis phone number. It turns out to be the number of the rectory of a Catholic parish there—name of St. Jude's. Nobody there admits to knowing this guy or anything about the fire. Two days later, we get a letter from an organization calling itself the Society for the Preservation of Catholic Dogma, or SPCD, claiming responsibility for the arson. You think your magician-slash-gambler might moonlight as a zealot arsonist for a shadowy para-religious organization?"

Joan frowned. "I wouldn't think so, under normal circumstances, but nothing about this case—if it is a case—seems normal. What's the story on this secret society?"

"Apparently it formed in response to the election of Pope Francis. The SPCD is about as anti-reform as you can get. More so than Opus Dei, and that's saying a lot. The membership, as far as we've been able to determine, is made up of clergy and laity. Apparently, some of them are in positions of power in the Church or in society or both."

"No surprise there. They'd have to be to stay secret and continue to pull off terrorist acts without getting busted. What about the folks at St. Jude's? I assume you checked them out."

"Yes, ma'am. And they all seemed straight up and narrow. We also checked out Gilbertson six ways from Sunday—no pun intended—and he was somewhere in the boonies of Missouri the night of the arson. Five hundred miles away with an airtight alibi. Plenty of witnesses. We found out then that he's some sort of clown, which I personally find creepy as hell. But aside from that, he's about the furthest thing from a religious activist I can imagine. And he's not all that bright. Vague, I guess you'd say, though I suppose that could be an act."

Joan thought it funny that such an intimidating man as Edward Mathews was creeped out by clowns. She started to comment on it, but the door of the office swung open and a young officer entered with two paper cups full of coffee that turned out to be pretty decent.

After he'd accepted their thanks and left, Joan said, "So, you haven't connected Gilbertson to the arson."

"No. His fingerprints weren't on the car or its contents. Nor was his DNA. We can't make any connection to Gilbertson except his name on that note. But he does seem to be connected in some way to the SPCD. We aren't ruling out the possibility that there are members of the Society high up in the Chicago Archdiocese."

Joan felt the hairs stand up on the back of her neck. *By the pricking of my thumbs . . .* "How high up? You don't think the cardinal—"

"Not personally, no. What I know of the man, he's by the book—meaning the Good Book. But the chief and I passed along to him what we've gleaned so far, thinking maybe he might have seen some suspicious activity in his bailiwick."

"You told the cardinal about the note in the stolen car?"

Mathews nodded, sipping at his coffee. "Yes. He was pretty stoic about the whole thing, but I could tell the arson and its connection to St. Jude's and the SPCD had him twigged. He asked us to keep it quiet but stressed that he wants us to get to the bottom of it, wherever it goes."

So, the cardinal had known about this yet said nothing last night. Why? Was it because he didn't want someone else at the dinner to hear it and knew she'd be getting the intel from Mathews today? She might just have to ask him about that so she didn't let something slip in front of the wrong person.

"Doesn't sound like a man who's covering up shit," she said, "but the guilty usually try real hard to look innocent. Sometimes they try a little too hard."

"That thought had crossed my mind. Which is why I think it's pretty weird when the chief tells me last night that the mayor and the cardinal both want me to reveal our connection with Gilbert. Guess that tells you a bit about the power of the Catholic Church here in Chi Town. These are not, I repeat not, the kind of stories we tell out of school in Chicago."

"Or Las Vegas, for what it's worth." Joan tapped a fingernail against the side of her coffee cup. "Is it possible you could share some of your intel on this secret society with me? If our magic clown is a member, it might be pertinent to our investigation."

"I'll email you a synopsis. It's not for public consumption, so—"

She nodded. "Use with discretion."

"One more thing that's not in the official report," he said. "You ever hear of a guy named Francis Xavier Coughlin?"

"Can't say that I have."

Mathews's mouth twitched. "He'd be disappointed to hear that. He's big in the Chicago area. Real estate developer. Massively wealthy, massively powerful politically, and massively Catholic—old-school Catholic."

Joan raised an eyebrow. "SPCD old school?"

"We have nothing concrete, but let's just say that his public rhetoric and theirs are awfully similar in very unsettling ways. Cardinal O'Connor can tell you more about the guy—probably more than you want to know, actually. The two of them have tangled more than once over Church reform and tradition in recent years. It would not surprise me to find out that Coughlin was a card-carrying member of the SPCD. I think, at the very least, he's supportive of their activities. If Gilbertson is one of their operatives or is on their radar for some other reason, Coughlin might take exception to your poking around him."

"Hell, Ed—can I call you Ed?—Gilbertson flat out invited us to come take a poke."

"Yeah. Which is pretty weird if he's a member of the Preservation Society. So's his habit of giving large donations to victims of priestly abuse. The SPCD holds that most of the priests were innocents seduced by sinful congregants and should never have been prosecuted."

Well, that was an interesting wrinkle. "Maybe our man, Gilbert, isn't a member of the Society. Maybe he's on their hit list."

They wrapped up fairly quickly after that, each agreeing that they'd call the other if anything broke that would bear on their part of the investigation. Joan gratefully accepted the synopsized version of the police report on the SPCD's record as a sponsor of homegrown terror. It didn't tell her much beyond what Ed had told her—that the SPCD had implicated itself in three firebombings, some costly vandalism, a few vague death threats, and some fiery hate speech, mostly directed at progressive clergymen, up to and including Cardinal O'Connor and the pope himself.

Mathews walked her down to the foyer and saw her out. As they shook hands in parting, she asked him, "Are you really creeped out by clowns, or were you kidding?"

"Not kidding. I hate clowns."

"I guess a lot of people share that particular aversion. What was it, a childhood trauma?"

Mathews snorted. "Adult trauma. Ever hear of John Wayne Gacy?"

For a second, Joan didn't get the connection, then she tumbled to it. "Right. Gacy, the serial killer. He part timed as a clown, right?"

Mathews nodded. "Did kiddie parties to make money. Worst sonofabitch in living memory."

"And now we've got Gilly the Clown, who seems to be a serial Good Samaritan."

"Makes you wonder if the world isn't upside down sometimes, doesn't it?" said Mathews, then ordered up a car to take her back to her hotel.

As she watched the Chicago streets glide by, Joan Firestone couldn't help but wonder what the hell she'd gotten herself into. She took out her cell phone and punched in Cardinal O'Connor's private number.

Chapter 5

Jack made it his business to reacquaint himself with the late Ruth Gilbertson by poring over the medical records and personal information he and Dr. Bernstein had compiled during the course of their study of her "stigmata." The records had been digitized, so he'd been able to access them from his laptop through the MSM intranet.

Her maiden name had been Ruth Czworniak, and she'd told the doctors that she'd learned to read palms from her aunt, a first-generation Polish immigrant. Her husband, Rudy, had been a childhood sweetheart from her old neighborhood and had worked in the stockyards. He'd been killed in a freak accident after only four years of marriage. They'd had one child, Gilbert, who was five when Jack and his mentor had examined his mother.

Ruth had been devastated by her husband's death but had come out okay financially because of Rudy's union affiliation. There had been a huge settlement and a decent pension that she collected as his spouse. Jack recalled that she'd told them she had no real need to work, but she'd kept up the fortune-telling even though she didn't need the money. She wanted to help people, she said. And it gave her some extra cash to indulge her fondness for birds. Jack had the image in his mind of the petite woman with a flock of sparrows perched on her head and shoulders.

He shook his head at the memory. A devout Catholic who read palms. He'd asked about that seeming contradiction, whereupon Ruth had earnestly informed him that the Church was no stranger to magic; indeed, it had historically sponsored special Church magicians called theurgists. He wondered if she realized that, even in the heyday of Church wizardry, she'd have been burned as a witch simply because she was a woman.

Ultimately, Ruth Gilbertson sought the aid of doctors only because the stigmata was disrupting her business. Having your fortune told is one thing, having the fortune-teller start spouting messages from the Blessed Virgin and bleeding on her tarot cards while doing it is something else again.

Stigmata were a source of debate in both the religious and medical communities. Oddly, they weren't limited to Catholics or even to Christians—something that had always puzzled Jack. Sam Bernstein had once told him that, early in his practice, he'd seen an elderly Jewish man in an insane asylum who was able to make his hands bleed on command.

Jack was intensely skeptical of stigmatics. Since most scholars agreed that Christ was crucified with nails through his wrists, why did they bleed from their hands? Jack suspected it was because they had accepted the Bible story of Doubting Thomas touching wounds in Jesus's palms and had seen countless religious artworks that showed them there. That the majority of episodes occurred during moments of religious ecstasy was evidence of a deep-seated emotional component. In Jack's opinion, just because science had not yet discovered the reason for certain instances of stigmata (the ones that were not flat-out hoaxes) did not mean they were miracles, simply a strange pathology that had not yet been defined.

Then there were Ruth's alleged psychic abilities. Jack had learned a fair amount about fortune-tellers during his year with the Harris Brothers, so he knew how to speak Ruth's language. They'd hit it off pretty well. He hadn't introduced himself to her as a skeptic because he was curious about her experience and figured if she saw him as an ally, she'd open up to him. She had, to a degree that exceeded his hopes. He knew fortune-telling was a con game, but Ruth didn't. To her, the ball gazing, palm reading, and tarot cards were simply different ways of accessing information that was hidden behind material reality.

Jack had been confused by Ruth—still was. He couldn't doubt her sincerity; in her own mind, she was doing God's work and doing it legitimately. And though he knew fortunetellers gleaned their insights from holding a hand, asking questions, and reading faces and body language, Jack had to admit that Ruth Gilbertson seemed far less watchful than the palmists he'd studied before. In fact, when he'd asked her to demonstrate her process by reading his fortune, she'd spent most of the time either looking directly into his eyes or with her eyes closed, and she hadn't asked him any questions.

No, that wasn't quite true; she'd asked him one question, but not until the end of the reading. She'd said, "You're not a believing man, are you, Dr. Madison?"

No, he was not a "believing man." But he'd hedged a bit, not wanting her to shut him out. He'd used the question as a jumping-off point to ask Ruth about how religion played into her act. (Of course, he hadn't called it that.) Had she done something to bring on the stigmata?

"No, doctor," she'd told him. "I would never have *asked* for something like this. I want these spells of mine to stop. That's why I came to you and Dr. Bernstein."

Her "spells" were unusual. They came on unexpectedly, typically in the midst of working with a client. She described them by saying she was "suddenly inside the other person's mind."

"Then I would see secret things from their past," she'd told him. "Things they were embarrassed about or would never discuss with anyone—like petty crimes, affairs, and such. Sometimes I can see future events, too. But I only tell them things that are positive or that I can see will work out. You don't want to make people really sad or angry."

That was in the transcript Jack now studied, looking for . . . he wasn't sure what he was looking for.

MADISON: Who suggested that these spells were visitations from the Virgin Mary?

MRS. GILBERTSON: That was me. Someone asked me who was giving me these messages. I knew the person was a devout Catholic and it was very important—very important—that they pay attention to what I was telling them, because otherwise their career plans would fail. They did pay attention, thank God, and things turned out fine, but they told a bunch of other folks that I was getting these messages from the Virgin and . . . well, it sort of took on a life of its own. It must be something like that, Doctor, don't you think?

MADISON: What do you think, Ruth? Do you have some idea where the spells come from?

MRS. GILBERTSON: Well, maybe from my—my guardian angel.

MADISON: Your guardian angel? I don't follow.

MRS. GILBERTSON: You know how Native Americans have animal spirit guides? So do I. I think of her as my totem. She protects me

and keeps watch over me—ever since Rudy died. She came to me the
day of his funeral and stayed.
   MADISON: Really? What sort of . . . animal is your spirit guide?
   MRS. GILBERTSON: Why a bird, of course.

Jack paused in his reading, remembering how startled Ruth had looked
when he'd asked her that. She'd seemed embarrassed suddenly, as
if he might think messages from the Virgin Mary were completely
acceptable but scoff at her if he thought they came from an animal
spirit guide. He remembered how hard he'd had to work to hide a
smile as he adjusted the image in his head to make her look more
like a dainty Morticia Addams with a raven whispering "nevermores"
into her ear.

   The diagnostic tools of the nineties were not what they were today;
ultimately they had made no diagnosis and had affected no cure. But
now, going through the file, Jack came across a note Sam Bernstein
had appended to Ruth's chart that he hadn't paid much attention to
twenty-five years before. During his final neurological exam, Sam
thought he might have heard a soft to-and-fro murmur over Ruth's
right temporal cortex. He'd opined that this finding, in combination
with unusual blood pressure readings, might indicate the presence of
some sort of arteriovenous malformation of the brain. It was a stab in
the dark that the medical team had never discussed because Ruth had
disappeared the next day. She'd checked herself out of the hospital
"against medical advice," as the nurse's notes succinctly put it. That,
of course, stopped any further study of her stigmata.

   Jack had forgotten about that note, which made him wonder what
else he might have forgotten. He had several boxes of Sam Bernstein's

observations that he'd kept after his mentor's death. He kept them in a walk-in closet just off his home office. He'd looked through them several times through the years, seeking insights, but had never looked for anything specifically on Ruth Gilbertson. Now, he dug out Sam's files and spent about twenty minutes going through them before he found a folder with Ruth's name on it.

Back in his office, he skimmed notes that detailed his partner's frustration that the woman had left suddenly before he had been able to develop a working hypothesis about her condition. Paper clipped to the back of the folder was a sealed envelope addressed to Jack with Sam's signature across the flap, and dated several days after Ruth had left the hospital. There were two letters inside.

The first was a short note from Sam Bernstein to Jack.

Jack,

I don't know if you will ever open this envelope but reasoned that if you ever went through Ruth Gilbertson's records carefully, you would find it. The other letter in the envelope is a note Ruth left for me. Please, read it. As you and I discussed on several occasions, I haven't the faintest idea how or why her palms bleed. On a rational level, I do not think it has anything to do with religion, but at the end of the day, who knows? I just wish we could have spent more time with her. I hope what she said in the letter to me (about what is going to happen to your wife, if you indeed ever have one) never occurs.

Sam Bernstein

. . .what is going to happen to your wife . . .

Jack's throat closed up suddenly and emphatically. The second letter lay, folded, atop his computer keyboard. He looked at it now as if he expected it to burst into flames or leap up and attack him. He swallowed the tightness in his throat and picked up the note. It was written in pencil on a sheet of lined paper. It read:

Dear Dr. Bernstein,

I have decided that I am leaving the hospital, and Chicago also. Me and my little boy will go live near my brother in Missouri. I really don't know why my hands start bleeding and I swear to you that I can't figure out any of the stuff with the Virgin or if she's the one talking during my trances. For some reason, tho, I'm pretty sure that the bleeding is all over and done. I know that none of you believe that I can see into the future, but sometimes I can. I think that my days are numbered, and I know that nobody can do anything about it. Not even you doctors, smart as you are. Right now, I just want some good years with my little boy and some peace and quiet.

I have to tell you that I like young Doctor Madison, but I have some reel bad thoughts about him too. He had me read his fortune, but I only told him a thing or two about it. Here's what I really saw. He is going to get married in about a year and will have two daughters. His wife is going to die in a bad accident about the time his girls get grown up.

Please don't tell him this, cause all he'll do is worry and I don't think there is a thing that can be done about it. This is one of those

*times when I am reel sure about the future for him, so I am writing
it down for you or someone· else to prove someday that I am not a
liar or a fony nutcase. Also Doctor Madison is going to run into
Gilbert again, and I can only hope and pray that he will be able
to help him. Gilbert has some bad trouble in his future too. I don't
know what its going to be but it will be something like my spells and
hands—only worse.*

*Don't worry about me. Thank you for being so nice to me and
trying to help but its not in the cards.*

Respectfully,
Ruth Gilbertson

It has to be a fake.

That was Jack's first impulse. But the paper and envelope were
clearly aged, the glue on the flap dried to cracking, and the signature
was Sam's, as was the handwriting on his brief note. Jack rocked
back in his desk chair and tried to think logically. The voice of
reason told Jack that someone had planted this here recently, but
another voice—perhaps the voice of reason—pointed out that he'd
only discovered it because of a set of circumstances so bizarre that
imagining someone had manipulated those circumstances was more
irrational than the alternative. Assuming the age of the envelope and
Sam's handwriting had been faked, someone would have to have
put it in his office while he was at the hospital or in class *and* his
secretaries were out.

His secretaries. Might one of them . . . ?

He banished the thought as swiftly as he had it; he'd known both
Keenan and Angela for years. Angela had been a childhood chum of

Katy's, and Keenan was the son of a colleague and friend. He trusted both with his royalty checks, for God's sake. He couldn't imagine they could be bribed, though he supposed they might've been threatened. *Get a grip, Jack,* he told himself. *You're drifting into conspiracy territory.*

And he was doing it, he knew, to avoid thinking the unthinkable—that Ruth Gilbertson had actually predicted major milestones in his life. He had, in fact, met Carolyn three months after Ruth left Chicago. They'd married within the year, and she had died when Katy and Irene were nineteen and twenty-one.

A taste like ashes in his mouth and fighting nausea, Jack put both letters back into their envelope, tucked it into his jacket pocket, and went for a long walk. His head felt somewhat clearer after that; he'd made a decision to park Ruth Gilbertson's prophecies in a dark corner of his mind and concentrate on her son. With that in mind, he took a cab to Chicago Magic—a storefront that catered to experienced amateur and professional magicians. It was in a still-impressive brick and stone vintage building with studiously ornate architectural details that gave it an air of regal shabbiness.

On Saturday afternoon, a lot of the old-timers came around to swap tales, catch up on what was new in the world of magic, and opine about its worthiness to be called magic. Jack went in hoping that a particular veteran magician would be in the informal seating area among the shelves of books on magic. He was not disappointed. Wilfred Benson was holding court among the stacks. The Admiral, as he was known, had just turned eighty and had been a magician for over sixty-five years. No one seemed to know where the nickname came from; Benson had been in the navy in WWII but was never an officer, much less an admiral.

The tall, portly magician sported white hair and a thick handlebar mustache that he kept died black and waxed to stiffened perfection. He wore white suits and walked with a variety of ornate canes. Jack suspected he collected them like rock stars collected guitars; he'd never seen him with the same one twice.

Admiral Benson was a legend in the art of magic. He claimed that his father had been in vaudeville and that, as a little boy, he had known all of the famous magicians of his father's generation—Blackstone, Dunninger, Cardini, Dai Vernon, and Bert Allerton—and spoke of them as if they were family friends. Jack's guess was that only about twenty percent of what the old codger said was true, but he was brash and genuine and funny, and beloved by one and all. He also possessed an encyclopedic knowledge of magic and magicians that had served Jack well during the research and writing of his books. And that was precisely why Jack had sought him out.

When he entered the seating area, Benson was in the midst of a tale about his days working cruise ships and his nights with lonely widows—a performance he was giving for about a half dozen aspiring magicians. The old man glanced over at Jack, smiled, and lifted his hand in greeting . . . then frowned.

"Excuse me a minute, ladies and gents," he told his rapt audience. "I need to speak to my young friend here for a moment. I'll finish that story some other time."

Jack was amused that, at fifty, he could be anyone's "young friend." Context was everything. He answered the Admiral's beckoning gesture by crossing the "parlor" to take a seat next to him in a leather club chair.

"God Almighty, Doc, you look like someone just walked over your grave. What's the matter?"

Jack grimaced. "It shows, does it? I didn't mean to interrupt—"

"Nonsense. I was just winding up some astute observations on the connection between magic and romance."

Jack quirked an eyebrow. "Magic and romance."

"Well, naturally. You think puppies and babies are chick magnets—or hunk magnets for the ladies, I guess—magic is far superior. And you don't have to feed it or change its diaper."

Jack grinned in spite of himself at the words "chick magnet" coming out of his old friend's mouth. "Wilfred, I need your help. Specifically, I need information."

The Admiral spread his hands in a gesture of openness. "Anything. What's got you spooked?"

"Well, I can't yet go into any real detail, but I need you find out anything you can about someone for me. Not quite in your league, but you may have run into him over the years or can find someone who has. His name is Gilbert Gilbertson—stage name Gilly the Magic Clown. I think he lives at least part time in Springfield, Missouri—was raised there, anyway—and I know he attends magic conventions on a regular basis. Goes to Vegas maybe once or twice a year. Performs during the conventions on open stage nights. I need to know everything you can possibly find out about the guy—his schtick, his reputation, affiliations. Anything you can tease out. If you find out anything, please call me." Jack held out his personal contact card.

Wilfred took it, frowning. "Shit, Jack. What's this guy done?"

"I can't really discuss it, Wilfred. All I can say is that he has some connections and some . . . behaviors that have gotten the authorities pretty wigged out."

"You too, by the look of it. How'd you get dragged into this?"

Jack waved his hands. "Hocus pocus. I'm apparently the resident subject matter expert in the Chicago area on . . . what this guy does. There are a couple more things I'd like to ask, if you're available."

Wilfred snorted. "Do I look like I've got somewhere else to be? What did you have in mind?"

"I'd like to introduce you to the detective from Las Vegas who's investigating Gilbertson—for reasons I can't divulge without consulting her," he added before the old man could ask. "Tomorrow around noon at the Drake? I'll buy you lunch."

"Ah, an offer I can't refuse."

"I'd also appreciate it if you could come by the House of Magic tomorrow night around nine. I think this guy is going to show up, and if he does, I would love to have you around. Can we keep all of this between you and me?"

"Doc, I don't know what this is about, but you've got me more than a little curious about Mr. Gilbertson. Trust me, the Admiral will get to work ASAP on sussing out this guy. Although, as you suggest, magic clowns are hardly my specialty. I'll be at the Drake at noon tomorrow with bells on. And I wouldn't miss seeing this guy at the House for all the tea in China."

"'Sussing out'?" Jack repeated. "Wilfred, where are you picking this stuff up? Awhile ago you used the term 'chick magnet.'"

The handlebar mustache wriggled with apparent glee. "You see the average age of my audiences these days? They call me Admiral Wil. I'll introduce anyone who calls me Willie to my cane. Other than that, I like their lingo. It's fresh, young, h—"

Jack pointed a finger at the Admiral's nose. "Don't you dare say 'hip.' That word was in when I was their age. And their *lingo*, my old friend, is like a uniform they wear." Jack rose to go.

"You, sir," said Admiral Wil, "are becoming a curmudgeon. You're older in the head than I am."

Jack sobered. "Life does that to some of us."

Or death does.

Joan was waiting outside the Drake hotel when Jack arrived for their scheduled powwow. She stood on the glittering sidewalk in a pool of sunlight making banners of steam with her breath, apparently with great delight. His eyes caught on her as he got out of his cab; he found it hard to look away.

They walked down to Oak Street Beach and sat on a park bench at the water's edge. The wind had died down, and the late afternoon sun shone off the few remaining sheets of ice along the shore. Lake Michigan was calm and gleaming—a mirror for God to admire himself in.

If there is a God, Jack added reflexively.

He gave Joan a report on his day so far, beginning at the end with his enlisting Admiral Benson's sage aid. Only then, and with more uncertainty than he'd felt about anything in recent memory, did he show her the letters he'd discovered among Sam's papers. She read them over carefully while Jack watched her face. It went through a series of emotions that he thought included puzzled, incredulous, and plain old gobsmacked. When she was done, she looked up at him with an expression that was entirely opaque—her cop face.

"How good was her prediction?" she asked.

Jack breathed deeply of the wintry-warm air. "On the money. Right down to the timing of our marriage and the relative age of the girls when Carolyn died."

"Do you think it's a forgery?"

Did he? He *wanted* it to be a forgery, but—as he reminded himself and anyone who heard him speak or read his books—conforming to human whim was not reality's job.

"I don't know. I think I'm too disturbed by it, whatever it is, to be logical. If it's real, it challenges everything I know—or thought I knew—about reality, which is disturbing. And if it's a forgery that was planted recently in my private home office without either of my secretaries being any the wiser, then it means someone is willing to go to extreme lengths to make me *think* that it's real, which is, in some ways, even more disturbing. What I *can* tell you is that the paper looks suitably aged and the handwriting looks like Sam Bernstein's handwriting. And the way the note is written sounds like Sam."

"What about Ruth's note? I notice she misspelled some words and her grammar was wonky sometimes. Did she talk like that, too?"

Jack nodded. "She'd only had a high school education, and I gather she wasn't the best of students. She planned all along on growing up to be Rudy Gilbertson's wife. She was unlettered, not stupid. She understood things about human nature that made me feel . . . out of touch."

Joan folded the letters and slid them back into the envelope. "Is there someone at your university who can analyze these to determine if all the components are the same age? Theoretically, someone could have distressed some paper, then scared up an old envelope to stick it in. The only thing they couldn't fake would be the ink. If the ink is from the same era . . ."

Jack nodded again. He felt as if he were entering a strange swamp in a dense fog. A "here there be dragons" area of unknowns. He did not like it. Not one bit. He was a scientist. Under normal circumstances, he would have not given those two notes more consideration than it would have required to get them to the university's forensic chromatography lab. But the subject of the letters struck at the core of who he was and what he believed. He was completely off balance.

"Jack," said Joan softly, when he hadn't spoken for several long moments, "I can see this has really gotten to you. I understand why. I can't wrap my mind around it, either. I wish there was something I could do to help."

He took the letters back and tucked them into an inside jacket pocket. "Thanks. I don't know if I'm more upset by the idea that Ruth's prediction was true clairvoyance or by the fear that if I had seen it earlier, I might have prevented Carolyn's death."

"Jack, you can't think like that. You read what Ruth said—she didn't believe it would have helped."

"Maybe she was wrong, Joan. She wasn't omniscient. Maybe, if I'd known—"

"What? You would've sealed your poor wife up inside her house and never let her go anywhere?" She leaned back and gave him a long assessing look through those amber eyes. "I dunno, Doc Madison, but knowing you even as short a time as I have, I've got to believe that your Carolyn was no Princess Buttercup. Correct me if I'm wrong, but I'd say she was probably as smart as you are, stubborn, and very much her own woman. You think she'd go for that Sleeping Beauty routine?"

No, she wouldn't have. Jack sucked in more barely warm air and tried to think straight. Getting the letters analyzed by the university forensics lab was the logical thing to do. So he'd do it.

"If it's a fake," he said slowly, "it means that someone, for some reason I cannot at this moment fathom, knew I was going to be involved in this case and created and planted these letters suspecting that I'd go through Sam's papers and find them. Why? To drive me away?"

"As if," Joan said wryly. "But stop and think about that. Granted, Cardinal O'Connor knew this was coming days in advance, but no one else knew he was going to call you in until yesterday—at a stretch, the day before. And even then, there would have been no way to know that you'd agree. Not with a vacation booked."

"They might have been hedging their bet. If they moved the moment they knew Tom was thinking of calling me in . . ."

"That would have given them a day and a half to create a forgery good enough to fool you and plant it in your private office. And it means that this someone would have to be among the cardinal's closest associates."

Jack looked at her. "Maybe that snooty young priest who serves as his steward. But why? Why would he care if I was involved or not?"

Joan shrugged, then gave him a saucy look from the corners of her extraordinary eyes. "Maybe he doesn't like you because you're such a heathen."

Jack laughed.

She sobered then and reached out to lay a hand on his forearm. The gesture flushed a flurry of conflicting feelings from hiding and sent them darting every which way, like a bevy of confused quail.

"I have something to tell you," she said. "I don't know that it bears on Gilbertson's deal with the casinos, but it's tied into all this somehow. The cardinal and mayor conspired to set up a meeting this morning between me and the CPD's head of violent crimes. A Commander Mathews. Gilbertson's name came up in connection with an arson case—a women's clinic here in Chicago."

"What?" Jack gave up trying to track the flushed quail and gave Joan his entire attention. "How was he involved?"

"He wasn't. Or at least, the cops can't make a case that he was." She explained the strange circumstance of Gil Gilbertson's name being on a slip of paper in a stolen car along with a phone number that connected to St. Jude's parish in St. Louis. "Here's where things get even weirder. The arson was claimed by an organization called the Society for the Preservation of Catholic Doctrine—a seriously conservative group of traditional zealots who dislike the pope and anyone who sides with him."

Jack felt as if a piece of cold iron had settled in the pit of his stomach. "Like Tom O'Connor?"

"That thought crossed my mind, and also that your buddy the cardinal knew all of this when he sent me to CPD headquarters. So, on the way back to the hotel, I called the cardinal and had a little chat with him. Turns out he didn't mention any of this at dinner because he wasn't sure he could trust all of his guests, and because some of it was not his to divulge. Bottom line: there is a slender connection between a nasty secret society and the subject of our investigation. No one's sure yet what it is, but my guess is it's not a friendly one. And Commander Mathews mentioned another player who may be involved in some way. A real estate tycoon named Coughlin."

Jack nodded. "Francis Xavier Coughlin. Yes, he's quite the local icon."

"Were you aware of his church politics?"

"You mean the fact that he's frequently and loudly at odds with the pope and the general direction of the Church? Yes. What's his connection?"

"This is for your ears only, but both Mathews and Cardinal O'Connor suspect he might be associated with this secret society in some way."

"As public and outspoken as he is?"

Joan tipped her head to one side so that a banner of gleaming black hair fell across one eye. "Sometimes the best hiding place is out in the open."

She was right about that. "Sleight of hand. Distract the audience into looking right at you with something splashy—"

"While you do something not-so-splashy where they're not looking. No one's saying this guy is definitely connected to the SPCD, but his politics are their politics, and what Gilbertson's doing with his legally won money could have gotten their attention."

Jack had no idea what any of this meant but trusted his subconscious would worry about it until something fell out. He shook his head. "Give me some sane news; what did you get from your folks at the LVMP?"

"Not a whole lot. Gilbertson was raised in Hunterton, a small town between Springfield and Branson, Missouri. He's thirty and single; no family that anyone knows of. No criminal record. Graduated from high school in Springfield. Credit cards and bank accounts show no unusual activity. Most of his spending has been in the Springfield area, St. Louis, and Vegas, where it appears he shows up whenever there is a magic get-together of almost any sort. He's a shift manager at a Burger King and pays taxes on about fifteen thousand a year extra on his earnings as an entertainer. Ruth Gilbertson died in Hunterton sixteen years ago, when he would have been fourteen. Cause of death was a stroke. No record of her having married again or having any other children. Gilbert was her only heir and got almost seven hundred thousand after taxes. He has one bank account in Springfield with almost a million in it, all interest from the original money. Drives a three-year-old Chevy. No record of home ownership; address is a rental in Springfield. Never in the armed services." She gave Jack an oblique look. "I suspect, Doc, that we're going to be making a trip to Missouri."

"If it's still necessary after tomorrow night. It's possible we could get a lot of our questions answered when he shows up at the House of Magic."

"You mean *if* he shows."

"You think he'll bail?" Jack asked.

Her eyes half closed as she considered that. "Actually, no. I . . . I'm reasonably sure he'll show."

Jack smiled. "Premonitions, Detective Firestone?"

Again, the charming head tilt. "If you want to call it that," she said.

"I'll call it intuition. So, in aid of that, why don't we have a quiet dinner and talk about something other than the Gilbertsons? My guess is that we will be spending plenty of time immersed in their lives in the next few days."

"Sounds like a plan."

Jack walked Joan back to the Drake, then went to the gym to work out for an hour. His intent was to give his subconscious the opportunity to pick over the information tumbling through his brain. He ended up thinking about Joan—or perhaps trying not to think about Joan. He was full of curiosity about her, about what made her tick, about what she was like beyond her role as a career detective.

He was also full of a strange, nervous guilt at being attracted to a woman so soon after Carolyn's death. And such a woman; she was so different from Carolyn . . . and yet like her in ways that went deep beneath the surface. Qualities of character, perhaps.

Well, that, and she was undeniably sexy. She wore her skin with an earthy, sensuous dignity that Jack felt viscerally. He was curious to see Joan in a relaxed environment. Would she wear her gray suit and sensible pumps to dinner?

Chapter 6

Joan did not wear her gray suit and sensible pumps out to dinner. She wore skinny jeans, tall boots, and a quilted jacket over a pale green sweater that made her skin seem to glow. She'd dressed up the low neckline of the sweater with a simple strand of fresh water pearls and had French-braided her hair, something that impressed Jack immensely. It boggled his mind that some women could construct those intricate plaits without being able to see what they were doing. His daughters had both mastered the French braid. It made him wonder if Irene, who was following in her father's footsteps, might be able to perform surgeries behind her back as well.

Jack took Joan to Rocco's, a small, out-of-the-way Italian place in Little Italy. It was sort of a landmark—an old building with big windows across the front, a big bar with a giant TV just inside the entrance, and several dining areas with white linen covered tables. Oil paintings and photos of Italy dappled the walls. There was an old-school pizza oven set into the wall next to the open kitchen doorway through which waiters and busboys bustled madly.

As usual for a Saturday night, Rocco's was jam-packed, but since the Bulls were playing, the crowd was moving out to get to the game as Jack and Joan arrived. On the way to their table, Jack saw Denny Brauer, a neurologist from the University of Illinois and Cook County

Hospital, having dinner with his wife and some friends; he stopped to say hello and introduce Joan. He wasn't blind to the glances Denny and his companions exchanged at seeing him with an attractive woman—a black woman. There was another exchange of glances when he explained that Joan was a detective working a case he was consulting on.

He wondered, as the hostess seated them, if Joan had noticed all the nonverbal communication. He considered asking but didn't, afraid it might make her uncomfortable. They ordered their meal and talked about what Joan thought of Chicago and Jack thought of Las Vegas. Chicago came out on top in that competition.

They'd noshed on appetizers and were waiting for their entrees when Denny Brauer got up and rushed out of the restaurant, cell phone in hand.

"Looks like your friend got called away," Joan observed, following Jack's gaze. "Happen to you a lot, does it, Doc?"

"Not as much as it used to. But, yeah, it's part of the life."

"Same here," she admitted. "Meals, sleep, concerts, workouts—everything you can get yourself involved in, the job will interrupt."

"Yes, but in your case, the interruptions can be life threatening. Mine, not so much." Jack grimaced. "Well, at least they're not life threatening to me. Does that bother you—the idea that any given call might put you in danger?"

She shrugged, drawing Jack's attention to her cleavage. She was well-endowed and curvaceous. He wondered if she wanted him to notice that.

"I don't really think about it anymore. I did when I was in academy, of course. You do then. Everybody does. There's this mosh pit of anxiety and anticipation in your belly, and you're imagining what it'll be like to be out in the street. After as many years as I've spent on the force, the kind of work I do now . . ." She shrugged again. "Like I said, I don't mind it. I suppose if I had a husband and kids I might, though."

Jack stared down at his salad plate. "No, um, attachments? Cat, gerbil, significant other?"

She shook her head. "None of the above. How about you? Your kids are both out of the house now, right? Is that hard?"

Jack was struck by the insight that question implied—it wasn't just a pleasant inquiry, it was directed at him and his situation in particular.

"It is hard," he admitted. "Especially mornings . . . and nights . . . and weekends. The quiet times that I'm still not used to spending alone."

"So, you work a lot more than you did before."

It wasn't a question.

"And I pester my daughters on any weekends they don't come home, yeah. We're planning a father-daughters camping trip this summer. When they were kids, Carolyn and I took them camping, fishing, and hiking all over the place. In fact, Carolyn and I met when I was headed for a Canadian fishing trip; we were seated together on a flight from Yellow Knife to Cambridge Bay on Victoria Island." He felt himself drifting back in time and brought himself up short. "What's your favorite vacation?"

Joan laughed. Her laugh was like her speaking voice—deep, rich, resonant. Her teeth were white against her cafe-au-lait complexion. "*Not* camping. Don't get me wrong, I love the mountains and the pines, but I hope to never see the inside of a tent. I demand a comfortable bed and a functional shower. I'm more the ski resort type."

"You ski?"

"I do."

"Fish?" He found himself hoping she'd say yes.

She shook her head. "Never done it. I have played tennis. I like to swim. But I'm more into watching other people do sports. Baseball, basketball, some tennis. But, no, I have never relished the idea of sitting by a body of water waiting for a bite. My relationship with fish has always been a bit ghoulish. I like to eat 'em."

Now it was Jack's turn to laugh aloud. "So, what else do you do for fun?"

She hesitated, giving him an assessing look, as if debating whether to reveal something. Then she said, "Actually, I've been attending college part time."

"Let me guess—law?"

She shook her head emphatically. "Nope. I've already got a criminal justice degree from UNLV. Now I'm working on my Masters in Twentieth Century American Music."

"American music? So, Gershwin, Copland?"

Her smile was blazing. "Two of my favorites. But more than that, of course. Blues, jazz, rock—all of it."

Their entrees had just arrived when Jack's cell phone went off in his pocket. He considered ignoring it, but he could no more ignore a call than Joan could. He pulled the phone out and glanced at the screen, frowning; it was Denny Brauer.

"You gonna answer that, Doc?"

Jack glanced up to see Joan watching him, her fork poised over her plate.

"If you don't mind . . ."

She made a gesture that said, Answer it, already.

He did. "Denny, what's up?"

"Jack, thanks for picking up. I'm over at County in the ER. I know you're not on call—I tried your pager first—but I really need an emergency consult. Could you come over?"

Jack looked across the table at Joan. "It's Dr. Brauer. He's got an emergency on his hands."

"Like I said," Joan told him, setting her fork down, "that's the life."

"I'll be there ASAP," Jack told his colleague, then glanced down at the two plates of untouched food. "I hate to eat and run—I really hate to eat and run from Rocco's—but you can stay—"

Joan stood and lifted her purse from where she'd hung it on the back of her chair. "Hey, I've got a belly full of salad and those tasty appetizers. Maybe we can take a rain check on dinner."

"You sure?"

"You betcha. This gives me a chance to see Dr. Jack Madison in action."

Jack explained the situation to Rocco—who served enough doctors to be used to having customers called away in the middle of a meal. By the time he'd settled the bill, their food had been packaged and bagged and placed in Joan's capable hands. They grabbed their coats and caught a cab to Cook County Hospital; it was now officially Stroger, but Jack doubted he'd ever call it that. Neither, he was willing to bet, would the many young doctors who trained there in what was probably the best—and busiest—trauma center in the world.

Jack was prepared to show his ID when they arrived at the ER's admissions desk, but a security guard approached before he had even gotten anyone's attention. The man greeted Jack with a broad smile.

"Hey, Dr. M! Where you been? I saw you on TV the other night. You've come a long way since we were both pimply-faced kids over here. I tell everybody I taught you everything you know."

"I can't argue that, Cletus."

Jack held out his hand for Cletus to shake, but the guard pulled him into a back-slapping hug. He caught the surprise on Cletus's face as he stepped out of the embrace and knew he'd just spotted Joan.

"This is Detective Firestone," Jack introduced her. "We're working together at the moment."

"Hello, Detective," Cletus said appreciatively. "May I say you don't look like any detective I ever seen."

"You may say that," Joan told him, "which is the secret of why I am so damned good at my job."

Cletus's smile widened as he turned back to Jack. "Doc Brauer told me you were coming. I'll take you back."

The trek to the heart of the ER revealed Cook County in all its glory. Ambulances disgorged a more or less constant stream of injured, who were swept into triage by paramedics. There were gunshot wounds, heart attacks and attempted suicides, sick crying kids with worried parents, drunks, people who were obviously mentally ill. At least three young men had hands and heads wrapped in bloody makeshift bandages, a dozen people sound asleep in plastics chairs. All waiting. Waiting to see a doctor, an intern, a nurse—anyone who could help them. But the sicker patients kept coming and pushing back the waiting time for those less in need of immediate care. Some of them would be rerouted to urgent care centers nearby, but most would wait and hope for relief from their particular suffering.

The sound and turmoil was overwhelming; it was Union Station at quitting time, a Bulls game, and an after-Christmas sale at Nordstrom all rolled into one. Cletus ushered his charges through the chaos to a curtained-off cubicle along one wall of the ER's huge central core. Inside, Denny Brauer stood at the bedside of a young Hispanic man who was clearly close to losing a battle to respiratory arrest. He was cyanotic, fighting desperately to breathe, and thrashing on the examination bed while several members of a code team struggled to restrain him so they could intubate him and establish an airway. A second young Hispanic huddled with a resident in the rear corner of the small space, conversing in a frantic mixture of Spanish and English.

"Got it!" The shout came from one of the nurses on the code team. She'd gotten the endotracheal tube in; one of her colleagues started the ventilator.

The level of chaos in the room dropped precipitously, and Jack heard several people draw in the noisy breath they'd been holding, waiting for their patient to breathe again. The patient, too, relaxed suddenly, his body going limp in a relief Jack suspected he'd have nightmares about for years to come.

Crisis over, Denny turned to Jack and Joan, his eyes going to the detective. "I'm sorry," he said, "but your lady friend will have to wait outside. HIPAA requirements—"

Jack opened his mouth, but Joan displayed her badge, reaching across him to offer Dr. Ellis her hand.

"Detective Joan Firestone," she said with subtle emphasis on the title. "Las Vegas PD. Jack and I are working a case together."

Jack cringed a little mentally. HIPAA requirements aside, he suspected that Joan did not much care for being introduced as his "lady friend."

"Oh," Denny said, "fine, then. Jack I'd like you to meet our neurologist resident, Dr. Henry Ellis. I'll let him fill you in on this case." He canted his head toward the young man on the bed.

"Dr. Madison," the resident acknowledged him, "thanks for the consult. I'll try to piece this together as best I can; my Spanish isn't all that good. The patient is Pablo Ruiz. Nineteen years old. His cousin here says he arrived in Chicago late this afternoon. I have reason to believe he was smuggled in on a big rig carrying fertilizer or something similar. His cousin says that when he picked him up, Pablo complained of pain in his left leg, but they couldn't see anything wrong with it. On their way to the cousin's house, Pablo started seeing double and became disoriented. Didn't know where he was or why. He became confused and combative and then began to drool uncontrollably. At this point, his cousin brought him to the ER. The intern started an IV, did some blood gases, and called me. By the time I got here, he was struggling to breathe."

Jack catalogued the symptoms, which spoke of growing toxicity. "How long from the time he came in and intubation?"

"About half an hour to forty minutes. We started nasal oxygen immediately. He is hyper-salivating and has bilateral ptosis."

Jack glanced at the patient's face. His eyes were closed now, so he'd have to take Ellis's word for the ptosis, or drooping eyelids.

"I called Dr. Brauer," the resident was saying, "when I saw Pablo's blood gases. His breathing became increasingly difficult and his throat closed up about ten minutes after Dr. Brauer got here. I called a code five minutes ago."

"Neurological exam?"

Ellis nodded. "No localizing signs or symptoms. Can't see his retinas, but his pupils are equal and slow to react to light. He's completely disoriented, probably at least partially due to his hypoxemia. I think that it and the salivation are associated with profound pharyngeal spasm; the anesthesiologist said the whole mouth and throat were very constricted and he had a hell of a time relaxing him. The patient also has the most impressive fasciculations that I have ever seen: neck, chest, and shoulders. His left leg, which was hurting him, seems normal. No swelling, no redness."

Jack glanced at the young man in the bed again. "He's not showing any sign of fasciculations now."

"Excuse me," Joan said quietly, "but what exactly is a fasciculation?"

Jack was surprised to hear her voice coming from so close beside him. "A twitch," he explained. "You know those annoying twitches you sometimes get under your eyes?"

She nodded.

"Imagine that all over your body." Jack turned back to the resident. "Ask Pablo's cousin where he and the truck he rode in on came from." He turned to Denny Brauer. "May I have a closer look at him?"

"Please."

Jack moved to the bedside and pulled the light blankets away from the boy's left leg. He began a careful examination, starting at the hip and moving down toward the ankle. He became vaguely aware that the resident had come to stand at the other side of the bed.

"He says his cousin and the truck came from Mexico. Near Dolores Hidalgo, wherever that is."

Jack nodded, his attention still focused on Pablo's leg. "Good," he murmured.

"There was no swelling," Denny reminded him.

"Not looking for swelling. Looking for punctures. Judging by the symptoms—including the lack of swelling—I'm about ninety-five percent sure this kid has been bitten by a coral snake, which we will never find and we sure can't ask him about until we can stabilize him. Any more specific neurological exam will be screwed up by the muscle relaxants he's been given, and I can see no benefit from a brain scan."

Jack straightened and let out a pent-up breath. There it was, above the left ankle, effectively camouflaged by dirt, leg hair, and a well-placed mole. He turned the ankle so his colleague could see the tiny wounds.

"If we could find the snake that made that, we'd know for sure. You know, 'red and yellow, kills a fellow.'"

"'Red and black, you're okay, Jack.'" Denny recited the second clause of the old reminder used to distinguish dangerous snake species from benign.

"Unfortunately, the chances of locating that truck and finding a reclusive coral snake in a load of fertilizer are slim and none, and slim just left town."

"What do you recommend, Jack?"

"There's coral snake antivenom that works for most victims. They'd have it at the Lincoln Park Zoo. He's your patient, Denny, but if it were me, I'd take the chance and give him *Micrurus fulvius* anti-venom as soon as you can lay your hands on some. If this is a coral snake bite, the high risk of cardiovascular collapse in the next few hours is a compelling reason to try the anti-venom. I'll be your defense witness if we're wrong."

Brauer turned to the resident. "We need to get someone to the zoo ASAP. Call ahead; tell them what we need."

"Micrurus fulvius," Hank Ellis repeated. "Got it." He disappeared through the curtains.

Brauer shook his head. "Jack, I'm embarrassed that I missed the significance of those puncture marks. As I think back, these symptoms are pretty classic for a neurotoxin, but we missed it. I'm going to start pretreatment with antihistamines while we're waiting for the anti-venom." He turned his attention to an attending nurse. "Pretest for sensitivity and give him something for tetanus. Be watchful for anaphylactoid reaction and delayed serum sickness."

The nurse was off as if her sneakers were rocket powered.

Denny turned back to Jack."What made you think of snake bite? You don't get much of that here in Chicago."

"I worked in a carnival years ago. We had all kinds of snakes, and I, being married to medicine and with more curiosity than I'm sure is healthy, had to know all about the toxicity of their venom. Besides, there was a bareback rider I had an insane crush on, and I figured it would impress the hell out of her if I could roll that sort of useful information off the tip of my tongue."

Jack heard Joan's laughter again. It tickled his ears very pleasantly.

"And now," he said, "since you seem to have this under control and we've got a dinner to finish, we'll be heading off. I'm going out of town in a day or two; if you need a consult while I'm gone, Fred Applebee over at Loyola knows more about snake bites than anybody in town. Give him a call and he'll be here in a New York minute. He loves this stuff, and you and your resident probably have a paper for the Archives of Neurology."

Denny Brauer grinned. "AFM, Jack. Can we put you on the paper as co-author? It should get us some attention."

Jack grimaced. "Yeah, but maybe not the kind you want. We have a number of colleagues who feel I am a shameless glory hound."

"What is AFM?" Joan asked as they made their way back through the tumult of the ER to the cab stand.

Jack felt his face flush with sudden heat. Good God, was he blushing? "Another Fucking Miracle."

"So, I guess it's a compliment then, huh?" Joan was silent for a moment, then asked, "Do some folks really think that about you—that you're a glory hound?"

"Alas, 'tis true."

"It bothers you," she surmised.

Damn, but she was sharp. Jack shrugged. "Not really."

"Dude," Joan said dryly, "your pants are smoldering."

They'd emerged into the cold night air, and Jack's surprised laughter rode out on a cloud of steam.

Joan angled a glance at him. "What?"

"First time in my life anyone's called me dude."

He hailed a cab and gave the driver instructions to take them back to the Drake.

"Are you hungry?" he asked as he slid into the car.

"No, sir. I figure I'm having roast pork with morels for breakfast tomorrow." She rattled the bag she'd been carrying.

"It's a bit early to turn in. Is there anything you'd like to do while you're in Chicago? Play tourist? Take in a show?"

She was quiet for a moment, then said, "I would love to hear some honest-to-God Chicago blues. Is that something you can arrange, Dr. Madison?"

Jack smiled. "I believe I can."

They dropped the bag of interrupted dinner off at the Drake, then took their cab over to Buddy Guy's Legends on South Wabash. Thanks to Jack's acquaintanceship with the bar manager, they were able to get a couple of seats at a table just to the left of the stage. The place was crowded, exuberant, and filled to the brim with the music of the Chicago R&B Kings. The light was low but for the stage and the "wall-o-guitars" behind the bar, both of which were artistically lit.

Jack hadn't been here since Carolyn's death, and felt a certain bittersweetness to coming here now with Joan. He found himself wondering if anyone he knew was here and what they would think of him showing up with a beautiful African-American woman in tow. He banished the thoughts and tried to let the music roll over him in warm waves.

"I've dreamt of coming here for years," Joan said when the Kings took a break. "The talent that's performed here: Bessie Smith, Blind Lemon Jefferson, John Lee Hooker, Charlie Parker." She smiled brilliantly and shook her head, her eyes sparkling like a kid's at Christmas. "Damn it, Jack, those are people I'm studying in school and they all played right here in this city—in this room. I've seen my share of brilliant musicians in Vegas, but this—*this* is where jazz and blues and R&B grew up."

Her enthusiasm was infectious and mesmerizing. Jack studied her in the warm, muted light and felt his attraction to her as part of the atmosphere of the place. It filled up his entire core and wrapped itself around him so suddenly and completely that he had to fight the urge to reach out and take her hand. Instead, he flagged down a passing waitress so they could order drinks. She wanted beer. He ordered himself a glass of red wine.

The house sound system had come on when the band's break began and was now rolling into "Good Night, Irene" by Lead Belly.

"This has always been one of my favorite songs," Jack said. "In fact, it's how my daughter, Irene, got her name."

"Now, I never would have taken you for a hopeless romantic, Jack Madison. I'd've thought you'd have a girl named Coral after your favorite reptile."

"I never," Jack objected, "said coral snakes were my favorite reptile. I actually prefer puff adders, but I think Puff is an unacceptable name for a girl. It lacks gravitas."

Joan laughed, then made a gesture toward the speakers from which "Good Night, Irene" flowed like warm honey. "This is the Capitol Record release, recorded right after the war. A lot better sound quality than the Huddie Ledbetter version from the thirties. But man, that older version has got somethin' goin' on. It hurts to think how much amazing music is either lost or barely heard because we didn't have the technology to preserve it."

"You weren't kidding about how much you love this stuff."

"Blues were a pivotal part of twentieth-century music, Jack. They paved the way for jazz, for rock and roll . . . Every musician stands on the shoulders of the ones that came before. It's history. If slaves don't come to the US with their tribal tunes, we don't have gospel, blues, jazz, or rock as we know it. There would have been no Elvis, no Chuck Berry, no Beatles, no Hendrix."

The Kings retook the stage and talk ceased. Mindful of the time, they left after that set and caught a cab back to Joan's hotel.

"Hey," Joan said as they crossed West Chicago Avenue, "wanna walk the rest of the way? I think it's only three or four blocks."

Jack agreed, and they paid the cabbie and got out. Clouds had rolled in and the temperature had risen a bit. All in all, it was a pleasant evening for a walk. Jack offered Joan his arm. She hesitated for a moment, then slipped her arm through his. They ambled up Lake Shore Drive in companionable silence, drawing the occasional sidewise glance. Mostly people ignored them.

"Ever date a black girl?" Joan asked suddenly.

The question startled Jack. "Ah, no. But then I didn't date much of anyone before I met Carolyn. Between medicine and magic, I was a bit on the nerdy side. She thought both those things were pretty cool. Most women—of any color—didn't. And my female co-nerds at school were every bit as perpetually exhausted as I was. You ever date any white guys?"

"A few. Nothing serious."

"You noticed some of the looks we were getting," Jack guessed.

She tipped her head to one side in a gesture Jack found increasingly charming. "The race thing is different on the Left Coast than it is in the Heartland, isn't it?" she asked cryptically, then fell silent.

Did she feel it too? Jack wondered. He thought she was attracted to him but possibly had the same yellow caution tape wrapped around her that he wore. He honored her silence—or maybe he was just avoiding the implications of her question.

He gave up trying to examine his own feelings and instead hummed a tune that seemed appropriate to the occasion.

Joan stopped dead in her tracks and turned to face him. "'On Such a Night as This'!" she exclaimed, her eyes shining again. "I am all over surprised that you even know that song, Jack. Hardly anyone in my classes at school knew Marshall Barer's music before they studied it."

Jack felt as if he'd done something marvelous and clever for which that smile and that sparkling gaze were his just reward.

Joan turned on her heel and began walking again, pulling Jack along, and as she walked she sang the song. Her singing voice was, like her laughter, rich, warm, and seductive. Jack realized he was almost quivering with emotions he couldn't possibly sort out with her so close.

"You blow me away, Joan Firestone," he said, though he was pretty sure he hadn't intended to say it aloud.

They were approaching the glittering facade of the Drake now, and Jack found himself wishing she'd invite him up to her room . . . and wishing, just as hard, that she wouldn't.

"I'll say good night here," Joan told him. She released his arm and turned to face him.

He felt bereft, colder. The words "May I come up?" hovered on his lips. He realized how viscerally he wanted her.

Joan flicked a glance toward the street. "That cabbie's eyeing us like he just knows one of us is a fare."

Jack followed her gaze. "Yeah, I can see that. I'd hate to disappoint him."

She'd meant to distract him, but he was suddenly unwilling to be distracted. He turned back to her and met her eyes. She didn't move. He didn't move. Jack felt the pull of her, like gravity, like a tide. He swayed toward her, lowering his head for a kiss.

Their lips were all but touching when she put her hands firmly on the lapels of his coat and leaned away from him. "Whoa, Doc. Too much beer, blues, and buzz for one night. I'm a little off balance here. Better for both of us to keep this professional, don't you think?"

What did he think? That she was probably right. That he didn't care just this moment.

She seemed to read that conclusion in his face and took a step back from him. "Yeah. You're rebounding from the worst possible kind of separation, and we are, both of us, too damned old for this shipboard romance stuff. Good night, Dr. Madison, and thanks for a wonderful evening. I'll see you at noon tomorrow. I'm really looking forward to meeting the Admiral. Seems like he'd be a real hoot."

Jack nodded, welcoming the change of subject. He, too, was off balance. "Yes. Yes, he is that. I think you'll enjoy him."

He went home, then, to his empty house and failed to sleep until nearly dawn.

Chapter 7

Jack was up by eight a.m. Sunday morning and had gone down to the kitchen to make coffee when his cell phone rang. He leaned over the phone where it lay on the countertop to peer at the screen. Irene.

He hesitated. He'd awakened this morning with a raging erection and last night's near kiss flooding his memory. He had not, just this moment, been thinking thoughts he wanted to share with his daughter.

"C'mon, Jack. Get a grip," he told himself and answered the phone. "Irene, sweetheart! How's my favorite eldest daughter?"

"A little worried. You didn't call yesterday. You said you'd check in when you got to the islands. I was getting ready to call your hotel—"

"Ah. About that. I'm still in Chicago."

She was silent for a beat. "Daddy, you're supposed to be lying on a beach sipping piña coladas. Why are you still in Chicago? And don't just say 'something came up.'"

"Well, damn. That was pretty much what I was going to say. Something did come up. Tom . . . called in a favor."

"Must've been a pretty big favor to keep you away from the Virgin Islands."

He was suddenly hyperaware of how much he had not been looking forward to the vacation that much. Too much alone time. He gave Irene an edited version of the case he was working on with the lady detective from Las Vegas: odd-duck magician making the casinos and the Church nervous by performing seemingly miraculous feats. He didn't mention the big donations to abuse survivor organizations.

"If he's not cheating, what can law enforcement do?" Irene wanted to know.

"Probably not much," Jack admitted. "But from my point of view, it's fascinating. What this guy has done so far is pretty impressive."

"So, what's this detective like? Is she a PI or FBI or—?"

"Las Vegas PD. Fraud Division. She—ah—works the casinos busting cheaters."

There was an awkward silence, then Irene said, "Uh-huh. So, what's she *like*? I've never met a woman detective. Is she, like, all pantsuits and cigarillos?"

"Good night, Irene! What would make you think that?"

"Well, is she like Agent Scully, then? Which, I guess, makes you Fox Mulder." She made a raspberry sound.

"More like Scully. She's in her late thirties, early forties, I guess. Attractive—"

"*Attractive*," repeated Irene with emphasis. "How attractive?"

Damn. His palms were sweating. He did not—*did not*—want to discuss another woman with his daughter so soon after her mother's death. He snagged a coffee cup from the drainboard next to the sink. "She's pretty, I guess."

"You guess. Hair? Eyes?"

"Yes, she has both."

"Daddy."

Jack sighed and poured coffee into his cup. "Black hair, kind of dark amber eyes." He vividly recalled all but falling into those eyes last night.

"Sounds exotic," said Irene. "What's her name?"

"Joan. Her name is Joan. Firestone."

"Like the tires?" Irene's voice had taken on the quality of a doctor absently asking a patient about their symptoms while filling in diagnostic data. ("How bad is the pain on a scale of one to ten?")

"I . . . yes. I guess so. Irene, why are you asking me all th—"

"Oh, Daddy, she's *gorgeous.* 'Pretty, I guess.' You're a terrible liar."

Dude, your pants are smoldering, said Joan's voice in his head.

"How the hell do you know what she—"

"It's called the Internet, Dad," she said. She sounded . . . gleeful. "You're the one who taught me how to do effective searches."

"Irene Constance Madison, you're stalking me."

"No, I'm just being a good daughter. Looking out for your best interests. Do you like her?"

He was speechless. "She's . . . very nice. Strong. Smart."

"Interesting?"

Beat. "Yes. She's actually really into music. Working on a degree."

"Is she working on you?"

"Irene! For the love of Pete! Your mother—"

"Is gone, Daddy." Irene's voice was subdued suddenly. "You're still living in this world. I know you. You're not a solitary kind of guy."

"She's from Las Vegas. She's a career cop. Head of her division. And I'm not really interested in a—a shipboard romance," he finished, using Joan's words to him.

"You *are* interested in her." There was that glee again.

Jack sighed. "I . . . I'm attracted to her, yes. But there's no there there, as they say. We just sort of . . . click in some weird, offbeat way."

"Well, you know what they say: never look a gift click in the mouth."

"No one says that, Irene."

"I love you, Daddy. I'll see you and Katy during spring break." And she hung up. There was even glee in that.

Jack arrived at the Drake just before noon to find Wilfred Benson already ensconced in the lobby with Joan. They were chatting and laughing over coffee like old friends. The Admiral's cane du jour had a cat's head handle in sterling silver. Joan wore a vivid plum colored sweater and a long black skirt. Jack wondered absently how big her suitcase was.

Benson saw him and waved him over to join them. "Doc, you are a scoundrel. You didn't warn me your detective was a beautiful woman." He shot Joan a sidewise glance. "A *sassy* woman. Do you know what she said to me? She said she knew me on sight because you told her if she saw an old duffer who looked like Colonel Sanders on steroids, she had the right man. Did you really describe me as Colonel Sanders on steroids?"

"I'm afraid I did," Jack admitted. "But you sort of do."

"I," Wilfred said archly, "am the original. Colonel Sanders was a pale imitation. Note the anemic quality of his facial hair."

"Well, since you two have taken care of the introductions, let's get something to eat; I'm starving."

Joan gave him a searching glance. "You just get up, Jack?"

"Not just. I mean, I slept in a bit this morning. I've had coffee. How about you?"

"Been up long enough to have a swim, a bite to eat, and go to early Mass at Holy Name Cathedral. I saw that Cardinal O'Connor was scheduled to give the eleven o'clock mass. Too bad I had to miss that. It'd be interesting to see him in action."

"You're Catholic?"

"Raised Baptist, mostly, but I'm pretty nondenominational . . . and curious."

They went over to the Four Seasons Hotel for Sunday brunch at Allium. The three of them got more than a few stares on the way across the street. Jack reflected that they probably looked like a joke going somewhere to happen. *Okay, so, a southern gentleman, a blues singer, and a stuffed shirt walk into a bar . . .*

Jack was convinced that Sunday brunch at the Four Seasons was in the top ten in the world. Every kind of breakfast from meat, egg, and pastry to sushi and dim sum, smoked salmon and caviar. All served with any beverage a patron might desire, up to and including champagne. All this was laid out in one of the most elegant dining rooms in the Midwest.

"Wow," Joan said quietly, "so this is what y'all call a brunch buffet in the Windy City. Vegas has a thousand buffets, but nothing like this. There goes the diet."

Jack chuckled. "We'll have a light supper: burgers, cheese fries, and malteds at Johnny Rockets."

"Oh, there's that mean streak you've been hiding. I suspected you were a sadist at heart. I bet that's why you like poking people with sharp tools."

Once they were seated at a table near the front window with plates piled high with food and an inexhaustible supply of coffee, the Admiral wasted no time getting to the subject of their meeting. "I've been asking around. Gilbertson's not your typical magic clown. Is there anything more you can tell me about your interest in this guy?"

Jack opened his mouth to answer, but Joan cut across him.

"Admiral," she said, "I can't tell you much except that it broadly concerns a potential gambling scam."

"Joanie, my jewel, I've already figured out it was something like that. Why else would Jack be working with a cop from Vegas? But my instincts tell me there's more than that to it. I suspect you can tell, my dear, that the world-famous Admiral was not born yesterday."

Joan smiled. "You are a perceptive man, Wil. As you suspect, there is much more to our interest in Gil Gilbertson than just a little hanky-panky at the slots. And I'm sure you understand why I can't divulge everything and why we need you to keep this entirely confidential." She leaned toward him slightly, laying a hand on his sleeve. "Tell me, Wil, what do you mean when you say Gilly isn't a typical magic clown? I'm not even sure what the word 'typical' means when it comes to clowns."

Jack hid a tickle of annoyance. Even he wasn't so privileged as to get away with calling Wilfred Benson "Wil."

"Magic clowns are typically more clown than magician," the Admiral explained. "They do kids' birthday parties, hospital and charity work, school shows, and things like that. Their acts have lots of balloon animals and self-working magic: milk pitchers, hand puppets, flowers that spring from colored scarves. All relatively simple magic tricks you can buy at the store and learn in the course of an afternoon. Don't get me wrong—some clowns are marvelous entertainers, but most are not really accomplished magicians, nor do they aspire to be. Recent rumor has it that Mr. Gilly has suddenly blossomed as a magician's magician."

"Rumor?" Jack repeated. "What sort of rumor?"

"First of all, he's been around Springfield for years, doing the things I just described, but not all that well. Even the off-the-shelf stuff he did was shaky—man had no self-confidence and it apparently showed. Seems he's wanted to do more for a long time; he joined the Springfield Ring ten years ago and attends their meetings regularly."

"Ring?" Joan asked.

Wilfred nodded. "As in linking rings. I'm sure you know the trick."

"Take two rings, tap 'em together, and suddenly they're interlocked?"

Another nod. "Rings are regional magic clubs. There are rings all over the country, mostly made up of members of the International Brotherhood of Magicians. IBM members are serious amateur or semiprofessional magicians who meet on a regular basis to show off for each other, talk shop, drink, eat some junk food, and get away from their mundane lives and significant others. Often they have a visiting lecturer. It's a gig I've done on occasion."

Joan flashed him a smile. "I don't doubt it."

Benson preened his mustache. "I spoke with Lew Gleason and Charlie Thomas, hoping for something on our man, Gilbertson. Lew owns Gleason's Magic Shop in St. Louis, and Charlie was international president of the IBM six years ago. He lives in Springfield, as it happens. They're thick as thieves, those two. Seems this fellow Gilbertson is a member of the Springfield Ring. Charlie attends most of the meetings, and Lew goes over three or four times a year, mainly to remind them that he owns the closest real magic emporium. They said Gilbertson doesn't contribute much at the meetings—sort of a watcher. Apparently, the few times he's done anything resembling magic, it was routine self-working stuff done poorly."

"Why do they keep him on then?" Joan asked.

The Admiral shrugged. "He shows up, pays his dues, and brings food and beer. Anyway, Charlie said that, about two, three months ago, Gil started doing card fans and productions. Not just regular card fans that you can buy off the shelf, but the kind that require real skill and can take years to learn. He said the entire group was dumbfounded and that Gilbertson was as good, if not better, than anyone Charlie had ever seen. And that's saying something; this guy has been around the magic block a few times and seen a lot of card men."

"Gilbertson didn't drop any clues about what caused his sudden improvement? Did he brag about a new mentor, maybe?"

"Not a peep. But all of a sudden he has a newfound confidence, an air about him, Lew says. And he does the Miser's Dream." He turned to Jack. "Get this, Doc, he does it with a big, clear crystal ice bucket. It's usually done with a rigged metal champagne cooler or a metal can," he added for Joan's benefit. "Lew and Charlie both tell me they have never—I repeat *never*—seen anyone as good with his hands. Filled the container with close to a hundred silver dollars and never made any moves to get to loads. They were both blown away, and the guys in the ring—all of whom know enough to understand how good this guy was—were similarly impressed. On both occasions, as soon as he was done, Gilbertson lost all his aplomb, got the jitters, and left the meeting."

Joan frowned. "I know what card fans are. I've seen Lance Burton perform them. But what's the Miser's Dream?"

"The Miser's Dream is a pretty rare trick," Benson told her. "Jack knows. Personally, I've only seen it done well by maybe ten performers in my whole life. It was invented by a famous turn-of-the-century American magician named T. Nelson Downs. He wrote about it. Classic book—*Modern Coin Manipulation*."

"Catchy title," quipped Joan.

Jack chuckled. "Hey, Downs was a magician, not a writer. Fifty years ago, his book was standard reading for any stage magician."

"Let me just say," the Admiral continued, "that we magicians do not usually discuss how a trick is done; however, the Miser's Dream is different. Anyone with an IQ over 60 knows that no one is actually pulling money out of thin air and that it has got to be sleight of hand—and done well, it is fabulous sleight of hand. Here is how it goes: the magician rolls up his sleeves, holds a bucket in one hand, and starts pulling silver coins out of the air, from his ears, from behind his neck, etcetera." He mimed the motions. "Sometimes he'll call someone from the audience up to the stage and pull coins out of *their* ears. Each coin is thrown into the bucket—usually a metal bucket—so the audience can hear it hitting the bottom or side."

Joan nodded. "I get it. The bucket is opaque. Which is why it's significant that our man Gilly did it with a transparent container."

Wilfred gave Jack a sidewise glance. "She's a smart one. The trick requires two entirely different sleights. First, the magician never actually throws a coin into the bucket. He never lets go of the coin; he palms it so that the audience can't see it until he produces the next apparently new coin."

"But he's just recycling the same coin, right?"

"Precisely. Second, the coins that fall into the bucket come from a device called a load that the magician has hidden in his coattails or some other convenient place. Sometimes the champagne bucket is rigged to hold the coins and release them one by one as the magician pretends to throw them into the bucket. The coordination between the fake throwing of the coin and the sound of it hitting the bottom of the pail must be perfect and takes years to master."

"So then the clear glass ice bucket lends some serious pizzazz to the show," Joan guessed.

"And a whole new level of complexity," added Jack. "I've seen it used a couple of times by real old-school stage pros. Blackstone did it live several times a day."

Wilfred was nodding, a back-in-time look on his face. "My father did it for a while in his vaudeville act and taught it to me. And, I will humbly add, I did it as well as anyone in my pre-arthritic years. As I said, it is rarely done well today, which is why both Lew and Charlie were so impressed with Gilbertson. The Miser's Dream requires a pure technical dexterity that, according to my compadres, Gilbert Gilbertson had shown no evidence of until an IBM meeting two months ago. Yet, when he did the Miser's Dream, his sleights were undetectable."

Jack drew in a long breath. "That's . . . well, it's impossible, isn't it?"

Joan glanced from one man to the other. "Why is it impossible? What does that mean—the sleights are undetectable?"

"Our witnesses," Jack explained, "are two professional magicians intently watching another performer to see what sleights he's using, hoping to maybe see something they can use in their own acts. Apparently, neither Lew nor Charlie could tell what Gilbertson was doing with his hands."

The Admiral nodded. "Precisely. So, I'm agog, Jack. How could a guy like this become a major league finger flinger overnight?"

That was indeed the question, Jack thought as they continued their meal, during which the Admiral regaled them with stories about his long career in the world of magic. A tale about how he fell off the stage while trying a flying carpet trick had both members of his audience in stitches.

"I don't know about the both of you," the old man said at length, "but I'm stuffed and we've been here for over two hours. I will see you tonight at our assignation at the House of Magic. I am beside myself with curiosity." He excused himself and left the dining room, tapping his cane energetically on the marble floor.

Joan watched him go, admiration and affection warming her gaze. "He is every bit as much of a hoot as I expected. Maybe more. What a character. I don't wonder you idolize him."

"Do I?" Jack asked, surprised.

Joan set her elbows on the table and leaned toward him. "Fess up, Doc. You'd like to be him in thirty years or so, am I right? He's what you might have been if you'd chosen magic over medicine. A legend."

"Hey," Jack objected, "I'm a legend now . . . Doctor Debunk, Medic Magician. The guy half the university medical staff wishes would STFU."

Joan laughed. "Do you even know what that means?"

Jack grimaced. "I'm only fifty, Joan. I got my first computer in the late eighties and have purchased every new iPhone since day one. I'm fluent in Twitter and Facebook, and I even have my own Flickr account."

"Which, I bet, is full of pictures of your daughters and magician friends . . . and very big fish."

He toasted her with the last of his coffee. "Damn, you're good."

They walked off brunch along the waterfront, ambling side by side in the afternoon sunshine, eyes narrowed against the aggressive sparkle of light on the thawing lake.

"So," Joan said at length, "what's the story on this place we're going tonight?"

"The House of Magic is a restaurant-cum-theater. Food's nothing special, but on any given night it hosts a diverse and interesting array of pro and semipro magicians and their friends and fans." He shrugged.

"In other words, it's a social hangout for the magic community. Sunday nights are reserved for card-carrying magicians like members of the IBM, so tonight it'll be mostly Chicago guys and their families, but past practitioners and friends of friends get in, too."

"Which is why you get in, I expect. Sounds like you're almost as much of a fixture in the magic community as your friend Wil."

"Hardly. I'm a semimundane that they agree to tolerate because of my checkered past. Anyway, most of the staff at the house are into the art as well; even the bartenders do tricks. It can be a challenge just to get a drink some nights. There's also a special auditorium for sleight-of-hand performances, and the dining room features a fully equipped stage for professional illusionists. You'll enjoy it, even if Gilbertson doesn't show up."

They walked along in silence for a while, then Joan said, "Want to talk about last night?"

Did he? Not really. Hell, he didn't really even want to *think* about last night, but now that she'd brought it up . . . "I guess all there is to say is that I had a wonderful time and I'm sorry if I came on too strong. I haven't been with a woman since Carolyn died and, so far, I haven't been at all interested. But if I were to tell you that you don't interest me—that you don't attract me—I'd be lying."

He wasn't looking at her but caught her nod from the tail of his eye.

"Me too," she admitted. "I was awake half the night thinking about it. Or trying not to, I guess. And I think there are some things I need to say to you before this goes any further."

"Oh, God," Jack said wryly, "the four most dreaded words in the English language: we need to talk."

"Don't joke, Jack. I don't want to pretend there's nothing there, nor do I want to start something that gets out of hand and screws up our working relationship. I need to be straight with you."

"Okay. Sorry. Please, say what you need to say."

She gave a big sigh. "I'm forty-two years old, never married, never really wanted to, and my window of opportunity for having kids is rapidly closing. Guess I've pretty much given up on the whole marriage and family thing. My job, my education, and music are my whole life. Once I get a degree, I'm going to retire from the force and get myself and my pension out of Vegas. I love the job—don't get me wrong. Solving cases, catching cheats, that's a good career to have. But I hate the place, and I don't like many of the people I have to deal with day to day. I don't date guys on the force, and I lead a pretty quiet life outside of work. Yesterday, when you got out of the cab in front of the Drake, you looked at me in a way I . . . well, I haven't had a man look at me that way for a very long time."

"I find that hard to believe."

She shook her head. "I get appreciative and predatory and calculating looks all the time. What I don't get is *that* look. As if I were a—a sunset instead of a steak. You know what I mean?"

Jack remembered the moment vividly. "You *were* a sunset."

"See? Now, there you go, saying stuff that makes me feel things I'm not sure I want to feel just now."

He shoved his hands into his coat pockets and looked skyward; clouds billowed and birds darted, sunlight glancing off their wings. "I know just how you feel."

Now she did look at him. "Jack, we are worlds apart. Literally black and white, cop and doctor, rough cut and sophisticated."

"Well, I wouldn't exactly describe myself as 'rough cut.' More 'unadulterated.'"

"Jack, you're doin' it again."

He grimaced. "Sorry. Go on."

"You are, I'm sure, one of the hottest single men in Chicago. I'll bet within weeks of your wife's death, widows and divorcees started showing up in droves. And you have the pick of the litter. Smart, rich, sophisticated women."

Frowning, Jack stopped walking and turned to look at her. Where was she going with this? She stopped too but shifted her gaze to the lake so he could only see her face in profile.

"Here I am," she said, "a chubby black woman you've known for less than two days and I'm flirting like a damned schoolgirl who doesn't know any better. I knew it wasn't right. We're professionals working a case together, and I think—no, I'm certain—that we should just forget about last night and work hard to keep this professional. Otherwise, one or both of us is going to get hurt. And I'm not willing to be hurt right now."

Jack opened his mouth and surprised himself with the words that came out. "Joan, let's not just dismiss this out of hand—and you're not chubby; you're curvaceous. You're ravishing . . ."

She swung around to fix him with a glare that should have singed his eyebrows. "Shut up, Jack. We're like Chicago and Vegas. Thousands of miles apart and separated by a mountain range of differences. Chicago is a real city; Vegas . . . well, Vegas is not a real place. It's filled with drifters, con men, cheaters of all kinds, and greed."

He shook his head, taken aback by her vehemence. "I don't understand—"

"What I'm telling you is that I long ago lost the ability to trust. And trust is something I need in a relationship. That's why I went to the cathedral this morning, believe it or not: to put this before God. To ask Him if I was kidding myself and should just take *this"* – she made a gesture that took both of them in—"at face value."

Jack stepped back quickly from the issue of trust and whether he was thinking of a relationship or just a hook-up. He took the opening she'd given him to change the subject. "And here I thought you weren't religious."

She had that gimlet gleam in her eye now, which he decided he did not like aimed at him. It made him squirm.

"Knowing how you feel about religion, I suspect that's a disappointment to you. Which is just one more way in which anything between us that wasn't purely physical would be doomed. News flash, Jack: religious and spiritual are two different things. I went to church because I needed to pray. I went to *that* church because I was curious. It was a good choice; the spiritual atmosphere helped me get my head on straight."

"So, God helped you get your head on straight and told you not to trust me?"

She shot him another pointed glance, then turned and started walking again. "Have you ever prayed, Doc?"

He was "Doc" again. She'd put miles of distance between them with that single word.

"Not since I was about twelve."

"Then I doubt you'd understand. Now that I've said what I wanted to say, I'd like to get us back to business. I didn't sleep well last night and we have a long evening ahead of us, so I'm going back to the hotel for a nap."

"I don't get to say anything?"

"Like what?"

Jack made a broad gesture of sheer frustration. "Like . . . I don't have any assumptions about where this attraction would go. Like you, I was pretty much blindsided by it. And I'm . . . conflicted, I guess. That's not a feeling I'm used to, and it's one I'm pretty sure I don't like. Which is not to say that if you wanted some company during your nap, I'd say no."

She actually rolled her eyes. "You couldn't just let it go, could you?" She turned her back on him and walked away toward the Drake, throwing the words, "See you tonight" back over her shoulder.

Jack tried to unroot himself to go after her—tried to call out an apology—but his feet were stuck to the pavement of the walkway, and the words were stuck in his throat.

Better this way, he told himself, and went to hail a cab.

Chapter 8

Cardinal Archbishop O'Connor said Mass and gave the homily at eleven a.m. that Sunday morning at Holy Name Cathedral with two members of the United States Congress attending. A local TV station had been invited to televise the service as a feed for other local channels.

Tom O'Connor would admit to God and no one else that he suffered the tiniest bit from nerves for the first time since he'd been a young priest subbing for a well-respected bishop with the stomach flu. His closing comments, which he had practiced in the sanctity of his private study, were meant to be a blockbuster message to person or persons unknown, and he had no real sense of how they would be received.

He began his comments by affirming his position as the head of the Chicago Archdiocese and cardinal archbishop of the Church of Rome. He avowed his unwavering support for the doctrines and official teachings of the Church and the responsibilities he held in common with his congregants as a citizen of the United States. He reminded those gathered of his service in the armed forces prior to becoming a priest, of the vows he had taken to uphold the Constitution and respect the law of the land. With those affirmations out of the way, he came to his point.

"Recently," he told his congregation, "I issued a mandate to the clergy of the archdiocese to remain aloof from politics. That they reject the clamor of partisanship and the magnetic pull of material and earthly concerns, and refrain from endorsing or publicly supporting specific political candidates and positions . . . or denigrating candidates they did not support. There is a distinction between the opposition of conscience to what one feels is immoral legislation, and public contempt aimed at persons one associates with it."

He could see heads nodding, brows furrowing, lips compressing. They knew this was a veiled reference to his having censured a priest who publicly mocked a political candidate from the pulpit. The cardinal knew that the case had divided believers all over the archdiocese.

"We are called upon by our faith," he reminded his listeners, "to love even those we perceive as our enemies, and to recognize that, as written in the Old Testament book of Ecclesiastes, 'All things equally happen to the just and to the wicked, to the good and to the evil.' I want to make it very clear that I support the separation of Church and State suggested by the Constitution of the United States. Christ Himself said we must 'Render therefore to Caesar the things that are Caesar's; and to God, the things that are God's.' That is the word we shall abide by while I remain your archbishop."

He paused for a beat, then said, "I'm sure most of you are aware that there have been criminal assaults against women's clinics in this city that either perform abortions or offer referrals to services that perform them. Let me be clear: I do not condone abortion. But, as much as I oppose this practice, I oppose even more any individual or any group that takes the law into their own hands and carries out or even *threatens* violence against these facilities, their staff, or their patients."

He had let his voice rise on these last words until they rang in the lofty vault overhead. There was complete silence as the words settled into the audience.

"There is never justification," the cardinal continued, "for people of faith to pursue illegal actions, let alone those intended to inflict injury or even death on other human beings, regardless of how sinful we imagine them to be. If their sin is great, how much greater is the sin of violating Christ's greatest commandment to love without distinction? A commandment upon which He says all others depend. A commandment that is exemplified by these words: 'He that is without sin among you, let him first cast a stone.' Therefore, the Catholic Church should and will cooperate with authorities in any and all areas involving unlawful behavior. Such behavior on the part of Christians can only soil the Church, and beyond that, the throne of God Himself."

Again, he paused to survey the congregants' upturned faces, gaze lingering here and there, reading, assessing. Were they here, any of those good Catholics who had set the Lake Haven women's clinic ablaze? Would they be at all chastened by his words? He doubted it. Zealots were hard to convince of anything that ran counter to their beliefs, even if one quoted them chapter and verse of scripture or, as Christ had observed, performed miracles for them. *If they hear not Moses and the prophets, neither will they believe, if one rise again from the dead.*

"It will be no surprise to those who know me well that I have chosen to make these comments in the presence of two distinguished members of the Congress of the United States and that I have invited the media to record my remarks." He acknowledged both groups with a nod of his head. "I am firmly convinced that my sentiments are not only in alignment with the teachings of our Lord, but are in concert with the thoughtful opinions of most American Catholics. My words were chosen with prayerful care and are not to be parsed and reinterpreted according to partisan whims. Which is why I do not intend to discuss my comments with any entity, including the media, secular or religious. I have shared what I feel compelled by the Word of God to believe. You deserve no less than to hear it from my lips. Thank you for your attention this morning. May God bless each of you and our great nation."

He made the sign of the cross, then stepped down from the pulpit in a silence so palpable, he felt it as a subtle pressure on his face. The silence maintained until he reached the center of the apse and stood before the altar. Then someone stood and began to applaud. They were joined by others, until virtually the entire congregation was clapping . . . with a few exceptions. Tom noted them. Most were people he knew. He wondered if any of them were inclined to arson.

He signaled the organist, who launched the cathedral's immense Flentrop pipe organ into a trenchant chorus of "Holy God We Praise Thy Name," during which Tom made his way slowly up to the sacristy where he removed his ceremonial robes. Father Lyons was waiting to help him, but in a state of muted agitation that made Tom edgy.

"Father," he said after a moment, "would you be so kind as to find Senator Farraday and Representative Hogan and invite them to join me in my private study?"

Lyons said nothing but merely nodded and left the room, fidgeting with his rope belt. Tom sighed. Lyons was a man of uneven temper and strong opinions that leaked out no matter how hard he tried to stifle them. That he had chosen to enter the Franciscan order was a source of great bemusement to his cardinal. Perhaps it was an indicator of self-awareness.

Tom had donned a less opulent set of robes and was about to leave the room when his cell phone buzzed, nearly walking itself off the side table he'd set it on. He answered, wishing the electronics could convey the humor of the caller. A second later, he doubled down on that wish; the caller was Francis Coughlin.

"O'Connor, you duplicitous sonofabitch! D'you think I wouldn't get the damned coded message you wedged into the end of your service this morning?"

"No," said Tom imperturbably. "In fact, I was certain you would get it . . . at least eventually, through the grapevine. I'm only surprised by the fact that you actually watched the sermon yourself."

"Of course I fucking watched it. You don't just invite politicians and the press to a run-of-the-mill Sunday litany. I knew you had something up your sleeve, Cardinal." The last word came out in a sneer.

"That makes sense. What about my coded message has you so exercised, Francis?"

"You damned well know what. Standing up for those abortion mills. If God had His way, every last one of them would be roasting in hellfire. As far as I'm concerned, the bombers are doing God's work."

"Ah. I see you failed to get the *uncoded* part of the message."

"Which was what? That you're a liberal apologist?"

Tom chuckled. "I should hope I'm liberal. After all, the word does mean broadminded and generous. The uncoded part of the message, Frank, is that you cannot offset the sins of others by committing a worse sin of your own. Breaking Christ's commandment to love unconditionally is, by His own Word, the greatest sin. If I were you, I'd be more concerned with righting my own wrongs, not someone else's."

"You sound more like that damned pope of yours every day," Coughlin snarled. "Or maybe he sounds like you."

"I am honored by the comparison. Did you have a particular reason for calling me, or did you just want to vent?"

"I wanted to warn you, Your Apostate Eminence."

Tom waited a beat. Clearly, Coughlin felt an ominous silence was appropriate here. "About?"

"I can't do a damned thing about that joker in the Vatican. But I might be able to do something about you."

"Threats, Francis? Really? Do you imagine that you can make me fear you?"

"Do you imagine that I can't have you removed from the picture?"

"Oh, I have every confidence that you can remove me from the picture, as you put it. But I think you won't, because if you did, the Holy Father might simply assign someone to Chicago that would make me seem tame. Better the devil you know."

"I don't give a rat's ass what the Holy Father does."

"A lie. You care deeply what Pope Francis does because it infuriates you. Ironic that you share a name. Ironic, too, that you share with him a desire to preserve the true faith of the Church—you just have very different ideas about what that is."

Coughlin did not miss the oblique reference to the SPCD's agenda. "Whatever it is you think you know," he said, "you would be stupid to share it with the authorities. Don't make trouble for me or I'll find it necessary to return the favor."

"Really? A moment ago you were threatening to *kill* me, Francis. Are you walking back your threat? Now you're merely going to make trouble?"

"I'm not walking back a fucking thing, you smug bastard. You are defending the indefensible. Those clinics should all be burned to the ground. Every last one of them."

"Yes, you said that. Look, Francis, I have a meeting with the two legislators who attended Mass today. I really must go. But I'd like to ask you to think about something."

"Yeah? What's that?"

"Since you clearly believe in neither the authority of the pope nor the Word of God, why are you Catholic? In fact, what makes you identify as a Christian at all?"

Tom cut off the resulting pyroclastic flow of obscenities and tucked the phone into the pocket of his cassock. He stood for a moment, contemplating the call. Was Frank Coughlin actively and directly involved with the SPCD, or was his defense of their activities merely an affectation intended to impress or distract? It was possible, Tom reasoned, that he would never know.

He left the sacristy and made his way across the second-floor gallery toward his office, wondering at his own temerity. Francis Xavier Coughlin was not a man one itched to cross. He was a billionaire many times over and had been known for his ostentatious support of the Chicago Archdiocese . . . until Tom had been assigned as archbishop and refused to be impressed with the way Coughlin wore his religion on his sleeve like a set of crucifix cuff links. The real estate mogul gave money, now, only to more conservative movements within the Church.

He was also a political player. In that effort, he was quite bipartisan— he bought anyone willing to be bought and worked to compromise or embarrass anyone who refused, irrespective of party. In the darkest corners of the business sector, he was "Fast Frankie" and was suspected of all manner of dark pursuits and crimes that had never been proven. His friends called him "Franny." His employees knew that if they were caught doing anything Fast Frankie considered morally questionable— getting a divorce or committing an act of debauchery that might result in a divorce—they would lose their jobs and be blacklisted in whatever line of business they were in.

Tom supposed he ought to be afraid of such a man, but he wasn't. Frank Coughlin had begun his empire as a slumlord, and a slumlord he would always be, regardless of how many other businesses he made money in. It was his family Thomas O'Connor prayed—and feared—for. Coughlin and his wife had eight children, the oldest of which had just gone off to college. He wondered occasionally what they thought of the patriarch of their family. He supposed that they loved him, but Cardinal Archbishop Thomas O'Connor solemnly admitted before God that he could not imagine that feat of Christlike proportions.

"Forgive me, Lord," he murmured, crossing himself. "I am just not there yet."

He breezed through the half-open door of his office to find Senator Janice Farraday of Iowa and Representative Steve Hogan from a nearby district in Indiana seated at a small, round conference table in the lee of a stained glass window and a floor-to-ceiling bookshelf.

"Your Eminence," Farraday said as Tom seated himself across from her, "I was not expecting anything like this today. Thank you for saying what you did. I hope it will work toward healing some of the rifts that have occurred in this country in recent years. You did not mention the radical religious right, but I'm sure the connection won't be missed."

Tom smiled wryly. "Yes, well, subtle I am not."

Representative Hogan was young for having risen to his position in government, handsome and earnest. "I guess," he said now, "the senator and I had better be prepared to respond to questions. You may have ducked the media, but they'll be waiting for the two of us outside in droves. Any suggestions, Senator? I'm a bit new at this," he added in a mild note of self-deprecation.

Real or feigned? Tom couldn't tell, which meant that the young congressman was either sincere or very good at appearing to be so.

The senator shook her head. "No, I'm only going to say that I support most of what the cardinal said and that I have to rush to catch a plane. I suspect both of our parties will have carefully crafted responses by later this afternoon. Too bad we can't be as blunt as you, Cardinal."

Hogan turned a seemingly admiring gaze on Tom. "No kidding. You sure do know how to stir the pot, Your Eminence."

"Had to be said, Congressman. And anybody who knows me is already well aware of my feelings on virtually everything I said this morning. I figured it was time to stop beating around the bush and get it out in the open. If you think you have some tough questions ahead of you, wait until the calls from Rome start. I could be transferred to a cloistered monastery in Slovenia by tomorrow for all I know. You two go out and face the vultures with their cameras and microphones. I'm going to reflect and pray a bit, then head back home to face the music."

Janice Farraday rose, looking bemused. "Calls from Rome? Surely Pope Francis would have no quarrel with your message today. He's very much about going by the Book, as it were."

"Ah, yes. But the calls I'll get won't come from the pope. My fellow cardinals have no compunction about letting me know when they disagree with me."

Tom bid his guests good day, then sat for several minutes in prayer and contemplation before he rose to collect Father Lyons and head back to the rectory.

Collecting the Franciscan proved to be more difficult than he expected. He was not in the main sanctuary nor in the choir loft. Tom pulled out his cell phone and tried Lyons's number. He got voice mail. Vaguely annoyed, the cardinal was at the point of giving up and leaving Lyons to find his own way home when he heard a muted exclamation from the gallery level. He went back upstairs, realizing as he stepped out onto the gallery, that the voice was Lyons's, that it was coming from the sacristy across the gallery to his left, and that he was undoubtedly hearing one side of a phone conversation. That explained why he'd been unable to reach Lyons by cell phone.

Tom strode down the gallery toward the sacristy. As he drew closer to the closed door, he caught a word here and there as Lyons punctuated them with zeal.

"Are the networks? . . . saw it live? . . . No, sir. . . . me? What? . . . Yes, sir . . . outreach . . . *Protestants?* . . . Yes, sir."

Tom frowned, wondering what the conversation was about. There was a lull as the other person spoke at some length. In that time, he reached the door.

"Yes, sir, as you said, it's time for outreach," Lyons said, his voice hard with resolve. "The enemy of my enemy is my friend."

Tom supposed that was one way to frame ecumenism. He rapped the door smartly with his knuckles. "Father, the car is waiting," he said. "Please wrap up your call and come down."

There was a beat of silence, then, "Of course, Your Eminence."

They were riding back to the rectory in the cardinal's car when Tom's curiosity got the better of him. "So, Father Lyons, are you interested in pursuing interfaith work? I hadn't thought it inspired you."

Lyons looked positively stunned. "Interfaith . . . ? No, Your Eminence. I would not—that is, I would never . . . We are servants of the True Church. All else is—is false and satanic. Please, Eminence, I'd beg you not to require me to do interfaith work."

Tom started to open his mouth to ask what he had overheard, if not Lyons accepting a request to take part in an ecumenical effort, but intuition stopped him. He had not been mistaken about the deference in Lyons's voice during the brief snatch of conversation he'd overheard. He had clearly been speaking to someone he considered his superior, but had uttered no honorific titles. Who might he defer to other than a superior clergyman?

"No worries, Father Lyons," Tom said. "I can see you are not my man." *Possibly in more ways than one.*

Chapter 9

The House of Magic was located in a restored Victorian mansion on North Dearborn. The only signage was a small brass plaque on the door, which was tended by a guy who reminded Jack strongly of Lurch from the Addams Family. Guests stepped into a foyer that had no visible access to the interior of the club. All three interior walls were covered in floor-to-ceiling bookshelves. The only other furniture in the room was a Victorian-era chair and a matching side table on which sat a candelabra and a skull with a candle inside.

Lurch asked everyone who arrived in this anteroom for the "secret" password. It was always "Houdini," and return visitors knew that. Newbies didn't, and got a kick out of the resulting drama.

Jack was tickled that he and Joan happened to step into the club's foyer in the wake of just such a group of first-time visitors.

"The password?" The doorman regarded the newcomers with an arched expression.

"Password?" the man leading the group repeated. He glanced around at the other three members of his party. "I don't . . ."

"Watch this," Jack murmured close to Joan's ear.

The doorman glowered. "You don't know the password, sir? Have you an invitation?"

"Uh, yeah. Yeah, here."

The man handed over a large cream-colored card, which Lurch eyed suspiciously, even turning it over to scan the back and sniffing it. Finally, he turned to the skull and held the invitation in front of it as if the thing might be able to read it. The skull's eyes blazed hotter for a moment, sending flickering light out through its eye sockets, then its mouth opened slightly.

"Houdini!" it screeched in a tone that sounded like a parrot in an echo chamber.

The visitors jumped and giggled, and the sepulchral doorman handed back the invitation.

"Very well. You may enter." He touched the candelabra. Its arms lowered, and the bookshelf behind the doorman turned on a pivot to allow the visitors entrance. They went through the door chattering like magpies, their eyes almost as incandescent as the doorman's skeletal sidekick.

The doorman turned back to his next set of guests.

Jack grinned. "Houdini," he said and produced his invitation.

The doorman checked it, noted their host's name, and nodded. "Good evening to you both. Admiral Benson is already here. I believe he went up to the dinner theater."

The bookshelf repeated its dance, letting Jack and Joan into the House of Magic. It was a little after eight—they had dinner reservations for eight thirty—so Jack led Joan on a brief tour of the place. They began with a drink at the bar, the back wall of which was covered with hundreds of autographed photos and posters of magicians. One of the bartenders was doing simple rope tricks that Jack had seen many times before. He pretended to watch anyway, but was really watching Joan watching the performance. She had worn a vibrant ruby red cocktail dress that fit her curves as if it had been molded to them.

Uncomfortable with where his thoughts were headed, Jack suggested they continue their tour of the House of Magic. Drinks in hand, they went down to the Closeup Club—a two-story circular room with a dozen tiers of seats situated in a remodeled turret. The centerpiece of this extraordinary room was a sort of intimate theater in the round that held only a green satin-covered table and several seats. Here, magicians did table tricks—cards, coins, and other intimate sleights of hand.

"Huh. It's like an old-fashioned surgical amphitheater, isn't it?" Joan remarked. "I see why they call it the Closeup Club."

"I wouldn't know about old-fashioned surgical theaters," Jack said wryly. "That'd be before my time."

A magician was taking a seat at the table now. Jack started to suggest they continue their tour, but Joan had already slid into a seat in the top row of the audience. Jack hesitated, then sat next to her. The magician—whom Jack hadn't seen before—did a selection of card routines that he recognized—Four Ace, the Ambitious Card, Card-to-the-Wallet—before moving to dealing perfect poker hands.

Jack was about to comment about the quality of the magician's work when Joan leaned toward him and murmured, "This guy deals seconds, bottoms, and false shuffles pretty well. But I've seen better."

Jack hadn't. He stifled a niggle of irritation. Magic was his bailiwick. "So much for trying to impress the lady. Let's go get another drink before dinner."

On the way to the bar he couldn't quite contain himself. "I thought that guy was pretty good. You've really seen better? Or were you just counting coup?"

She shot him a puzzled glance. "Jack, compared to some of the guys we catch in Vegas, he's about a C plus. He'd last about fifteen minutes in one of our hotels if he tried any of that stuff. Of course, he's telling stories and misdirecting; neither of which is possible when video cameras are recording your every move, magnified in high res. I suppose that distracts a lot of people."

"You really think he's not as good as some two-bit hustler?"

"Jack, this guy's playing Marco Polo at a tourist pool party. Our guys in Vegas are swimming in shark-infested waters." She hesitated, then added, "I've trained for years to catch cheats, Jack. It's my job. I wasn't trying to rain on your parade. I think maybe I ought to just keep my non-case-related comments to myself."

Suddenly and emphatically, Jack felt like a jerk. "No, Joan. This one's on me. Of course, you'd have seen better. You're right. This guy's livelihood doesn't depend on fooling people who are professionally trained not to be fooled. Your Vegas card shark does. I just hadn't thought of it that way before."

She rewarded him with one of her one thousand candle-watt smiles, and his momentary irritation evaporated.

The dinner theater was on the second floor in the core of the house. The tables were set on broad tiers that formed a semicircle around a stage big enough to hold most magic acts, including props and two or three people.

Despite the size of the room—which was quite full—Jack was able to locate the Admiral without half trying. He was seated at a table with a party of five, apparently in the midst of a story that had his rapt audience laughing uproariously. His snowy hair gleamed in the low light, and he gestured with a cane whose jeweled head flashed and sparkled.

Rather than join the party, Jack chose a smaller table nearby where Benson could see them. He and Joan waved; the old man acknowledged them with a twinkle, not even pausing in his story.

The moment they'd seated themselves, table hoppers appeared to entertain them with small, intimate magic tricks.

"Good grief," Joan said after the third one had left their table. "They make it hard to read the menu. How'm I supposed to get fed if they keep interrupting the hunt?"

"It's a ploy," Jack told her. "The hungrier you are and the harder you've had to work for it, the better the food tastes. Don't order fish."

"Why not?"

"Sunday night. Worst time for fresh fish anywhere, especially the Midwest."

She laughed and applied herself to the menu. The Admiral joined them at the same time the waitress arrived at their table. She took Jack's and Joan's orders, then looked to their companion.

"The usual, Barb," he told her. "Surprise me with the sides."

"Ooh," Barb said, "taking your life in your hands."

"I live for danger . . . Any sign of our guy?" he asked as the waitress sailed off toward the kitchen.

"Not yet," Joan said. "But then, I gather he likes to make a mysterious entrance and a hasty exit. I wouldn't expect to see him hobnobbing with the clientele before the show." She checked her watch. "Which should start in about twenty minutes."

It didn't start in twenty minutes. They'd finished their dinner and had ordered coffee when there was finally some activity down near the stage. A group of folks—mostly house magicians—had gathered along the front at smaller tables, the better to see what the performer of the evening was doing. Admiral Benson excused himself and went down to join them, the better to catch any potentially important gossip.

The stage was small but elaborately decorated. The proscenium arch was bordered with intricate carvings of mischievous elves, djinn coming out of bottles, bizarre animals, and ghosts of all kinds that shone as if the aging wood had captured some residual magic from the myriad performances there. It was a perfect stage for magic. The bright red satin curtains were opened and, with the exception of a small table and a couple of chairs upstage left, the stage was bare.

Jack realized that though the remaining dinner guests were few, the gathering at the stage apron was the largest he'd ever seen for the nine p.m. show on a Sunday night. Every one of the table hoppers was there, along with the other house magicians and performers he'd seen at other venues around town. He also recognized the sleight-of-hand artist from the Closeup Club. Clearly, someone had spread a rumor that something special was going to happen tonight. He wondered if the rumor monger was Gilbertson himself.

When the murmurs from the assembled multitude down in front had reached a fever pitch, Gilly the Magic Clown appeared from the stage-right wings. Jack assessed him with interest. He was of average height, but that was the only average thing about him. He was portly, with abnormally pale skin and flaming red hair. He wore thick horn-rimmed glasses and a ridiculous Aladdin costume made up of a voluminous pair of harem pants and a spangled vest that revealed a doughy torso with a smattering of red chest hair. His costume was all topped off with a bright gold turban. He carried a huge, round straw basket.

All conversation stopped.

So did Gilbertson. He gawked at the audience for a moment as if their presence surprised him, then continued to the center of the stage where he set the basket down and asked if someone would kindly turn up the stage lights. His voice was as pallid as his complexion, but it did not waver or crack. Gilbertson thanked the unseen lighting tech that had honored his request, and turned to face the group of snickering magicians, who had apparently decided to take this as a comedy routine.

In a voice that challenged the sound engineer to keep his mics from feeding back, the would-be magician announced himself. "My name is Gilbert the Great—King of Cards, Rajah of Ropes, and Master of Mystery. For your enjoyment, I am going to perform the Hindu rope trick as it was always meant to be done but has never before been accomplished. I am confident that you will be amazed."

"He doesn't *sound* confident," Joan murmured. "He sounds like Piglet."

Jack glanced at her askance.

"Y'know—Winnie the Pooh's little sidekick?"

"I have two daughters, Joan. I know Piglet intimately and can recite most of his dialogue from any given Pooh book or video."

The magicians in attendance apparently agreed about the comic nature of Gilbert the Great; they erupted with laughter at the ludicrous sight he presented—trembling but solemn—in his cartoon getup.

Gilbert ignored them entirely. He took the woven lid off the basket and removed a thick braided rope, then draped the coil over his shoulder and tilted the basket on its side to reveal the empty interior. The snickers died down as the magicians focused on the trick. Gilbertson placed the basket upright upon the stage floor, then climbed in and stomped around inside of it as if to further prove its emptiness. Then, he covered the basket with its fitted top, walked around it several times, and removed the lid.

Like a jack-in-the-box, out popped a dark-skinned, black-haired boy of about fourteen dressed only in a loincloth. He was almost as tall as Gilbertson, leading Jack to wonder how he'd fit inside the basket.

Of course, if there were a drop-bottom in the basket and a trapdoor on the stage, he wouldn't need to fit. Jack made a note to check the stage floor after the show.

The magicians, who were roughly ten feet closer to the stage than Jack and Joan, were accustomed to seeing people and animals appear and vanish, but even they seemed impressed by the trick. A number of them exchanged glances, followed by nodding and even a smattering of applause.

Gilbert quieted them with a wave of his hand. The gesture was confident, even imperious. Jack glanced at the younger man's face. His expression had changed subtly as well. He no longer looked the least bit timid.

Gilbertson took the rope from his shoulder and tossed one end of it into the air. The bound end disappeared behind the top of the proscenium, and the rope stood, straight as a rod, from ceiling to floor. Several of the magicians in the audience leaned out over the apron, straining to see up into the loft. Jack only barely restrained the urge to go down to join them.

Those who'd peeked into the rafters sat back, shaking their heads. Gilbertson pointed at them. "Do you see any wires? Hooks? Supports?"

"No," said the man from the Closeup Club. "I didn't see anything but the end of the rope."

The rope ignored all this; it remained upright, like a snake with rigor mortis, its lower half coiled and its upper half stretching upward about fifteen feet. Now, the boy walked over to the rope, grasped it with both hands, and easily as a monkey, began to climb.

Of course, thought Jack. *He'll just climb up into the loft.*

But he didn't simply disappear behind the proscenium. He began to fade when he was five feet off the stage, gradually becoming less and less solid until—by the time he reached the top of the arch—he had completely disappeared, quite as if he'd climbed up into a fog bank. But there was no fog onstage, no smoke, no mirrors, nothing but the rope, the basket, and one oddball magician-clown.

The magicians applauded tentatively, as if they thought they'd been told a joke but weren't sure they were supposed to laugh. Jack, for his part, had never seen anything like this, and he'd seen nearly every kind of vanishing act there was. Gilbert bowed, then moved to stand next to the coiled rope, gazing up into the theater loft. He squinted. He waved. He scowled prodigiously, then shouted, "Hey!"

A voice—ostensibly the boy—answered from the darkness of the loft, speaking in a language Jack didn't understand but that he suspected was Hindi. Gilbertson answered in kind, his tone quarrelsome. He made gestures at the stage to indicate the boy should come down this instant. The boy answered with heat, which caused Gilbertson to shake his fist at the distant rafters. He moved to the basket, reached in, and drew out a curved scimitar. He put the dull edge of the blade between his teeth and, with amazing grace and agility, shimmied up the rope. Like the boy, he became progressively obscured until he vanished from sight.

There was dead silence in the room; the magicians' knowing smirks and smiles were gone, but from the remaining diners, Jack heard murmurs of disbelief.

"It's all smoke and mirrors," said one man. "They're hiding up in the rafters. There's catwalks up there, I bet."

The words had no sooner left his mouth than a great ruckus sounded from the theater loft—sounds of a ferocious struggle. Then, without warning, severed and bloodied parts of the boy's body—his limbs, torso, and finally his head—tumbled from the top of the rope onto the floor. Blood and gore were scattered about the stage; the arms and legs were still moving and, unbelievably, the eyes in the boy's bloody head were blinking and looking about, while from his mouth came a chant in the strange language he and Gilbert the Great had been speaking.

As the audience reacted with exclamations of horror or disbelief, Gilbertson, also covered in blood, faded back into sight as he descended the rope. The bloody scimitar was still clenched in his mouth. The moment he set both feet on the stage, the rope collapsed back onto its coil, as if guided by unseen hands. Gilbertson dropped the sword, then collected the severed pieces of his assistant's body as if he were gathering cord wood. He threw them one by one into the basket. With this grisly task complete, he uncoiled his turban, wiped the blood from his body with it, and tossed it into the basket as well. Finally, he replaced the lid.

"This guy is making me very nervous," Joan murmured.

Jack could tell. She had placed her purse on the table and laid her hand atop it as if she might need to open it at a moment's notice. He realized that must be where she kept her service piece. It certainly wasn't concealed under the clinging cocktail dress she was wearing.

Gilbertson had begun to pace round and round the basket, making arcane hand gestures and muttering something completely unintelligible.

"What the hell is that?"

Joan's voice pulled Jack's attention back to her face. She was staring to stage left with a puzzled frown on her brow.

"What's wh—?"

"On the chair to Gil's left and behind him."

Jack looked. Where there had been nothing a moment ago sat what looked like a very large, dark bird. From here, with the lighting as it was, Jack couldn't tell what kind of bird it was or even what color it was. He could tell only that it was bigger than any hawk or macaw he'd ever seen and that it was alive. Its head moved with quick, precise movements as it apparently tracked the scene on stage.

He opened his mouth to say he had no clue what that was when Gilbert the Great stopped pacing and faced his silent audience with a beatific smile that transformed his round face. He reached down and removed the lid from the basket. Out jumped the boy, wearing the turban in addition to his loincloth. All were spotlessly clean.

Magician and sidekick smiled broadly and took a deep bow; Gil added an exaggerated flourish. When they straightened, he spoke again, his voice now sonorous and forceful.

"Ladies and gentleman, the Hindu rope trick, as interpreted by Gilbert the Great."

The gathered magicians jumped to their feet, applauding wildly. With no acknowledgment of their praise, Gilbert and his assistant picked up the basket, rope, and sword, then, instead of exiting into the wings, descended the steps on the side of the stage and walked toward the back of the dining room. Neither of them so much as glanced at the audience until they reached the tier on which Jack and Joan were seated. The boy kept walking, but Gilbertson took a detour to pass by their table.

He paused to offer each of them a sketch of a bow. "Dr. Madison, Detective Firestone. Thank you for coming. Doctor, it's good to see you again. I hope I'll see you in Vegas in about a week. And detective, it's nice to see that the two of you have finally met."

He winked at Joan, then hurried away before Jack could ask him how he had managed the trick. Jack and Joan both rose to follow him. They exited the dinner theater into an empty hallway.

"You take the back; I'll take the front," Joan said and headed toward the front of the club.

Jack wheeled around and headed in the opposite direction. He saw no sign of Gilbertson in the building. He quickly checked the men's room at the rear of the building; it was empty. At the rear of the huge house was a conservatory that ran the entire width of the first and second floors. Four sets of French doors opened onto an exterior deck and thence, to the parking lot. The parking lot was only one-third full. The magic clown was nowhere in sight.

Jack returned to the dinner theater to find Joan standing down by the stage talking to Admiral Benson and several of the magicians who'd seen Gilbertson's performance. Three of the house magicians were pacing the stage, looking for blood or any other physical trace of the trick.

The Admiral, looking more disconcerted than Jack had ever seen him, turned to Jack as he approached. "How'd he do this, Jack?" he asked, sounding shell-shocked. "There are no trapdoors on this stage. There are no rods or pulleys. There is not even a catwalk up there." He pointed up into the stage rigging.

"Wil," said Joan, "did you see the bird? On the back of the chair up there?"

Wilfred nodded. "It was an eagle. A golden eagle. Chet and Maggie saw it too." He gestured toward two of the magicians currently prowling the boards.

"I didn't," said one of the other magicians. Jack recognized him as one of the table hoppers who'd entertained them before dinner. His name tag said Brendon. "But then, I was trying not to take my eyes off that basket."

There was something ironic, Jack thought, about Wilfred Benson asking him if he knew how a trick was performed. "I have to tell you, Admiral, that was the most intense fifteen-minute routine I have ever witnessed. And, believe me, try as I might, I don't have the faintest idea how he did it."

"What did he say to you when he came to your table?"

"He said he remembered me from when he was a kid, that he hoped to see me in Vegas, and . . . and that he was happy Joan and I had finally met. As if it were something he'd wanted to happen."

"Or predicted?" asked Joan. "Like his mother . . . predicted things? Like he predicted his wins in Vegas?"

They stood in silence for a moment, while Jack fought the sensation that he was one of those doomed knights trying desperately to climb a glass mountain to love and fortune. Reality was no longer obeying the laws of physics, or Jack Madison's expectations. For every step his mind took up the slippery, deadly slope, it slid back two.

"Well," said Wilfred at length, "I can finally die a fulfilled man. The Hindu rope trick, exactly as it was imagined for ages but probably never, until tonight, performed. Jack, I just don't know what to say. If I hadn't seen it, I wouldn't believe it. You wrote about this trick, didn't you, in that piece in the *Inquiring Skeptic*?"

"I did. Lectured on it, too. There are theories, of course, the most rational of which involve mass hypnotism." Staring at the solid boards of the stage floor, Jack chewed the inside of his lip and turned ideas over in his head. "About twenty years ago, my mentor, Sam Bernstein, studied a colleague's account of three missionaries who claimed to have seen a variant of the trick performed outdoors by an Indian magician."

"Outdoors?" repeated Joan. "Doesn't that make the trick damn near impossible?"

"You'd think, wouldn't you? These men had made a sixteen-millimeter home movie of the whole thing. It showed the Indian gentleman standing next to his coiled-up rope the whole time. Just standing. None of what these three men described having seen happened. The magician didn't even attempt to toss the rope into the air."

"What did they describe seeing, exactly?"

Jack stifled a wriggle of discomfort. That was the one facet of the case that occasionally gave him a case of the weirds. "They described exactly the same thing: the magician tossed the rope up, it stood upright, the magician climbed it, disappeared, then reappeared and climbed back down."

Joan's brow furrowed. "How's that even possible—that they described exactly the same thing? Is that how hypnosis works, because it sure doesn't describe mass hysteria."

"I've never heard of anyone hypnotizing more than one person at a time."

"Meaning, you don't know."

"I know how hypnosis works," protested Jack. "I just don't know how *this* hypnosis works." *And it bugs the shit out of me,* he didn't say.

"But it *was* hypnosis, right?" Joan gestured at the stage.

"As opposed to what?" Jack asked. "Gilbert actually hacking a teenager into pieces, then putting him back together again?"

"Might explain why some of us saw the eagle and some didn't," said Wilfred.

Jack shook his head. "No, I think Brendon was right: I think some folks didn't see the eagle because they were focused on various parts of the trick. I mean, part of it is sleight of hand. But here's the thing that's bothered me about those three missionaries all these years: Sam Bernstein interviewed each of these men separately, and they were in complete agreement on what they saw. Complete. Agreement. I haven't really admitted it to myself until this minute. But even hypnosis doesn't explain that."

"This is going to be all over the magical community by midday tomorrow," Wilfred predicted. "This act was slicker than greased owl shit. By far the best stage illusion I have ever seen. He could make a fortune with that act."

"Which begs the question," said Joan, "as to why he is investing so much energy in shortening the already brief and troubled life spans of Vegas casino owners."

"He'll see us in Vegas next week . . ." Jack repeated. "Another prediction? I wonder what sort of magic trick he'll pull off there? This one, or the kind that gives the Casino Association ulcers."

"I'd lay odds," said Wilfred, "that he's going to be in town for the Cavalcade of Magic next weekend. As it happens, so am I, so I'll see you in Vegas next week, too. For the now, I need to get my old bones home to bed."

"How did he know, Joan?" Jack asked on the cab ride back to the Drake. "How did Gilbert know that *I* was going to be going to Vegas next week?"

"Your guess is as good as mine," she said, sounding distracted.

She shifted her position and Jack felt the warmth of her thigh against his.

He pried his attention away from that and returned it to a niggling sense he'd had in the few moments that Gilbertson had stopped to speak to them. "He's not well."

"Who? Gilbertson?"

Jack nodded. "He's unnaturally pale and has no muscle tone, but there's more to it than that. He had a sort of pinched look around the eyes, a tightness in his jaw, as if he were in pain. I don't know how else to describe it."

Jack could feel her smile even though he couldn't see it in the flicker of light and darkness. "A sixth sense, Doc? You?"

"Don't you have a cop's sixth sense?" he asked her.

"I do. But I also believe I inherited something-something from my Cherokee grandma. It's what tells me that Gilbert the Great is not a bad man, not a criminal, and most definitely not involved in those clinic fires."

"What does Grandma's something-something tell you about me?"

She looked out the passenger side window to where the facade of the Drake loomed over the sidewalk. "You, sir, are dan-ger-ous."

"But not a bad man."

She didn't answer that. The cab had pulled into the hotel drive, and she popped open her door as soon as it stopped, then turned toward him.

"See you in the morning, Doc. Eight thirty? That ought to get us to the airport in time to catch our flight."

"Eight thirty it shall be," he told her.

She hesitated, meeting his gaze for a frozen moment before she did the unexpected—she leaned forward and kissed the corner of his mouth. Before he could react, she was on the sidewalk and the door had closed behind her.

"Where to?" the cabbie asked.

Jack gave his address, wondering again what he and Joan were getting themselves into.

Chapter 10

"I seem to have overpacked," Joan told Jack as she lifted her luggage off the baggage carousel at Lambert International Airport. To her large suitcase and courier bag, Jack had brought only a single, large carry-on.

Jack shrugged. "Never met a woman who didn't. I have everything I need for a week or so: two pairs of pants, two shirts, a sweater, an extra tie, underwear, a bathing suit so I can work out in the pool, pajamas, and a toiletries kit. What else do I need? The hotel has a laundry, doesn't it?"

Joan put her hands on her hips. "Well, let me go all sexist right back at ya. Men! Did you ever think that you might have need of some more casual clothes, or do you do everything in that blue blazer?"

"Hey, I said I brought a sweater."

"A sweater. That's your idea of enough casual clothes."

"No. The bathing suit is my idea of enough casual clothes. The sweater is because all hotels are overrefrigerated—winter, spring, summer, and fall. Besides, we're here on business, and this is standard issue for at least two of my functions—doctor and professor. The sweater is the writer me. I also have a couple of suits at home for more formal occasions—weddings, funerals, that sort of thing—but I find this outfit quite utilitarian. And easy."

"And boring."

Jack's eyebrows rose, but he didn't argue.

They picked up their rental car and drove to Gleason's Magic Shop, which was in a modest mall in a middle-class St. Louis neighborhood of older brick homes and equally mature trees. Gleason was just turning over the OPEN sign on the glass door when they arrived, and unlocked the door to let them in.

The shop was in one immense room with a long glass counter along one side. Joan noted that only half of the store was dedicated to magic. The other half held practical jokes, costumes, and masks, along with kids' starter magic sets and books. Obviously, Lew Gleason needed to appeal to a wider audience to survive. The magic half of the store and the area behind the counter were filled with boxes of cards, linking ring sets of various sizes, rigged coins, oriental boxes and vases, ropes, brass tubes, cups and balls, and sundry other devices. The walls were covered with reproduction posters of Houdini, Blackstone, and other famous and mostly dead magicians.

"You're out early," Gleason observed as he retreated behind his counter. "I don't often get customers before noon."

Jack glanced at Joan before introducing himself and Joan as friends of Wilfred Benson, adding that the Admiral had recounted his conversations with Gleason about Gilbertson. He didn't mention that Joan was a detective, which was fine with her. She'd play that card only if she felt she needed to.

"Dr. Jack Madison?" Gleason repeated, eyes widening. "I've read your books. Love 'em." His eyes flitted to Joan; she thought she saw unease or suspicion in them. "So, Miss Firestone, are you a writer too, or a magician, maybe?"

"I'm a musician, actually. And a research hound. Never met a mystery I didn't want to solve."

"And you're hoping to solve the mystery of poor old Gilly?"

"That's our intent, Mr. Gleason," Jack said. "I'm researching a new book, and Joan is giving me a hand."

The older man narrowed his eyes and gave both of them a pointed look. "Call me Lew. And I'll just bet you have some swampland in Arizona that is gonna make me a fortune, don't you, Doc?"

Jack laughed. It was a warm, easy sound. "Ask me no questions, I'll tell you no lies, Lew. The Admiral said you saw Gilbertson do the Miser's Dream and were mightily impressed."

"That's the understatement of the year. It was like nothing I've ever seen. And he did some card fans that were even more impressive. Have you ever seen a YouTube video of Cardini?"

"I have."

"As far as I am concerned, there was never anybody as good as Cardini. Gilly made him look like a birthday party trickster. I just cannot figure out how he got that good between one month and the next. If that's what you came here to ask, I got no answers."

Joan suspected only Gilly could answer that one, but she asked Gleason to describe what he saw Gilbertson do anyway. He added little that Wil Benson hadn't told them, but his astonishment was palpable. When he described how Gilbertson worked with the crystal champagne bucket, Jack stopped him several times to ask pointed questions about what, exactly, the newly expert magician was doing with his hands.

"I'm telling you, Doc," said Gleason at one point, "his hands never moved away from the container. He never reached for a load, never misdirected our attention, nothing like that. He simply executed the trick and made it look—well, like real magic."

"Do you think it might have been mass hypnosis?"

Gleason snorted. "Well, if it was, he somehow hypnotized everyone in the room into seeing exactly the same thing. And we're talking about professional and semiprofessional magicians here. Guys—and gals—who do those tricks themselves and know them inside and out."

There was a moment of awkward silence as Jack and Joan digested all of this, but as Joan opened her mouth to ask another question, Jack beat her to it. "Lew, have you seen Gil Gilbertson outside of ring meetings?"

Gleason nodded. "On occasion he drops in here to buy books, check out new tricks. Quiet fella. Never says much except to talk about a book or a magician he particularly admires."

"So, you don't know if he has any close friends?"

"Never seen him with anyone. He's always been a loner and real shy . . . although he sure has been bolder with his newfound skills. Still hasn't made any real friends in the ring, though. He's bold onstage, but as soon as he steps off it—" Gleason snapped his fingers. "It's like someone flipped a switch. He goes right back to being . . ."

"The mouse that roared?" suggested Jack.

Gleason nodded. "Pretty much."

"Besides those new skills," asked Joan, "is there anything unusual or odd about him? Something that changed about the same time his abilities changed?"

"Now that you mention it, yeah. Just about every time I see him, lately, he's popping aspirin or Advil."

"At ring meetings he's doing this?" Jack's sudden urgency was like static in the air.

Gleason nodded. "Here, there—like I said, every time I see him. Doesn't drink much. In fact, he brings beer to the meetings, but I've never seen him actually drink any of it. Maybe he's religious? Don't know."

Jack asked about particular card fans that Gilly had done. Joan wasn't sure if it was professional curiosity or if there were some clues he was looking for. She was more curious about the way he'd reacted to the subject of Gilbertson's consumption of painkillers. She asked him about it when they left Gleason's shop a quarter of an hour later.

"It just seemed odd. At the same time he develops all this talent where he's shown none before, he develops chronic pain of some sort." He shrugged.

"What do you think it means?"

Jack smiled. "I got nothin'. So, are we off to Springfield?"

Joan hesitated, wanting to get what she had to say just right. "Not until we get something straight. I'm leading the investigation, so let me ask the nonmagical questions, please."

He frowned at her over the roof of their rental car. "Look, Joan, this is not a pissing contest. We'd sort of adopted the 'me, writer; you, researcher' paradigm, so I took the lead. I'm sorry if you think I'm stepping on your toes. You call the shots from now on."

Joan sighed. "Don't get me wrong, Jack—your presence is helpful. With your reputation, and with these people, you give me an in I wouldn't otherwise have. But, with my law enforcement experience—not to mention my badge and rank—there are circumstances under which I might get answers you couldn't."

"You would have pursued the comment about painkillers?"

Joan stifled a flutter of annoyance at how arch that sounded, and said, "Trust me, a subject snacking on pain meds is not a detail I would let pass. You may be an experienced neurologist and magician, but I've done countless investigations. In this dance, let me lead."

"Yes, ma'am. Got it. You lead. Would you also like to drive?" He gestured at the driver's side door.

"No, sir. You may take the wheel for the first shift. I'll drive after lunch."

Joan studied Jack's face as he started the car. She did not miss the tightening of his jaw, nor was she naive about what it meant. He was a control freak—that much was clear. She wondered how long it had been since he'd had to take instructions from a superior. She was about to say something off topic to distract him from their butting of heads, when she saw something that caught her attention.

"Well, that's odd."

Jack looked up to follow her gaze. "What?"

"Old Lew is closing up his store when he's only just opened it. And he seems to be in a big hurry."

"What do you want to do, Detective?"

Joan rolled her eyes. "My gut says we should follow him. His leaving right after our visit might be entirely coincidental, but I'm thinking not."

Gleason turned right on the sidewalk outside his shop, facing away from his watchers and heading for a public lot at the end of the block. Jack started to pull away from the curb, but Joan put a hand on his arm.

"Give him half a minute. The last thing we want is to do a crawl-by and have him see us."

She counted down in her head, going by instinct, then gave Jack the go-ahead. They arrived at the cross street just in time to see Gleason pull out of the lot and turn right, into the neighborhood. Jack turned the car up the side street and settled in at the speed limit, leaving a comfortable buffer between them and the target car—a silver-blue Honda of indeterminate age. He even let another car come between them.

Joan was impressed. "You're pretty good at this cloak and dagger stuff, Doc. Ever considered a career in law enforcement?"

"Not even for a second."

Six blocks and three turns later, Gleason pulled into another parking lot. All the hair on the back of Joan's neck stood at attention. The lot was sandwiched between St. Jude's Catholic Church and the church rectory. Jack drove straight past the driveway and pulled to the curb half a block down. Joan watched in the side view mirror as the magic store owner hurried to the front door of the parish rectory and, after a moment, disappeared inside.

She let out a long breath. "Well, that's something." A moment ago, the only thing connecting Gil Gilbertson to St. Jude's parish had been his name scrawled on the same scrap of paper as the parish phone number. Those connections had just doubled.

"I don't get it," Jack said. "What's going on?"

"Honey, I wish I knew."

They hung around St. Jude's for about twenty minutes when Joan finally decided it was time to leave.

"Can't see that we're going to learn anything more this way. I'm thinking we should get over to Springfield before it's too late in the day."

Jack looked back over his shoulder at the manse. "I don't suppose this is just a wild coincidence."

Joan gave him a look. "What do you think?"

They had lunch at a Steak 'n Shake along I-44. They gave their order to a big guy in a too-tight white shirt and tiny white hat with the company logo on the front. Joan had a salad; Jack had the Frisco Melt Special, in which the main ingredient seemed to be cheese. It inartfully obscured two hamburger patties and some kind of special sauce, and clung lovingly to the butter-soaked sourdough that embraced it. Hence, Frisco, Joan guessed.

"How do you eat that crap and stay thin?" she demanded. "Aren't doctors supposed to set a good example for us lesser humans?"

"Guess it's good genes and working out. And 'do what I say, not what I do' is my motto, as far as patient advice is concerned." He grinned at her across their table and took a big bite of the burger.

"I think I've gained five pounds just watching you eat that thing. I'm going to look like that poor guy behind the counter if I hang around with you much longer. When I get back to Vegas, I'm gonna lose at least twenty pounds. Scout's honor."

"You look good to me just as you are. Especially the—ah—super-structure." He made a gesture that indicated the part of her he could see above the table top.

Joan pushed down her irritation and gave her attention back to her salad. Superstructure. Well, at least that was a reference to her breasts that she'd never heard before. *Probably should give him props for novelty, but . . .*

"Bag it, Jack," she said, her voice breezy but brusque.

The drive from St. Louis to Springfield took four hours total, what with the stop for lunch. The first half hour after the lunch break passed in near total silence. Joan's expression was closed, and Jack—knowing that his recognition of her feminine charms was not appreciated—wondered what had possessed him to make such a remark. He'd been married for so long, he suspected his single-guy skills had stagnated at the frat house level.

At length, Joan asked him how his daughters had taken his decision not to go on vacation, which led him to talking about both of his girls ...and Carolyn. He talked about his late wife's work in anthropology, his pride and elation at her academic success, what a great mother she had been.

He opened up to Joan, wondering if that were part of her success as a detective—presenting a solid, calming presence and a listening ear. He still felt a dull ache in his heart when he talked about Carolyn; he sometimes doubted it would ever go away entirely. But somehow, with the motion of the car, the sun-washed landscape fleeting by beyond the windows, and the warm presence of the woman at the wheel, Jack felt as if a few more pieces of his self had been restored to their rightful place.

He asked Joan about her own family and learned that she was half Cherokee on her father's side. He'd been Jimmy Firestone, a Native rights activist and musician.

"His momma—my   Grandma Joy—was a Cherokee wise woman," Joan told him. "A witch, for all intents and purposes. She worked magic, she did. And made jewelry. She made this." She tugged at the silver chain she wore around her neck, and the red, opalescent stone suspended on it flashed fire into the intimate confines of the car.

"It's beautiful," Jack told her, not mentioning that he'd already admired the way the fiery cabochon lay between her breasts and made her skin look like velvet. "Fire opal, if I'm not mistaken."

Joan nodded, returning the pendant to its place in her décolletage. "Grandma called it a firestone. Our family namesake."

Jack glanced at Joan's earlobes and saw that she'd paired the opal with a set of plain silver earrings. "It'd be nice if you had earrings to match."

"Trust me. I haunt the Vegas pawnshops every chance I get, looking for its mates. Never yet seen anything I liked. The settings are always so froufrou. Usually gold."

"You could find the stones you wanted and get custom settings."

She laughed. "Not on my salary, I couldn't."

Jack was happy to have the atmosphere of ease between them restored. He sat back and enjoyed the drive.

Entering the Ozarks was to move through another world—green, vivid, and perfumed with cedar. It was a place you might believe fairies or brownies existed, or that communities of mysterious wise women, like Joan's grandmother, lived off the beaten paths and conversed with forest animals.

Tourist traps dappled the forested hills that embraced the famously dragon-shaped lake. Chief among them was Branson—a woodland Vegas, without the gambling. The roads were crawling with tour buses and lined with cheap motels and campgrounds . . . and fundamentalist Christian churches. Among the early-blooming dogwoods and evergreen cedars peeked pointedly evangelistic billboards with messages like "Jesus is Lord" and "Repent and be Saved."

That might have been what prompted Joan to ask, "You know, I can understand why you've said and written some of the things you have about religion, but the degree of hostility in your work goes beyond that, doesn't it?"

Jack realized he hadn't articulated his core beef with organized religion for so long that it no longer hovered on the tip of his tongue.

"I guess it's just that the Church is more concerned with fake miracles and accepting all of the dogma mandated by Rome on blind faith than they are with what their own Holy Book teaches. Frankly, the Church supports too many things I've spent my adult years debunking. Belief in angels and demons, exorcisms, miracles. I think that the old men who run the Church—some of whom are, in my opinion, outright senile—spend way too much time scouring the world for evidence that supports some ridiculous alleged miracle and not enough asking what Jesus meant when he answered the question about eternal life with the parable of the good Samaritan. If they dedicated half the time they spend worrying about women in the clergy to doing good works, we'd live in a much better world."

"Wow! You say that in your books? I thought you were just debunking the demon-y stuff. I can see why they get pissed at you; you don't hold back. Are you sure you're not being just a bit too harsh?"

He considered that. "Maybe. I've certainly been accused of dogmatism myself, and being a pot calling the kettle black when it comes to tolerance, in general. Tom O'Connor has told me that I'd have more credibility in some quarters if I was more accepting of the many good things the Church does. But, look—" He gestured out the window at yet another preachy billboard—this one citing an Old Testament passage full of the wrath of God. "While the rest of Christendom is fiddling, these fundamentalists are gaining ground all over the world. Just look at that bullshit. Is that the message of the same Jesus who spoke of loving one's neighbors and of the virtue of forgiveness?"

Joan glanced briefly at the billboard. "I wouldn't say so. Jesus notoriously changed some of those old-school laws. Said it was because people were less hard-hearted."

Jack was just getting started. "People are getting elected president of the United States by born-again Christians with a lot of help from the conservative arm of the Catholic Church. Think about that. In my opinion, these people are even more dangerous than those old farts in Rome who fast-tracked Pope John Paul the Second's sainthood. A saint—the guy who was the champion of the ultra-right wing of the Catholic Church?"

"And you've said all this in your books."

"Using more eloquent words. See why I'm on their shit list?"

Joan shook her head. "You must have been a real fan of *The Da Vinci Code.*"

Jack shrugged. "I wouldn't call myself a fan, but I think Brown did the service of bringing the mythos of Mary Magdalene into more public view. Students of religion have known about that stuff for a long time, but Dan Brown made it popular knowledge. Not that long ago, he would have been burned at the stake for that. Honestly, I think if Jesus Christ himself came back to earth and said it was okay for women to be priests or that stem cell research was fine with him, a significant portion of the College of Cardinals would want to crucify him all over again."

Joan glanced over at him, then laughed. "Lighten up, Dr. Thunder-brows. This stuff only makes you angry, and you're not going to change anyone's mind about God. Leastwise, you're not going to change mine."

Startled, Jack turned to look at her. "That wasn't my intention, to change your—Dr. Thunder-brows?"

Her mouth curled up at the corner and one eyebrow arched as her gaze slid sidewise to meet his for a heartbeat. Then, they were both laughing.

"Truth is," Jack said, when their mirth spent itself, "I'm more agnostic than atheist. I don't hate religion, per se, but I detest what some human beings have done in its name. In my opinion, the leaders of most religions are wonderful people who give huge helpings of their time and energy to aiding others. People like Tom. The world is a better place for them. They have what I sometimes wish I possessed: the simple and pure faith that something better is out there awaiting us and that we have the capacity to help build it. Something that gives meaning to life."

"'And they shall beat their swords into plowshares and their spears into pruning hooks. Nation shall not lift up sword against nation; neither shall they practice war anymore,'" Joan quoted. "Book of Isaiah."

"Something like that. That builds hope. The thought of a driving life force that has created us for good works, kindness, and charity, that wants us to form a worldwide brotherhood of man—who can argue with that? But when you get into the 'my way or the highway' mentality that permeates so many religious groups, that's where I lose it."

"Preach it, brother," said Joan. "I hear you. I do. When it comes to that sort of thing, I'm as big a skeptic as you are. But it seems to me that the problem isn't faith or religion, it's dogmatism. It's zealotry. The kind of zealotry that makes that Catholic hate group go out and burn women's clinics."

Jack was quiet for about five minutes. She was right. He was occasionally—well, okay, frequently—both harsh and broad in his condemnation of religion. He was, in a word, intolerant. Ironic, because that was one of the things he most hated about religious zeal—its intolerance of the other, of change, of diverse points of view.

"You sound like Irene. She often tells me the same thing."

"She religious, is she?"

"She'd say she was a person of faith, but of no particular faith tradition."

"Ah. She's one of those unaffiliated folks that the atheist groups are trying to claim."

Jack shook his head. "Irene is no atheist. Katy . . . Katy I'm not sure about. Mostly because I think Katy's not sure." *And neither am I.*

The flicker of sunlight through the trees, the warmth, and the sense of being in a cozy cedar chest made Jack feel every hour of sleep he'd lost tossing and turning the night before thinking about Gilbertson . . . and Joan. He gave into the soporific effects and slept, awakening only when Joan pulled into the parking lot of a Residence Inn in downtown Springfield.

They got rooms, then went out for dinner at one of those franchise steak houses where they knew they'd at least get a good salad and a drink, even if the meat was far from prime. Joan was the only African-American patron in the restaurant, and as a racially mixed couple, they garnered a fair number of stares. Nothing overtly hostile, but lots of lookie-loos—far more than they would have ever gotten in Chicago. Even their waitress gave them some long, searching appraisals.

Jack was unaware that his discomfort and growing anger was showing until Joan said, "After awhile you get used to it."

He looked up from his menu and met her eyes. They were deep, calm, and glinted with wry humor.

He shook his head. "I don't think I *could* get used to it."

"You won't have to."

"What does that mean?" Stupid question. He knew damn well what she meant.

A second later, she confirmed it. "Jack, people in this room are already thinking what you've been half hoping for. That we're sleeping together. Well, not *sleeping* together," she added with innuendo curling her lips. "If you think this is hard getting used to when you're not actually part of a mixed-race couple, imagine what it would be like if you were."

"I didn't mean . . ."

"Of course you didn't."

Was that regret in her voice or disappointment? Jack hated the thought of either. He changed the subject. "What have you got lined up for tomorrow, fearless leader?"

"I want to check out where Gilbertson lives, his neighbors, where and who he works with, and if possible, some of the guys in this ring he belongs to. I'd also like to learn more about what else he does in his free time besides attend magic conventions and ring meetings. I have the name of a hospital here in Springfield where he's volunteered entertaining sick kids for the last few years; I'd like to talk the staff there. I think we should have a conversation with the ex-IBM president, Charlie Thomas. We should also make a quick trip to Hunterton to talk to anyone who might remember Ruth. If we could find someone who knew her well—maybe even at the end of her life—that'd be a real bonus."

"How do you intend to find these folks?"

"She was religious. I'd start with the local churches, beginning with the Catholic parishes."

Jack nodded. "Of course. I'm sure I can find out if Thomas is in town and will meet us."

Joan smiled. "Well, sure you can. Any excuse to explore the magic back alleys of greater Springfield."

"Bus-ted."

Dinner was thoroughly okay. The food was plentiful, if bland. Back at the hotel after dinner, Jack asked Joan if she cared to come to his room to watch TV for a while.

"They've got Netflix," he told her.

She burst out laughing.

"What? What's so funny?"

"You just reminded me of this guy—years ago—who tried to pick me up in a bar. I was on duty and nursing a virgin daiquiri when this howling drunk guy figures the fates have decided I need to come home with him. His gotcha line after I politely turned him down was, 'But, baby, I got HBO!'"

"Great. I remind you of a howling drunk who thought having HBO was enough to get a beautiful woman to have sex with him."

"If it's any consolation, Jack, you've made a tempting offer. But we really did have a long day and we've got more of those ahead of us. I think it's best for everyone concerned if we just go to our separate rooms and get some sleep."

He nodded. "Yeah, of course. You're right. I'd tell you I didn't mean it as a—you know—as a come-on, but I'm pretty sure I did."

"I'm pretty sure you did too," she said. "Good night, Jack."

He watched her walk away, mesmerized by the sway of her hips, the way her thick, glossy mane lifted and rippled with each step. He wanted her . . . and he wanted not to want her.

As if she knew he was standing there, gawking like a horny high school boy, she swung around when she reached her door two rooms down and gave him a long, level look. There was nothing come-hither about it, nothing coquettish or smoldering, but somehow that look—that sober, thoughtful, longing(?) look—made every hormone in Jack's body rise up with one accord. He raised a hand in a parting gesture, then hurriedly unlocked his door and went inside.

He distracted himself by kicking off his shoes and turning on the TV. He washed his face, brushed his teeth, put on the black track suit he used for pajamas, and stretched out on the bed to watch the news. He failed at this simple task; his mind kept returning to dinner at the steak house, sitting across from Joan under the withering stares of other diners. Why had he said that: *I'd never get used to it?* Was it true? If he had begun a relationship with Joan—or at least fallen into bed with her—would those stares have shriveled his lust or killed his fascination with her?

He thought about it as the news anchors gabbled and the on-the-scene reporters nodded between grim retellings of tragedy. Would the censure of other people make him rethink his attraction? He sat up on the realization of what Joan must think of him. One moment he was proclaiming his desire for her—hell, he was wearing it out in plain sight—and the next, he was weirded out by mob bigotry. It bothered him, suddenly and deeply, that Joan might think what he wanted was a dangerous secret liaison that he would be afraid or ashamed to admit to in public. That he was merely thrill-seeking at her potential expense.

Had that been the content of that long, solemn look she'd given him right before he fled?

He was standing and heading for the door of his room before he'd half registered that he'd moved. He did not give himself time to think or put on his shoes. He padded down the hall in his stockinged feet and tapped lightly on Joan's door. He heard music from inside and tapped again. The music stopped. He tapped even more lightly. There was a long, aching silence.

Just as well, he told himself. He wasn't even sure how he'd say what he wanted to say. He'd turned away and taken a half step down the blandly carpeted corridor when the door of Joan's room opened and she peered out at him. She was wearing a fleece robe with long sleeves and a gathered bodice that accentuated her curves. It was in a shade of pale green that contrasted with her skin. She was stunning.

"Jack? Something wrong?"

"Yeah, as a matter of fact. Me. I'm wrong. What I said at dinner. That was wrong."

She looked at him for a moment—that same, solemn look that she'd directed at him earlier. Then she stood back and opened the door wider. "If you want to try to explain that remark, you should probably come in."

He did. Her room was identical to his but smelled of her perfume. She moved to the chair stationed in one corner of the room with a small side table next to it. A cup of hot tea sat on the table, steaming into the light of a reading lamp. A book lay unopened on the arm of the chair. He felt vague guilt at having interrupted her winding-down process.

"So, what did you get wrong, Doc?" she asked, lowering herself into the chair.

He pulled up the matching ottoman and perched on its edge, facing her. "I got *me* wrong, for one thing. But I don't think I got you wrong."

She rolled her eyes. "Well, that was illuminating."

"Joan, tonight at dinner, what I said about not getting used to being stared at . . . I didn't mean it as a white man being seen with a black woman by a room full of judgmental eyes. I meant if I were you, if I were the odd man out—or the odd woman out—it would be hard to get used to. To not have it irk me, or even hurt me. Being the white man at the table with you was easy by comparison. That I *could* get used to."

"And this is the epiphany that got you to come roaring down the hall in your jammies?"

"I didn't roar," Jack began, then looked up and saw the wry twist of her mouth. He stopped. Took a breath. Started again. "Here's the deal: I was afraid you interpreted what I said to mean that I was up for . . . for shagging you on the QT and pretending we were 'just working together' in the public eye. I was afraid you might think I was looking at you as forbidden fruit, a—a heady thrill—that I was ashamed to be linked to you . . . intimately, or that I was squeamish about it, or—"

She leaned forward and put a finger to his lips to stop the flow of words. "I admit it, Jack. I did think that. All of it. Hush," she added when he tried to speak again. "At dinner . . . the situation just reminded me of one more thing that puts us in different worlds. Well, that's not quite true. You'd fit in fine wherever you went. Not just *pretend* to fit in, like I do. I, on the other hand, would be a fish out of water if I were to hang with you and your brain trust buddies. You *would* be ashamed of me."

"Bullshit," he said, pulling her hand away from his lips and holding it in both of his. "I'd never be ashamed of you or for you. You're brilliant. You just pretend to be ordinary or ornamental to fit in so you can do your job. You're a—a chameleon. And my buddies like to drink beer and go fishing or loiter around magic shows and tell themselves they could do that trick better than the guy onstage."

"Jack, this isn't fun and games. At least, not for me. I get that you're coming off a huge loss and that maybe, for you, a little YOLO fling with an unlikely stranger—"

Now, he put his finger over her lips. "This doesn't feel like a fling to me, Joan. I don't know what it does feel like. I just know I am incredibly attracted to you and that right now, I really, really want to kiss you."

She stared at him for a moment, her own desire clear in her eyes. Then she looked away, shook her head, and simply said, "Jack . . ."

"Tell me you don't want it too."

She met his gaze again. "You know I can't. It'd be a lie."

He leaned into her then, slowly, giving her time to pull away, half afraid she would, half afraid she wouldn't. He felt the tension in her hand as it telegraphed her indecision. By the time their lips touched, they were both quivering.

Instead of pulling away, Joan leaned into the kiss, returning it with interest. Jack groaned and dropped to his knees in front of her, bringing their bodies together. He gathered her against him, pressing himself between her legs so she could feel how badly he wanted her. In response, she took his head between her hands and deepened the kiss.

When she wrapped her legs around his waist, Jack thought he'd go through the roof. He scooped her from the chair and rolled with her onto the bed, half wondering how people did this in the movies—how they wriggled out of clothing before things got messy. He lost track of everything after that stray thought, knowing only that they were suddenly skin on skin, then joined in a single rhythmically writhing entity. Jack felt as if his body were not his own; it belonged, in the moment, to this woman and his hunger for her. She fed and devoured him in equal measure, crying out in pleasure and passion again and again. He thought he growled.

Afterward, they lay entwined until Joan extricated herself and disappeared into the bathroom with a murmured, "Need to clean up."

Jack stared at the ceiling, feeling as if he'd just stepped into a new room in his life. He was tingling with spent excitement that discharged like static across his skin. In that exalted state, he was hit with the sudden realization that he had no idea what Joan did for birth control. He felt vague guilt at having not considered that. Before he could formulate how he could ask about it—possibly apologize—Joan was back. She'd put on her robe again and caught her hair up in a clasp.

"I was hoping you'd be naked when you got back," Jack told her.

"I was hoping you'd be gone."

Jack chuckled, sleepily. "Sure you were."

"I mean it, Jack. I think you should go back to your own room and get some sleep."

"Well, I'm pretty sure neither of us will get any sleep if I stay here." He felt an erection growing at the thought.

"Jack . . ."

The tone of her voice made him sit up, studying her face. Her expression was distant; the passionate woman he'd just coupled with was gone.

"I don't—is this because I didn't . . . take precautions?"

She laughed without humor. "No, Doc, it's because *I* didn't take precautions."

That froze him for a moment.

Joan made a dismissive gesture. "I'm not talking about birth control. In my line of work, a monthly period would be a good deal worse than inconvenient. I get a shot every three months to take care of that.

I meant, I didn't take precautions against *you*. I didn't want that to happen; I just didn't try hard enough to stop it."

He smiled. "I'm not sorry about that."

"I am. I am royally ashamed of myself. I've never been into one-night stands—"

Jack rolled off the bed, only half conscious of his nakedness. "No! Not a one-night stand. I sure as hell don't want it to be just one night."

"A one-week stand, then. Look, Jack, you caught me with my guard down. There is no future with this and, right now, I'm all about my future. Now, I'm gonna go back into my bathroom and take a nice, hot shower. I think it would be best if you'd go back to your room and get some sleep." She turned and disappeared into the bathroom.

Sleep, Jack thought as he hastily dressed, was unlikely to happen tonight.

Chapter 11

Gilbertson's apartment was a small, dark one-bedroom on the second floor of an extremely modest apartment house on the outskirts of Springfield. Joan showed her badge, and the manager let them in without objection; Jack suspected the fact that Gilbert hadn't been around for over a month didn't hurt.

"Is this strictly legal?" Jack asked Joan as they stood in the middle of the tidy but spartan living room.

"Well, that's a good question. I suppose we should've gone to the local PD and asked permission, but . . ."

"Better to beg forgiveness?" Jack finished the thought.

Was it really? He wondered about that. He'd considered begging Joan's forgiveness this morning when they'd met for a breakfast during which neither could meet the other's eyes. But he wasn't sorry about the hot sex on its own merit; he was only sorry that she was sorry. And of course, he wondered what Carolyn would think of him.

"I'm pulling your leg, Doc," Joan said, moving to stand in front of the floor-to-ceiling bookshelves that dominated two walls of the small room. "I actually did ask permission. Or at least the chief of the Vegas PD did. Called Springfield and told them we'd be coming and that we were working on a case involving one of their citizens.

And, since the landlord opened the door for us with no objection, we are not required to get a warrant."

Beyond the bookshelves, which also covered two walls of the bedroom, the rooms were sparsely furnished with furniture that looked like it came from an upscale hotel . . . from the 1960s. In the living room was a rust-colored love seat, a matching upholstered chair, and a side table—all mid-century modern, Jack thought—arranged in an L on a charcoal gray carpet. Opposite the chair was a small plasma-screen TV on a pedestal with a DVD player underneath it. The remote for this was set perfectly on the right arm of the chair, where the owner's hand would fall on it when he sat down. The windows had no curtains, just blinds, closed.

Every book on Gilbertson's shelves was about magic or magicians. Likewise every DVD. There were biographies, histories, how-to books on practicing magic, books on specific types of tricks. The arrangement in the bedroom echoed the living room, with two walls taken up with full bookshelves packed with texts on magic. Some were quite rare, and Jack suspected Gil had spent a considerable amount acquiring them. A neat pile of magic magazines was stacked on the side table in the living room; more occupied cardboard magazine boxes on the bedroom shelves. The wall decorations were dedicated to magic, too; old stage posters of famous magicians like Houdini and Blackstone were lovingly hung in wooden frames. A couple of them seemed authentic.

One large cabinet in the living room held a collection of simple magical items: cups and balls, linking rings, silk flowers. It was a bit sad, Jack thought. Clearly Gil Gilbertson loved magic better than magic loved him.

The bedroom closet had few things in it: one summer-weight tan suit, several pairs of slacks and shirts, and a clown costume in a dry cleaner's plastic wrapping. The bathroom was nothing special. It was clean and tidy with a small carpet and matching towel hung neatly on the bar. The eye-popping items were on the étagère over the toilet tank: Costco-sized bottles of over-the-counter painkillers like naproxen, ibuprofen, and acetaminophen. And, in the medicine cabinet was a row of prescription bottles.

"Sumatriptan, in its varied forms," Jack told Joan when she gave him a questioning look.

"Which is?"

"Migraine medication. Our magic clown has killer headaches."

Joan checked the jumbo bottles of painkillers on the étagère. "These were all purchased within the last two months."

"Yeah. The scrips are all recent, too."

Joan made a thoughtful noise and went back into the living room to take a closer look at the books. Jack followed her.

"These are all well-read. See the bookmarks and tabs?"

She took one volume down and leafed through it. Not only was it tabbed, but it was full of sticky notes—layers of them, covered with dense, cramped script. Gil Gilbertson was a good boy who did not scribble in his treasures.

Jack turned to give the room a once-over. "Some of this makes sense and some doesn't. How come a guy with as much money as he has in the bank lives like this? The furniture is high end, but it's old. He could afford a much better apartment. My guess is that he could live pretty well here in Springfield on just the interest from his inheritance."

Joan reshelved the book. "Makes sense to me. When he buys, he buys quality, but my guess is he doesn't replace it until it falls apart or is obsolete. The TV is small, but it's state of the art. Ditto the DVD player. The books are new or rare and all well-kept. I think it's pretty clear; magic is about the only thing that matters to our guy. That's where he puts his money when he spends it. That, and travel. I see OCD all over this place, too."

"That did not escape my attention," said Jack. He'd half suspected that Gil Gilbertson had obsessive compulsive disorder before they'd set foot in his apartment. "Did you see how the dishes were arranged in the kitchen cabinets? And I've never seen such neatly stacked silverware in my life. I'd bet dollars to donuts that if he walked in here after we'd left, he'd know exactly what items we touched. That book you just put back will catch his eye the minute he walks in the door."

Jack moved toward the kitchen, drawn by a single framed black-and-white photo on the breakfast bar. He recognized Ruth Gilbertson and a boy of ten or so—Gilbert. They stood on the front porch of a white farm-style house smiling, with their arms around each other. Judging from the foliage and flowers framing the porch, it was summertime.

He listened, staring at the picture of Gil and Ruth, as Joan went through drawers. He wasn't thinking of the Gilbertsons, but of last night. Joan had asked him not to do that—not to think about it, not to talk about it. How was he supposed to honor her wishes when he wanted nothing more than to repeat the experience tonight? When he wanted to understand why they couldn't?

Right now I'm all about my future, she'd said. Why would that future rule him out? There were such things as airplanes, after all. Telephones. The Internet. Skype.

"Don't think there's any more to find out here," Joan said, breaking into Jack's reverie. "They've already got copies of all of the credit card and bank statements back in Vegas. There's nothing else."

On the way back to the car she said, "You never get used to going through another person's home. No matter what the reason. I always feel like I'm violating them. This place was unusually sterile, though. Most of the time there are more personal photos, keepsakes, odds and ends. Usually when you go through a place like this you find something hidden or tucked out of view. Not here. Notice that his refrigerator was almost empty? Like he wasn't planning to come back for a while."

On the way out they stopped by the manager's unit and asked him if Gilbertson was friendly with any of his neighbors. The landlord—a brawny fellow Jack guessed was in his thirties—snorted at the absurdity of the suggestion.

"Are you kidding? I've never seen him even give the time of day to anyone around here. Only times I've ever seen him when he wasn't coming or going was when I was doing repairs in his unit. He's not the social type. In fact, he's kind of a weirdo. I mean, half the time when I see him, he's dressed like a clown. What's up with that—you got any idea?"

"Yeah," Jack said. "He's a clown."

"You're shittin' me."

Nettled by the guy's attitude, Jack said, "He volunteers to do magic for the sick kids over at St. Mary's hospital."

The jackass had the good graces to look a bit shame-faced. "Yeah? Huh. I mean, I didn't think anything of it, but my girlfriend saw him walking in and out in his clown suit and got all freaked out. Said all she could think of was one of those serial murderers like in horror movies. He hasn't done anything—you know—violent, has he?"

"Now, why would you think that?" Joan asked. "Just because he's a little odd, that's no reason to think he's a whacko . . . is it?"

"Oh, not *me*," the guy said. "My girlfriend, you know."

"Right." Joan pulled a card out of her purse and handed to the landlord. "As far as we know, Mr. Gilbertson has never done anything even remotely violent. We just want to talk to him about a situation he may have knowledge of. If you see him or hear anything about him, give me a call, would you? That'd be a big help."

The guy squinted at the card. "Sure thing, Detective Firestone."

As they strolled back to their rental car, Joan murmured, "Looks like someone else is interested in Gilbertson, or maybe they're interested in us."

That brought Jack up short. "What?"

"When you get into the car," she told him, "take a look at three o'clock."

Jack did just that as he slid in behind the steering wheel. At three o'clock was a nondescript silver sedan with a couple of men sitting in it. Joan had rounded the car to the passenger side and, before Jack could guess her intention, she turned and strode briskly over to the other car as if on a mission.

"What the hell," he murmured under his breath.

The car didn't peel out as he half expected. Nor did bullets fly. Still, when the driver rolled down his window at Joan's approach, Jack felt his throat tighten in apprehension. Joan flashed her ID, then chatted with the occupants of the car for a moment. After a brief conversation, she returned to where Jack sat white-knuckling the steering wheel.

She slid into the passenger seat, then watched as the sedan pulled away from the curb. "Said they were from the Springfield PD and were just checking to see that everything was okay. Gave me some cock and bull story about problems with the tenants here. I didn't ask for any ID, but I'd bet my mortgage that they are not with the police. Those guys were not cops."

"Did you think they might be when you marched over there?"

"Nope. Did you?"

"I didn't know who they were, but—do you do stuff like that all the time? Take chances like that?"

She turned and gave him a double-barreled look. "Yes, as a matter of fact, I do. It's my job."

Jack kneaded the steering wheel, realizing that he still had what Irene referred to as "the yips." If that look meant what he thought it meant, this was a test he was about to fail. "To do crazy shit?"

"Jack, I'm a police detective . . . and the granddaughter of Ahyoka Firestone. Of course I do crazy shit."

"I thought you said your grandma's name was Joy."

"Bet you were good at dodge ball. Her Cherokee name—Ahyoka— means 'she brings happiness.' Everybody called her Joy."

Jack forced himself to relax, taking his hands off the steering wheel. He flexed his fingers. "So who do you think those guys were, if not Springfield's finest?"

"I'm not going to speculate, but I have a feeling we'll be finding out. Let's keep moving. We're going to do a little dance, hopefully lose our tail." She gave him another look. "You want me to drive?"

"I'll drive. Just give me directions."

She grinned at him. "Sure you wanna take directions from a bossy Firestone woman?"

"Not a problem, Detective," he said, even though it was.

Joan directed him through driving around the block twice, cutting through an alley and backtracking. Then she coached him through a circuitous route to the Burger King where Gilbertson worked. Joan had intended to ask for the store manager's contact information but found the man himself—a Jamal Brooks—was in. Brooks was a tall, athletic-looking black man dressed in slacks, a white short-sleeved shirt, and a tie rather than the company uniform.

"Nothing bad's happened to Gilbert, I hope," he told them after inviting them back to his office. "We haven't seen him for close to three weeks. He took time off—I figured to go to one of his magic conventions out west, then never came back to work. Is he all right?"

"He seemed fine the last time we saw him," Joan said, "though we are a bit concerned about his health. It seems he has very bad headaches—possibly migraines. Do you know anything about that?"

Brooks frowned. "Now that you mention it, he did take quite a few sick days this winter. He's always had problems with headaches, but in spite of that Gil is a great employee. He's worked for me for three years. Always here on time, no trouble working longer if I need him. Does anything that's asked of him; even works the kitchen and the front in a rush or if we're a man down. He helps train the new kids, absolutely trustworthy with the money, and very polite to our customers. I've offered to promote him to assistant manager several times, but he always refuses. Says he doesn't want all that stress." Brooks gave Joan an uneasy look. "Is he in any trouble? Do you know if he's coming back?"

"He's not in trouble," Joan said smoothly. "But he may have information that we're seeking about something that happened in Las

Vegas during the last convention he attended. We're honestly not certain when he'll be back."

Jack was impressed. She'd managed to tell the unvarnished truth, but so vaguely that it imparted no information.

"Is there anything unusual that you've noticed about Gil in the last few months?"

Brooks shook his head. "Just the headaches getting worse. I've noticed him popping those headache pills more and more often and rubbing the side of his head. Told me that the bright lights were starting to bother him. I guess I should've figured it was migraines."

"Which side?" Jack asked.

He'd been silent so far, and the suddenness of his question seemed to startle both Joan and the manager.

"Excuse me?"

"Was there a particular side of his head that he seemed to favor when he'd get one of his headaches?"

"Uh . . . left. That mean something?"

"It might."

"My partner has a background in medicine," explained Joan.

"Oh . . . You know, there was one other thing. I'm not sure if it means anything, but not long before Gilbert took off, there was a big, loud drunk in here. Gilbert was getting him his order and being his usual nice self. He was like that. No matter how obnoxious people got, Gil never lost his cool. Anyway, this guy had a little girl with him and he was getting mean with her. Gilbert did something totally out of character for him, given how shy he was. He outright told the drunk to stop being mean to the little girl. The drunk got all bent out of shape and started yelling at Gilbert, swearing up a storm. Thought

I'd have to call the cops. All of a sudden, Gil gets a real funny look on his face—real serious—and he starts staring at this guy."

"Staring at him?" repeated Joan. "Like he was getting angry?"

"No. There was no anger in it at all. Just real . . . intense. Like he could see through the guy. The drunk was getting madder and madder, though, and then—just out of the blue—the guy grabs his throat and starts yelling, 'I can't breathe! I can't breathe!' And he falls down on the floor and starts thrashing all over the place. The little girl starts crying and screaming. Pretty soon the drunk turns blue and stops moving. I thought for sure he'd given himself a stroke or something."

"A stroke wouldn't have caused those symptoms," Jack said, caught Joan's warning look, and asked, "What happened next?"

"It just passed." Brooks snapped his fingers. "Just like that, the guy gets his wind back, and after a minute or so he gets up. He was pretty shaken, pretty unsteady, but he was okay."

"And Gilbert was doing what during this time?" Joan asked.

"Staring straight at him. Never flinched. And when the guy's on his feet again and leaning on one of the tables, Gil says, 'Had enough, asshole? I told you to be good to that girl. And I want you to remember this for the rest of your life, because I guarantee that if you ever yell at her again like that or lay a finger on her, you're going to have another seizure. Even if I'm not around. Only it won't stop like this one did. Got it?' I swear to you I could not even imagine those words coming out of Gil's mouth. But he was like . . . like a different person."

"What'd the drunk do?" Joan asked.

"He was scared to death. He grabbed that little girl and ran out to his car. Gil pulled out his cell phone and called the cops on him for driving under the influence. Gave his license number, the whole deal. They had units in the area. Got him before he'd even managed to make it to the end of the block."

"And after that, what did Gilbert do?"

"He went back to being Gilbert. But, you know, now that I think back on it, he had a really bad headache right after. I figured it was from the stress. You know, adrenaline and all."

He hesitated, looking from Joan to Jack and back again. "This is going to sound really bizarre, but it almost seemed as if Gilbert made that seizure happen somehow. He said he thought the guy had just worked himself into a tizzy—that's what Gil called it, a tizzy—and had a—a spell of some sort. But it was surreal, the way he just stared at him." He shifted his gaze to Jack. "You're like a doctor or something?"

"I am a doctor, actually. A neurologist."

"Is it possible that Gil just staring at that guy could, like, freak him out so badly he had a seizure?"

"You mean a hysterical reaction—like a panic attack?"

Brooks nodded.

"I suppose that's possible, yes."

Brooks seemed relieved. "So, nothing spooky, right?"

Jack shared a glance with Joan, then smiled and said, "Nothing spooky, no."

Joan turned her attention back to Brooks "How long was this before Gilbert left for his vacation?"

"A couple of days."

"Did he ever say anything to you about his personal life? Maybe mention his other job?" Joan asked.

"You mean the clown gigs? Oh, I knew he had that job at the hospital and that he did some kids' parties, too, but Gilbert, he's so shy, he didn't talk much about it. Once in a while one of his buddies from that magic club or the hospital would come in for a bite, but Gilbert didn't get very chummy with them."

"Girlfriend?"

"None that I know of. Don't think he's gay. I just think he's plain scared of women. Some of the older gals that work here tease him sometimes and he gets all flustered and retreats into that shell of his. Gilbert's a good guy, though. Strange, maybe—a bit weird, maybe, but he's okay. I trust him. There's not an ounce of deceit in him. You know what I mean?"

Chapter 12

Not an ounce of deceit in him.

Jack pondered that on the drive over to St. Mary of Nazareth Hospital. It was, he realized, absolutely true. For all his mystery, Gilbert Gilbertson had been completely truthful about his intentions, about where he would be and when, about what he would do when he got there. Which was one big, hairy ball of cognitive dissonance—in layman's terms, bewildering.

"I was thinking," Jack said as they pulled into a parking space at St. Mary's, "this might be a situation in which my medical background could be of benefit."

Joan gave him a sidewise grin. "I was thinking exactly the same thing. Why don't you take point on this one?"

"You're not going to snatch that football away now, are you Lucy?"

She took a deep breath, her breasts rising and falling with the movement. Jack found he could not look away.

"Jack, remember what you said the other day—that this isn't a pissing contest? I never thought it was. I don't operate that way. I know people who do, and it sucks, so I try real hard not to be one of them. This is about who has the best chance of getting results out of a line of questioning."

167

"Understood," he said and mentally kicked himself for having unintentionally insulted her.

They went straight to the office of the hospital's director of nursing. Jack introduced himself as Dr. Jack Madison, professor of neurology at Midwestern School of Medicine, and asked to see the director. A few minutes later, a middle-aged woman wearing a white lab coat appeared from an inner office and invited them in.

"I'm Alice Blanton," she told them as she motioned them to seats across from her desk. She seated herself behind that desk, steepled her fingers, and said, "I've heard of you, Dr. Madison. You're quite the sensation on the talk-show circuit."

Well, that was unexpected. The words were delivered without heat, but Jack was suddenly aware that this was a Catholic hospital in which he was about to ask for favors a "sensation on the talk-show circuit" might not be easily granted.

Before he could respond, Ms. Blanton asked, "So, how can I help *you*, Doctor?"

Jack did not miss the subtle stress she laid on the penultimate word. "My associate and I are here to inquire about Gilbert Gilbertson. I understand he volunteers here in the pediatric ward."

Her eyes suddenly flashed suspicion. "What exactly is it that you want to know . . . and why?"

"We're trying to find Gilbert. We just spoke to his boss, who told us he's been suffering debilitating headaches and has not been to work for weeks. His manager is worried about him. We thought perhaps you might have some idea of how we can reach him."

"So . . . he's a patient of yours?"

"Not exactly, no. We were seeking to speak to him about another matter, and the headaches came up in conversation. I knew his mother,

Ruth, and was part of a medical team investigating a related condition that she came to us for."

Alice Blanton crossed her arms. "Ruthie died years ago."

"Yes, I know. Look, Ms. Blanton, it's complicated. But we really need to find out as much about Gilbert as we can and, if possible, find him."

"This isn't some stupid reality TV thing, is it?"

"No, I promise you, this is not reality TV. Just reality. It's important."

Jack could almost hear the gears turning in Alice Blanton's head as she weighed the situation. He saw the subtle thawing in her body language.

"Mr. Gil works for us on the pediatric oncology and burn units. He's been doing it for as long as I've been here, and he is wonderful with our sick children. They love him and his jokes and tricks. He's been gone about a month and I don't know where he went. Kids really miss him."

And so do you, Jack thought. That was real emotion in Alice's blue eyes.

"Is there anything you can tell us about his work here?"

Her lips curled wryly. "I can. I'm just not sure you'd believe me." Before Jack could comment, she added, "Wait here a moment. I'll be right back."

"What was that about?" asked Joan, following Blanton's departure with curious gaze.

"Don't know, but we'll find out."

Ms. Blanton returned shortly with a middle-aged man in surgical scrubs with a file folder in one hand. He held out the other to shake hands with Jack and Joan.

"Dr. Madison? I'm Frank Simpson; I'm a surgeon here at St. Mary's. I run the burn unit. I've been wanting to contact you but couldn't quite work up the gumption to do it. Your dropping by is like . . . kismet."

Now, Jack was intrigued. "Really? Why, exactly?"

"They say, 'One picture is worth a thousand words.'"

Simpson opened the file folder and laid it on the edge of Blanton's desk. Inside was a stack of eight-by-ten color prints of a burn victim. The shots were close-ups of the child's torso, showing a blasted landscape of burnt flesh that covered the child's entire back from shoulders to buttocks. The sight was shocking enough to make even Jack wince. He heard Joan stifle what sounded like a whimper.

"This is a picture of a twelve-year-old patient named Mitchell. Mitchell was transferred up here from Northern Arkansas seven weeks ago. This is, as you probably know, an extensive third-degree burn. Electrical. One we sometimes refer to as fourth degree because of the deep soft tissue and bone involvement. We spent the first two weeks just keeping this poor kid alive. This next photo is after my first debridement."

The new photograph showed charred muscle and bone, after the skin and subcutaneous tissue had been removed.

Jack sucked in a breath through his teeth. "I don't see many burns these days," he said, "but I can see how serious these are. Has this got something to do with Mr. Gilbertson?"

"That's what I'm getting to. Gilly is a great hit on the burn unit. Visits all the kids regularly and knows how to cheer them and their parents up. He's a real asset to our program. I don't know him very well—he's intensely private—but he's always there for the kids. All of us, doctors and nurses alike, appreciate what he does for them. As soon as Mitchell arrived, Gilly latched on to him and spent a lot of time with him from the moment he got out of ICU.

"The last photo I'm going to show you is why I wanted to call you. I had Mitchell scheduled for more debridement and some skin grafting for a Friday morning, four-and-a-half weeks ago. The night before the procedure, Gilly was in Mitchell's room for about an hour. His mother, who had been saying the rosary, had fallen asleep in a chair while he was in the room. I got a panicked call from the nurses when they changed Mitchell's dressing about two hours after that. This is why they called."

He flipped to a third photo. It was Mitchell's back again, the dressing removed: the boy's burns were essentially healed. There were a few raised liner streaks, but otherwise the boy had fresh, healthy tissue from his neck to his lumbar region.

Jack felt as if he were on a carnival ride that had unexpectedly dropped fifty feet. He took the photo from the folder and stared at it. He had to work to keep his hands from shaking.

"That's not . . . it's not possible."

Simpson ran a hand through his wiry hair. "I know your reputation, Doctor. I know you believe this is a hoax—a case of mass hysteria. I swear to you, it's not. Everyone on the burn unit witnessed this . . . transformation. This miracle. Every nurse, every doctor, every intern. Plus Mitchell's mom and dad. We even brought in specialists from a couple of teaching hospitals in St. Louis. They all saw it. We sent Mitchell home a week after this last series of photos was taken. I can show you his lab workups, the notes of the specialists, everything. No one knew what to think, because no one had ever seen a spontaneous healing like this before."

"Pathology specimens?" Jack murmured.

Simpson nodded. "I debrided this kid; we've got the pathology specimens to prove it. This was more than full epidermal thickness; the muscles themselves were burned." He raked his fingers through his hair again and perched on the edge of Alice Blanton's desk, looking down at the photo Jack still held. "I know how you feel about miracles, Dr. Madison. They're unfalsifiable. But this one . . . this one isn't."

Beside Jack, Joan cleared her throat and asked, "Did you talk to Gilbert about this, after the fact?"

Simpson shook his head. "No. We tried to reach him, but he'd left town; wasn't answering his phone for the first week after, then his number was disconnected."

"Did you ask the boy what he did?"

"Yes, of course. Mitchell said he was doing some card tricks, then stopped and just stared at him . . . and he hummed a funny song. Mitchell said he started feeling some tingling in his back. He said it felt like what happens when your arm has fallen asleep and is waking up. Now, remember, a lot of nerve endings had been flat-out destroyed, so this wasn't even remotely possible. Frankly, if I'd walked into the room at that moment and Mitchell told me that, I'd chalk it up to some phantom sensation. Anyway, Mitchell said the tingling turned into itching, and then he suddenly felt normal. Like before the accident. Like nothing had ever happened. As you can imagine, I've been in shock for the last month. Nurses, too. We were just starting to get over it when you showed up."

Jack swallowed, handing the last photo back to Simpson. "Uh, can you give us contact information for the boy's family? I'd . . . we'd like to speak directly with Mitchell if we could."

Alice Blanton shook her head. "They've gone back to Arkansas, Doctor. And they made it clear they do not want to be contacted by anyone except hospital staff. They were adamant about that. They don't want their lives to become fodder for social media and conspiracy theorists."

"I can understand that, but if you tell them I'm a neurology specialist—"

"No, Dr. Madison. I cannot give you access to that child. I'm sure you understand that, too."

He did understand. "Trust me, I do. Can you tell us anything else about what happened between Gil and the boy? Maybe something the boy said that seemed inconsequential at the time or overly imaginative . . ."

Simpson snorted. "Everything he said seemed overly imaginative— except that I realized it was probably true."

"Like?"

"Well, the gazing thing. Mitchell said he felt as if Gil was looking through him, inside of him, like he had X-ray vision. Or that silly song. Mitchell said it was 'Itsy Bitsy Spider.'"

"What about the bird, Frank?" Blanton prompted.

Jack felt as if he'd been yanked out of already cold water into an ice bath. "Excuse me, what?"

Simpson nodded. "Right. Okay, this is probably going to sound overly imaginative, too. Mitchell said that Gilly had a big bird with him. A bird with dark feathers. He said he thought it was an eagle."

"An eagle the size of a Saint Bernard," added Alice Blanton. "Mitchell's words, not mine," she clarified when Joan threw her a startled glance. "He asked Mr. Gil if that was his pet. Gil said it was a guardian."

"A guardian of what?" Joan asked.

Blanton shrugged and spread her hands. "I haven't the foggiest."

"No one else saw the bird?"

Both medics shook their heads.

"Mitchell said Gilly took it with him when he left," said Dr. Simpson. "Or rather he said the bird *disappeared* when Gil left."

"That was his word?" asked Jack. "Disappeared?"

"Yes. I thought that was just . . . well, you know. I thought he'd made up an imaginary creature to help him cope. A giant eagle like in *Lord of the Rings* or *Harry Potter* or something. You know, a guardian spirit. Now, I don't know what to think."

Joan leaned forward in her chair. "You said you consulted external experts. How far beyond the medical community does this go? Did the local media get involved?"

Blanton shook her head vigorously. "Sister Claire, who is technically in charge of the hospital, called the mother superior of her order about it, and I believe both spoke to the bishop in St. Louis. I gave the Sister a copy of the photos to give to them and a written report but haven't heard anything back. In the meantime, Sister Claire instructed us not to discuss this with the press or, really, with anyone outside the hospital."

"Actually," said Dr. Simpson, exchanging glances with the nursing director, "she strongly discouraged us from even discussing this among ourselves. She suggested we turn over our records on the case to her, but . . . we kept copies."

Alice Blanton was visibly uncomfortable. She brushed at nonexistent dirt on her desk and looked down at the screen of her laptop. "Your coming here, Dr. Madison—well, that just seemed like a sign that we were supposed to share it with you."

A sign. From God, Jack supposed, and bit back a glib remark.

Frank Simpson looked at him. "Have you ever seen anything like this, Doctor?"

"No, Frank. I have not. I've seen all manner of remissions—all of which, in my opinion, could have been explained scientifically. But this—this is a new one to me." He glanced at Joan. The expression on her face was guarded. He had no idea what she was thinking. "Joan, do you have any questions you'd like to ask?"

"I'd like to talk to the nurses who discovered the healing," she said, "and it occurs to me to ask, Ms. Blanton, if any of your young cancer patients have had unusual recoveries."

"Not unusual, no. We do have an excellent survival rate here, something we owe to our superb pediatric oncologists and nurses . . . and, of course, to prayer." Blanton looked directly at Jack as if daring him to say something to challenge her.

He wouldn't dare.

They interviewed the nurses who had been the first to discover Mitchell's sudden recovery. Neither of them had seen the alleged Saint Bernard–sized eagle. Jack might have written it off as a child's desire for a mighty protector, but he'd seen a big, dark-feathered bird on stage with Gilbert at the House of Magic. Jumbo eagle or not, the bird existed as part of the puzzle that was Gil Gilbertson.

Expecting an emphatic no, Jack asked Alice Blanton for copies of Mitchell's photos. He was surprised when she handed him a thumb drive and said, "I downloaded these while we were talking. I may be doing this against orders, but Sister Claire only said we needed to keep this between the medical staff at this hospital. You're someone's medical staff and you're at this hospital, and I'm going to think of you as a consulting expert. These are only the photos. There's nothing here to identify the patient by. You understand."

Joan's iPhone began to sing "Stormy Weather" in a sultry female voice. She checked the screen, then hastily left the room to take the call.

"Of course," Jack told the nursing director. "We're glad to have any help we can get."

"I also put transcripts of the interviews with the attending nurses on there," she told him, "as well as Frank's testimony and the timeline he established. I hope it's helpful. I hope nothing bad happens to Mr. Gil. He's a dear man. A godly man."

Joan appeared in the office doorway. "Gotta go, Jack," she said. Her eyes said more.

Something's happened.

They thanked their hosts for their cooperation, then Jack followed Joan out into the hospital's manicured forecourt. She made a beeline for the parking lot and their rental car.

"What is it?" he asked. "Who was the call from?"

"That was Cardinal Tom," she said tersely, never breaking stride. "Francis Xavier Coughlin is dead."

Jack stopped walking. Joan went several steps beyond him before she stopped and turned back.

"Dead?" Jack repeated. "What—murdered?" With Frank Coughlin, that seemed almost likely. The man had certainly made his share of enemies.

"Tom said it appeared he died suddenly while strolling the grounds of his estate. The ME completed his autopsy about half an hour ago. Well, damn."

Jack felt the skin between his shoulder blades tingle as if ants were crawling on it; Joan looked over his shoulder at something on the street behind him.

"Let me guess—our phony police detectives?"

"Uh-huh. Now I'm dead certain they're not cops. I never told the Springfield PD that we were going to visit St. Mary's. They've been surveilling us."

"What do we do now?"

Joan turned and strided purposefully toward the car again. "We go buy us a couple of burner phones, we get someplace very private, and we call your friend Tom back. He said there's more, but he doesn't trust our current mode of communication."

"Holy shit," said Jack.

"Precisely." Joan reached the car first and unlocked the driver's side door. "Hop in, Doc. I'm driving."

Chapter 13

"It was neither a stroke nor a coronary that killed Frank Coughlin," said Cardinal O'Connor an hour later.

He was on speaker phone in Jack's hotel room, his voice emanating from the burner Joan had placed on the ottoman. She sat cross-legged on the bed; Jack perched tensely in the chair.

"Then what?" Jack asked. "What was the cause of death?"

"Massive, widespread trauma."

"Can you be more precise?"

"According to the ME's report, Coughlin had complete fractures of almost every large bone in his body, including his skull. The ME said his brain looked like scrambled eggs. That's verbatim, not in the written report."

"Can we see the written report?" Jack asked.

"I'll do you one better. I've spoken to the mayor; he's given the Cook County Medical Examiner permission to speak to you about the findings. I think you know her—Charlene Merkle."

"Sure, I know her well."

"You can call her directly at this number," said Tom and gave the number, which Joan scribbled down on hotel stationery. "Use the burner phone for this one. I hope you get something useful."

Tom rang off, and Jack immediately dialed the ME, putting the call on speaker the moment Dr. Merkle picked up.

"Hi, Char. It's Jack Madison. Cardinal O'Connor suggested I call you regarding a certain autopsy report."

"Well, hi, Jack. Long time no see. I'd love to do some catching up, but I think I ought to get right to the point." Charlene's voice was a creamy contralto that seemed somehow out of keeping with the nature of her work and the smart-ass attitude he remembered so well from their previous encounters. "So, here's the deal: Frank Coughlin died in his own backyard about five minutes after his usual morning exercises. Now get this: virtually every large bone in his body was fractured, including his skull in multiple locations—his brain looked like corned beef hash—"

"Tom said you'd compared it to scrambled eggs," Jack observed wryly. "Did he get the wrong food group?"

Char snorted delicately. "Not at all. I did say 'scrambled eggs,' but I try to avoid overusing good metaphors. And in addition to that, his liver, spleen, and both thoracic and abdominal aorta were torn to shreds."

"Attributable to what, do you think?"

"Jack, it looked like he had been dropped from a great height. Hell, I've seen people who've fallen from the top of Sears Tower that had less internal trauma."

Jack shook his head. "Is that even possible? Did he have any external wounds?"

"Indeed he did. He had odd wounds on both shoulders—front and back. Fresh wounds that looked as if he'd been hoisted up on meat hooks or something similar. There was one wound on each side in the back, just inside the shoulder blades, and three on each side in front beneath the clavicle. Each about three inches deep."

"Where exactly was he when this happened?" Jack asked.

"He'd left his home gym and personal trainer and was walking through the parkland behind his house. The trainer's the one who found him when she followed him about five minutes later. She didn't see anything. Just found him lying dead on the grass. And get this: he left an impact crater."

"So we're not thinking he was beaten to death?"

"First of all, the security at Frank Coughlin's place is extraordinary. Second, the injuries are too massive and general to have been inflicted during a beating. Also, there was fresh ecchymosis distributed evenly over only the posterior side of the body. Normally we see that in people who've jumped from extreme heights. The impact forces blood into the tissues."

Jack worried his lower lip. "You think someone may have sent a drone to literally pick Coughlin up and drop him?"

"Right now, that's the only possibility I can think of."

Death by drone? But why? "What do you think it means?"

"I haven't the foggiest, Jack. This is some truly weird shit. Now, I gotta run. Bodies are piling up in the hall."

"Tsk. I thought you ran a tighter ship than that."

She gave him a Bronx cheer and hung up.

Joan looked at him askance. "What is ecchymosis?"

"Extensive bruising, in this case probably postmortem." He picked up the burner phone and punched in Tom's number. "We need to talk to the good cardinal again."

When they had Tom O'Connor back on the line, Jack asked the questions he couldn't ask the ME. Questions about why rather than how.

"Okay, I'm stumped. Char Merkle made a case for Coughlin being dropped from a great height. By a drone or something. What are we looking at here, Tom? Mob infighting? Power struggles inside the SPCD?"

"Possibly the latter. It could also mean that God works in mysterious ways. Coughlin was a dangerous man."

"I'd observe," said Jack dryly, "that whoever had him killed is even more dangerous."

"Granted. Which may explain why my young associate has been so on edge since we got the news about Coughlin's death."

Jack frowned. "I don't get it. Why—"

"I have recently come to form the suspicion that Father Lyons is a bit of a mole. It's been clear for some time that his personal ideology does not jibe with the more liberal tone struck by our new pope. And I've overheard at least one conversation that was, shall we say, unsettling. He has always been a bit too studious in his avoidance of even discussing Coughlin."

"Lyons reacted strongly to his death?"

"More than that, he was in an agitated state even before I told him—a condition that seemed to come on right after I got the phone call from Commander Williams about Coughlin's demise."

"You think he was eavesdropping," said Joan.

"I'm almost certain of it. When I hung up from that call, Lyons was in the front hall, pocketing his cell phone. He was white as a sheet and his lips had disappeared." Tom's tone was deeply ironic. "I am not so technologically challenged that I don't understand what's possible in terms of surveillance for an organization with deep pockets and a deeper network."

"But if Coughlin's pockets are the ones in question," said Jack, "is it possible that whoever killed him put a huge crimp in the Society's line of resources?"

"I don't suppose for a moment that Francis was the only underwriter of the Society's efforts. There are others whose pockets are every bit as deep, and likely to inherit Lyons's loyalties if they were, as I suspect, with Coughlin."

"Is there any chance he's listening now?" Jack asked.

"The number I gave Detective Firestone is a burner phone I picked up this morning. I'm in my car at the moment. Alone. I'm planning on being extremely careful, my friends, and I suggest you do the same. Use your own phones only if you don't care if someone overhears you . . . or you want them to."

"Okay," said Jack when Tom had hung up. "Here's the big, fat, obvious question: what does an organization that burns women's clinics and thinks their new pope is a 'nope' want with Gilbert the Great?"

"Mm-hmm. And who hates their head guy enough to murder him? Someone who's a champion of the Catholic Church, a fan of Gilly the Magic Clown, or a rival within the Society?" Joan took the thumb drive Alice Blanton had given them and tossed it onto the bed next to the burner cell phone. "I'm wondering if Sister Claire might know."

"Sister Claire? What would she—" It struck Jack, suddenly, that a group like the SPCD might be awfully interested in someone who could do miracles on the fly and who had become a high-profile donor to what they might construe as an anti-Catholic cause. "You think Sister Claire might have mentioned Gil's activities to the wrong people?"

"Or she's a Society insider herself. Think about it. Why is she so tight-lipped about Mitchell's miraculous recovery? That's hardly the behavior I'd expect, under the circumstances. Miracles are the stuff of faith, Jack. The Church is in the business of miracles. They're usually at great pains to announce them, not hide them under the proverbial bushel."

"The boy's family might have put pressure on the hospital," Jack suggested.

"Yeah, but they told *us* everything, and we still have no idea how to get to him. They could even have gone to the press and not given up the boy's location. But Sister Claire shut it all down. She even told her staff not to talk about it among themselves. That's pretty extreme."

"And it bothered the hell out of Alice Blanton."

"Indeed it did."

Jack raised an eyebrow. "You want to see if we can talk to Sister Claire?"

"Or maybe the bishop in St. Lou. I gotta wonder if Sister Claire really contacted him or her mother superior about Mitchell's miracle. But before we dive headlong into that, I want to eat something. Then I'd like to keep our meeting with Charlie Thomas and, if there's time, take a side trip over to Hunterton and talk to the head of the local parish. Sound like a plan?"

Jack nodded, wondering about the nature of the SPCD's potential involvement in Gil Gilbertson's seemingly supernatural abilities. What might they want with a miracle clown? Was he a hero to them, a potential saint, or something else?

Michael Lyons felt as if reality had taken a sudden vacation. He recognized his first reaction to hearing of Francis Coughlin's death as denial but knew he had no time to wallow there. He pushed himself swiftly through the next several stages of loss by locking himself in his room to pray and think. Perversely, calm brought anger. The emotion surprised him, because it had no target. Was he angry with God for removing one of His own lieutenants from the field of battle?

When he had calmed himself enough to think clearly, Lyons called Coughlin's right-hand man, George Farrell. Farrell surprised him by picking up after the first ring, as if he'd been waiting for Lyons's call, as he should have been.

"You've heard?" Lyons said tersely.

"Heard?" snapped Farrell. "I was just pulling into the drive when the ambulance rolled up. I saw his body, for Christ-sake! I had to hold Liz while she unraveled. Thank God the kids weren't home."

"What happened?"

"Damned if I know. They said it looked like he had a coronary or a stroke or something, but . . ." Farrell made an indistinct noise that sounded like teeth grinding.

"But what?" Lyons asked.

"His body looked weird. I mean, they covered it up before I got a real good look at it, but I saw that he was bleeding from both shoulders. Looked like bullet holes to me, but Hillary said she didn't hear anything. Neither did that bimbo personal trainer of his. Jesus Lord, I still can't believe Franny was keeping her right there on the premises. Right under Hillary's nose."

Lyons stiffened at the unexpected aside. "Focus, Mr. Farrell. This is not the time to be speculating about Mr. Coughlin's sins. Are you saying this looked like a hit?"

Farrell snorted. "Oh, hell, I don't know. I mean, he sure didn't die of natural causes. That much is certain."

Farrell rambled on about the amount of blood and the havoc that had been wrought on Coughlin's body, but Lyons wasn't listening. He was calculating his next moves—the Society's next moves. If Franny Coughlin's death was an assassination, they needed to find out who was responsible and why. A rival faction in the Church, perhaps? Or was this the result of Coughlin's business dealings? Lyons hoped it was the latter. If Coughlin had been murdered because of his questionable commerce, then his death would likely be the end of it. If it was related to the activities of the SPCD, that was a different matter. That had implications for the survival of the entire organization.

"Mr. Farrell," Lyons said, cutting off the other man's flow of words, "we need to regroup. Gilbertson is still out there, and Dr. Madison and that detective have gone to Missouri to investigate him."

There was a moment of taut silence, then Farrell repeated, "Missouri?" Then a beat after: "Do you think they know about the boy?"

"I'm almost certain of it. Two of the brothers tailed them to St. Mary of Nazareth, where they spent several hours."

Again, the silence, during which Lyons thought he could hear the gears turning slowly in Farrell's head. He had wondered often how George Farrell had been elevated to his position as Francis Coughlin's second. When Farrell spoke again, though, he said something unexpected.

"Actually, Father, it might be a good thing for Madison to stumble across the Miracle Boy."

"How could that possibly—"

"You read what Madison wrote in that last book of his, right—that he's never seen a miraculous cure of severe burns? Well, what happens if Dr. Atheist has to come to the conclusion that this is a real, honest-to-God miracle, huh? I mean, if he's going to be honest—"

"Who says he will be?"

"It's his stock in trade, Padre. He prides himself on his honesty. So, he comes out, say, and says that, yeah, the little Catholic magician did a real honest-to-God miracle. Maybe he even writes a book about it. How's that not gonna help the Church?"

"*If*, Mr. Farrell. *If* Gilbertson is somehow performing 'honest-to-God miracles,' as you call them. There are other possibilities. It is written that in the last days false prophets will appear, able to perform signs and wonders that can deceive even the elect."

"I think you're missing the big picture here, Father." Farrell's voice took on a patronizing tone that set Lyons's teeth on edge. "A miracle is a miracle is a miracle, and the fact that this kid was healed must mean that God had a hand in it, right? I sure don't wanna make an enemy of God. Do you? Besides, Gilbertson's never made any claims to be anything more than a magician and a clown. He sure *seems* to be doing God's work."

Lyons had resisted thinking of it that way. Perhaps it was time for him to stop resisting. As rumors about Gilbert Gilbertson had filtered into the Society, Lyons had been skeptical and fascinated by turns. Until they had heard about the healing at St. Mary of Nazareth, he had been convinced the man must be an extraordinarily skilled charlatan. A terse call from Sister Claire had severely muddied the waters. If Gilbertson's miracle was real, then was Farrell right—was the only possibility that he was doing these things in the name of God? It was true that he had never claimed to be more than a man. He had done his miracle quietly, even secretly, and disappeared from sight immediately after. He had made no attempt to capitalize on his good works. That, too, was the hallmark of the righteous.

"Besides," Farrell added, putting Lyons's own thoughts into words, "signs and wonders is one thing. Healing is something else. That's God bailiwick, isn't it?"

Lyons wasn't convinced of that, but he was convinced of one thing: whatever Gil Gilbertson was, the Society must know. If Gilbertson was a legitimate miracle worker, he must be protected. If he was not, he must die.

"Whatever Gilbertson's role is," Lyons said, "we must work to keep the cardinal and his cronies from taking him off the battlefield before we figure out who or what he is and whom he works for. Until we understand the part he plays in the affairs of the Church and the fate of the world, he must not be interfered with. Call a meeting of the Council. Tonight in the alternate location."

"Sure thing, Padre."

Lyons hung up, cringing at the other man's lack of respect for the officers of the Church. He would deal with that later, he decided. Now he must consider next steps. He thought back to the last meeting Francis Coughlin had convened. It was before they had known the full import of Gilbertson's activities at St. Mary's Hospital. Coughlin had been livid with volcanic zeal.

"I want that damned clown's head on a pike!" he'd roared. "On a *pike*, d'you hear me! How dare that backslid freak pass himself off as a miracle worker? He needs to die!"

He'd wanted to dispatch men immediately to carry out his demand, but Lyons had forestalled him. The "backslid freak" had not died; Francis Xavier Coughlin had. Was that the will of God, or someone else's will? Father Michael Lyons intended to find out.

Hearing a car pull into the drive, he pulled back the curtain of his bedroom window. The cardinal had returned from whatever errand had called him away. Lyons composed himself and went down to see if the cardinal had need of his services.

Chapter 14

Bishop Strickland had no idea who Mitchell was or why Sister Claire of St. Mary of Nazareth Catholic Hospital should call him about the boy. Neither did the mother superior of the good sister's order. That cast a whole new light on Sister Claire, though it did not implicate her in anything illegal. Nonetheless, in the parking lot of the Red Lobster in which they lunched, Joan had called Tom's burner and let him know that the news of the miraculous healing had never reached the higher authorities the hospital administrator claimed it had. Joan had no intention of looking into that further at the moment. She figured that was a job for Cardinal Tom. Jack disagreed and spent part of their lunch break arguing that they ought to go back to St. Mary's and corner Sister Claire in her office.

Joan gritted her teeth and calmly tried to dissuade him. "That's a sideshow to this investigation, Jack. The SPCD is peripheral to Gilbertson's dealings in Las Vegas. My job is to investigate how this guy is doing what he's doing and determine if he's running a scam."

"You know he's not," Jack insisted. "The experts in Vegas have sworn on a stack of Franklins that there was no mechanical meddling with the systems. None. And you saw the photos of that boy's back."

Joan raised her eyebrows at the seeming non sequitur. "Well, that's a first for you, isn't it, Doc? Are you arguing that Gilly is doing legitimate miracles? You, of all people?"

He stared at her, apparently at a loss for words. That was a first, too.

"I . . . I don't know what I'm arguing. Except that if the SPCD is involved in this, Gilbert's life could be in danger. Which, to me, means they are a legitimate subject for this investigation."

"Yes, but not the primary one. We've got an appointment with Charlie Thomas at his legal office at two. I intend to keep it. Are you thinking we should split up and cover more territory?"

Jack paused to consider that. Then he threw her a sloping grin. "Nah. I've seen enough badly written horror movies to know that the old splitting up thing never works out well for our heroes. People get eaten that way."

Joan laughed and relaxed back against the vinyl upholstery of the corner booth she'd chosen so she could watch the front door for their stalkers. She took a measured breath. Seemed like they were getting back on some sort of even keel after last night's stupidity. The half-formed memory of their coupling filled her with a combination of embarrassment and desire. Her temporary partner was hot, and clearly as attracted to her as she was to him. But that wasn't all he was. He was the first man she'd encountered who spoke jazz. He was interesting and smart and didn't treat her like a second-class human. Their clashes over who was going to lead weren't because he was a man and she was a woman, but simply because they were both people used to being in control and giving orders.

And none of that serves as an excuse for you falling into bed with him so damned easily, she told herself. She felt like an idiot. She wanted more out of life than a series of brief, go-nowhere romances or to be someone's experimental woman of color. Which was why the brief time she'd spent thinking Jack found himself unable to stand the attention of last night's lookie-loos more devastating than she wanted to acknowledge.

Okay, so he'd put that concern to rest, but she had to admit there was more to it than that. She wasn't built for casual relationships, and she couldn't imagine that Jack was looking for anything more.

"Then we'll stick together," she said, aware of the irony of her own words. "I figure with the nature of this business, two heads are better than one. Cheaters are in my wheelhouse. Miracle workers, not so much."

Jack snorted, almost doing a spit take with his coffee. "You think miracle workers are in mine? *Charlatans* are in my wheelhouse, Joan—people who only *pretend* to do miracles."

"Cheaters, in other words," said Joan. "I guess we've got that in common."

Back in the car on the way to meet Charlie Thomas, Jack asked casually where Joan had grown up and how she'd gotten into law enforcement. She started to compose the standard bland patter in her head, then scrapped it.

"I told you my dad was Cherokee. Mom is black. A mixed marriage was pretty tough back then no matter what color your skin was. So was being the product of same, even in LA. That's where they met. Riverside, to be more specific. He was in the army, stationed at Camp Haan; she was working in a restaurant he liked to go to. We traveled a lot when I was a little girl. He died in 1985 in a helicopter accident."

"Combat?" Jack asked.

She shook her head. "Stupid training exercise in Oklahoma. My mother and I moved back to LA. Grandma—Dad's mom—is still alive, and I see her whenever I'm home. After that, I guess I had a pretty normal upbringing in LA in a houseful of women. Grandma lived with us for a long time, and Momma has two sisters with families there that gave me a lot of support. I did well in school, joined pep club and choir and drama; I was gonna be the next Leontine Price or Aretha Franklin, maybe."

"Which means you've always loved music, then. So . . . law enforcement?"

She chuckled and shook her head. "Summer after graduation, I got stupid. I got involved with this guy—a bassist—who thought I was exotic. He talked me into running off to Vegas with him. Typical dumb teenage crap. He dumped me for a lounge singer who wanted to be on Broadway. Next thing I know, he's driving her to New York and I'm stranded in Sin City, too broke and embarrassed to go home. I thought of trying to get a gig as a performer, maybe singing backup or doing studio work. But it was suggested by just about every man I met that—being exotic and all—I ought to be willing to audition horizontally, if you get my drift. At that point, I felt like I'd made my quota of stupid life decisions. So, I applied for a job with the LVMP as a dispatcher and started studying criminal justice. It was four or five years before Momma and I got back on good terms. By then, I had set my sights on being a real detective."

"You and your mom are okay now, though, right?"

"We're good. I go home every six weeks or so to see her and the rest of the clan; they're proud of me now—especially since I've gotten involved in the scholarly side of music. Mom comes to Vegas once a year or so, but she hates it there as much as I do. She's seventy-two, but her health is good. She's sharp as a tack, and we're very close. We talk almost every day."

Jack nodded and gazed out the front window of the car for several beats before asking, "You mention me to her? I mean, that we're working together?"

That was not the real question and she knew it. "Oh, hell, Jack. I called her last night right after you left my room and told her I'd just hooked up with a famous neurosurgeon. I figured she'd appreciate how far I'd come from banging a bass player who dumped me for a classier piece of ass."

Jack turned to look at her, clearly stunned. "Joan . . . stop it! I . . . I'm sorry that happened to you. But you're one of the classiest—" He cut off, laughing. "There is no good way to finish that sentence. Let me try again. You're a class act, and your old boyfriend was a moron. Certifiable. Deserved to be lobotomized." After a beat, he added, "You didn't really tell your mom—"

"No. I mean, I've told her I'm working with you, not the other thing."

"Did she . . . What did she think of the situation?"

Joan snorted. "She asked me if I *liked* you. As if I were a fourteen-year-old staring down the barrel of my first high school dance."

"Yeah. My daughter kind of did the same thing."

Joan felt a tickle of something that wanted her to think it was prescience. Fate—or Grandma—whispering in her ear. She reached up reflexively and touched the fire opal that lay in the hollow between her breasts.

No, no, no, Joan Firestone. Don't you dare go all mystical on me. You are no wise woman.

Thomas was a partner in a fair-sized law firm. Jack thought he seemed like a nice enough guy, maybe a little full of himself. There were pictures of him all over the wall of his office, punctuated with framed awards and certificates. Jack remembered when his office had looked like that. He'd always thought that when the diplomas and board certifications came off a doctor's walls, it meant they'd finally grown up.

Thomas seated them at a small, round table bracketed by bookshelves. Joan had insisted that Jack take point during the interview. He did, making his questions seem to relate to the book he was allegedly writing (and might actually write, depending on how this whole thing turned out). Initially, Thomas didn't have much to add that the Admiral hadn't already shared about Gilbertson.

"He shows up at most of the ring meetings," the lawyer told them. "He's been coming for five or six years. He doesn't have much to say unless you get him into a discussion about the history of magic." He smiled; the expression seemed genuine. "He knows book loads about that. Almost worships some of the old legends. Knows his stuff about them, too." He paused, looked from Jack to Joan, and said, "Listen, I'd prefer not to beat around the bush. This isn't really about a book you're writing, is it?"

"I'm sorry?" said Jack.

"It doesn't take a rocket scientist to figure out from the questions you're asking that Gilbert is in trouble. He is, isn't he?"

"Is that a personal concern of yours, Mr. Thomas?" Joan asked.

He seemed to withdraw slightly, his eyes guarded. "He's my client. If there's any trouble, I need to know about it."

Joan reached into her jacket pocket and pulled out her badge. "Mr. Thomas, I'm a detective with the Las Vegas PD. Mr. Gilbertson has . . . come to the attention of our offices because of his activities there, which may relate to his recent increase in skill as a performer."

Thomas's eyes jerked from the badge to Joan's face. "Are you insinuating that he's—what—using his magic to cheat at gambling?"

"I don't know." She hesitated, then added, "He also seems to have drawn the interest of an organization that has a well-earned reputation for violence. There is some concern that his life may be in danger."

"Because of what he's done with his *magic*?" Thomas asked incredulously.

"I've said all I'm able to, Mr. Thomas," said Joan. "Do you know where Gil is, right now?"

The lawyer chewed his lower lip for a moment, as if deciding how open to be with them. At length he said, "No. I don't, and that has me worried."

"I think you're right to be concerned," Joan admitted. "Tell me, what sort of affairs do you handle for Mr. Gilbertson?"

"It's estate work, mostly. I was his mother's attorney before she died, so I've known Gil since he was a young teenager. To be honest, my concern is more personal than legal. I've grown fond of Gil over the years, and I know how vulnerable he is. So, for the record, if there is anything going on that could cause him trouble, I want to know about it. If you see him before I do, please have him call me."

Well played, madam, Jack thought. Joan had once more applied exactly the right incentives to get the information she wanted.

She'd unslung her purse from the back of her chair, which Jack took as signaling their departure. He was half out of his seat when she asked, "Has anyone besides us asked you about Gil recently?"

Charlie Thomas blinked. "Well, you know about the Admiral, of course. I gather that you sent him. Then there was that asshole Lew Gleason. He's a ring member too, and owns a magic shop in St. Louis.

He called me earlier this week and wanted to know if I knew where Gil was. Which I don't, and wouldn't tell that jerk if I did."

Jack sat back down, trading puzzled glances with Joan. He suspected he knew what she was thinking; what made these two magic club members enemies?

"What makes you call him a jerk?" Joan asked.

"Sells all that toy magic crap to gullible kids and then walks around like some sort of living saint. Sort of a Catholic holy roller, if you ask me. Brags about all of his righteous buddies in the Church in St. Louis—how they go to Mass every day, and how they're so goddamn good and everyone else is so bad. He even runs down fellow Catholics—members of his own church, and the *pope*, for the love of God. Like he's a member of some little True Religion Club. Asshole."

"Did you tell him *anything* about Gil? Any of what you told us?"

"Hell, no."

"Anything in particular he asked about?"

Thomas nodded. "He wanted to know if I knew anything about Gil's volunteer work at the Catholic hospital—St. Mary of Nazareth. Rambled on about a kid in the burn unit. To tell you the truth, he didn't make a lot of sense. He was talking as if Gil had done something weird to the kid. A miracle, he said. I got curious, actually, and called the hospital. No one there knew anything about it. They hadn't seen Gilbert for a couple of weeks at that point. Neither had I. He's not in good shape . . . his health, I mean."

That got Jack's attention. "Do you have specific concerns about his health, Mr. Thomas?"

"He's always been a bit frail, but in the last several months, he's looked especially bad."

"In what way?"

"Just ill. Pale, like he's ready to drop. He's always had headaches—sinus headaches, he called them—but lately he's seemed to be in pain more often."

The headaches again. Were they connected to the sudden blossoming of Gil's powers, or was he taking something that was causing them—something intended to increase his mental acuity, perhaps? Was it as simple as stress or something more dire like a brain tumor? There was no way to know without evaluating Gilbert firsthand, which increased Jack's determination to force their gadabout illusionist to hold still long enough to have his head examined.

For now, worrying about Gil's symptoms was futile at best. Jack turned his mind to Lew Gleason's peculiar behavior—specifically his scurrying from their interview to a parish connected to both Gil and a series of clinic arsons.

"You have a few more pieces of the puzzle than I do, don't you?" he asked Joan when they were back in the car and headed for Hunterton.

She frowned but didn't look up from the road. "What are you talking about?"

He ticked the items off on his fingers. "A series of clinic firebombings is somehow connected to both Gil and St. Jude's Church in St. Louis. Lew Gleason, who's awfully interested in where Gil is, scampers from an interview with us right to that very parish. He's a loudly pious Catholic who knows something about a miracle that Gil allegedly performed, knowledge of which, as far as we know, went no further than the hospital administrator. Are Gleason and Sister Claire both part of the SPCD? Because that sure seems likely to me."

She didn't answer.

"The Society is more than peripheral to this case, isn't it?" he persisted.

Joan was silent a moment more, then said, "I can't really speak to that, Jack. I think you need to talk to Cardinal O'Connor about it. Until he decides what you need to know about the Church's connection to this, there are things he's asked me not to reveal. I'm sorry about that . . . if it matters."

Jack smote the dashboard of the car in frustration. "You can't tell me what you know, and I can't help you any more than I have until you *do* tell me."

They lapsed into silence after that—a silence that carried them all the way to Hunterton.

Hunterton was fifteen miles or so off the road between Springfield and Branson. It was a farming town that served as a bedroom community for people who worked in Branson. There was one grocery store, a pharmacy, a Subway sandwich shop, hardware, feed store, elementary and secondary schools, a sheriff's office, and a couple of bars. A clinic on one end of the main street seemed to house a doctor and a dentist. And three churches served the community: a Presbyterian, a Baptist, and the Catholic parish of St. Peter's.

St. Pete had seen better days, Jack thought. Its school was obviously closed and the sanctuary needed a paint job, as did the rectory next door. The parish priest, Father Feney, was a wiry old Irishman with a shock of white hair, who welcomed his guests cordially and seated them in his shabby, comfortable parlor. He'd prepared coffee and served fresh-out-of-the-oven cookies. He was clearly one of those salt-of-the-earth clergymen who'd spent his whole life serving in the Lord's vineyard.

"Glad you're here, Dr. Madison, Miss Firestone." He looked at Joan with birdlike attentiveness. "I hear you're from Nevada."

Joan shot Jack a look. "You knew we were coming?"

"Yes, Miss Firestone, I got a call from the diocese office in St. Louis that you could be here soon. You're here about Gilbert?"

"Did they say how they knew we were coming?"

"No, though they did tell me to be circumspect." He smiled, and an impish light danced in the pale blue eyes that peered at them through the lenses of his wire-rimmed glasses. "But old Irishmen are never very circumspect. Not too good at following instructions, either."

"You've been serving here in Hunterton for some time, haven't you?" Jack asked.

"Thirty years, give or take."

"Then you knew Gil Gilbertson as a boy. Knew his mother, Ruth."

"Very well. Which is one of the reasons I'm going to be frank with you. Ruthie and her son joined our parish soon after their arrival. Gilbert was just a little tyke then. Kenny Corning, Ruth's no-account brother, lived with her part time, but he never had anything to do with the Church."

"Wait. Corning?" Jack repeated. "Ruth's maiden name was Czworniak."

"That's right. It was. Ken Corning was born Kovac Czworniak. He changed his name—every bit of it—because he didn't want people to know he was Polish. You have to remember that back then, immigrants from *that* part of the world were still very aware of the reasons their families had fled the homeland, and people in *this* part of the world were highly suspicious of anyone who might have rubbed shoulders with the USSR."

"Is the brother still alive?" Joan asked.

"No, Miss, he drank himself to death."

"Did Ruth have friends in the community? Someone else we might talk to about her and her son?"

The priest shook his head. "Ruth kept pretty much to herself. Didn't make friends easily. She put Gilbert in our school here, came to Mass two or three times a week, and never said much to me about her past life other than that she was a widow. Pretty well fixed, financially. Never took up with any men that I knew of."

At the mention of Ruth's finances, Jack asked, "Were you aware of what Ruth did to make money?"

Father Feney looked at him over the rims of his glasses. "You mean the fortune-telling?" He shrugged. "There was gossip. There is always gossip. This is a small town, after all. Though I'd swear it was bigger then than it is now. The people who live here do everything else in Branson or Springfield. Anyway, Ruthie had a way with people and animals. They seemed to naturally gravitate to her for help, for advice, for comfort. She had a great many guests from outside the community. Whether they were friends or clients, I certainly couldn't tell you. I only know that she was a good mother, constant in her faith, and that she gave generously but quietly to the Church."

He paused for a moment to push the plate of cookies—cake-like and tasting of molasses and nutmeg—closer to Jack and Joan. Then he looked up at them, catching them both in his bright gaze. "Before Ruthie moved here, I got a phone call from the office of the archdiocese of Chicago. They told me about her having the stigmata and asked me to let them know how she was doing and if anything unusual happened once she got here."

Jack felt as if someone had just walked over his grave. Someone in the Chicago Church was interested in the Gilbertson family that long ago? "Who?" he asked. "Who called you?"

"An administrative assistant, I believe, from the archbishop's office. I don't recall the name. Honestly, I can't even recall if the person was a member of the clergy or a lay employee."

"It sounds," said Jack, "like you're telling us nothing unusual did happen once Ruth got here. Did you ever see her stigmata yourself? Or her so-called totem or spirit guide?"

"No. Never. I mean, she talked about her totem—some sort of big bird, I gather—but I certainly never saw it. I rather fancied she just imagined it—a way of coping, you know." The priest gave him a look that was two inches from being sly. "And to be truthful, I should say that nothing unusual happened *right away.*"

Joan leaned forward in the heavily embroidered chair she occupied. "But something did happen. Involving Ruth?"

"Involving Ruth *and* Gilbert. You have to understand that Gilbert was a frail boy. Average student but sickly, and Ruth was overly protective. He got teased a lot by the other kids—bullied, really—and never had many close friends. He was with his uncle a lot when Kenny was in town. Kenny did card tricks and that sort of thing. I think that's how Gilbert developed his interest in magic. He'd do little magic shows for school events and Sunday socials, but he was never any good. Mostly, he just made a fool of himself." He seemed to go within himself for a moment, sorting through memories, perhaps choosing which ones to share.

"I guess it would have been thirteen or fourteen years ago," he said after awhile, "when Ruth started getting ill. Told me once she had real bad headaches. Refused to go to the doctor. She said what would be, would be, and there was no use in interfering. She was bedridden most of the last year of her life. That's when something happened that caused me to call Chicago.

"One afternoon, Gilbert was out on their front porch when three boys came up and started poking fun at him. Gilbert tried to go into the house, but these bullies blocked the front door and wouldn't let him back inside. Then they began pushing him around. He started crying, and Ruth came to the door. She told the boys to leave him alone. One of them spit at her and called her a witch. Said she should be burned at the stake. The other two dragged Gilbert to the edge of the porch and dumped him over the railing into the holly bushes. Theresa Whalen, who lived across the street from Ruth at the time, saw the whole thing from her front yard and called the sheriff."

Joan cocked her head to one side. "Because of the bullying?"

"No, because of what happened to the boys because of it. They went blind, Miss Firestone. The moment Gilbert hit those holly bushes and cried out in pain. All three of them. Couldn't see a thing. Not even light. Mrs. Whalen saw it all. One moment they were laughing, the next they were rubbing at their eyes and screaming. That's when Mrs. Whalen called the sheriff, while Ruth grabbed Gilbert and took him inside."

"What did the sheriff do?"

"What could he do? He called Dr. Bowen, the local GP, and took the kids over to the clinic. Doc Bowen examined all three of them. Said he couldn't find anything wrong with them other than that they were completely blind; he was pretty sure they weren't faking. He figured that if they were faking, they'd be pointing fingers at Ruth Gilbertson and her alleged witchcraft. All they could do was howl."

"Did they ever regain their sight?" Jack asked.

The old priest nodded. "Oh, yes. At about the precise moment their frantic parents got them into an ER in Springfield. Doc said it must have been hysterical blindness, but that didn't stop the gossip mill. I mean, really, hysterical blindness that struck all three boys at the same moment? How likely is that? Someone started the rumor that Ruth was a witch. Doc Bowen and I tried to put a lid on it, as they say, but folks were scared of Ruth. Which, of course, means they were angry at her, mistrusted her. Never saw her outside her house after that."

Hysteria. Mob mentality. Jack often marveled at the stupidity and ignorance of human beings. "And that's when you called the Chicago Archdiocese?"

Father Feney nodded. "Right after it happened. Naturally, they wanted all the details I had. I gave what I could, put them in touch with Theresa Whalen. That was the last contact I had with them. A few weeks later, Ruth's health failed. I gave her last rites and she died in her sleep the next day. Dr. Bowen said she must have had a stroke or maybe a brain tumor. Only Gilbert and Kenny and a few old ladies from the parish were at the funeral. Very sad. Ruthie was a good woman."

"What happened to Gilbert?" Joan asked.

"Kenny took him to Springfield. Eventually, the bank sold the house here in Hunterton. I heard that Kenny died a few years after that from liver disease, which was no surprise given the way he drank. I called Gilbert when I heard his uncle had died. He was polite and said that he was a senior in high school and was taking care of himself with a part-time job. That was the last I ever heard of him. Next, you're going to ask if Mrs. Whalen and Dr. Bowen are still around. The answer's no. The Whalens moved away to be closer to their kids; Doc Bowen died five or six years ago."

Frustration roiled in Jack's stomach as he and Joan thanked Father Feney and planned their next move. One of the kids who'd been blinded still lived in town and worked at the feed store. They interviewed him, but he had nothing significant to say except that the experience had changed his life. He was still convinced Gil's mom had blinded him, but he no longer thought she was a witch.

"I was the one in the wrong, you know?" he told them. "I was the one caught in sin. Being struck blind was my wake-up call. I figure it was the Lord who let me have it. And I deserved every minute of it. I was a little shit. No ifs, ands, or buts."

Silence ruled the car again on the drive back to St. Louis where tomorrow, bright and early, they'd board a flight and head west to Las Vegas. Both of them, Jack suspected, were using the quiet to introspect. He had no way of knowing what Joan was thinking, he only knew that whether he tried to ponder the strange connections between a sickly, introverted young man, a youthful burn victim, and a powerful underground conservative movement within the Catholic Church, his mind ultimately came back to hover around his feelings for Joan.

He now understood, with much more clarity, why she was so reluctant to enter into a relationship of any kind. A psychologist might have said she had abandonment issues. From her father dying when she was young, to some idiot thrill-seeker dumping her in the middle of nowhere where some additional idiots thought her best option was to trade on her sumptuous figure and exotic looks to become a glorified hooker, she'd been conditioned to be independent . . . or to lose herself in other people's expectations of her.

Jack thought about Irene and Katy and wished he could pray that neither of them would ever meet a jerk like Joan's manipulative, fickle bass player. The problem with men like that was that men like Jack had to reap what they sowed. He could kick himself for the sophomoric things he'd thought about Joan and even said to her during the first flush of his mad attraction to her.

Land mines, he thought. *Everywhere I turn, there are land mines.* Mr. Brainless Bassist might have set those mines, but Jack had tripped over them all on his own.

"Jack, there's something I haven't told you."

Those were the first words Joan had spoken since he'd taken the wheel for the drive back to St. Louis.

"Yeah, I got that memo. You clear this confession with Father Tom?"

"It's something else. Something the cardinal doesn't even know. Something I haven't told anyone. Not even my captain."

That sounded scary. "Joan, I'm not a priest. I'm not sure you should be confessing—"

"Shut up, Jack, and listen. Remember I told you that Gilbert came by my office the morning before he started his winning streak?"

"Yeah, I remember."

"This is going to sound really weird," she murmured. "I fell asleep while he was in my office, and when I woke up, he was gone. Must have been out for about ten minutes. I've never done anything like that before. Can't imagine why I did it then. And now I'm starting to wonder if . . . if Gilbertson had something to do with it. If he caused it in some way, for some reason. If he messed with my head."

Jack was at a loss. "I . . . don't know what to say. Are you sure you weren't just tired and bored? I mean, Gil's voice does have that drone-like quality . . ."

"No. I wasn't abnormally tired. I'd had my coffee, eaten a good breakfast. And I found what he was saying pretty damned interesting— or at least strange and kind of funny. But it was like I developed narcolepsy. One minute I was asking him a question about what he expected me to do about any of this, and the next I was waking up with my head on my desk like a kid in detention."

Jack glanced sidewise at her. She looked worried; her brow was knit and she was rubbing the firestone, her hand pressed to her breast. Jack shifted uncomfortably in his seat. "Has it happened since?"

"Nope."

"Well, as far as I can tell, your head is just fine. Honestly, it does sound as if he might have hypnotized you. Maybe he was afraid you'd arrest him or call the local HHS office and have him hauled off to a shrink."

She turned to look at him, hopefully, he thought. "Just making good his escape?"

"Yeah. Why's it bothering you so much?"

"I thought about hypnosis. It made me wonder if he might have fed me some sort of posthypnotic suggestion. It's a pretty unsettling feeling, thinking someone might've planted something in your head with no idea what it might be."

Jack had to admit that was a rather alarming idea. "Look, this is Gilly the Magic Clown we're talking about here. A guy who, as far as anyone who knows him is concerned, wouldn't hurt a fly. A guy who sounds like Piglet."

"Uh-huh. As I recall, it was a guy who sounded like Piglet who turned out to be a mass murderer in that Star Trek episode."

Jack couldn't help but smile. "I remember that episode. Turns out the mass murderer actually *was* Piglet—or at least the actor who voiced the cartoon character."

"See? Stranger things, Jack."

She was smiling at him, and he realized he had just learned something important about her. When she had something bothering her, giving her the room to get it off her chest enabled her to move on. Which made him wonder if getting off his own chest what was bothering him would have the same effect. He decided to give it a whirl.

"You knew about Mitchell before we even went to St. Mary of Nazareth, didn't you?"

Joan took a deep breath, let it out. "I knew, yes, that Gilbert was alleged to have performed some sort of miracle there. I didn't have all the details or know that Sister Claire was the one who issued the gag order, or that Lew Gleason was involved in some way."

"And you knew because Tom knew."

She nodded.

Nope. Venting at Joan had not assuaged his ill humor at Tom's lack of trust in him. Which meant when they got to their hotel, he was going to have to take it up with the man himself.

Chapter 15

When they'd settled into the airport hotel in St. Louis, Joan opted to simply get a bowl of soup and go to bed, citing their early flight. Jack swallowed his frustration, ordered room service, and spent several minutes deciding whether to call Tom O'Connor using the burner or his own cell phone. Reasoning that whoever might be listening was well aware of where he and Joan had been, he went for the latter, calling the landline at the cardinal's manse. Father Lyons answered and told Jack he would see if the cardinal was free.

Tom didn't keep him waiting, nor did he pretend he didn't know why Jack was calling. "So, I suspect you're mad because I didn't tell you more of what was going on."

"Something like that."

"Jack, I figured if I'd gabbled at you about a miracle healing and the weirdness with Ruth Gilbertson it might be too much. That you'd just throw up your hands and stomp out of my house. This burned boy seems like the real McCoy—the recipient of a legitimate miracle. Did you talk to the parish priest in Hunterton?"

"Yes."

"Then I suspect you've heard the parable of the blind bullies. I dropped the ball on that and should have had someone go down there when it happened, but there was a lot going on here at the time and it fell through the cracks. Off the record, what do you think about the young burn victim?"

What did he think? Hadn't he just spent the better part of the day trying to figure that out? "Tom, in strictest confidence, this might be the closest thing I have ever seen to justifying the word miracle. Frankly, I'd have a hell of a time ever convincing anyone that it isn't . . . if I ever wrote about it."

"Will you write about it?" Tom asked; Jack could hear the smile in his voice.

"I don't know. Maybe. But the signal thing to me, Tom, is that your interest in Gil Gilbertson predates his activities in Vegas by decades. Or at least, your interest in his mother."

"Yes, that's true. Her case was startling, to say the least. I was sorry she felt the need to disappear the way she did. I'm not exactly sure why she did that. Maybe she just didn't want the attention that being seen as a walking miracle would bring. I can understand that. Certainly, Mitchell's parents didn't want that sort of exposure. I'm glad to hear you don't think we were crazy to be impressed by his case."

"Tom, anyone who sees those pictures, assuming they are authentic, can't help but be impressed. I'm at a loss to explain them." He was also at a loss to understand why Sister Claire insisted on killing the story. "There's something I'm not getting here. Miracles are a good thing for the Church, aren't they? I mean, healing a poor child in a Catholic hospital? I would think that would be great optics for the secular world and a real shot in the arm for true believers."

"Yes, you would think that, wouldn't you? And if one of the doctors or nurses in that hospital had performed the miracle or if a statue in the lobby had performed it, you might be right. But some minds have trouble with the idea that God does miracles that don't involve devout Catholics—true believers, as you put it. Or that they could happen under the regime of a pope who's seen by some as flouting the dogmas of the Church."

"When he's reading his lines straight out of the Gospels?"

There was a tiny, strange noise on the line, as if someone had let out a pent-up breath. A shiver ran up Jack's spine. It didn't take clairvoyance to know that someone was probably listening to their conversation. The shiver was followed by a flare of annoyance.

"Did you hear about the bully Gil vanquished at the burger joint he works at?"

"No," said Tom. "I hadn't."

Aware of their eavesdropper, Jack related the incident with some relish, dwelling on the meanness of the man toward the little girl, Gil's standing up to him, the bully suddenly gasping for breath, and Gil's threat that he could see him wherever he went and would know if he ever harmed the girl again.

Now, a tiny click sounded across the connection. Jack guessed Father Lyons had heard about all he could handle. He smiled. "So, St. Jude's parish and Lew Gleason; what's the connection? And why is Joan keeping some of what she knows from me?"

"Jack, are you in your hotel?"

"Yeah, why?"

"Is Detective Firestone there?"

Jack felt a shaft of dismay tighten all the muscles in his chest. "Here? You mean, in my room?" *Jeez, Jack. You sound like a guilty school boy.*

There was a second of loaded silence on the other end, then Tom said, "I meant, is she in her room at the hotel."

"Yes. She's just down the hall. Room 312."

"Great. I'll talk to her, clear her to tell you whatever you want to know. By the way, if you hadn't talked to Father Feney, I was planning on telling you about Ruth's situation there in Hunterton."

"You mean you were going to tell me that you called Feney and asked him to keep an eye on Ruth and Gilbert? That was you, wasn't it?"

"Yes, that was me. Or rather it was Father Powell—now Bishop Powell—acting on behalf of the diocesan office."

Jack frowned. "Powell? Powell knew about Gilbert before too?"

"Yes and no. He knew Ruth Gilbertson had a son—they attended his home church, but he didn't make the connection between the boy and the generous altruist in Vegas until the letter Gil wrote surfaced."

"That's a rather amazing number of coincidences, isn't it?"

Tom chuckled. "Is it coincidence, Jack?"

Jack hated it when Tom went all metaphysical on him. "Oh, what—the hand of God?"

He heard Tom's long-suffering sigh as a bit of static in the connection. "Ruth was going to Powell's church when she manifested her stigmata. I arranged to send her to Sam Bernstein while you were his protégé. You and I became friends, and because of the nature of your work, I called you when Gilbert surfaced again in Las Vegas. What coincidences do you see in any of that?"

"Why Las Vegas?" Jack said. "Why not Reno or South Shore Tahoe or Atlantic City or any other place gambling is legal and lucrative? Why Bishop Powell's bailiwick?"

"I should think that would be obvious, Jack. Gil Gilbertson loves magic and longs to do it well. Las Vegas is the magic capital of the world."

Jack had to allow that made sense, but another angle to this niggled, and that was the fact that Gilly the Magic Clown was sending all of his gambling winnings out of Vegas to abuse survivor groups in other parts of the country.

He hung up with Tom and tried to watch TV but couldn't concentrate. He found himself in the uncomfortable state of mulling his feelings for Joan Firestone, feeling a conscious need to come to some definite understanding of them. He was not a man who tolerated uncertainty well.

All right. Fine. There was the sexual chemistry, of course, but he'd have to be as dumb as a post to not know that his attraction to the detective went light-years beyond that. Though they were from far different backgrounds, they spoke a common language: music. And she could actually *do* music, not just study and appreciate it as he did. She knew a great deal about sleight of hand, both in its entertainment application and in its mundane use as a means of fleecing the unsuspecting. She was beautiful—stunning, actually—but her physical beauty did not obscure the beauty of . . . oh, all right, her beauty of *spirit*. She was intelligent, perceptive, made connections between ideas more easily than most people Jack knew, and she learned quickly. He respected that. He respected her.

All great reasons to admire another human being, but what Jack Madison was feeling as he thought of Joan Firestone was neither mere admiration nor mere physical attraction. Was it infatuation? Was it fondness?

Was it love?

He wriggled away from that idea mentally. They'd known each other such a short time . . .

Yes, but longer than you'd known Carolyn when you came to the conclusion that you wanted to marry her.

Well, there it was. The real reason he was questioning the emotions that clamored to be examined. In a word: Carolyn. What would Carolyn think of him tumbling head over heels in love (or lust) with Joan Firestone?

She'd think it was just like you to do that; it's the way you fell for her.

He tried to imagine the two women meeting each other, and knew without doubt that they'd get along like bagels and cream cheese, beer and pizza, coffee bars and bookstores.

But what would Carolyn think of him moving on? That was the real question. And because he couldn't ask Carolyn that, he did the next best thing; he called Irene.

She picked up on the second ring. "Hi, Daddy," she said. "How goes the sleuthing?"

"It goes. Learning a lot about . . . a lot of things."

"Ah, I feel a new book coming on."

"Entirely possible. We're flying to Vegas tomorrow and will be in the air a good part of the day, so I thought I'd check in."

"Uh-huh. 'We' meaning you and the lady detective?"

"Yeah. Joan. Her name's Joan Firestone. I told you that, right?"

"Yes, you did. You also told me she was attractive."

He found himself suddenly at a loss to know what to say next—a truly unsettling circumstance. "Yeah. She is. Very attractive. She's also smart and funny and stubborn and loves jazz. She's getting a degree in musicology."

"Wow. She sounds amazing."

"She is. Amazing. Irene . . . look, here's the thing: I'm very attracted to Joan. Getting to know her over the last week or so . . . she's really gotten to me, I guess. And I don't really know what to do about it. Where to go with it."

"Oh, Daddy," said Irene softly.

"I keep wondering . . . what would your mother say? If she's . . . if her soul or spirit is still . . . what would she think?"

Irene snorted. "She'd say, 'Isn't that just like your father?' She'd say that was just the way you fell in love with her."

There was a long moment of silence, then Jack asked, "And what do *you* think, Irene? What would Katy think?"

"That you deserve to be happy, and if being with Joan Firestone makes you happy, then you should be with Joan Firestone. I love that name, by the way. It sounds strong and sort of mystical at the same time."

"She's both. I think she's a Cherokee medicine woman like her grandmother."

"Cherokee medicine woman! Well, I'm impressed. I didn't think you believed in that sort of thing. Is she opening up new vistas for Jack Madison, skeptic?" Irene had a way of cutting to the heart of things.

"Yes. Yes, between Joan and this case we're investigating, I'm lousy with new vistas."

"Does she like you as much as you like her?"

"I hope so. I think so. But she's . . . she's a skeptic herself. About relationships. She's never had one that lasted. I don't think she believes they *can* last."

"Well, I guess you're just going to have to get in there and convince her that she's wrong. You know volumes about lasting relationships." She was silent for a second, then asked, "Is that what you want? A lasting relationship?"

Did he? He thought about Carolyn—about how life had been with her presence in it. "I think . . . I think, yes. I think that's the only kind I'm cut out for."

"Well, speaking of relationships, my boyfriend is sitting across the table from me wondering when he's going to get to be the main man in my life."

"Boyfriend? I didn't know you had . . . You're on a date? I'm sorry—"

She laughed. "Daddy, it's okay. I love you. And it's not really a date; it's just us going out for dinner and a midnight movie. We both hate dating."

"Well, I'll say good night then and let you get back to your undate."

"Good night, Daddy . . . Jared."

"What?"

"His name is Jared. Love you. Talk soon."

She hung up, and Jack lay back against his pillows and tried to wrap his mind around how fast things were changing in and around him.

Chapter 16

As bad as the commuter flight was from Springfield, the flight to Vegas was even worse. Their departure was delayed for two hours because of unsettled weather, and the airport was jammed. They upgraded to first class and spent the wait in one of the VIP lounges, sipping coffee and chatting.

Joan suspected Jack was as aware as she was of the bull moose in the room (as Grandma Firestone would have said)—the one subject they would not talk about. So, instead of trying to explain why she was distancing herself from him, she brought up their conversations with Cardinal O'Connor the night before.

"The cardinal tells me you think Mitchell's healing is the real deal."

Jack looked annoyed. Whether it was real annoyance or feigned, Joan couldn't tell.

"I told him that in confidence, but yes. I'd say the evidence points to a spontaneous healing of the boy's burns. And it also points to our magic man as being a catalyst in some way."

"A magic man," Joan added, "whose mother apparently had ESP or clairvoyance or the gift of prophecy or whatever."

"Or whatever," repeated Jack.

"What do you know about all that?" Joan asked. "ESP, clairvoyance, that sort of thing?"

Jack gave her a look. "You could read my books."

"Can you give me a thumbnail sketch?"

He took a long sip of his coffee, then asked, "Ever heard of the mimic octopus?"

"The what? No, although I can guess from the name what its claim to fame is. It chameleons, right?"

"Uh-huh."

"And it has what to do with ESP?"

"It may seem as if I'm digressing a bit, but bear with me. The thing that makes the octopus so fascinating to human scientists is that its brain seems to work so differently from ours that we probably can't appreciate it fully. In a lab setting, mimic octopi have been caught on security cameras waiting for humans to leave, then escaping their tanks to raid those nearby for shrimp and other food fish. And you're right. They're called mimics because they can completely change their body to virtually any color they wish. And they can change shape—and I mean really change shape. They can rearrange themselves to look like fish, sea snakes, rocks, coral. Needless to say, this requires a very advanced nervous system."

Joan digested that. "Okay. I think I see where you're going with this. You're suggesting Gilbert's brain—and possibly his mother's—is wired differently than a normal human brain."

"Something like that. Our preconceived ideas about how the mind works are often restricted to how most humans and other mammals think. So is our understanding of the central nervous system. But what if there are humans whose minds simply work differently enough that what they do seems like magic?"

"You think that might explain miracles in general? I mean the kind that Jesus and Buddha and people like that are said to have done?"

"It's possible, I suppose. I mean, look—you sing. You can snatch a note out of the air and have it come out of your mouth. You told me you hear harmonies."

She nodded.

"I can't do any of those things. Your ability to sing harmonies—heck, to find a *melody*—is a mystery to me. What if there are minds that can . . . I don't know, bend light so a camera can't make out their face, or accelerate healing by exciting cell production, or . . ."

"Or see into the future occasionally?"

He made a face but said, "Possibly. During my gap year, I took time to travel to universities that were carrying out scholarly work on a variety of ESP-related topics: telepathy, clairvoyance, out-of-body experiences, telekinesis, and so forth. I have kept reasonably up to date on writings about these things in respected, peer-reviewed journals. The bottom line is that the more I study it, the more confused I become."

Joan smiled crookedly. "You? Confused? That's worth the price of admission."

"Don't be mean. Yeah, I sometimes have an inflated sense of my own grasp on reality. As a scientist, do I believe extrasensory perception exists? Yes, but only in some narrowly defined instances. I'm willing to entertain the idea that Ruth's apparent gift of prophecy might be a natural ability to see a dimension of the time continuum that most people don't. Like your ability to hear harmonies that I'm deaf to. I'm willing to acknowledge that this ability might be as inconstant and unpredictable as, say, an AM radio signal."

Joan puzzled over that for a moment, then had a minor epiphany. "You mean like the way I'm in Vegas listening to my radio at night and suddenly realize the station is broadcasting out of Chicago."

"Bingo. But no one's used AM radio freakishness to practice pure hokum, and I know of no other field in which science has been as much corrupted by hokum as ESP. No other field in which misguided zealots, intent on their own agendas in spiritualism, religion, the occult, you name it, have tried to inject their fantasies into rigorous science. No other field in which statistical analysis has been misused." He tapped his finger on the table to punctuate his points. "And yet, in other instances, it has been held to impossibly rigid standards by the scientific community. Standards they'd never hold a physicist to who was predicting invisible particles to explain another phenomenon. Standards so high that in any other discipline, no one could ever publish anything. The Higgs boson would still be a pipe dream."

"In other words, people who pick up faraway radio waves are okay, but people who get time waves from the future are nut bars?"

Jack nodded. "Exactly. A lot falls into the zone where there is, to me, nothing all that special involved. Animals knowing that an earthquake or hurricane is coming, for example. That's not magic; it's the ability to connect with signals—minor earth tremors or subtle changes in barometric pressure, for example—that humans cannot feel or sense. At least, not most of us. So, I acknowledge that there are times when certain people know that something is going to happen by instinct, or through an ability to read signals that the rest of us don't get."

"Like all those gamblers who tell you they know when a particular slot machine is going to pay off?"

"I don't think anyone can do that on a consistent basis, but yes. I've heard enough stories, by people I trust, to believe that it occasionally occurs. Why? I don't know. I just know that it's so. There are people who have the documented ability to predict random number generating, and there are a few who, from time to time, can do it with incredible precision. Obviously, if it were predictable, they'd be multimillionaires—"

"You mean, they'd be Gilbert," said Joan.

Jack blew out a gust of air and stared down into his coffee cup. "Yeah. With Gilbert, all bets are off. And Ruth . . . if the letter she left for Sam . . . if she really saw Carolyn's death . . ."

His voice staggered to a stop, and Joan felt her heart contract painfully. There was no way this man was ready for another long-term relationship, but she realized at that moment that she wanted him to be. To have that level of love and commitment invested in her was something she realized she wanted. If she hadn't seen her parents together, didn't remember how they were, she wouldn't think it was possible, wouldn't think it had been possible for Jack Madison.

And might be again? She clamped down hard on that thought. *No, ma'am, you are not going down that rabbit hole today.*

"So, how do you test for ESP?" she asked. "Is it really like that scene in the first *Ghostbusters* movie? Cards with symbols on them— triangles, wavy lines, and all that?"

Jack smiled and nodded, and Joan was gratified to have pulled him out of a possible funk. "Pretty much. There are probably thousands of flawed studies in which something gave away the game: a tester's body language or unintentional marks on the backs of the cards or cards that weren't opaque enough. And, of course, there's plain cheating. But also, respectable scientists have done solid studies that seem to prove that some subjects can see what the tester is seeing a statistically significant number of times, beyond the toss-up of pure chance."

"What do you think it is? I mean, if you were to guess."

"There's some evidence that electrical currents disrupt a subject's ability to read the tester's mind. That would indicate that what's actually happening is that the subjects are able to pick up the electrical signals being generated in another person's brain and interpret them. Like picking up a Chicago AM station in Vegas."

"I get it," said Joan, and realized she did get it. "Just a different way of using our nervous system. That might explain two people thinking of the same thing at the same time or finishing each other's sentences. They literally tune in on each other's frequency. They say that happens with people who've been married a long time."

Joan regretted the words almost as soon as they left her lips. Jack was smiling, but she saw a sadness in his eyes.

"Yes. Yes it does," he said quietly.

Joan hastened to pull the conversation in a different direction. "That might explain Ruth. But what about Gilbert? He's more like that guy who claimed he could bend spoons with his mind. What was his name—Uri something?"

A spark of disdain flared in Jack's eyes. "Uri Geller. That's pure bullshit. These spoon benders are strictly sleight-of-hand artists claiming supernatural ability."

Joan laughed. "I saw Bobcat Goldthwait at the Bellagio years ago. I remember him saying, 'I can bend forks with my mind, but only at Denny's. And you have to look away for a little while.'"

Jack grinned. "That about sums it up."

"So that's it? Jack Madison's Handy Dandy Explanation of ESP?"

"That's it. Part science, part craft, and lots of BS. But that's after years of study. Now I'm trying to fit Gil and his mother into what I already know." He frowned, introspecting.

Joan studied his face, looking past the handsome exterior, and thought she divined a bit of what he was thinking. "But it doesn't fit very well, does it?" she murmured.

He shook his head, eyes still distant and unfocused. "No. Think about the guy who couldn't breathe, and the three boys who were temporarily blinded. Both of these might be explained as hysterical events triggered by some sort of suggestion. I've seen cases of hysterical blindness triggered by extreme stress." His eyes came into focus on Joan's face and he met her gaze. "But, Joan, I've never seen or heard about it happening to multiple people simultaneously. Maybe a stage hypnotist has caused a few people to think that they can't see, but that's entirely different than what happened in Hunterton to those three boys. Certainly nothing close to a hypnotic trance was involved there; nor in the Burger King incident. Angry people don't take to hypnosis. Their emotions are too excited, too much in control. Hypnosis relies on relaxation and emotional detachment."

"Yeah," Joan said, "I see what you mean. And then there are Gil's magic acts. Did he suddenly grow a lifetime of craft, or did he have it all along and was hiding it?"

"Neither makes sense. And it doesn't explain the rope trick. I have no idea how he did it—if he even did it at all."

"What do you mean, 'If he did it at all?'"

"I know this is going to the postulation phase, but could it have been mass hysteria? Like the missionaries Sam interviewed? I don't think so, but it is at least a logical explanation."

"And the slot machine and keno games?"

"Well, okay. The electrical impulse thing again."

That raised Joan's eyebrows. "He read the machine's mind?"

Jack laughed and finished off his coffee. "When you put it like that . . ."

"And the boy with the burn? You said something about exciting cell growth . . ."

He got that faraway look again. "I guess the question is: is it possible for something to awaken some primitive neurological ability to change shapes the way the octopus can—or in Mitchell's case, to regrow tissue like some animals can regrow body parts?"

"Does anything grow back spontaneously in humans besides hair and nails?"

"Only the liver, but that doesn't happen overnight. How did Mitchell's cell regeneration happen so quickly?"

"Isn't the bigger question how Gilbert caused it to happen so quickly *in another person*?"

Jack looked at her, meeting her gaze and holding it. "Actually, the bigger question is: how did we come to be sitting here asking these questions?"

Joan was wary of that look and that tone. "Meaning?"

Jack sat back in his chair and began folding and unfolding the paper napkin that sat beside his coffee cup. "Let's see if I can figure out what led from something that happened twenty-five years ago to now. Twenty-five years ago, something caused Ruth Gilbertson to manifest stigmata and begin receiving messages from the Virgin Mary—or from somewhere. She came to then Bishop O'Connor's attention through the parish priest, now Bishop Powell. He sent her to Sam Bernstein, which made me part of the effort to understand what was happening to her. In the process, I met Gilbert. Ruth left Chicago suddenly, for reasons that are unclear, and moved with Gilbert to Hunterton—pretty much the backside of nowhere. Tom O'Connor kept tabs on them, receiving information about strange goings-on from Father Feney. Years later, Gil grows up, moves to Springfield, joins a Magic Ring, and starts going to Vegas for magic conventions. Out of nowhere, during one of these conventions, he suddenly begins to manifest capacities beyond anything he's done before. Not just skill with magic, but a bunch of other abilities as well: seemingly some form of deep manipulation of other people and machines. So far, so good?"

Joan nodded, watching his face.

"Someone alerts Tom O'Connor."

"Bishop Powell," said Joan, "once he made the connection between Gilbert and his mother."

"Okay. So, Vegas is suddenly full of concerned parties: the Casino Association, the bishop, and the police. Representatives of those parties—including you—arrive in Chicago to consult with Cardinal O'Connor, the man Powell figures knows the most about the Gilbertsons . . . and me."

"And you."

"Where does the SPCD fit into this?"

"We're honestly not sure. Cardinal Tom knows they're keeping an eye on Gilbert, and us, too, now. They probably would like to know why we're interested in Gil. Their interest is in the miracles. Question is, exactly why? Is it friendly interest or something else?"

"And you knew all this from the get-go."

"Not all of it. I didn't know about the connection between the SPCD and St. Jude's until Captain Edwards told me. I shared that with you right away, though I wasn't sure I should."

"Bishop Powell," Jack murmured.

"What about him?"

"He's the first one to report Ruth's stigmata, and he's there when Gil suddenly displays the skill of a master magician. Ruth runs to Hunterton. And Gilbert just runs."

"D'you think he's SPCD?"

"I don't know. But he's something. I mean, maybe he somehow was just in the right place at the right time. Or maybe he . . . catalyzed these abilities the Gilbertsons display in some way."

'That doesn't seem likely, does it?"

Jack laughed. "I ask you, my dear detective, what about any of this seems at all likely?"

She joined him in laughter. "You have a point."

They landed in Vegas at noon Pacific Standard Time with the rest of the day to kill. They caught a cab to the Bellagio where they checked in briefly with Arnie Rosen in the admin offices before Jack went down to the lobby to check into his room.

"Join me for dinner?" he asked before Joan could effect an escape. "I'd kind of like to forget the case tonight and just relax. Talk about . . . other things. Maybe check out the local music scene. I'm sure you know where jazz is happening."

"I have a better idea," Joan said. "I'll invite you to dinner. At my place."

"You're offering to cook for me?" Jack asked. "Oh, I don't know, Joan. You know what they say about a man's stomach."

"I do. Is it true? Is that the way to your heart, Jack Madison?"

There was a note of solemn inquiry in that, despite the fact that she was giving him that sweet, crooked smile that he realized he'd become addicted to and would do almost anything to cause.

He met her gaze levelly and adopted the same quietly serious tone. "Joan, you have already found the way into my heart. Your being able to cook, on top of all of your other talents, is just gravy." He grinned, lest he seem *too* serious. "See what I did there? Cooking? Gravy?"

He could almost see her gauging her response. In the end, she fixed him with a narrowed gaze and said, "It's more than gravy, boy-o. It happens I am one world-class cook. Which you are going to find out firsthand. If you are appropriately worshipful of my culinary chops, I may let you take me out on the town after dinner. I'll text you the address."

"Anything I can bring?"

"Just your appetite and the aforementioned worshipful attitude. And don't be late. I'll expect you at five, sharp."

After Jack checked into the Bellagio, where Arnie Rosen had arranged one of the high-roller suites for him, he went down into the casino and played a little blackjack, winning about a hundred dollars. He poked through some of the stores in the underground galleria. Then he went to the spa and worked out a bit, took a nap, then showered. During all that time, he tried hard to not overthink the evening ahead. He knew how he wanted things to go, and it took a modicum of detachment for him not to turn his hopes into a plot. He had room service bring up two bottles of wine to take with him and had the concierge call him a cab.

Joan lived in a nice, tree-lined suburban area. Her house was a seventies' style split-level ranch, the kind with the sharply peaked roof and tall, narrow windows that hinted at the vaulted ceilings within. It sat on a big lot with lots of flowers and a manicured lawn.

"This is fantastic, Joan," he told her when she met him on the wide, flagstone porch. "You don't think about Las Vegas having quiet, refined residential areas. How do you find time to keep the lawn in such good shape?"

She laughed, opening the front door to him. "I pay my yard guy well and occasionally ply him with baked goods. I've had the same landscaper for almost ten years. Actually, I arrested him on a DUI, but when I found out he'd been laid off from his prior job and was trying to start up a gardening service, I gave him a little break. He's always been grateful to me. He's done pretty well for himself. I used to be his only client. Now I'm probably the poorest."

Jack stepped across the threshold and took in the high-ceilinged entry and the clean lines of the living area beyond. "I know a little bit about the real estate boom here; this place must be worth a fortune."

"It is. Best investment I ever made. I bought it fifteen years ago and it's probably appreciated ten times, maybe more. Even on a detective's salary, I'd never be able to buy anything like this today. It's away from the neon glow, I know a fair number of my neighbors, and it's close to the university. I'm lucky."

The house was tastefully furnished with furniture that reflected the tenant—sturdy, with clean, graceful lines. Mission style mixed with Asian, dark woods, art that flattered the sage green walls, pictures of family and friends, lots of books, and overall open, light, and airy. He gave the woman herself a longer look. She'd opted out of business attire in favor of a UNLV sweatshirt with a V-neck, and a pair of skinny jeans. Her hair was braided and fell over one shoulder. It took him a moment to realize that she wasn't wearing any makeup. This was Joan off stage, he realized. She was showing him her unvarnished self in her own space.

"Thank you," he told her solemnly.

"For what? You haven't eaten yet. How do you know you'll want to thank me after you do?"

"I mean, thank you for inviting me into your . . . your sanctum. Thank you for letting me see this side of you."

She looked at him for a moment. "You're welcome. This *is* my sanctum. It's what makes living here in Vegas tolerable." She tilted her head to one side. "You bought wine."

"I did." He held it out to her. "Best I could afford."

She took it and gave his attire a critical once-over. "And you didn't wear that damned blazer."

"Jeans and a sweater seemed more appropriate to the occasion. I wanted to fit in."

She smiled and carried the wine into the kitchen, from which indescribably mouthwatering smells were wafting. Dinner was a seafood gumbo with a big salad, crusty French rolls, and fruit. With the case off the menu, they talked about a host of other things, from art to music, from Chicago to Las Vegas.

"Las Vegas the Damned," Jack called it. "It's changed a lot since the first time I was here. More slot machines. More families. More people, period. Also, years ago, people dressed up here. Tuxes and gowns. Now the outfit I see most of in the daytime is cutoff jeans and flip-flops. People on the streets drink alcohol openly; hookers try to proposition men who are obviously with their wives and children. It looks seedier during the day than I remember."

Joan rolled her eyes expressively. "Yeah, but it's still someplace to go, someplace to say you've been, somewhere to lose your money . . . or yourself. Oz with slot machines."

Jack laughed. "That's one of the best descriptions I've heard yet."

"Oh, don't get me started on this place. I'm way too jaded. Jack, it's a gilded sepulchre, a trashy, overly ornate tomb. It's an utter lie, a fantasy. Sleight of hand writ large, from the fake Luxor pyramid to the fake Eiffel Tower to the fake indoor gardens at the Bellagio. I think that's why so many magic conventions are held here; it's the perfect town for make-believe. And behind all the neon and fake fronts is a lot of desperation. Bishop Powell is right. The underbelly of Las Vegas—the *real* Las Vegas—is full of desperate people barely hanging on."

"Is there anything about the place you like?"

"Besides my house?" She thought about it. "Yeah. The fountain in front of the Bellagio. That dancing water with its music and lights is the best show in town. And it's free."

"Best things in life are, they say."

After dinner they worked together to clear the table and clean up. For Jack, it was a weird juxtaposition of the familiar and the new. Helping with after-dinner chores was familiar; doing it in this sleek kitchen with this woman was surreal. Once the dishwasher was loaded, they retired to the living room with glasses of wine and settled on the couch in front of the modern, white brick fireplace.

Jack raised his glass in a toast. "You were right about your cooking, Joan. It's not just gravy. A toast to the fact that you cook the way you sing."

"Thank you. Are you having a good time?"

"Can't imagine anything better . . . except maybe being able to repeat the experience on a regular basis." He found it hard to look at her as he said it, so he watched her face from the tail of his eye.

She tilted her head and studied him. "A regular basis? In the week or so you'll be here?"

He turned to face her, setting his wine glass carefully on the long, low coffee table. "I was hoping for more than that. Longer than that. You see, I've come to the conclusion that I'm not really into one-night stands either. Or two-week stands."

She continued to study him. "What are you saying?"

"I'm saying there are some awfully good colleges in the Chicago area where a promising musicologist could pursue her post-grad work. If she was of a mind to do something that wild and crazy. Because you'd have to be wild and crazy to give up this place." He glanced up toward the high-beamed ceiling.

He watched her pull back into herself, her gaze falling into her wine glass. "You know I want to get out of here. Not out of this house, but out of this *place*. So, you're not suggesting anything that's all that wild and crazy. It's the other part of it. I . . . I think you know how I feel about you—"

"Do I? I know you're physically attracted to me. And I know you're a little afraid of that attraction. Or maybe you don't trust it. Or trust me."

She glanced up at him, then back down. "Jack, I know you're struggling with your loss—"

"No. I've stopped struggling, Joan. I've spent a lot of time thinking about you and me . . . and Carolyn. And here's what I figured out: when I fall in love, I fall fast and deep. I did it with Carolyn, and I think I've done it with you. I wanted you the moment I first saw you. And I regret that I acted like a randy teenager because of it. It's just that the sexual fizz was so strong, it blotted out anything else. And I figured a woman your age, unmarried and not gay . . . well, that's last week's news. I wanted you and I wanted to be with you and I was afraid it was what you said—rebounding. But it's not that, Joan. I'm not rebounding from Carolyn. I've come to terms with Carolyn."

"But when you talked about her this morning—about Ruth's letter and all—you were so sad."

"Well, of course I was sad. I'm sad I lost her. But I'm happy I found you."

She nodded, still watching her wine as if it might feed her her next line. Then she looked up at him and smiled. "Grad schools, huh?"

"Northwestern. University of Chicago. DePaul. Fine establishments with top-notch music schools."

She set her wine glass down next to his, and he felt his pulse kick up a notch.

"Look me in the eyes, Jack. Look into my soul as I say this."

He looked. The prospect was blinding.

"I'm going to make love to you tonight, but when we get into that bed together—from that moment—I'm yours. Here or in Chicago. For as long as you can look at me and say you want me. I am going to give myself completely to you. Everything. But there's a catch."

He swallowed. "And that is?"

"From that moment, you also belong to me. I can't do this if it doesn't go both ways." She reached over and took his hands in hers. "Jack Madison, skeptic, I love you."

Jack smiled. Turned on, smitten, exalted—all of the above—he pulled her into his arms and murmured into her ear, "Joan Firestone, medicine woman, I love you right back. You are making me believe in magic in ways even our buddy Gilbert can't do."

She laughed breathlessly. "Oh, you silver-tongued devil, you."

As she'd done in her hotel room in Springfield, she took his face between her hands and kissed him so thoroughly he felt as if his entire body was on fire. He was surprised when she disentangled herself and got up from the couch.

"Finish your wine," she told him. "Then come back to my bedroom in about fifteen minutes. I'll be waiting for you."

"With bells on?" he teased.

"Maybe not even that much," she said, and disappeared down the broad hallway toward the back of the house.

"How will I know which room it is?" he called after her.

Her laugh was sultry. "Follow the Gershwin."

When Jack entered the master bedroom exactly fifteen minutes later, having followed the strains of *Porgy and Bess* down the hall, he'd already taken off everything but his jeans, and padded in, shirtless and barefoot. The room was lit with candles, and the bed had been turned down. Joan was nowhere in sight, but the door to the en suite master bath was closed, and light crept beneath it across the polished hardwood of the floor. He could hear her singing along with "Bess, You Is My Woman Now."

Jack took off the rest of his clothing and lay down in Joan's bed. He was already hard with desire, and seconds later, when she emerged from the bathroom, he thought he'd burst. She was wearing a white silk dressing gown that hung open, displaying every curve. Her hair, loose around her shoulders, just skimmed the tops of her full breasts; her nipples peeked, dusky rose, from the snowy white of the peignoir. Jack found it difficult to breathe.

She crossed to the bed with a cat's grace and turned in a circle, sliding the gown from her shoulders as she moved in rhythm with the music. Candlelight licked the milk chocolate contours of her body, highlighting every mound and curve and flirting seductively with every shadow. It danced in the fire opal pendant—now the only thing she wore.

"God but you're a cruel woman," Jack said, his voice a husky whisper.

She turned to face him, smiling. "Cruel to be kind, Dr. Madison."

He wanted to simply pull her into the bed and storm her, but this was her domain. She set the tone and tempo for their lovemaking;

it was scored by Gershwin with the slow, deep passion of American jazz. She smelled of vanilla and spices, felt like silk and velvet, and tasted like good wine. Loving her was to court sensory overload. When she had touched and tasted every inch of him and offered herself in return, she pushed him back against the pillows and simply engulfed him. In their mutual moment of release, Joan bent to press her lips to his and caught his groan of pleasure in her mouth; Jack, having entered into her being, found he didn't want to leave.

He felt bereft when she lifted herself from his body and drifted into the bathroom to clean up. *Porgy and Bess* had given way to a Gershwin medley: "How Long Has This Been Going On" was the first song that registered on Jack's overwhelmed senses. He sat up, retrieved his jeans from the foot of the bed, and rummaged in the pockets, pulling out a small leather jeweler's wallet. He laid this on Joan's pillow.

She was smiling when she came out of the bathroom. Smiling and naked. Jack felt unexpected stirrings beneath the sheets he'd pulled over himself.

"What's this?" she asked, her hand on the little leather envelope.

"Open it."

She looked at him. "Jack, what have you done?"

"Open it," he repeated.

She sat on the edge of the bed and opened the jeweler's wallet, unsnapping it and flipping up the flap. "Oh, Jack, they're . . . they're perfect."

"No, you're perfect. They merely match your necklace."

Joan held the earrings up in the light of the candles. Flame leapt from the hearts of the twin fire opals, seeming to spark a response from the pendant between her breasts. "Where did you ever find them?"

"Antique jewelry store in the Bellagio. Put them on."

She did, going to the full-length mirror between the bed and the bathroom to admire them. Jack took the opportunity to admire her, taking in how amazing she looked in nothing but a necklace and dangle earrings.

She returned to sit on the bed. "Jack, they're beautiful. No one's ever given me anything like this in my life."

It took Jack a moment to realize that she was crying, her tears blazing in reflected light as they raced silently down her cheeks. He gathered her into his arms and held her to him, pulling the comforter over them both. When she stopped crying, she kissed him. One thing led to another and they were making love again before Jack had barely registered that he *could* make love again. It was every bit as astonishing as the first time.

"Bess, you is my woman now," Jack whispered, before sleep claimed him.

Chapter 17

Joan and Jack met with Chief Spader in his office just after noon, then went from there to Arnie Rosen's office at the Bellagio. Gil Gilbertson was there before them, pacing the room, when Rosen ushered them in.

The magician immediately came over and shook Jack's hand. "Dr. Madison, I'm sorry I didn't spend more time talking with you in Chicago, but I had to run that evening. I'm glad to finally meet you again; it has been a long time. Thanks for being here."

Rosen, his face tense with anger, told his admin to hold all his calls, herded his guests into a small conference room that adjoined his office, and invited them to sit at the table. It was obvious to Jack that he intended to run the show, despite the fact that Joan had requested Jack take lead when it came to dealing with Gilbert.

Rosen's cheeks had no more than grazed his chair when he launched into a verbal attack on the hapless young man. "Mr. Gilbertson, I am sure you're aware that patrons of our casinos and hotels are, under Nevada law, guests. As your host, we have the prerogative to disinvite you."

Jack narrowly avoided rolling his eyes. *Disinvite?* What was that, Arnie's word of the day?

"The Casino Association does not know how you have won so much of our money, but from our perspective, it was not done fairly and, as far as we are concerned, we no longer want you as a guest in Las Vegas, nor any part of Nevada."

Jack coughed and glanced sidewise at Devin Spader. The chief looked a bit surprised at Rosen's tone but didn't say anything. Jack wondered why he was being so quiescent.

Arnie marched on. "I know Dr. Madison would like to spend some time with you, but I think the two of you should do that elsewhere, far away from here. So, to cut to the chase, I would like you to leave Las Vegas, and the state of Nevada, as soon as possible. I think it will solve many problems. If you will agree to do this, we will give the Catholic Church all winnings not already transferred to your bank. That's the deal. Would you agree with me, Chief Spader?"

"Well, I wouldn't state it quite so baldly . . ."

Joan gave her boss a sidewise glance. "Actually, Mr. Rosen, what you're suggesting is highly illegal."

"Or unconstitutional," Jack added.

"The *local* church?" asked Gil. He seemed completely unruffled by Rosen's little speech.

"Excuse me?" said Rosen.

"Will you give the money to the local church?"

"Yeah. That's the deal."

"Then, no deal," said Gilbert mildly. "Besides, I'm afraid it's not that easy. I can leave town and you'll still have a very big problem on your hands."

"What kind of big problem?" asked Spader.

There was a spark of something un-Gilbert like in Gilbert's pale eyes. "The problem of me breaking the bank in Las Vegas, and in this whole state. If that's what you guys want to happen, I assure you, I'll make it happen. You'll be bankrupt in a few weeks." This little speech was delivered in Gil's most inoffensive Piglet voice, which somehow made it almost chilling.

Rosen's face went red. "Don't threaten me, pal. You're biting off way more than you can chew."

Jack opened his mouth to speak, but Gil raised a hand, motioning for him to remain quiet.

"Thank you, Dr. Madison, but I want to handle this. Mr. Rosen, first of all I would like to give you a bit of a warning. Bad things have happened to people who threaten me. Horrible things. Things that I cannot control."

Rosen's face went bright red. "Why you little pipsqueak! Don't you dare talk back to me, you son of a—I'll say whatever I want!"

Spader, eyes narrowed, reached over to put a warning hand on Rosen's shoulder.

Jack raised both hands in a calming gesture. "Arnie, I am telling you this with every bit of sincerity that I can muster. Listen to what this man is saying."

Rosen nodded, getting redder in the face by the second. He had clenched his fists.

"Thank you, Dr. Madison," said Gilbert. He returned his attention to Arnie Rosen. "I take it that you can see the outside of the Bellagio via your security system?" He pointed to a row of TV screens on the wall opposite the door of the conference room. They were blank at the moment.

"Yeah. What of it?"

"Humor me for a minute, would you? Turn them on so we can see the people coming into the hotel from the outside. Go ahead, Mr. Rosen, indulge me."

Rosen looked at Spader, who simply crossed his arms and frowned. Oddly, Rosen then turned to look at Jack as if asking his opinion.

Surprised, Jack shrugged. "I can't see what you've got to lose."

"You wouldn't," murmured Spader.

Jack flicked the police chief a puzzled glance, noting that Joan was also regarding him intently.

Rosen picked up a remote control that had been sitting in the middle of the table near a triangular speaker phone and turned on the surveillance feed. In seconds, they were looking at the exterior main entrance of the Bellagio. As was the case at almost any time, day or night, a large numbers of visitors were passing through its doors into the hotel/casino.

Gilbert gestured at the screen and said, "Now, Mr. Rosen, pick out a person. Any person you wish, man or woman, young or old. Take your time—however long you want. When you pick that person, follow him or her inside."

"Cut the crap, Gilbertson. I'm starting to get pissed," Rosen said.

Spader shook his head. "Arnie, I sympathize with your position, but you really must try to control your temper. There are two police officers in the room. Please try to remember that."

"Yes, Mr. Rosen," Gil said reasonably. "I'd think you'd want to be careful about threatening me in front of a police chief and a detective." He turned to Joan. "Detective, perhaps you might ask Mr. Rosen to go along with me for a minute; he might listen to you. You've seen what I can do close up."

Joan gave Arnie Rosen a look Jack suspected could strip paint. "I think we ought to hear him out, Mr. Rosen. I'd certainly like to see what he wants to show us."

But Rosen pounced on Gilbertson's words. Looking back and forth between Jack and Joan, he asked, "What does he mean, you've seen what he can do close up?"

"Jack and I," Joan told him, "have had the pleasure of seeing Mr. Gilbertson—"

"Gilbert, please," said the object of Rosen's angst.

"Gilbert, then. We've had the extreme good fortune of seeing Gilbert perform some truly world-class magic in the last week or so. His abilities are off the charts. I think if you want to understand what he's capable of, you might want to play along for the moment."

Rosen glared at Joan for a second or two, then sat back in his chair and straightened his tie. He glanced up at the TV monitors, then pointed at one. "Okay, wise ass," he told Gilbert. "I pick that woman, there. The one with the pink sunglasses, in the blue sweat suit." She was hard to miss.

"Please, follow her inside," Gilbertson said. "It may take a few minutes for the payoff, so let's just relax, shall we?"

Gilbertson rocked back in his chair with a cherubic smile on his face as Rosen selected a series of cameras to follow the woman as she made her way into the club and onto the casino's main floor. For a certified milquetoast, Gilly the Magic Clown behaved like the most confident man on the planet.

"Good job, Mr. Rosen," he congratulated their seething host. "It looks as if she's headed for the quarter slots. Let's see how she does and, please remember, you picked her out of the crowd."

"Don't patronize me," Arnie snapped.

The woman had, indeed, wandered over to the banks of quarter slot machines. She looked around, clearly trying to choose a machine. In a moment, she settled on one.

"Oh, good," said Gil, rocking forward and putting his elbows on the table. "Blazing Sevens. That's a nice big jackpot. You know, my guess is this lady that Mr. Rosen chose is going to have a very pleasant afternoon. Very pleasant, indeed."

As her unseen audience watched, the woman put her slot player's card in the Blazing Sevens machine, inserted a twenty-dollar bill, and punched the Maximum Play button. On the first pull, a bet of seventy-five cents, she hit the progressive jackpot. The lights on top of the machine flashed and music started playing. Fellow slot players flocked to see what was going on. At first the woman didn't seem to realize what had happened, but when she saw the three big triple flames on the pay line, she looked up. Her audience could see the dawn of comprehension in her eyes; she had just won a progressive jackpot worth a little over $147,000. She jumped up and down, screaming with excitement.

Arnie Rosen's mouth opened and the color drained from his face. Spader's reaction was more subdued but still incredulous. Jack and Joan traded knowing looks. Jack had realized what was going to happen the moment Gil asked Rosen to pick a random guest. He knew Joan had too.

Gilbertson stood. "You see?" he said, pointing at the still celebrating gambler, his voice rising further into the soprano range. "See what you have on your hands here? Do you see? She's not a plant, Rosen. You picked her out yourself."

"Yeah, but she was dressed like an Australian's nightmare. Maybe you planted someone that obvious just so's I'd pick her."

Gil's carroty eyebrows rose exaggeratedly toward his receding hairline. "Want me to do it again? Maybe on the fifty-dollar slots? How about another real big progressive jackpot? How about five or

six tonight? Here at the Bellagio? Maybe at Caesar's? Pick anyone
at random, Mr. Arnie 'Big Shot' Rosen. I will make them win. And,
make no mistake, I can do this from Texas as easily as I can from
here. Or jail, since that's what you have on your mind, Captain Spader.
Want to try me?"

He turned his glittering gaze on the police chief, and Jack felt a
chill skitter down his spine. *Is he reading people's minds?*

Just then, Rosen's admin slipped into the room, apologizing profusely,
and handed her boss a note. His mouth was open to scold her, but his
gaze had dropped to the note, and he froze. "Some guy just won the
mega-jackpot at the Venetian on the one hundred-dollar slots. That
payoff is one million dollars . . ." His voice was airless with shock.

Everyone in the room turned to stare at Gilbert, including the admin,
who no doubt wondered why everyone else was gawking at the pale
young man in the brown suit.

"Gil," Jack said, "was that you?"

Gil shrugged. "Sorry folks, needed to do that. People who play the
hundred-dollar slots don't need the money, so I think this guy is going
to decide to give it away. I think it will be . . . to a woman's shelter."

Jack marveled again at how rapidly Gil's demeanor—his whole level
of energy—had changed. He even *looked* bigger and more imposing.
Or was that part of the aura he cast? One of his peculiar new talents?
Jack realized he'd begun to doubt his own perceptions.

Rosen made a quick preemptory gesture that sent his admin scurrying
back to her desk.

When the woman had gone, Joan got to her feet and swept the group
with her dark gaze. "Chief, Mr. Rosen, can I ask you to join me in
the outer office for a moment?"

Rosen and Spader exchanged glances, then the police chief stood and beckoned Rosen to follow Joan into his office. The three of them were gone for perhaps thirty seconds, during which time Jack watched Gil, and Gil simply sat down in his chair, humming something Jack recognized as a Gilbert and Sullivan tune: "I Am the Very Model of a Modern Major General." It was at once ludicrous and appropriate.

When the others returned to the conference room, Rosen was the first to speak. "Okay, Mr. Gilbertson, you have our attention. I offer my most sincere apologies. I'm sorry I came on so strong. Let's all sit down and talk this through. Clearly, we should have had Dr. Madison begin the conversation this afternoon, so I'm gonna defer to him. Doc, you have something to share with us?"

Jack waited for the rest of the group to reseat themselves, but they'd no sooner done so than Gilbert got up to pace, his confidence making a swift slide toward agitation. Jack waited a beat, then said, "Gilbert, why don't you come on over here and sit down? We're going to get this straightened out, I promise." He watched Gilbertson for a moment more, then asked, "Gil, does your head hurt?"

Gilbert turned, rubbing at his temples. "Yes. Yes, it does hurt. It always does when I . . . you know."

"Yes, I know. Your mother got these headaches too, didn't she? I couldn't help her because she left Chicago too soon, but I can help you, if you'll let me. I know you want something, and I don't think it's to bankrupt Las Vegas. I think you can do that if you wish, but I get the feeling money doesn't mean much to you."

"Thanks, Dr. Madison, you seem to understand me pretty well."

Gil returned to his chair and sat down. His face had lost a lot of its color, and his eyes had begun to take on a haunted look that Jack saw often in the eyes of chronic pain sufferers.

"I know Mom trusted you and Dr. Bernstein. That's why I was so intent on getting you involved in this, Dr. Madison. But help me? I don't think that's possible."

"What makes you say that?"

Gil's gaze swept the two men sitting across the table from him. "I don't want to talk about it here."

Jack shook his head. "I understand completely. We'll have a private conversation about it later. I . . . I want you to understand up front, Gilbert, that I was hired by the Las Vegas Casino Association to figure out what's going on with you. But as a physician, I am morally and legally bound to keep your medical information strictly between you and me."

"That's very professional of you, Doctor, and I would not expect anything less. But honestly, that's of no concern to me. Yes, I do want to speak with you about some of my health problems, preferably in private, but if you feel it's necessary, you may share what you wish with the detective—and even with these two gentlemen. I'm good with that. I really don't care about my privacy. I only want one thing: to finish what I've started. But because I require time to do that, do you think you can give me something for my headaches?"

"Yes, I can prescribe any number of painkillers, some targeted to migraines. But, I've got to know a bit more about what's causing the headaches before prescribing specific long-term treatment. A lot's changed since Sam treated your mom. We know much more about the brain and about pain. I'm hopeful I can offer you real help."

Gilbert gave Jack a rare smile. "I appreciate that you want to try. Look, Dr. Madison, I'm not the threat any of you think I am. I have a really simple request to make. Simple, but . . . well, I'd like to go into that later with you and Detective Firestone. Right now, I need to rest. I'd like to go to my room at the Mirage." He checked his watch, then looked to Jack. "It's two thirty. Could you have someone deliver the medicine for my headache to my hotel?"

Rosen's mouth popped open and his brow furrowed thunderously. Jack raised a hand to keep him from saying anything to Gilbert. The last thing they needed was to have Gil get agitated again.

"Yes," Jack said, "I'd be happy to do that. Do you need anything else?"

"I'd like it if you and Detective Firestone would join me for dinner this evening. Say about six? I'll let you know then what I need to do, and the help that I need to get it done. It may be a bit tricky, but I know the four of you can do it."

"Mr. Gilbertson . . . ," Spader began.

"I assure you, this is all legal, Captain Spader. I haven't broken any laws, I haven't cheated, and I won't cheat. And if you play along, Mr. Rosen, I won't deplete any more of your Casino Association's hard-earned money. So, can we talk about it this evening after dinner?"

Spader raised his hands. "Look, Gilbertson, you need to realize that you're asking for an awfully long leash. I demand to know the nature of what you're going to ask of Dr. Madison."

"You will. At the right time. I assure you, it's nothing illegal," Gilbert repeated. "It's got to do with my magic. With my stage act. I really don't want to say more than that."

He was rubbing his temples again, and Jack could tell from the glassy look in his eyes that he was in severe pain and having trouble concentrating.

"I understand, Gil," Jack told him. "We'll see you at six. I'm going to call in some medication for you immediately and have it delivered to your room at the Mirage. I have a request to make of *you*, now.

I'd like to have a chance to get a full history of your headaches, to examine you, and run some tests. Tomorrow, if possible. May I make arrangements to do that at a local clinic?"

Gil pondered that. "Let's see, the Cavalcade of Magic starts on Saturday and I don't want to miss any of that, and there will be some get-togethers tomorrow evening, but I guess tomorrow during the day would be all right." He met Jack's eyes and nodded, decision made. "I will place myself in your hands for a bit, Dr. Madison, but as I said, I think you are in for a disappointment. As Mom used to say, 'What will be, will be.' You may be able to help the pain, which I will really appreciate, but I expect that will only be temporary."

Jack turned to Arnie Rosen. "Can you spare someone to take him over to the Mirage?"

Rosen looked as if he'd resist, but in the end, he threw Spader a look and nodded. He assigned a couple of security guards to return Gil to his hotel, while Jack arranged to have a prescription filled and sent to the Mirage. When Gilbert was gone, Jack dropped any semblance of a doctor's bedside manner and focused on Rosen.

"Arnie, you complete asshole. You came real close to blowing this whole situation sky high. You don't know about Gil what Joan and I do. Trust me, if you'd pushed him too far, there could have been some real fireworks."

Rosen had the good graces to look contrite, but Spader was still pondering Gil's display of power. "I don't believe this," he said. "That woman must've been a plant."

"How?" asked Rosen. "You think he had three hundred plants out there waiting for me to pick one? But say she's a plant: how does that make her able to control the damned machine?"

"Some sort of electronic gadgetry, maybe? Did you search him—?"

"Of course we searched him," Arnie snarled. "And I don't know of a gadget made that can do *that.*" He stabbed a finger at the TV monitors.

Spader shook his head. "No. There's got to be an explanation for these things—the woman in the casino, the boy in the burn ward, all of it. There is a nonmagical, nonmiraculous explanation for Gil Gilbertson, and I'm going to find it."

"Do you think there is a nonmagical explanation?" Joan asked Jack as they made their way back down to the lobby of the Bellagio sometime later.

"Well, I suppose that depends on what you mean by magic. Maybe Gil just understands physics on an instinctive level that most of us don't."

Joan nodded. "Arthur C. Clarke on magic and technology. Yeah, but really, do you think it's all a trick?"

"No, I do not. On no level do I think this is a trick. Mitchell certainly wasn't a trick. And by the way, I thought we agreed not to mention him to Spader."

Joan gave him a startled look. "Jack, I didn't. I assumed Rosen passed the information along."

"Where would he have gotten it?"

"You didn't tell him?"

"No, and I'm reasonably sure that Cardinal O'Connor would not have brought it up. Which leaves—"

Joan's eyes narrowed. "Bishop Powell. I'm looking forward more and more to having a chat with him."

Jack felt his cell phone buzz in his breast pocket and pulled it out. It was Hillary, his secretary.

"Hi, Hill."

"Hello, Dr. Madison. I've got a few messages for you."

"Fine. I assume they must be important."

"I'm sorry, Doctor. I can't hear you on your cell. Could you call me at the clinic from a landline?" She hung up.

Jack stared at his cell phone as if it had done something rude. "That's strange."

"What's wrong?" Joan asked.

"She said she couldn't hear me. I could hear her fine, notwithstanding all the buzzing and dinging from the casino. She told me to call the clinic from a landline, but the clinic should be closed now."

"The cardinal?" Joan asked.

"He'd use one of the burners, wouldn't he?"

"Would he, if he thought you might be in public when he called?"

Jack turned on his heel and headed for the concierge. Joan followed. After asking about any guest courtesy phones or pay phones in the hotel, he headed down a hallway behind the registration desk. Each one was in a fancy hardwood kiosk that reminded Jack of the confessional he'd been required to use as a boy.

He chose one and had Joan linger watchfully at his back.

"I'm sorry about that, Dr. Madison," Hillary said when he reached her at the clinic. "I received a call from the cardinal fifteen minutes ago, and he wants you to call him from your secure phone. I hate to bother you, but he was adamant that you speak with him ASAP. Doctor, does this have anything to do with that Mr. Gilbertson?"

Jack felt the hair rise up on the back of his neck. "Hillary, how do you know about Gilbertson?"

After a moment of silence, Hillary said, "Doctor, he was in your office last Friday morning."

"He was what?"

"Don't you remember? The young gentleman that came to see you last Friday? He didn't have an appointment, but I managed to fit him in before you took lunch."

He had no memory of Gilbert visiting his office.

My God. Last Friday.

He fought down an icy panic, deciding there was no sense in upsetting Hillary by saying he didn't remember Gil's visit.

"Oh yeah, Gilbertson. Right. How'd you manage to work him in?"

"Oh, he said he only needed about fifteen minutes and that you were a friend of his family. That was true, wasn't it?"

"Yes. It was. I am a friend. Hillary, why did you think he might be involved in . . . what the cardinal wants to talk to me about?"

"Mr. Gilbertson mentioned the cardinal, actually. He said he was a mutual friend, something like that. Just chitchat, you know."

"I see. Well thanks, Hill. I'll, uh, I'll tell you all about it when I get home." He hung up and turned to look up at Joan. "We need to get someplace private. I'm not sure of my room here. Or our car."

Joan nodded toward the front of the hotel. "Take a walk around the fountain?"

The water falling into the Bellagio's big reflecting pool was loud enough to foil potential eavesdroppers but not loud enough to overwhelm conversation. Jack got out his burner phone and dialed Tom's.

The cardinal picked up on the first ring. "Jack," he said, "thanks for getting back to me. I just learned a few things that I think you need to know. I don't want to sound too alarming, and it could be nothing, but they may have some bearing on your investigation. I'm scheduled to be in San Francisco this weekend for a church function. Is there any chance you could meet me there? I could come to the airport."

Jack did a quick mental rundown of his increasingly tight schedule. "I'm examining Gilbert in the morning and meeting with Powell in the afternoon, but I could probably catch an early evening flight. Yeah. Sure. Are you sure we can't do this over the phone?"

"I'm reluctant to do that. I'm pretty sure Lyons is aware that we're taking steps to keep secrets from him, which means that—if he is part of SPCD—he may try harder to surveil us."

"Can't you just fire him or reassign him or something?"

"I could. But why would I? Right now, he's where I can at least keep track of him during his working hours. May I remind you of that old aphorism: Keep your friends close—"

Jack nodded. "And your enemies closer. I hear you."

"Good. I will be at the United Airlines Polaris Club at SFO—seven p.m. on Saturday evening. Let's meet there. And Jack, you can mention this to Detective Firestone, but please ask her not to say anything about it to Captain Spader or to anyone else. *Especially* Spader."

That gave Jack a chill. "Spader knew about Mitchell, Tom."

There was a moment of silence, then Tom said, "I regret to say that does not surprise me."

"You clearly were not the one who told him."

"No, I wasn't."

"Powell?"

Tom sighed. "I fear that may be the case. Jack, you and Ms. Firestone should toss your burner phones and get new ones. This could be a tempest in a teapot, but we need to talk face-to-face. When you meet with Powell, be very circumspect in what you tell him. I'll see you on Saturday evening in San Francisco." He hung up.

Jack pocketed the phone and stared at the water playing in the reflecting pool while Joan leaned on the marble balustrade watching his face. At length he said, "Tom wants to meet with me face-to-face on Saturday night. He can't say why."

She nodded, her lips pressed tightly together. For the first time since Jack had known her, she looked deeply concerned. "What about Spader?"

"I hate to say it, but my old buddy, the cardinal, doesn't trust your boss."

She straightened. "Jack, I don't like this. I was watching Captain Spader during our meeting just now. I've known the man a long time, and it was clear to me that he doesn't like you or Gilbert."

Jack shook his head. "Why? Why would he not like me? I just met the man."

"He's a devout Catholic for one thing, and a great admirer of Bishop Powell, for another. I think you have got some real enemies in the Church, Jack, and I'm beginning to wonder if Captain Spader isn't one of them."

He nodded, only half hearing what she was saying. His mind had not yet let go of what Hillary had told him. He felt Joan's hand on his arm.

"Jack, what's wrong? You're white as a sheet."

"When I spoke to Hillary just now, she told me that Gilbert was in my office last Friday morning, before Tom even involved me with this. And . . . damn it, Joan, I can't remember anything about it." He met her eyes. "Nothing. Not even that he was in my office, much less what we might have discussed."

She drew in a long breath. "Oh, honey, I know that feeling all too well."

Chapter 18

So that they'd have a place to speak freely, Joan rented a car. Jack checked out of his room at the Bellagio and stowed his belongings in the rental with plans to move them to her house. Arriving at the Mirage early, Joan stopped in at the hotel's security office, first asking Jack for his personal cell phone.

"Why?"

"Security reasons." She held out her hand, snapping her fingers when he hesitated.

He gave her the phone. She carried it into the security office where she sat down across the desk from a handsome black man whose great height Jack could easily guess from the way he dwarfed his desk and chair. He watched as Joan handed over his phone and hers, as well as her keys. She spoke with the man for a few moments, then shook hands with him before returning to join Jack in the lobby.

"What was that about?" he asked.

"That's Roscoe Smith, an old friend. He's ex-LVMP and someone I can trust to keep a secret for me. He's the best in town when it comes to checking for surveillance. I've asked him to check out your room at the Bellagio, my car and house, and both our mobile phones. My guess is he won't find anything, but after the cardinal's call, I think it's wise to check. Frankly, the big casinos are so paranoid about security that it would take a real pro to bug a room in one of them, and my place has a top-notch security system—one Roscoe installed with his own two hands—but better safe than sorry. We'll rendezvous after dinner."

They met with Gilbertson twenty minutes later and found a quiet corner in one of the casino's restaurants. He looked much better, Jack thought. His color was good, his eyes clearer, his voice subdued but steady.

"Thanks for the pills, Doctor; I took one an hour ago and it really helps."

"Glad to hear it," Jack told him. "After I check you out tomorrow, we'll see if this is the best medication for you, but for now, you can take one every four hours if you need it."

"Thanks for being patient with me. When I do something like that little slot machine demonstration for Mr. Rosen and Captain Spader, it really wears me out. I'll probably eat a lot tonight." He smiled shyly, then added, "I ate two ribeye steaks and slept for eighteen hours straight after my gig at The House of Magic."

Jack made a mental note of that. Clearly, whatever phenomenon was in action with Gil, it drew power, for lack of a better word, from his physical resources and depleted them. Curious.

They ordered dinner and made small talk—mostly about magic—until the food had been delivered to their table, then Jack gave Joan a look he hoped she'd interpret as "ball's in your court." Jack was dying to ask Gil why he'd been in his clinic the Friday before they'd embarked on this wild ride, and why he had no memory of the visit, but he didn't want to do that if it would derail the discussion of Gilbert's terms.

Whether she caught the look or not, Joan engaged the young magician. She was solicitous without fawning over him, and her gentle touch seemed to draw him into her confidence. He tucked into his dinner and started talking between bites.

"I really just wanted to get their attention. I needed to do it so that they would take my request seriously. I don't want to bankrupt them, but they are the only people who can get me what I really want."

"And what's that, Gilbert?"

He put down his knife and fork and folded his hands in his lap. "I know this is going to sound trivial to you, but I want to perform at the closing show of the Cavalcade of Magic with all of the big stars present: Penn and Teller, Lance Burton, David Copperfield, David Blaine, Criss Angel, the whole lot. I'll bet anything that most of them have already heard about my Hindu rope trick in Chicago. All of them are scheduled, and I want them to see what I can do. I'm going to need at least an hour, and that's a lot of time, but I'm certain that Mr. Rosen can arrange it . . . if you can persuade him to."

Jack and Joan exchanged glances. Whatever Jack might've expected Gil to demand, it certainly wasn't this. And yet, he had to admit, given what he knew about Gilbert Gilbertson, it made perfect sense.

"I'd say you went a long way toward persuading him today," Jack told him.

"Yes, but I'm sure he thinks it's something monetary. That I want money to go to a particular charity . . ."

"Abuse survivors," said Joan, watching Gil's face.

Gil's eyes darted toward her, then dropped. He nodded.

"Are you a survivor, Gil?" Joan asked gently.

Jack was thunderstruck. It had never occurred to him that Gil's interest in that particular cause was personal. Something niggled at the back of his mind, but Gil's reaction to the question distracted him.

The guy's face went red then white, and he picked up his silverware and began carving his steak with quick, almost frantic strokes.

"I—I really want all of the magic stars to be there to see me; that's very, very important. Be sure Rosen knows that. Too bad the Amazing Randi won't be in town; I'd love to call his bluff. I thought I'd stay away from mind reading and ESP, though—do just plain old-fashioned magic—but now I'm having second thoughts. What do you think?"

Gilbert was rambling, which led Jack to believe that Joan had hit the nail squarely on the head. He decided to play bad cop—or at least pessimist cop. "Your request is hardly trivial—for you or for the Casino Association. I'm sure that the Cavalcade organizers have the closing show programmed down to the last minute and would undoubtedly resist a change that would put them off by an entire hour. Bear in mind that even Mr. Rosen might not be able to convince them to slip you in."

Gil licked his lips. "I'm sure you're wrong, Doctor. I'm sure he's the one person that *can* convince them. That's why I've been working on getting Mr. Rosen's attention. If he wants to do this badly enough for me, he'll find a way. That's the way things work here in Vegas. And I think he understands that I'm not going away unless he gets this done." He was starting to get agitated and his voice was rising, both in tone and in volume.

Joan reached over and put her hand over Gil's. "Gilbert, I guarantee you that you have Rosen's attention. Right along with the attention of all the people who run Las Vegas and have an interest in preserving their collective wealth. Rosen is spooked, and I'd be willing to bet that he would be very persuasive to the Cavalcade organizers."

Gil's gaze fell on their joined hands and he seemed to relax. He smiled wanly. "I saw what you did there, Detective. The pun, I mean—'I'd be willing to bet'?"

She smiled in return. "I thought you'd catch it. You're a smart guy."

"And clever," added Jack. "I'm curious, Gilbert, why was your face blank on the photos and videos? Did you do that on purpose?"

He gave Jack the closest thing to a grin Jack could imagine his face making. "Just one more way to—what did you say, Detective—spook everyone. I mean, that probably kept Chief Spader up at night, right?"

"Me too," Jack admitted. "I'd love to know how you did it."

"Maybe I'll share that someday. Just not now."

"Is there any particular reason that you need a whole hour?" Jack asked. "Why not take less time to do one impressive trick that would get you more gigs and gradually build up your reputation?"

Gil shook his head. "It's not that simple. First of all, ever since I was a little boy, I've dreamed of doing a real, world-class evening of magic. It's the one thing I want to do before I die."

"Gil, you're barely thirty," Jack observed. "You've got many years in which to hone your craft, perform, get a reputation—"

Now, Gilbert fixed Jack with a gaze so solemn it made the rest of what he'd been going to say curdle in his throat.

"No, Doctor. I think I have little time left. Very little. If I don't do this now, I will never do it. I have spent my whole life, up until the last three months, having people make fun of me when I do anything beyond the most bonehead easy kids' tricks. What I'm going to do at the Cavalcade aren't tricks. I'm going to do *real* magic. I am going to do this one great show, and I want the best magicians in the world to be there to see me do it. I want them to remember it for the rest of their lives. Twenty years from now, I want people to still be talking and writing about Gilbert the Great."

Talk about spooked . . . The nape of Jack's neck crawled, and he barely kept himself from reaching up to rub it. Gil's talk of impending doom reminded him viscerally of the letter the man's mother had written when she'd bailed on Sam Bernstein and hightailed it to Hunterton. But she'd had almost a decade. Deep down in the depths of his mind—or soul, he supposed Tom would say—Jack decided he didn't want Gil to be right. If there was a way to save the younger man, he was determined to find it.

"That's the history of magic," Gil was saying, his eyes unfocused, his voice taking on an almost musical rhythm and tone. "The great act, the special evening, that time when everything is just perfect. That's what they are going to see." He seemed to come back to the here and now, his eyes flitting to Joan, and he dropped yet another bombshell. "One more thing. And this is absolutely necessary: no videos, no TV, no cameras. Tell Rosen I'll know if they're there, and if they are, I walk. And from that moment on, there will be no losers in Las Vegas."

Joan retrieved their phones from Roscoe Smith and got a full rundown on what he'd found. Joan's house was clean, but her car had been compromised with a tracking device. Her phone was clean; Jack's wasn't.

Roscoe explained how it had been tapped, then added, "Did a reverse trace on the tap. Looks like it originated somewhere in Southern California. You want me to sanitize the phone?"

Joan considered that. "No, leave it. It might be something we can use to our advantage."

She called Rosen from their rental car and gave him the full story on Gilbertson. As Jack had warned, he first said it was impossible. Then he went ballistic, his voice rising to the point that Joan knew Jack could hear every expletive. She managed to calm him down and get him to agree to sleep on it.

"But remember, Arnie, the longer you wait to pull the trigger, the harder it's going to be. I really think even waiting until morning could be catastrophic. You know what's at stake. If there are suddenly no losers in Las Vegas, pretty soon—"

"—there'll be no Las Vegas. Damn right I know what's at stake! But it's my damned decision to make."

"Yes, Arnie. Yes, it *is* your decision. And in the final analysis, you'll be accountable for it. Likewise, you'll be accountable if something should mysteriously happen to Gil. I sure don't envy your position."

There was a hugely pregnant pause on Rosen's end of the line. Then he said, "Damn you, Detective."

"Damn *me?* Why damn me?"

"Because you're right. And I hate that you're right. I'll make the calls now. Come see me in the morning, you and your fancy boyfriend."

"Who said he was my boyfriend?" she asked, half amused, half embarrassed.

"Do I look like I was born yesterday?" Rosen asked sarcastically, and rang off.

"Is he doing it?" Jack asked when she'd popped her phone back into her purse.

"He's doing it. And speaking of doing stuff. How'd you like to come take a dip in my hot tub? I happen to know you brought a bathing suit with you."

Jack gave her an aggrieved look. "You're going to make me wear a bathing suit?"

Half an hour later, they were sitting on Joan's back patio in her hot tub, sans bathing suits. It overlooked a long, narrow lap pool and the rolling green of a section of golf course. Far and away loomed the shadowy bulk of the Nopah Mountains, like great sleeping dragons guarding Las Vegas's glittering treasures. Joan had put music on, and they were being serenaded by a variety of performers from her eclectic library: Frank Sinatra, Cole Porter, Irving Berlin, Gershwin, Beach Boys, Billie Holiday, Glenn Miller, Santana, Copland.

"What got you interested in music? Not your bass player."

"Mom. I cut my teeth on the music she listened to and sang along with. Did impromptu concerts on our coffee table."

"So, what's your master's thesis?"

"I'll give you the CliffsNotes version. I got the germ of an idea when I was listening to Cole Porter's 'Anything Goes.' Specifically, the lyrics. It suddenly dawned on me that one of the most unique things about twentieth-century American music is that, in many ways, it tells the story of American society and culture. So that's what I wrote about. The music we're listening to right now is in a collection I cited in my thesis."

Jack nodded. "I caught Chuck Berry, Leonard Bernstein, and Louis Armstrong."

"Mm-hmm. And Rodgers and Hart, Bing Crosby, Sinatra, Fats Waller, Muddy Waters, Hoagy Carmichael . . ."

"So, who makes the list and who doesn't? How'd you choose?"

"I asked who really contributed to the story of the American twentieth century. My classmates argue about it all the time, my professor wants me to write a book about it, which, as soon as I retire from this detecting business, I'm going to have a shot at. My black friends think I'm insane and a traitor for naming all these white folks who, in many ways, copied styles that began in slave culture. Cultural misappropriation, they call it. I call it just creative humans using the tools, resources, and inspiration available. Art shouldn't have a racial bias."

"You constantly amaze me, for so many reasons." Jack leaned over and kissed the tip of her nose. "Not the least of which that you would put Hoagy Carmichael on that list."

She gave him a severe look. "Jack Madison, don't you dare pick a fight you can't finish. 'Stardust' defined a whole generation of Americans during the Great Depression. I write of it as a tonic for troubled times."

Jack gazed out over the golf course toward the mountains. "We could sure use a tonic right about now. This case is . . . a little depressing, if I'm honest about it. Gil's mom died of whatever it was that gave her premonitions. Now, Gil thinks he's dying too. And as much as I hate to admit it, he may be right."

"I think I may have an antidote for that depression, Doctor." Joan stood up, water cascading from her naked body, and was completely gratified by Jack's response to her antidote.

Chapter 19

The UNLV Neurological Institute was an impressive new facility within the University of Nevada Medical Center, dedicated to the diagnosis and treatment of brain and spinal diseases. Jack arrived a bit early on Saturday morning and was met by Dr. William Pittman, chairman of neurology. Jack knew Bill Pittman both by reputation and acquaintanceship. They had sat in on each other's seminars at several neurological and general medical conferences.

Bill was a decade older than Jack—a big, gregarious Englishman who reminded Jack of Alfred Hitchcock. He greeted his American colleague expansively, shaking his hand with a firm, two-handed grip.

"Hallo, Jack! Welcome to UNNI. I don't know exactly why you're here—and I shall honor your request not to ask—but I wanted you to know that we are at your disposal. I and my entire team are available all day for anything you need."

"Thanks. It's most gracious of you to make yourself available, and on a Saturday morning, too. And, no, I cannot go into some of the details about this patient, but as far as his neurological workup is concerned, I'd love to run things by you for a second opinion as I progress. Also, legally, since I'm not licensed to practice medicine here in Nevada, I am going to request that you order any necessary tests after I go through my differential diagnosis with you. If you think it necessary, I will ask you to corroborate my physical findings."

"Jack, it would be presumptive of me to cross-check your physical findings—your reputation precedes you, and there are few neurologists in this country who would not trust your medical opinions. But you are most kind to make the offer. I'll be here in my office whenever you need me. Right now, let's go down to the clinic, and I'll introduce you to Betsy Novak, my nurse clinician. She knows the lay of the land and will be available to you all day."

By the time Gilbert arrived an hour later, Jack felt comfortable with the diagnostic tools and the layout of the clinic. The first step of the process was an interview with Gilbert to discuss his symptoms—headaches, mild visual disturbances in his right eye, and a ringing in his right ear that pulsated with his heartbeat. All of his symptoms were exacerbated by anxiety or anger, and his headaches worsened when he drank even a little alcohol. When the headaches had first begun, four years earlier he said, coffee helped them, but it no longer had any effect. He had no signs of any motor or sensory loss anywhere in his body.

Up to that point, the symptoms pointed to migraine, which accounted for the fact that his earlier consultations with physicians had resulted in a medicine cabinet full of sumatriptan derivatives. He said he'd even tried shots with less and less relief.

Then other symptoms had kicked in, symptoms that no migraine sufferer Jack had ever examined had reported: premonitions, the ravenous hunger that followed the sort of mental effort he put into the rope trick or the Miser's Dream . . . or healing the young burn victim.

"Describe that effort for me, if you can, Gil," Jack requested. "What's going on in your head while you're doing these things? What are your feelings—your thought processes?"

"Clarity," Gil said without hesitation. "It's as if everything becomes crystal clear. I can see how it's done—whatever it is. I can see the—the connections between all the elements of the situation, whether it's how a magic trick really works or how cells regenerate, heal, grow. I'm sorry I can't describe it any better than that. It's just . . . I see how all things connect." He wove his fingers together as he said the words, the way a child might make prayer hands.

"Then, afterward, you're exhausted and famished," Jack observed.

Gil nodded. "The more effort I expend, the more food and sleep I need."

Jack pondered all of this as he conducted a physical examination of his unusual patient. He began by listening to Gilbert's head with a stethoscope, and what he heard was puzzling. It was what neurologists call a bruit—a to-and-fro, machinery-like sound that was audible anywhere on the right side of Gil's skull. It was especially loud over his right ear. Jack examined Gil's eyes with a scope and saw some abnormal pulsations in his right retina. With a diagnosis taking shape, he checked Gilbert's right jugular vein; it, too, showed similar pulsations. He sat back on his stool, the stethoscope unheeded in his hands, his eyes focused on nothing.

"What is it, Doctor?" Gil asked. "I can tell you've found something."

Jack brought his eyes into focus on his patient. "I *suspect* I've found something. It's called an arteriovenous malformation. It's a condition in which a group of arteries in the brain feed directly into the veins draining blood out of the brain without going through the usual capillaries that supply cerebral tissue. This creates a lesion in the brain tissue. It usually has some form of neural tissue in it—most often, nonfunctioning tissue. AVMs are almost always a congenital defect but often don't show symptoms until the third or fourth decade of life."

"I'm in my third decade," Gil observed mildly.

Jack nodded. He thought back to Sam's note about Ruth and his suspicion that she might be suffering from the same condition. He'd even heard a faint murmur on the same side of her brain, although they'd never worked that out. Ruth may have died when the AVM began to leak blood. If detected soon enough, a variety of surgical procedures could correct the malformation. Ruth hadn't stuck around to find out if her life could have been saved.

Would her son?

"Gil," Jack said, "have you experienced any signs of weakness on your left side or any loss of sensation?"

"You've been listening to my right side."

"Yes. The right side of the brain controls the left side of the body, to put it simply."

Gil shook his head. "No. I've never had anything like that."

"Seizures? Blackouts?"

"No, Doctor. Neither."

As much as Jack wanted to rush Gilbert into an MRI machine, he made himself complete the physical exam. It was normal. No cardiac or pulmonary problems except for a rapid pulse rate, no signs of thyroid or adrenal disease, a normal-sized liver, no edema, normal reflexes, normal blood pressure, and no problems with his bones or joints. He was moderately obese and in poor physical condition—Jack couldn't shake the image of him shimmying up a rope as if it were nothing.

Taking a different tack, he asked about Ruth. "What do you know about your mother's condition? Specifically, the stigmata. You were aware of that, right?"

Gil seemed to withdraw slightly, but after a moment of silence, he answered, his voice subdued. "I didn't understand about the stigmata until the last few weeks of her life when she told me about that. She . . . she seemed to be trying to warn me about what might happen to me when I grew up. I just figured it wouldn't happen to me because I had nothing to do with the Church or religion in general. Mom . . . Mom loved the Church. She didn't love what was happening to her—the premonitions, the miracles. To be honest, Doctor, I think it frightened her."

"But you've done your own miracles, haven't you, Gilbert?"

"They're not miracles. I don't know what they are, but they're not miracles." His voice rose, and he rubbed his hands on his khaki pants. "It's just clarity, Dr. Madison. Clarity and mind over matter."

"Mind over matter. Is that how you kept your face from showing up on the photos and the surveillance videos?"

"Yeah, sort of. See, Doctor, I can sometimes control some things—electrical currents and machines. Slots and the keno game, digital cameras. People have electrical fields, too, right?"

"Yes. Our brains produce electromagnetic energy."

"I guess that's why I can control some things with people."

That was chill-worthy. "Like the man in the Burger King," Jack guessed. "The one who was abusing the little girl."

Gilbert nodded emphatically. "Yes. Like that. I hope to God that man learned his lesson. He was so mean to that little girl." He paused for a moment and studied Jack. "I can get a good feeling—sometimes—about certain things people are thinking, which is why I want to try out some mind reading on Monday. God, I sure hope that Penn Jillette is going to be there. Can you imagine a better guy to use to prove that I can read his mind?"

Suddenly Gilbert was all fanboy—fixated on the Monday evening show. It was if all of the other things were on a distant back burner, and he was just going through the motions here. He was giving honest answers, but he was divorced from what was really on his mind. It was like talking with a child.

"What about the boy with the bad burns, Gilbert? What about Mitchell? And what about your magic? How do you do those things?"

Gil's eyes seemed to snap into focus on Jack's face. "I don't know, Doctor. Maybe you'll be able to tell me. What's next?"

"Next," Jack said, "I need do to a blood workup and a high-contrast MRI. Have you ever had an MRI, Gilbert?"

He shook his head. "Do they hurt?"

"No. Some people find them energizing. They're, um, a bit noisy. I've had a patient describe them as like being in a cave full of bongo-playing monkeys."

"I'm good with that. I do want to be at a card manipulation session at the Cavalcade at two this afternoon. Is that possible?"

"Sure thing. I'll have Betsy take some blood samples, and I'll go order up the MRI. Why don't you go have a cup of coffee in the waiting area? It's pretty good coffee, all things considered. And I think there are still some donuts left."

Gilbert went out into the waiting room while Jack set up the next round of tests. He went into one of the staff break rooms after that and found that the coffee there was fresh and hot. He poured a cup and sat down to organize his thoughts and pore over the notes in his iPad. Ten minutes after he'd sat down, his cell phone rang. It was the Admiral.

"Hoped I'd be able to catch you, Doc. I arrived here in Sin City night before last and, as usual, am singing for my supper. Working—and talking—my tired old ass off. I have asked around a bit about that Gilbertson fellow. I did find out that he was here for a convention a few months back, and several of the guys tell me that he suddenly went from off-the-shelf kiddie parlor tricks to doing stuff that knocked their socks off. Literally overnight. One guy swears he did a Zombie Ball without the gimmick. Interesting thing is, he said some other guys have been asking around about Gil, too."

"Vegas police?"

"Notably. But Zombie Ball man told me that the two guys he talked to sure weren't cops."

Jack didn't want to talk any more about it on his compromised cell phone. The Admiral told him he was free for dinner on Sunday evening, so Jack asked him to join him and Joan for a further discussion. Jack didn't mention his side trip to San Francisco. If anyone was monitoring the call, he would do exactly what they expected him to do—make arrangements to talk to an informant. He hung up, wondering who had been asking questions about Gil, and why.

The question that loomed largest in Dr. Jack Madison's mind was, what had happened to Gilbert Gilbertson roughly three months ago that had turned him, overnight, from a lame clown into a world-class magical adept? Had something about Las Vegas triggered the change?

He went back over some of the other parts of Gil's story, trying to piece together a pattern. His mother had taken him from Chicago suddenly twenty-five years ago, when she was at the beginning of the end of her strange affliction. Now, Gil, emerging from hiding, was running to do the opposite—to go public in a very big way. What was the common factor? *Was* there a common factor?

Again, Jack's mind reached for something that promised to tie the loose ends together: Chicago, Las Vegas, miracles that weren't, sudden disappearances . . . mimic octopi. He felt as if he had his hands almost on the thing when Betsy came by and said that Gilbert was in the MRI machine; the tech and Dr. Fred Stoney, the neuroradiologist, were beginning the scans. It wasn't exactly an invitation to attend (attending physicians did not often sit in on brain scans), but in this case, he wanted to be there. He promised to be a good boy and sit quietly in the back of the room.

He entered the control room in time to hear the technician running the scan grunt in surprise. "Holy shit. That's . . . amazing."

Jack looked up at the displays along the top of the imaging controls where cross sections of Gilbert's brain were augmented with every pass the MRI machine made. There it was, in all its glory, being revealed slice by slice. The entire right half of Gilbert's brain was occupied by a giant arteriovenous malformation. It was lit up like a spaghetti tangle of neon by the high-contrast agent they'd injected him with. Jack Madison had never seen anything like it in all his years of practice.

He turned to Betsy Novak, who had lingered with him in the imaging suite. "Betsy, will you get Dr. Pittman down here stat?"

She nodded and went to do as he'd asked.

Fred Stoney turned to look at him. "Dr. Madison, this man essentially has only half a brain! How is it even possible for him to function?"

"Half a *normal* brain," Jack said. "We have no idea what's going on, if anything, in the side with the AVM. The mass is obscuring anything it's covering. Can you do functional imaging here?"

"Sure, but not until Monday. Can you get him in here then? I would like you and Bill to do the testing of his motor and sensory skills while we image him. And by the way, I get first dibs on this paper since I did the MRI."

"Paper? What paper?" Bill Pittman stood in the open doorway of the imaging suite. "Christ, Fred. We don't even know what we're dealing with here." His eyes traveled to the displays. "How is this possible? I looked at your exam report, Jack. It shows your patient to have moderate to serious migraine symptoms." He pointed at the screen on which the AVM was growing in size with every sweep of the scanner. "He shouldn't be capable of describing his symptoms to you. He shouldn't even be walking and talking. Hell, Jack. This man should be a vegetable."

That assessment fell into a silence so profound that when the technician at the controls of the MRI machine spoke, the sound of his voice made Jack jump.

"What the hell? What's that?"

The doctors all glanced up at the displays, but the tech was pointing at the glass panel through which they could see the large central room of the imaging suite where Gil Gilbertson lay within the MRI machine's tubular maw.

Flung against the pale gray wall behind the machine was a shadow. It was rounded, smooth, as if someone had hung a sheet or maybe a lab coat on a convenient knob.

"Obviously, it's the shadow of a piece of equipment—" The words died in Dr. Stoney's throat as the shadow moved. Stoney leapt to his feet. "There's someone in there with him! Stop the machine, Terry. Good God, who'd do that? Don't they realize the danger—?"

The tech paused the scan, and Drs. Stoney and Pittman entered the lab while Jack watched from the control room. He fought the urge to see the shadow as the silhouette of someone wearing a cowl or burnoose—the sort of thing generations of artists had depicted the Virgin Mary in.

The two doctors advanced along the side of the machine toward the interloper. Any second, Jack expected they would flush out a maintenance person who hadn't realized the room was in use on a Saturday. But just before they cleared the machine, the shadow moved again. Jack had the impression of a large, hooked beak and a flap of great wings before the shadow swept upward and vanished.

"Damn," said the technician. "I think we're haunted."

Gilbert, of course, had seen nothing from the confines of the MRI machine. He had been quite happy within it and came out looking refreshed and relaxed, although puzzled by the fact that the three medics questioning him seemed so concerned.

Jack, for his part, had no intention of mentioning giant eagles and how they related to miracle burn cures or impossible stage acts . . . or possibly unsolved murders. But it did occur to him that an eagle the size of the one whose shadow had appeared on the wall of Dr. Stoney's imaging suite must have talons that strongly resembled meat hooks.

Almost as soon as he had the thought, he dismissed it as the fantastical gabbling of a tired mind. He really needed to get more sleep. Joan Firestone was good for the soul, but she was hell on his efforts to get adequate rest.

"Gil Gilbertson is a sick man." Bishop Powell made the statement with a vehemence that contradicted the sorrowful cast of his face, now thrown into stark relief by the sun streaming through the window of his rectory office.

Jack thought for a moment he was referring to the younger man's migraines and almost let his own facial expression give away his surprise, but the bishop went on without pause.

"You'd have to be sick to steal money from the needy in one city to give it to a group that almost certainly includes opportunistic scammers."

"Scammers?" repeated Joan. "Surely you don't think—"

The bishop raised a hand. "I'm not saying they're *all* on the take. But it's become almost fashionable to deplore the Church, and leaders like Cardinal Archbishop O'Connor don't help when they unquestioningly and uncritically support the contentions of these people."

"I really don't think that's what the cardinal is doing, Excellency," Jack argued mildly. "I've known him to be a pragmatic and rational man whose interest is in justice being done. It's not as if you can build a court case on contention alone. Nor is it easy for the victims of molestation to come forward."

"I'd agree with you," Powell said, "about the few who have a legitimate grievance. But there are simply too many of them with claims going back decades to convince me that even a slender majority of them are legitimate. Certainly, someone who had really been . . . compromised might have been traumatized in the process. But, in cases where there has been no trauma, the argument that coming forward is emotionally scarring doesn't wash, does it?"

Joan sent Jack a fleeting look that eloquently said, *Do you believe this guy?* Aloud, she said, "Bishop, may I assume that you've chatted further with Arnie Rosen about the impact Gil's activities have had on your charities?"

Powell nodded. "Yesterday, as a matter of fact. He said there might be an end in sight. That, for one thing, Gilbertson believes he might not be long for this world. I wasn't sure whether he was threatening suicide or if he had some medical condition that gave him that idea."

Jack didn't miss the openly curious look in the bishop's eyes. He ignored it. "Did Rosen happen to mention Gilbert's request?"

"Request! Demand, you mean. An entire hour at the Cavalcade of Magic . . ." He shook his head. "Absurd."

"Pardon me, Your Excellency," Joan said, "given the high stakes for your Church and its charities, I'd think you'd encourage Mr. Rosen to honor Mr. Gilbertson's request."

The bishop's lips compressed. "I *did* encourage him, in fact. But if Gilbertson is in ill health . . ." Again, the meaningful look at Jack.

"Your Excellency, you know I can't comment on that," Jack told him. "I'd be violating patient-doctor privilege."

The bishop's pale eyes glinted. "Meaning you're treating him? Officially?"

Joan cut in, relieving Jack of the necessity of being rude. "Actually, it's not Gilbert's future we came here to ask you about, sir. It's his past. During a recent meeting with Mr. Rosen, my chief, Devin Spader, asked us about a situation in Missouri involving Gil and a young man we know only as Mitchell. I'm not even sure that's his real name. You know who we're talking about, don't you?"

The bishop was clearly startled by the sudden shift in topic. He blinked rapidly and sat up straighter in his chair. "I'm not sure I know—"

"Please, sir," said Joan. "Your honesty would be appreciated."

Now the bishop's face went red. "Of—of course I will give you my honesty. Yes, I know about Mitchell. His . . . circumstances caused quite a stir among my colleagues."

"We were under the impression that the head of St. Mary's Hospital explicitly directed her staff and others not to discuss his case even among themselves."

"Well, yes. That's so, but she's the one who told me about the situation herself."

"And did you then share it with Captain Spader?"

The question fell into a leaden silence. Bishop Powell simply sat and stared at the detective as if she had spoken to him in a foreign tongue. A clock ticked somewhere in the room; cars rushed by in the street outside. No one spoke until the bishop cleared his throat, rearranged his robes, and said: "I believe I may have mentioned it to the captain. He was—er—intimately involved in the Gilbertson matter . . ."

"Which, at this end, has nothing to do with a burn victim in Missouri, I'd think," Joan observed.

"The young man's . . . attitudes and behaviors were a subject of great speculation at this end, as you put it. I felt sharing that situation with Captain Spader was appropriate under the circumstances."

"I see. Did you share it with anyone else?"

Blink. "I . . . I don't . . . I may have."

"In spite of Sister Claire's wishes to keep the story under wraps?"

"Sister Claire did not lay upon me a particular burden of secrecy. In fact, she . . . indicated that I was free to share the story with . . . select individuals."

"Like Captain Spader?"

"Yes."

"Others?"

"I told you, I may have shared the story with other individuals."

"Can you be more specific?"

"Other than Captain Spader, I shared the story only with leaders of the Church."

Jack was frustrated with the bishop's too-careful choice of words. "What leaders?" he asked.

"I'm afraid I can't be more specific."

"*Won't* be more specific, you mean," Jack said, exasperated. "Joan, we're wasting our time here."

She turned her head to fix him with a dark, unreadable gaze. "That's not your call, Dr. Madison." She turned back to Powell. "How long have you known Gil Gilbertson, Bishop?"

"What?"

"It's a simple question. How long have you known Gil Gilbertson?"

"Some years."

"You knew him as a child, didn't you? You knew his mother, Ruth, as well. They were members of your parish."

The bishop was rearranging his robes again. "Yes. I was the one that brought Ruth Gilbertson's condition to then Bishop O'Connor's attention."

"Did Gil seem to you like a normal little boy?"

"He . . . he seemed like a nice child. He was quiet. Well behaved."

"Obedient to authority? Accommodating?"

The bishop was startled into meeting Joan's eyes. Jack watched in fascination as the color leached out of the other man's face.

"I never heard his mother complain of his behavior," Powell said after a moment.

"Do you know why Ruth Gilbertson took her son and left Chicago so suddenly twenty-five years ago?" Joan asked.

"I would assume it had something to do with her condition," he said. "Wouldn't you?"

"She was in the beginning stages of being treated for her condition when she left, wasn't she, Jack?" Joan asked.

"Yes. Yes, she was. Her leaving was unexpected."

Joan stood suddenly. "I think we've taken enough of the bishop's time, Jack. We'll be in touch, Your Excellence. I'm sure we'll have more questions in a day or two." She gave the bishop her polite goodbyes and led Jack from the room.

"That man is far too careful with his words," Jack said when they'd returned to their car. "He never answered even one question in a straightforward way. He barely managed not to lie to us. You're thinking the same thing I am, aren't you? That Powell was the real reason Ruth left Chicago. That she left to save her son from the priest that was abusing him."

Joan's face wore a thunderstorm. "Yeah, and I'm also thinking that I'd like to go home and take a shower."

Chapter 20

Jack met a worried-looking Tom O'Connor at seven p.m. on Saturday in the United Polaris Club off the main concourse rotunda at SFO. The two men grabbed some coffee and found an out-of-the way corner where they could talk privately.

"Why are we meeting like this, Tom?" Jack asked. "What couldn't be said over the phone?"

Tom was visibly uneasy. "I'm sorry, Jack, but I'm afraid I've gotten you into a big mess, and I want you to know as many details as I can fill in. I think this situation is potentially dangerous. You have my word that if I had known, I would never have gotten you involved. Never."

Jack was taken aback. "Tom, I trust you like a brother. And I'm a big boy, used to taking care of myself. So, no guilt. No apologies. I've got my own suspicions about what's going on, but I admit I don't see the danger. What'm I missing?" A thought struck him. "Did it turn out that Coughlin was assassinated?"

"Not in any usual sense, but that's tangential to what I need to say. It's the SPCD I'm afraid of."

"The Let's Go Back to the Dark Ages Society? Really? You think they're dangerous? All they've done so far is follow us around while pretending not to. They're no Opus Dei."

"There's more to them than meets the eye, Jack. They have more in common with the Society of Saint Pius X than Opus Dei."

Jack nodded. "I'm familiar with the Pius X. They believe that all popes after Pius XII were heretics."

"Perhaps most especially the last two popes before Francis. They also want a return to the Latin mass, fasting, and abstinence—in short, the Roman Catholic Church our great-grandparents grew up in. No concessions, no salvation outside of Catholicism, etc. They were fairly dormant for a while, but Pope John Paul II moved them to optimism. He stacked Church leadership with increasing numbers of right-wing bishops and cardinals, and the Pius Society started gaining significant momentum. That paved the way for groups even more radical and more secretive."

"Like SPCD."

"Yes. But Pius X is the model—a cadre of self-proclaimed martyrs on a mission to do God's will as only they can interpret it. Roman Catholic mullahs promoting their own version of Sharia law."

"Miracles," Jack said. "I remember that some fringe groups tend to be really focused on miracles. Which is where I began to part company with the Church. As I recall from my Church history, John Paul was fascinated by the Miracle of Fatima."

Tom leaned forward in his chair, his hands wrapped around his coffee cup as if it were trying to escape. "This is where we get into it. When the Virgin allegedly appeared to those children in 1917, she made three revelations. The first two dealt with a vision of hell, a second punishing war, and a prophecy that seemed to involve the rise of an apostate Russia. That is, if Russian leaders failed to heed God's warnings and return to faith. The third revelation wasn't made public until 2000. In it is a description of a pope being assassinated by a group of soldiers."

Jack saw immediately where Tom was going with this. "John Paul II survived a shooting in 1981."

"Yes. Which, of course, looked like a fulfillment of the prophecy. You have to understand that in his early days, John Paul was despised by the ultraconservatives; he spoke of Christian unity, did nothing overt to thwart the effects of Vatican II, reached out to Jews and Muslims, and of course, involved himself deeply in the fall of the Soviet Union. His persona, his good looks, and his ability as a speaker endeared him to the public. He became a worldwide hero, which is something, I think, he purposefully cultivated. After the attempted assassination, he was twice the hero; but he'd changed. I think he became convinced that God had special plans for him. Remember that the day he was shot was an anniversary of the Fatima vision, which only reinforced his belief that his survival was a special miracle and a personal message from God. And, of course, he believed he was the person most responsible for the fall of godless communism."

"Miracle worker."

"Indeed, yes. John Paul was obsessed with miracles. His particular hero was a friar-mystic called Padre Pio that John Paul viewed as a great and living saint of the Church. Within days of Pio's death, John Paul put him on the fast track to sainthood. Guess what his particular manifestation was."

"Stigmata?"

Tom nodded. "John Paul created saints in unparalleled numbers, which he was able to do by lowering the bar for canonization. It went from two or more unequivocal miracles, well-documented by unimpeachable witnesses and directly attributable to the intercession of the candidate, to only one miracle for which documentation was a nicety. And, of course, this was accompanied by a rejection of any form of liberalism. The Church became a creature of form over function—ritual over substance. And, of course, because he stacked the College of Cardinals with equally conservative theologians, it looked as if this trend would continue."

"The Society of Pius X must've been dancing with delight."

"They were. Then the pedophilia scandal broke. John Paul II took the view that the clergymen involved were innocent. He placed the entire blame on an irresistible external force—Satan. This was *his* church, and he was favored by God, so something like this had to be the work of the Devil. That's how Cardinal Law, and all of the others involved, hung on for so long; that's why the North American Church is suffering a loss of active membership to this day—plus a dearth of new clergymen and women, and one billion dollars in legal settlements. And it's not over."

"You're going to tell me," said Jack, "that this made John Paul even more of a hero to the fringe groups."

"Oh my, yes. He was their savior; he'd take the Church back to the days before Vatican II. When he died and Benedict XVI was elected, the Society of Pius X and its various spin-offs and satellite groups were practically salivating. Here was a leader even more conscious of doctrinal correctness than his predecessor. They seemed to believe that the lawsuits, the fall in contributions, the increasing skepticism among the laity could be solved by an even more trenchant dogmatism. They looked to Benedict to crack down on the wayward American Church."

"And then came Francis." Jack made an explosive gesture. "Boom."

"Indeed. But consider the state of seminarians when Benedict abdicated. Most of them were to the right of Opus Dei and have an increasing interest in the holy miracles of days of yore . . . and Armageddon."

Jack laughed. "I was wondering when you were going to bring up Armageddon. Is that what we're talking about here—that these guys are hoping to push the world toward its early demise?"

"Don't laugh, Jack. This is scary stuff. Very scary. Some of these kids remind me of members of the Hitler Youth Camps. Our very own Father Lyons among them."

That got Jack's sober attention. "You said you suspected Lyons of being with the SPCD."

"I knew he had a stick up his—" He caught Jack's look. "I knew he was doctrinaire. But I didn't suspect him of more until now. Now, I'm certain he's Society. He bugged my cell phone, my office, my study, and the sacristy at the cathedral."

Jack was stunned. "Jesus, Tom. I mean—"

"I know what you mean. It's that last one that bothers me most—he bugged the *sanctuary*."

"You put him on report, though, right?"

"I would have, but he's gone AWOL."

"To go off and start Armageddon, you think? What's that got to do with me?"

"Miracles, Jack. Miracles and prophecies. And more to the point, it's got to do with you and Gilbert. Here's this young nebbish guy who suddenly begins to do miracles just like his mother. A mother who had visions of the Blessed Virgin and who manifested the stigmata, which neither you nor Dr. Bernstein were ever able to disprove."

"We barely had the chance. She pulled a disappearing act."

"Irrelevant. Gil Gilbertson is a miracle worker and the son of a miracle worker who manifested stigmata just like St. Pio."

"Canon fodder," Jack punned wryly.

Tom didn't so much as raise an eyebrow. "This is the opportunity of a lifetime for these guys, Jack. Ruth's miracles are better documented than any in living memory, but better yet, her son is still alive and performing miracles so publicly it's even got the Vegas Casino Association and law enforcement paying attention. Enter Jack Madison, apostate pain in the ass. Miracles are the air Lyons and his ilk breathe, and you, sir, are publicly working to deprive them of that air, working to turn gullible souls away from the true faith. You just had another *New York Times* best seller. I'm not sure that you understand how much that has infuriated them."

"Okay, so I'm a minion of Satan. What else is new?"

Tom exhaled loudly. "Jack, focus. *They think they're helping to bring about the end of the world.* What's the life of one pain-in-the-ass author compared to that? Or a detective, for that matter? If Gilbertson is an asset—"

"I'm just an ass—yeah, I get it." Tom's words had sent a cold shiver scurrying down Jack's spine. He was suddenly regretting not bringing Joan with him. "You really think they'd harm Joan?"

"Lyons is a zealot, a fanatic of the worst sort, and I'm scared of him, Jack. I suspect that Bishop Powell is involved in this as well. In fact, I think he's got to be."

"Involved? I think he's one of the key figures. Joan and I suspect he's the reason Ruth Gilbertson left Chicago in such a hurry. We think he may have molested Gil when he was a kid."

The look in Tom O'Connor's eyes was one of horror. He sat back in his chair and looked away over the concourse, which was visible through a set of floor-to-ceiling windows.

"That thought . . . had never occurred to me. Dear God . . ."

"He's up to his neck in this, Tom. And judging from our conversation with him yesterday, he's running scared. I'm not sure why he brought Cardinal Munoz into the picture, but I think it might be because he wanted to maintain distance between him and Gilbert. So we wouldn't connect him with what happened twenty-five years ago."

Tom considered that. "It may also be a means of obliquely striking at Munoz. He wasn't subtle in letting me know that he's madder than hell that a moderate Latino is the new cardinal of LA."

Jack frowned. "Why would that—?"

"Las Vegas has to work within the framework outlined by the cardinal of Los Angeles." He made a dismissive gesture. "Irrelevant at the moment. What's relevant is that I have put you into a bad situation with some very unpleasant people. People who, in my opinion, could be very dangerous. They believe they are on a mission from God."

As Jack scrambled to take in the vast landscape that had just opened up before him, he filled Tom in on the interview he and Joan had had with Bishop Powell, then said, "If Powell is SPCD—or at least serving as an intel relay for them—and the Society is looking to Gilbert to be their hero, that must put Powell between a rock and a hard place. He's terrified of Gilbert—afraid he'll point a finger at him. The idea that Gilbert might be terminally ill made him downright perky."

"Where did he get that idea?"

"Sorry, I didn't tell you. I brought Gil into the Neurology Department at UNLV yesterday morning. He's not well. He has a rare neurological disorder—one his mother seems to have also suffered from." He gave the cardinal a thumbnail sketch of what the MRI had revealed.

"Could the condition be related to the miracles?"

Jack shook his head. "I'm tempted to think it is. It really does seem too much of a coincidence. Two people with the same rare condition and similar . . . abilities."

Tom sipped his coffee thoughtfully for a moment, then said, "If Powell told Spader about the healing at St. Mary's, you can be sure he had a reason. I'd be leery of Captain Spader. Do you think you can trust Detective Firestone?"

Jack could feel his face flushing. "With my life," he said.

"Oh, it's like *that*, is it?"

"Like what?" asked Jack defensively, then caught the twinkle in his old friend's eye and chuckled. "Yes. It's very much like that. I confess, Father, I'm in love with the woman. That's all I'm going to confess. So . . . what do you think our zealots will do next?"

"Don't know. But I wouldn't be surprised if some of them might be on their way to Las Vegas. I suspect they see Gilbertson as their Joan of Arc, and they are not going to let him get away from being recognized as a modern American saint."

"Do you think *they* murdered Frank Coughlin? Maybe some sort of—I don't know—internecine power struggle?"

"Certainly possible. Although, it might have also been connected to organized crime. Not their M.O., but who knows."

Jack struggled for a moment with his thoughts about Coughlin's death, then said, "This is going to sound batshit crazy, but I can't help thinking about the bird."

"The . . . bird?"

"The eagle. It turned up in Mitchell's room at St. Mary's; it appeared onstage the night we saw Gil do the Hindu rope trick, and . . . I saw it again yesterday in the MRI suite at UNLV. Or, at least, I saw its shadow. That bird's talons are as long as my pinky finger, Tom, and twice as thick."

The cardinal didn't answer but simply stared into his coffee cup.

Jack sighed. "You think I'm crazy . . ."

Tom cleared his throat. "How . . . how many toes does an eagle have?"

"Four, all told. Three in the front, a sort of thumb in the back."

Tom set down his coffee cup. "Ruth had a bird, didn't she?"

Jack swallowed. "How did you know about that? She talked about a bird in one of her interviews with me, but she called it a totem. I didn't think it was an actual bird. More like an imaginary friend for grown-ups."

"Gilbert mentioned it once or twice when he was a boy. I referred to it as a pet and he corrected me. He said, 'It's not a pet, Mr. Bishop. It's a guardian.'"

Jack wriggled his shoulders to chase away the chill that now scurried down the backs of his arms.

"A brain lesion," murmured Tom, his eyes on the concourse again. "Jack, are you at all familiar with the Book of Revelation?"

Jack blinked at the sudden change of subject. "Bits and pieces."

"When you have a chance, open up a Bible and read the beginning of chapter 13. See what you think."

"What has the Book of Revelation got to do with anything?"

Tom rose and picked up his computer bag from the floor by his feet. "To our zealous friends, a great deal. See what you think," he repeated. "Right now, I've got a speech to give."

"And the beast, which I saw, was like to a leopard, and his feet were as the feet of a bear, and his mouth as the mouth of a lion. And the

dragon gave him his own strength, and great power. And I saw one of his heads as it were slain to death: and his death's wound was healed. And all the earth was in admiration after the beast. And they adored the dragon, which gave power to the beast: and they adored the beast, saying: Who is like to the beast? and who shall be able to fight with him?"

Revelation 13:2–4

"You know, reading this now, as an adult, I feel as if I'm reading a synopsis for a fantasy novel. Why did Tom direct me to this passage?"

Jack glanced at Joan's face in the Skype window on his laptop; she looked more fascinated than perplexed. She was reading the same text he was, though in an actual book. He'd found a Bible site online.

"Maybe because you're dealing with a doomsday cult and this is about the end times? I assume he thought the metaphors and similes were meaningful in some way."

"Really? So, there's this hybrid leopard, bear, and lion—a leobelion, I guess you could call him. He's got multiple heads, wears tiny little crowns, and works for a dragon. What'm I supposed to make of that?"

"Don't be obtuse," said Joan. "The animals are symbolic of people or organizations. I'm sure you know that. In fact, it's been suggested that the Catholic Church is part of the mix—if you're a particular type of evangelical, at any rate. The dragon is Satan. So the beast is Satan's puppet."

Jack looked back at the previous verses. "With seven heads and ten horns wearing crowns to match?"

"Some scholars think that lines up with a series of powerful kingdoms and leaders that arose historically. There's another reference to seven heads and ten horns in chapter 12, too. Only in this case the dragon—who's menacing a woman—has them."

"What woman?"

Joan took a deep breath, looked skyward, and said, "The woman who is clothed with the sun and has the moon under her feet and who gives birth to a child who's caught up to heaven to protect him from the dragon."

"That's . . . pretty damned impenetrable."

"Mm-hmm. Which is why so many scholars agree that trying to decipher this stuff without a key is futile. They subscribe to the prophet Daniel's assertion that the words are sealed until the end of the age."

Jack continued to page through the Book of Revelation, flipping back to chapter 12 and looking for the verse about the dragon having seven heads. "End of the world, you mean," he said absently.

"End of the *age*. The original King James version of the Bible, for whatever reason, translated the Greek word *eon* as 'world' instead of 'age.' It's been fixed in the New King James Bible, but the Catholic Bible still says it's the 'consummation of the world.' Which apparently some folks take to mean the end of it."

"Consummation doesn't mean 'end.' It means 'completion'—and how do you know all this stuff?"

Joan grinned. "I have a fine collection of Bibles that I won in Sunday School, sir, with my name engraved in gold. For verses and biblical knowledge rendered."

"Impressive." Jack paused to consider how this related to their current situation. "Okay, so we're dealing with people who think all this prophecy—beastly leobelions and dragons, et al—is about the literal end of the world. And they see something about what's happening here as being relevant to the end times prophecies."

"I'm pretty sure that's Tom's message."

"Okay, so what about the beast is relevant . . ."

He looked at the passage again, reading it through carefully to the end. This time a pair of phrases in the middle of the passage leapt off the virtual page.

"Oh. Oh, hell."

Chapter 21

That Dr. Jack Madison had visited the university's Neuroscience Institute was not surprising. He was a neurologist, after all. That Gil Gilbertson had met him and spent the entire morning there was more than surprising. It was puzzling.

Michael Lyons's operatives had gotten as far as the admin station in the lobby, but lacking an appointment to see anyone, they'd been denied access to the labs and examination rooms. They had hunkered down in the waiting room, from which they had seen Gilbert in the company of Dr. Madison, and later a nurse, crossing a hallway in the part of building they could not access.

Lyons had authorized them to do whatever it took to find out why their miracle worker was being examined. He was fairly certain he knew why. The atheist doctor found it impossible to believe that there was any such thing as a miracle. He was looking for a materialistic explanation for the things Gilbertson was capable of doing.

He will find nothing, Lyons thought with a mental sneer. *He will be forced to acknowledge that miracles are real. Then others will listen.*

Lyons had no reservations about authorizing bribery, even theft, if it would get access to Gil Gilbertson's case files and give him proof that *this* young man was doing more than magic tricks. While Lyons waited for their report, he left his spartan cell in the Los Angeles facility the Society kept, and went down to the chapel to pray.

It wasn't a church, per se, but rather a converted warehouse in an industrial section of the city. It contained a small chapel, a dining/meeting room, and sleeping quarters for the disciples. Members wandered in and out; a few lived there full time. While at the Mother House, as they called it, they imposed severe deprivation on themselves, similar to monks of the Middle Ages. They slept on hard wooden pallets; food was bread and soup; they prayed nine times daily, starting at three a.m. A few went so far as to practice flagellation. All members, wherever they were, wore woolen scapulas under their shirts that caused constant irritation of their chest and back. A special few wore barbed wire wrapped around their legs.

A formal Tridentine Mass—performed in Latin as it had been for over sixteen hundred years—was celebrated daily, but in great secrecy. During meals, when members spoke to one another, the topic was most often the righteousness of their cause, the evil of virtually everything else, and The End.

Gil Gilbertson had added a new dimension to their fervor. One thing that the members of the SPCD and the legacy of Pope John Paul II had in common was a conviction that miracles had a special purpose in proving God's plans for man. And miracles were just what the SPCD needed right now—miracles that would prove God's plan was yet in operation, that the time of The End was fast approaching.

Lyons envisioned a great revival sweeping the world. A great return to the Church before what his Bible referred to as the 'consummation of the world.' So many of the prophecies had already been fulfilled, and now this unassuming young man was performing miracles that put Lyons in mind of an Old Testament prophecy in the Book of Joel about a time when God would pour out His spirit in the world. As Joel reported, "Your sons and your daughters shall prophesy: your old men shall dream dreams, and your young men shall see visions."

Gilbertson's mother had prophesied. Lyons had found people willing to testify to that. He quivered with anticipation of what her son would ultimately do.

On his arrival at the Mother House, Lyons had spoken to the gathered brethren of the Society. "I believe," he told them, "that Gilbert Gilbertson is no fluke. He has appeared, I hope and pray, for the propagation of the True and Holy Church. I am convicted that there exists real opportunity to recruit him into our sacred order. Imagine, my brothers, a devout and true Roman Catholic, the son of a holy Stigmatic, who has the power, given to him by Christ Himself, to heal the sick. Even as corrupt a soul as Dr. Madison, who is hell-bent on refuting all that we hold true, cannot refute Gilbert's God-given abilities. As pernicious as Madison might be, he is a national figure, so even his tacit verification of Gilbert's miraculous powers can further our holy cause."

He said this, though he had been, at first, a skeptic. But every report from the brethren in the field had convinced him and other leaders of the movement that Gilbertson was a sign from God. The fact that Madison thought him worthy of examination all but proved it.

Lyons felt his cell phone go off in the deep pocket of his cassock. He hurried from the chapel, saw that the caller was one of the brothers in Las Vegas, and hastened to his cell to take the call in private.

"What have you found?"

The voice of the young disciple on the other end of the call—who insisted on going by Brother Humility—was breathless. "Brother Matthew created a distraction that allowed me to gain access to the diagnostic room once the doctors had gone off to consult. There were brain scans still up on the screen, so I took photographs of them. I'm sending them through to you now in messages."

Lyons frowned as the images appeared on his phone. They showed high-contrast shots of a human brain. A data field in the lower right corner of the image declared it to be the brain of G. Gilbertson. And it clearly had something seriously wrong with it.

"I don't understand, Father Lyons," said Brother Humility. "What is that?"

"It appears to be a brain lesion of some sort," murmured Lyons. "A massive one."

"That would explain the evidence Matthew and I have found that Gilbertson is frequently in pain. His apartment medicine chest was filled with painkillers, and this doctor has prescribed even more. We saw them delivered to his hotel here in Vegas. Father, he . . ."

Lyons did not mistake the wonder in the young monk's voice. "What is it?"

"I overheard a couple of the doctors talking as they left the lab. They said that Mr. Gilbertson should be dead. That he should not even be able to walk and talk. What does it mean? Is this another miracle?"

"It means I must think and pray, Brother. Continue to watch Gilbertson. I will be with you soon."

Brother Humility's words niggled. Lyons hung up and opened the Bible app on his phone. He went to the Book of Revelation, thirteenth chapter. The words that first struck his eyes were these: *And the dragon gave him his own strength, and great power. And I saw one of his heads as it were slain to death: and his death's wound was healed.*

Those words were not about a latter-day visionary or miracle worker allied with Christ. They were about a different biblical figure altogether. Lyons's bowels quaked as he read through to the end of the passage.

And all the earth was in admiration after the beast. And they adored the dragon, which gave power to the beast: and they adored the beast, saying: Who is like to the beast? and who shall be able to fight with him?

An hour later, when Father Michael Lyons and two colleagues began their drive to Las Vegas, he was determined that *he*, at least, would fight the beast. There could be no healing for Gilbert Gilbertson.

Chapter 22

"Spader wanted to know where you were," Joan told Jack when she picked him up at the airport Sunday morning. "I told him you were catching up on email and doing some research about what might be going on with Gilbert. He asked me if you'd shared your diagnosis. I told him no. Then he wanted to know if you'd figured out how or why Gilbert is able to do what he does. I told him I hadn't the foggiest, which is God's own truth."

"Good. I'm pretty sure we don't want anyone in the SPCD to know about Gilbert's brain lesion."

"They might not even make the connection, Jack. Catholicism emphasizes tradition over scriptural scholarship."

He gave her a look.

"Okay, I'm just being a cockeyed optimist. What do you think they'll do? I mean, if they think Gilbert is a figure from biblical prophecy."

"That depends entirely on the depths of the chasm between them and reality." He hesitated, then added, "The Book of Revelation is a fascinating read. There seem to be several chapters that tell the same story using different imagery. That part in chapter 12 about the woman who gave birth to a man child . . ." He paused again, then quoted: "*And to the woman were given two wings of a great eagle, that she might fly into the wilderness, into her place, where she is nourished*

297

for a time, and times, and half a time, from the face of the serpent.'
I know that passage isn't about Ruth—she seems to have had more of
the eagle than just its wings—but it makes me think of her. Fleeing
to Hunterton with her child to protect him from a pedophile priest."

Joan's eyebrows rose. "Bishop Powell as the great red dragon?
Blasphemy, Doc. Bald-faced blasphemy."

Jack considered his next words carefully. "Joan, I need to run
something by you. It's going to sound crazy, but I have to get it out
there."

"Shoot."

"Ruth's stigmata and powers of prescience manifested suddenly
when Gil was a small boy, while they were living in Chicago. They
grew with the lesion in her brain until it killed her. Gilbert's powers of
kinetic manipulation and illusion manifested suddenly three months
ago, after he came to Vegas for a magicians' convention. Put another
way, twenty-five years ago, something happened in Ruth's life in
Chicago that triggered the growth of her AVM. Three months ago,
something happened in Gil's life in Las Vegas that triggered his. The
common thread—"

"Powell."

Jack nodded. "Three months ago, Gil came to Vegas. I think he
may have seen Powell and recognized him. Realized he was the head
of the diocese here."

"You're saying that what Powell did to Gil triggered the growth of
lesions that resulted in both Gil and his mother developing powers"—
she glanced sidewise at him—"as protection? A sort of fight-or-flight
response?"

Jack laughed mirthlessly. "Hell, I was hoping it would sound more
rational than that. But, yes: Powell triggered a fight-or-flight response

that shocked Ruth's, and then Gilbert's, brains so strongly that it precipitated the accelerated growth of AVMs in both cases."

Joan pulled into her driveway, set the brake, then turned to look at Jack. "But instead of turning them into vegetables before it killed them, it granted them protective powers . . . and a giant eagle?"

Jack thumped the back of his head against his headrest and closed his eyes. "God, Joan. I don't know. I really don't. I feel . . . completely out of my depth here. Damn it. This is neurology. This is my field of expertise. But right now, I feel as if I don't have a clue."

"So, what do we do?"

"We take one step after another until we get wherever it is we're going. We start by having a chat with Gilbert this evening."

Joan leaned over and kissed him lightly on the lips. "That's very philosophical of you, Doctor. I approve."

"You realize you're probably scandalizing your cross-the-street neighbor, right? He's standing at the bottom of his driveway, staring at us with his mouth hanging open."

"Ooh. I like that. Let's show him something that'll make him drop his teeth."

She kissed him thoroughly enough to make him forget leobelions, eagles, and the end of the world.

Jack and Joan arrived at Gil Gilbertson's room at the Mirage to find the young magician in a rather chipper mood. He immediately grasped Jack's hand and shook it emphatically.

"Doctor! This medicine you sent me is pretty good stuff. I still can feel a slight headache, but it sure has taken the edge off. I feel light as a feather. I was able to spend all last evening and this morning at the

Cavalcade. It's a great convention. No one knows me well enough to know that it's me who's doing the closing act tomorrow night—but word's out that something exciting is going to happen. I feel like I've got this fantastic secret that none of them could guess in a million years. If only they knew."

Joan took in Gilbert's flushed face and sparkling eyes. He was gleeful, maybe even manic—like a kid on Christmas Eve. She suspected maybe that was the net effect of having the volume of his head pain dialed back from a roar to a whisper. She remembered having a migraine after overindulging in champagne one New Year's Eve. When the pain had stopped suddenly, she felt downright giddy.

Gilbert burbled happily on as they seated themselves in the conversation area of his room. "I spent a few hours earlier with a Mr. Menkin from the convention. Mr. Rosen sent him over. Got everything set for the show tomorrow night."

"So," asked Jack, turning on his most relaxed bedside manner, "what's your favorite part of these conventions? I always enjoyed the amateur open stage performances: I liked to imagine that I could pick which of the newbies were going to turn out to be famous."

"Oh, I like the workshops and seminars on craft and method. Especially the close-up stuff like cards and coins. And history. I *love* hearing about the history of magic." He wrinkled his nose. "I notice there are a number of Gospel magicians this year."

"Gospel magicians?" repeated Joan. "What on earth are those?"

"It's really hokey. It's where the magician uses magic to preach. Do some magic to draw a crowd, then start using the tricks themselves to send a message."

"Such as?"

"Oh, like they'll link three ropes or three rings together to talk about the Holy Trinity. Very silly, in my opinion; nothing I'm interested in."

Joan used the opportunity to get a sense of Gilbert's current relationship with the Church. "I take it you're not very religious."

"Not really. I mean, I believe in God and all, but I don't like organized religion. Mom was in the Church, so I used to go to Mass every once in a while to pray for her, but I haven't been in months."

"Really? What made you stop?"

"Nothing in particular. I just don't believe in all that stuff."

Joan wasn't blind to the way his eyes dodged suddenly away from hers when he talked about the Church. "I hear you," she said.

"It's funny you would ask, though, because it's the second time today someone has brought it up."

"Second time today?" Joan asked.

"Yeah. I went to see Mr. Rosen about the Cavalcade, and Captain Spader was there along with an envoy from the archdiocese of Los Angeles. Captain Spader and Mr. Rosen were really nice to me, but this priest . . ." He shook his head. "I dunno. He just looked at me like I was a bug, you know?"

"I do know," said Jack sympathetically.

Gilbert turned his bright gaze on Jack. "I bet you do, huh? What with those books you write, I'll bet they don't like you at all."

"Back up," said Joan. "A priest from LA? Why would they be meeting with a priest from LA?"

Gilbert shrugged. "Because I sent so much money down there. He said the cardinal archbishop of LA wanted to thank me for contributing so much to their charities, but he didn't seem all that thankful. He was real intense."

Joan felt a sudden shift in Jack's energy. He leaned forward in his chair. "Did he give a name?"

"I don't remember it. Young guy, tall and bald. Looked like he shaves his head. He said something about being an assistant to a cardinal—Cardinal Munoz, I guess."

Jack glanced over and met Joan's eyes. "Lyons," he mouthed.

"And this priest asked you about your relationship with the Church?"

Gil nodded. "He asked if I were active. I said no, and he asked why I gave them all that money. I said I chose Catholic charities in memory of my mother. He asked if I liked the Church and if I still thought of myself as Catholic. I thought that was sort of funny. I told him I didn't *dislike* the Church and that I thought all religions were pretty much the same. Told him I hadn't thought about it, but I guess if someone needed me to write down my religion, I'd probably say Catholic. But only because that was how I was raised. He told me that he had heard from the folks at St. Mary's about Mitchell and the burn on his back and that since it was a Catholic hospital and all, he thought that I might still have some feelings for the Church. I told him Dr. Madison was the only person I was going to discuss my feelings about the Church with."

"Me?" Jack said, obviously surprised.

"You understand that faith isn't simple. That you're not just in or out. That Church and religion and faith aren't the same thing." He hesitated, frowned, then said, "And that's when he got really rude. He asked me how I could be that way when my mother had such a deep love for the Church and such a special relationship with the Blessed Virgin. That's when I told him that he didn't know a thing about my mother and her religious beliefs. Then I left. I think Captain Spader was mad at the priest, too. He followed me out of Mr. Rosen's office and apologized for him. He asked how I was feeling and if my tests had revealed anything."

"Did you tell him?" Joan asked.

"No. Why would I?"

"While we're on the subject," Jack said, "I'd like to discuss the results of your tests in more detail and set up some further testing." He looked at Joan. "Could you give us the room for a private doctor-patient conference?"

Joan rose reluctantly, but Gil waved her down. "It's all right, Doctor. Really. I give permission for her to stay."

"You're sure?" Joan asked.

Gilbert nodded soberly. "I consider you a friend. So, what's the verdict, Doctor?"

"Well, Gilbert, we don't have a complete answer yet—which is why I'd like to schedule some more tests—but you have some abnormal blood vessels in part of your brain that are causing your headaches. The good news is, I think we might be able to help you."

"Help how?"

"Well, there are some ways of blocking off these blood vessels . . ."

Gilbert interrupted him. "You mean surgery?"

"Not necessarily; there are some new ways that don't require opening the skull."

He nodded, seemed to go inside himself for a moment, then focused on Jack with a chilling intensity. "Doctor, I don't want any kind of treatment. I will never give my permission. I know that this is something very serious. In fact, I know that I'm not going to live much longer. And I don't care. You probably find that hard to believe, but I don't have any reason to live a long time, and I don't want to. All I want is to have people remember my magic—one big night, that's all I want. I know, deep down inside, and I think you do too, that I would never live through any kind of operation. So let's not go there. No more tests."

Joan watched Jack's face as Gil was speaking; she saw a series of reactions (up to and including anger) before he acquiesced. All he said was, "All right, Gilbert. I wish you'd let me do this, but I can't force you and I have to respect your wishes."

Gil nodded. "Thank you, Doctor. I appreciate that."

They left then, but Joan could tell Jack wanted desperately to talk Gilbert out of his fatalistic frame of mind. Wanted to so badly that he said, as they were crossing the threshold, "Gil, I wish you'd reconsider treatment. Please think about it, okay?"

Gilbert only shrugged. Jack opened his mouth to argue, and Joan put her hand on his arm, but before Jack could say anything, Gilbert spoke.

"There's another reason I think maybe I shouldn't stick around. I told you I can make people do things. I can affect them. I'm afraid I might really hurt someone—you know—in a fit of anger. Today . . ." He looked down at the carpet between his feet, shamefaced. "The priest I was talking about—the tall, bald guy—I was really angry with him, with the things he said. When he got rude toward the end, I decided to play a little trick on him. He was starting to get a twitch in his eye. I could feel when it was coming on and I sort of . . . kicked it into high gear. I made his whole face start twitching. He didn't know what to do, and Mr. Rosen and Captain Spader were staring at him real funny. He got all embarrassed." A sly smile curved his lips. "It was kind of a hoot."

Suddenly, he was laughing out loud—the uninhibited laughter of a child prankster. "And—and," he giggled, "he really hates you, Dr. Madison."

"How do you know that?" Jack asked. "How did you know his spasms were coming on? How did you make his face twitch?"

"I don't know. You see why it bothers me? Because I don't know. I just do it. I just have to focus on it—on the network inside his head. It's like electricity or water; things flow or build up like static, then discharge, you know? And getting inside people's heads is just too easy."

"How about Mitchell?" asked Joan. "Was healing his burns hard for you?"

Gil frowned. "Very hard. Off the charts. Actually, I was surprised it worked. But I was so happy for that little guy. You wouldn't believe how my head hurt after that, but it was worth it."

"You tried to heal the kids in the cancer ward, too, didn't you?" Jack asked.

Gil turned wide, round eyes on him. "How did you know about that, Doctor?"

Jack smiled. It was a sad smile. "I think maybe I'm beginning to understand you."

"Yeah, I tried a couple of times, but it didn't work. It was like I can make things grow, but I can't stop things from growing. Does that make sense?"

"Actually, it does." Jack hesitated, then asked, "Gilbert, can you tell me about the eagle?"

"The Guardian," Gil said.

"The Guardian. Do you control it?"

Gilbert's eyes were suddenly guarded, his distress palpable. "No. No, I can't. At least, I hope I'm not controlling it. I need to rest," he said, and shut the door in their faces.

They stood for a moment, staring at the blank wood, then Joan hooked her arm through Jack's and led him away.

"*'My candle burns at both ends,'*" she murmured. "'*It will not last the night. But ah, my foes, and oh, my friends—it gives such lovely light.'*"

"What was that?"

"Edna Saint Vincent Millay. That young man is writing his own obituary." She tilted her head so she could look up into his face. "I know it's hard, Jack, but you may have to let go of this one."

He met her eyes and she knew that was a forlorn hope. Jack Madison took his Hippocratic oath very seriously.

"Do you really think you can help him?" she asked.

"I don't know, Joan. I honestly don't. It's hard to imagine taking half of his brain out or at least shutting down all of its blood supply, but that's probably the only way to save him from this thing before it ruptures. And rupture it will, sooner than later."

Joan felt suddenly tired and heavy, as if her bones had been alchemically transmuted into iron. "I hate to think that. I like Gil. He's sweet and honest. I'd like to think you can save him. But I also think he doesn't want to be saved. That he's . . . content to be his own prophet of doom."

"I'm hoping he's just needlessly resigned to his fate. 'Needlessly' being the operative term. I've lost patients before, but never like this."

Joan squeezed his arm more tightly. "Then don't lose him. Make him see reason."

Jack looked at her, a rare uncertainty clouding his eyes. "And what if there's no reason to be seen? What if there really is no hope?"

Joan squeezed his arm. "Pray he makes it through his big night and that he really does stand Las Vegas on its head."

They were in the car on their way to meet the Admiral for dinner when Arnie Rosen called Jack. The first words out of the man's mouth were, "Did that sonofabitch tell you about all the crap he wants tomorrow night?"

Jack threw Joan a perplexed look, and mouthed "Rosen." Aloud, he said, "No, we didn't discuss it." He turned on the speakerphone so Joan could hear Rosen's end of the conversation.

"Did he tell you about the giant bird perch?" Rosen snarled. "Or about the circus wagon big enough for a fucking elephant? Or the experienced animal trainer?"

"No, he didn't mention any of that."

"Well he'll get them, but it's taken calling in every chit I've got to have it done. Menkin almost shit his pants, but I told him to give Gilbertson anything he wanted, anything."

"I think that was wise, Arnie."

"Wise, shmise. I just want this fucking nightmare over with. I'll see you tomorrow at the Rio." He hung up.

"Bird perch, I get," said Joan. "But circus wagon? Animal trainer? What's he going to do?"

"Give Las Vegas the most magical night of its life."

They dined at Carnevino—Chef Mario Batali's famous restaurant, which Jack thought looked like it belonged on an ocean liner from the golden age of steam, and where it was said one would find the best steaks in America. Admiral Benson met them there, abuzz with the rumors he'd been fielding.

"It's all over town that something big is up tomorrow night at the closing show of the Cavalcade. Mystery Guest." He framed the words with his hands as if they were on a marquee. "Everyone—or at least everyone who gives a rat's ass about magic is asking everyone else if they know who that is. I've heard all sorts of rumors, of course, most of 'em way off base, because who'd guess it's a mild-mannered Burger King shift manager who does kiddie parties on weekends?"

"Only most of them are off base?" asked Jack.

Benson grinned. "Believe it or not, a few people I've—er—overheard talking about it wonder if it might not be the same guy who did the Hindu rope trick in Chicago a week or so ago. And that there, lady and gent, is the big under-buzz. What a coup it would be for the Cavalcade if they could get *that* guy."

Joan rolled her expressive eyes. "That's ironic. Here Arnie Rosen is afraid the Casino Association is going to be seen as the goat because of Gilbert, when they might actually come out of this looking like shrewd operators."

"I heard Gilbertson did some pretty slick sleights here at the con," Benson said, "but I don't think most folks have put two and two together. The Casino Association will probably make money just on the mystery guest angle alone. Sure would like to know how you got him on the bill. I'm emceeing the show and got strict orders to keep the other acts short, sweet, and on time. And I mean orders. Some of the pros are pissed, some are curious, but they are all going to be there."

"Last time we talked," said Joan, "you mentioned that some other guys have been asking around about Gil. Asking what, exactly?"

"Oddly enough, they've been asking what he's done and why he's doing it." The Admiral ticked off the two points on his fingers. "First question makes me think they must be journalists, but asking why—that's just weird. Why does anybody do magic? Even street magic like messing about with the casinos for charity. You do magic because you *can*."

After his meeting with Tom O'Connor, Jack decided that Gil's rationale for his behavior was not something he wanted to pursue with their good friend Wilfred. Nor were he and Joan willing to share anything of what they knew of Gil's plans to possibly disappear large animals, though the Admiral tried to wheedle it out of them.

"Guess we'll just have to wait and see, Wil," Joan told him.

"Someday I'm going to get you two hammered and you're going to tell me all about this guy. You know a lot more about what's going on than you're saying." He gave Jack a sly look. "I heard a rumor that he can break the slots. Maybe I'll even tell you how to get that card to stick to the ceiling if you fess up."

"Ask me no questions, Admiral, and I'll tell you no lies. And if you don't think I know at least three ways to do the card on the ceiling, then you seriously underestimate me."

"Never let it be said that I did that." The Admiral raised his glass. "Tomorrow night."

Jack and Joan echoed the toast.

"Tomorrow night."

Chapter 23

The grand and gleaming Penn & Teller Theatre at the Hotel Rio had a seating capacity of over 1,400. It was sold out for the closing show of the Cavalcade of Magic—every seat taken. The evening's performers for the first half of the show were introduced by Admiral Benson, with his usual dry humor. They included the year's Best New Young Magician, who did a fine rendition of Dai Vernon's Symphony of the Rings, produced a chandelier with five lit candles, and performed some imaginative rope tricks. Next was a Japanese magician who did amazing productions of strand after strand of lighted electric bulbs of all colors and shapes—some while standing on his head. Lance Burton did his famous dove routine in which he produced over two dozen birds in a variety of ways, all from his seemingly empty hands.

Even so, the closing show was par for the course in one of these events, as far as Jack could tell. None of the performances were gasp-worthy, none of the comedy acts rolling-in-the-aisle hilarious.

At 8:50, the Admiral announced that there would be a short intermission and asked that the audience be back in their seats by nine fifteen. During the intermission, the semicircular main stage was completely cleared and reset with a large flip chart on an easel, and a simple card table that held a glass of water and a tall stack of fabric in bright colors. A folded wooden chair leaned against the table, while next to it was a large T-shaped stand, a clear plastic box—approximately four feet on each edge—and a round straw basket like the one Gilbert had used in Chicago for the rope trick. A ramp led from the center stage apron to the floor of the hall.

In the VIP seating closest to the stage were magic's royalty: David Copperfield, Penn and Teller, David Blaine, Lance Burton, Criss Angel, Mac King, and the Admiral, with a number of other famous magicians flanking them. Joan and Jack were seated three rows up, on the stage left side.

Promptly at nine fifteen, David Copperfield rose, walked up the ramp into the spotlights at center stage, and addressed the audience. Two immense displays flown to either side of the stage showed him in close-up.

"Ladies and gentleman, fellow magicians, and guests. While I have not personally seen our next performer, a number of you here this evening have had that pleasure. I am told by those who have seen him, both in Springfield and Chicago, that we are in for a special treat. So with no further ado, I present, from Springfield, Missouri, Gilbert the Great—King of Cards, Rajah of Ropes, and Master of Mystery."

Copperfield returned to his seat amid polite, enthusiastic applause. The applause had begun to wane when Gilbert appeared from the wings and made his way up a side ramp onto the stage. He was dressed in black slacks and a black short-sleeved shirt with no collar. He walked slowly into the spotlight where the audience finally got a look at the chubby, undersized, red-headed phenom. His pale complexion was washed out further by the spotlight, and he wore no makeup. He looked nervous and a bit lost.

Joining in the polite applause, Jack swallowed his own discomfort. He hadn't discussed the results of the morning's meeting with Gilbert with his colleagues at the Neurological Institute. The AVM was, if anything, denser and more complex than any Jack or his colleagues had ever seen, and they were all frustrated by Gilbert's refusal to undergo functional imaging. There was only the slimmest chance that the AVM was operable, and all were aware that surgery could as easily leave Gil Gilbertson a vegetable as restore his normal faculties.

Would it restore his normal faculties? Jack had to wonder, and to ask what was normal for Gilbert the Great? If shutting down the AVM meant him losing whatever bizarre abilities it seemed to bestow, would Gil be content to live life as a Burger King shift manager who sucked at anything more complex than a package card trick?

The young magician gazed out over the audience as if he could not believe so many people had stayed to see him perform. Or perhaps he was simply savoring the moment. He spoke, at last, in his clear, high-pitched voice, drawing a few titters from the crowd.

"Good evening to all of you," he said. "Thank you for allowing me to entertain you. The magic I perform for you this evening is in tribute to the greatest of magicians and done in the spirit of the amazing Siegfried and Roy, who brought the concept of the magical spectacle to Las Vegas and the world. My performance will have five elements: mind reading, manipulation, levitation, a mythic classic, and production of an animal. I think that is enough explanation. Prepare yourselves for things that you have never seen."

Gilbert was certainly no showman, Jack reflected. He sounded like a high school kid about to demonstrate a science project. Jack glanced at the professional magicians he could see in the front row; there were smiles, smirks, and a smattering of laughter.

"But before we get to the main event," Gilbert announced, "I'd like to warm up with a simple trick that is a staple of magicians at all levels—even for magic clowns like me. It's a rope trick, so I'm going to ask for the aid of the king of rope tricks—Mr. Mac King. Mr. King, would you please join me on stage?"

King rose as if he'd been expecting to be called upon and climbed the ramp to the stage.

"Now, I must disclose," Gilbert said when King had reached him and turned to face the audience, "that I asked Mr. King to help me with my first trick and requested that he provide materials for it. May I call you Mac?"

"Certainly," King said affably.

"Now, you're not a magic clown—"

"My wife would argue that point," King said, drawing laughter from the audience. "I keep telling her I'm a comedian, but she insists on calling me a clown."

Gil grinned. "Whatever you are, you are my idol. I believe that not only do you perform the best comedy magic act anywhere, you also are the current master of rope tricks, several of which cannot be duplicated by the best magicians in the world. Now, Mac, will you tell the audience what I asked you to bring with you tonight?"

"An ordinary length of rope and a pair of scissors," King said, drawing those items from the pockets of his blazer.

"Except for my written request that you bring these items with you tonight, have we ever met or communicated with one another?"

"Nope. First time I've seen you or heard your name."

"Would you please hand me the scissors, then stretch the rope out in front of you, holding it tightly at each end?"

King did as asked. The extended rope was about an inch thick and three feet in length. Gilbert cut it in half with the scissors so that two shorter lengths of rope now dangled from each of King's hands. The severed ends immediately began to unwind.

"Mr. Mac, can you guarantee that this is an ordinary rope?"

"Completely ordinary. I bought it at Home Depot." The audience laughed, and he added, "Seriously. Scissors, too."

"Would you please just roll the two pieces of rope into a ball? Then, squeeze them as tightly as you can between your hands."

King followed the instructions, crushing the rope in cupped hands.

"Now, open your hands, please."

King opened his hands. A single, three foot length of rope dangled from the fingers of one hand. He stared at it, then grasped the rope toward the bottom and yanked on it.

Gilbert smiled beatifically. "I think a seemingly simple trick is a good way to start an evening of magic. Don't you agree, Mr. Mac?"

King blinked. "Uh . . . yeah."

"Now, before you go back to your seat, would you please roll the rope up again?"

King did as Gilbert directed.

"Squeeze it, then open your hands once more."

What hung from Mac King's hands at the end of the trick was one continuous circle of inch-thick rope. Looking truly puzzled now, he ran the entire rope through his fingers, as if looking for the spot where it surely must be joined. He pulled at it several times . . . hard. At last he held it aloft and whirled it around over his head so the audience could see it clearly.

"That," he told the audience, "is the best rope trick I've ever seen. And believe me, I thought I had seen them all!" Still clutching the rope, he turned and shook Gilbert's hand, then returned to his seat accompanied by applause.

Gil surveyed the other pros with sparkling eyes and gave them a winsome smile. "I see Mr. Penn Jillette in the front row. Sir, would you be so kind as to offer me your assistance?"

Jillette pantomimed *"Me?"* He stood.

"Thank you, Mr. Jillette. Would you walk to the midpoint of the center ramp, please?" He pointed at a spot that would place the other magician in clear view of the audience.

"May I call you Penn?" Gilbert asked artlessly as Jillette hit his mark.

"Sure, if I can call you Gil."

Jillette's expression was guarded. Jack suspected he was not pleased to have been called out of the audience when he had no idea what he'd been called out for.

"Now, Penn," said Gilbert, "I have watched your stage show many times and seen your series on *Showtime*, read all of your books, and watched *Penn & Teller: Fool Us*. Would it be fair to say that you do not believe in true mind reading?"

"I think it would be fairer to say I think the entire concept is bullshit, just like the name of my show." The sarcastic response drew appreciative laughter from the audience.

Gil laughed too. "Just the answer I had hoped for, Penn. So, how can I prove to you that mind reading exists? That yours truly, Gilbert the Great, can actually read your mind?"

"Well, since you asked, I don't think you can. But you could start by telling me what I'm thinking right this minute."

"You are thinking: 'This fat little asshole is trying to make a fool out of me and I'm going to bust his chops. I can hardly believe that I let myself get talked into being a part of this fiasco.' Or ninety seconds ago: 'Wonder what time this'—what was the word you were using in your head?—'this jack-off will be through, and where will we go for dinner?' How's that?"

Penn's smirk disappeared. He looked shaken, but said, "Okay, that's pretty damn good, but you've got to admit, what else would I be thinking?"

The audience laughed.

"I know, Penn, that's the real trouble with mind reading. How does one know? I picked you because I think the audience would expect you to be the least likely accomplice to a mind-reading routine."

"Sounds like a safe bet."

"But in this routine, we're not going to write anything down. Nor will there be hidden notes or borrowed books or any of the usual stuff. Instead, think of anyone, anyone at all. Famous or not, someone you know or once knew. Just think about them for an instant."

Jillette nodded. "Okay, pal, I'm thinking."

Gil looked at him reproachfully. "I said think of only one person, Penn. In just that five seconds you thought of Albert Einstein, an uncle who played ball with you when you were little, your mother, and your childhood pet, a dog named Jessie. Trying to throw me off, weren't you?"

Penn said nothing. He simply stared at Gil as if trying to read him.

"Was I right?" Gil prodded.

Jillette cleared his throat, looking extremely uncomfortable . . . and curious. "Ah, yes, you were right. As weird as this sounds, I have to admit that is exactly what I was thinking. Exactly."

"And the dog's name was . . .?"

All of Penn Jillette's swagger was gone. "Jessie. His name was Jessie."

The audience broke out in applause and stunned murmurs.

David Blaine cupped his hands around his mouth and shouted, "Shill!"

Jillette turned to face the audience and raised his hands. "I swear to you, I am not shilling. I wouldn't. And you, Blaine, you damn well know I wouldn't. I have never even seen this man before tonight."

Gilbert was obviously having fun. His eyes were alight, his pale skin aglow; contented energy radiated from him in waves. "Well, let's try something else, something the audience can participate in. Mr. Blaine, would you pick out someone in the audience and ask them to take a bill out of their wallet? Anyone at all. Have them pull out any bill they want. Don't give them time to look at it."

Grinning, Blaine pointed to a guy seven rows up the central aisle and walked up to retrieve the bill himself. He was still grinning when he handed the bill to Penn Jillette. Meanwhile, Gilbert pulled the flip chart on its easel into the spotlight. He had a magic marker in his hand. The overhead displays went to a shot of the flip chart.

"Now, Penn, look at the serial numbers on that bill. Hold it close so no one else can see it."

As Penn Jillette carefully scanned the bill, Gilbert started writing on the chart—MN25635887326V.

"That's what you're thinking, Penn. But that's not what's on the bill. The real number on the bill is MN25666587373X." He wrote that beneath the first number. "Trying to fool me, were you? Would you show the bill to your friend, Mr. Teller?"

With a complete lack of resistance, Penn Jillette descended to the first row to show the bill to Ray Teller. Teller, looking utterly fascinated, studied the bill, checked the numbers on the chart up on the stage, and silently nodded assent.

"Thank you, Mr. Teller. By the way, ladies and gentlemen, we all know that Teller never speaks in public performances. Never. Right, Penn? Right, Teller?"

"Yes, that is correct," said Jillette, and Teller nodded vigorously.

"Do you think I can get him to say something to the audience?"

Jillette snorted. "Not in a million years."

Teller shook his head, and the audience laughed.

"Well, I can, but I won't. I respect you too much, Mr. Teller, and would not embarrass you; but, to be honest, you know I could, don't you?" Gil fixed Teller with his most direct gaze.

Teller was still shaking his head no, but his mouth opened as if he were going to speak. He put his fingers to his lips. Above his hands, his eyes were wide with surprise . . . or alarm. There was a tense moment in which he and Gilbert simply stared at each other, then Teller turned and gave a thumbs-up sign to the audience.

"Thank you, Penn and Teller. And one more time, on your word of honor, we have had no communication of any sort between us prior to this evening. Is that correct?"

Teller whispered something to Penn, and Jillette responded in a whisper, barely picked up by the stage mics. "Yes, it is."

"Give them a big hand, ladies and gentlemen!" enthused Gil as he waved the two men back to their seats. "Penn and Teller. One of the greatest magic acts in the history of Las Vegas."

The audience's applause was now enthusiastic and good-natured, even sprinkled with laughter. Gilbert had shifted into high gear, practically bouncing on his toes. He strode to the exact center of the stage, setting the flip chart off to the side, and stood beneath the spotlights looking electric with confidence. He snapped his fingers at the twin LED displays and they went dark, sending a murmur of curiosity around the hall.

"This audience, more than most, knows the difficulty of sleight of hand. Like some of you, my heroes in this ancient art have been immortalized, and we still speak of them today with respect and admiration. Cards, coins, billiard balls were their stock in trade. I thought long and hard how to pay them tribute. I finally decided on a combination of the Miser's Dream and the Great Cardini's amazing production of billiard balls. But with my own twist. They wore tails or coats. Notice my simple shirt and lack of sleeves."

He turned a full circle with his arms raised, as if to show that he concealed nothing, then said in a loud, clear voice: "Ladies and gentlemen, for your pleasure, the Croquet Ball Cornucopia. For this trick, I'd like to call on the amazing David Blaine to assist me."

Blaine, looking both skeptical and disgruntled, left his front-row seat and mounted the stage.

"Would you help me with the box, please?" Gil asked him, and moved to the oversized plastic container.

Blaine followed him and, together, the two men pulled the box to center stage. Gil then gestured for the other magician to stand on the opposite side of the box.

"I want to check it over first," Blaine demanded.

"Please do, Mr. Blaine."

Blaine walked all around the box, banging on the sides, inside and out. When he was done, he nodded and took the position Gilbert had indicated.

"Observe," said Gilbert, and proceeded to pull large, wooden, multicolored croquet balls literally out of nowhere. One after another, the balls simply appeared in his hands. There was no palming, no going to the pockets, no body loads—and the audience knew it. As he produced each ball, he would throw it into the plastic box where it was clearly visible as it was thrown in, and in which it made a solid clatter when it landed. He then started juggling the balls, five and six at a time. As he juggled, he continuously tossed balls into the box, yet the number of balls he juggled remained constant. He even tossed a few to Blaine who, stone-faced, dropped them into the box as well.

Soon the box was almost two-thirds full. Gilbert juggled the last six balls into the box, then held both of his hands together over it. More croquet balls cascaded out of his cupped hands into the box, filling it to the brim. Jack calculated there must be close to one hundred balls in the plastic container.

This performance was accompanied by a growing murmur of astonishment from the audience. By the time Gilbert had stopped producing croquet balls and turned to execute a deep bow, the murmur had become a roar. When it subsided, Gilbert turned to David Blaine and motioned at the collection of croquet balls.

"Mr. Blaine, would you pick a few of these balls at random and tell me what you are seeing and feeling?"

Frowning, Blaine did so. He dug down into the box and checked three balls in succession. "They're solid wood. Probably weigh a pound each." He held one of the balls up above his head, facing the audience. "This is legit."

Again, the audience roared. Gil moved to the top of the stage-right ramp as Blaine returned to his seat and beckoned to someone offstage. A pair of stagehands appeared to haul the box full of croquet balls away. Now Gil returned to center stage and turned his bright gaze on another of the pros.

"This evening we have seen Mr. Lance Burton, a man I admire immensely, do his dove act. This could be called a production, but it is so akin to manipulation that I wanted to include this during the current segment of my demonstration. So, here's my version. Mr. Burton, if you'd join me on stage?"

As Burton acquiesced, one of the stagehands brought the T-shaped stand out to the right of center stage. He handed Gilbert what looked like a thick leather arm band.

Gil faced the other magician. "Mr. Lance, you are no stranger to birds, but this one might surprise you. Would you please extend your left arm?"

Burton politely acquiesced. Gilbert fitted the leather sheath over the other man's arm and secured it. Next, he took a large, gold silk shawl from the stack of fabric on the card table. He showed both sides of the shawl to the audience, then draped it over Burton's extended left arm. Then, he simply stood back and watched.

Soon something beneath the shawl began to grow and show signs of movement. The growth stopped when it had reached a bit over three feet high, by Jack's estimate. As the something grew, Burton adjusted his stance several times, the expression on his face morphing from bemusement through bewilderment to alarm.

Gilbert faced the large object with a smile that transformed his pale face. He pinched a corner of the silken cloth and pulled it away with a great flourish. There, on Lance Burton's arm, sat a huge, majestic golden eagle. Jack was willing to bet it was the same eagle that he had seen on two other occasions. He felt Joan's hand on his arm, the pressure of her fingers as she telegraphed her own reaction to seeing the animal. Lance Burton, for his part, looked legitimately frightened.

"Don't worry," Gil told the magician. "She won't hurt you. She likes you."

The bird regarded the astonished audience with gleaming, raptor eyes, ignoring the thunderous applause that raced around the auditorium. Then, with a great thrust of its powerful legs and wings, the huge bird leapt from Burton's arm and soared into the dark vault of the theatre. Jack felt the gust of wind from those great wings from yards away.

Spotlights followed the eagle as it made a sweeping circuit of the auditorium, while the audience gave chaotic voice to its astonishment. The trick was potent in and of itself, but the sheer size of the bird Gilbert had produced made it more than that. Burton's doves were forgotten as the eagle, having completed its flight, swooped down and with a backward glance at Gilbert, lit on the thick crossbar of the T-stand.

Jack found himself transfixed by the bird's talons—as sharp and hefty as meat hooks. *What am I thinking?* he asked himself as he watched the stagehand move the stand and its passenger to upstage right. *That this bird murdered Francis Coughlin to protect Gilbert?*

Jack was pulled from his own confusion by the hushed silence in the room. The people in this audience were, for the most part, habitual consumers of magic. They had seen doves, rabbits, and the occasional duck or goose produced over the years but always with paraphernalia on the stage and by performers with enough room in their clothes for loads. But this unassuming and artless young man had produced this gigantic and rare bird quite literally out of thin air. This was something beyond immediate comprehension, even for this sophisticated—even jaded—audience. Applause perhaps seemed completely inadequate to the situation. The audience was silent, now, awaiting the next element in this extraordinary performance. Lance Burton, meanwhile, found his way back to his seat, looking dazed.

"Next, as promised, a levitation," announced Gilbert, turning toward the pros. "Mr. Copperfield, in my opinion you currently perform the best levitation in the world. Would you please assist me?"

David Copperfield glanced aside at his closest companions, then got up and warily approached Gilbert. The younger man motioned for him to stand next to him at center stage.

"Now, my friends, there are so many things I could levitate, I've had trouble deciding. Harry Kellar's wonderful Princess Karnac has been raised many times from a formal stage, so I dismissed using her. And the floating light bulb and dancing handkerchief have been done too well, too many times, by the Blackstones. So, I decided on the following concept just this morning." He turned to the senior magician. "Mr. Copperfield—David—could you be so kind as to bring that folding chair to center stage, unfold it, and sit in it?" He gestured from the chair to the spot he intended it to be set.

Copperfield hesitated only a moment before honoring the request. He collected the chair from where it leaned against the card table and carried it to the center of the stage. Before he unfolded it, though, he hoisted it over his head and turned completely around so that the audience could see it clearly. Then he unfolded it, running his hands over every surface, and sat.

Gilbert smiled benignly all the while. "Thank you, sir. Now, please, hold on to the sides of the chair. Ladies and gentlemen, here you see David Copperfield seated on an ordinary wooden folding chair. He himself picked it up and unfolded it. Did you notice anything at all unusual about the chair, David?"

Copperfield shook his head. "No," he said clearly.

"Please observe."

Gilbert began a slow circuit of the chair, muttering incomprehensibly and tapping his feet in a staccato fashion. Jack swallowed a chuckle. It was like watching a leprechaun or a Keebler elf flamenco dancing. As Gil made his second circuit, the chair and its occupant rose from the stage, slowly and steadily. There was no wavering or swaying as you would see if wires were being used. It was quite as if an invisible elevator were supporting the chair and its occupant.

In short order, David Copperfield, master magician, was seated six feet above the stage, his long legs dangling. Gilbert then walked deliberately beneath the chair so that it floated above his head. The magician made a slow 360, and the chair turned with him in perfect unison. Then he extended his arms to the sides and made a second turn while the chair remained facing the house, showing that no supports extended upward from the stage floor.

Gil faced front again at the end of this turn and, still standing beneath the chair, said, "David, would you be so kind as to wave your hands all around and above your head and to move your legs back and forth?"

"I don't want to kick you," Copperfield said.

"Good point," said Gilbert, and the chair rose even higher so that Copperfield's feet dangled clear of Gilbert's head.

The levitated magician first swung his legs, then let go of the chair and waved his arms slowly above his head and from side to side. Only now did Gilbert step free of the chair. He made a sweeping gesture, and the chair, with its obviously uncomfortable passenger, was transported across the front of the stage, allowing anyone sitting in the closest rows to see that there were no visible supports whatsoever. And then, as gradually as the chair had risen, it slowly descended back onto the center stage floor.

The thing had no sooner landed—to a chaotic roar of appreciation—when David Copperfield jumped up and ran to shake Gilbert's hand. His expressive face was eloquent with what Jack was feeling—shock and awe, mostly, but with a healthy dose of breathless exhilaration. One did not see such things without an electric thrill, regardless of how rational or blasé one was about life, the universe, and everything.

David Copperfield—a man who knew volumes about how seeming magic was done—pumped Gilbert's hand and said, "Mr. Gilbertson, I think it is fair to say that I've seen and done a lot of magic in my life, but this has surpassed anything I have ever seen or done. Thank you, sir. This was *spectacular.*"

"Thank *you*, David. Thank you, indeed. This is great praise coming from a man of your experience and skill. But, as the old saying goes: 'You ain't seen nothin' yet.'"

As Copperfield retook his seat in the audience, his face alight with interest, Gil showed his first sign of weariness. He rubbed his temples for a few seconds, then pinched the bridge of his nose.

"Uh-oh," murmured Joan. "Is he okay?"

Jack shook his head, fighting the urge to interrupt. Who knew what damage Gilbert was doing to himself by pushing so hard? But this was his night of nights; Jack wiped sweaty palms on his pants and bit his tongue.

Gilbert quickly regained his composure. He picked up the chair, refolded it, and leaned it against the card table. He then took off his shirt, picked up a length of brilliantly saffron fabric from the table, and wrapped it about his head in a turban. He retrieved the large basket and set it down at center stage. The audience stirred, murmuring, shifting in their seats. They knew what was coming.

Gilbert addressed them. "I know that many of you have heard that a short time ago I performed the Hindu rope trick—exactly as described by the Royal Academy over a hundred years ago—to a small audience of magicians in Chicago. This evening, you will all see this incredible mystery of the Orient, done in the way of legend. Often described but never accomplished—until I, Gilbert the Great, mastered it. Remember what you see, my magical colleagues, please remember it well—for I doubt that this shall ever be done again."

With that dramatic pronouncement, Gilbert the Great proceeded to do the Hindu rope trick, exactly as he had done it in the House of Magic eight days earlier. This time the audience did not interrupt to applaud, but sat in hushed silence. When the boy's severed body parts fell to the floor, some members of the audience gasped and had to turn away. Most horrifically, the boy's severed head rolled to within a few feet of the front row, eyes open and mouth shouting all the while in Hindi.

The applause began as Gilbert pulled the restored assistant from the basket. As the boy stood next to him on stage, bowing and showing the empty interior of the basket from which he'd risen, it reached a crescendo. The entire audience stood to heap praise on the small, pale wizard. For several minutes, Gilbert stood, face shining, and drank in the accolades.

Jack doubted that anyone else noticed the tightness around his eyes or the quivering of his jaw. Clearly he was in a lot of pain. Under the continued applause, Gilbert crossed to the table and drained the glass of water. Then he placed both hands on the table and leaned on it for a moment, seeming to gather his energy.

Jack considered, again, whether he should try to stop things here and now. Before he could form a conviction, Gil removed his turban and put his shirt back on. He then lifted the remaining fabric from the table, which turned out to be a parachute made of a deep red ultralight material that billowed as he carried it out to the center of the stage.

Once there, he called into the wings, "The circus wagon, please."

It was, indeed, an old-fashioned circus wagon with a cage inside it that appeared from the stage-right wings. Pulled by several men, it was barred and brightly colored, and decorated with gaudy paintings of a variety of animals: roaring lions and tigers, graceful circus ponies, elephants. The hands rolled it up onto the stage, pulled a ramp from the rear, opened the cage door, then spirited the other props away, leaving behind only the eagle on its stand.

Gilbert, meanwhile, spread his parachute out on the floor before the cage, then stomped back and forth over it until it lay flat. He then moved to stand next to the wagon. "Ladies and gentlemen," he said, "as you can probably tell, I am a tremendous fan of many of the performers here tonight and of famous magicians of the past. One of the things I often think about is those singular, great tricks that left people talking for years or decades after the fact, as I hope you'll talk about what you've seen here tonight. I think that perhaps the magic trick that I hear most frequently mentioned happened long ago, on a summer night in New York City, in a stuffy, too-warm banquet room. At the end of the meal, without leaving the table, Jewish magician Max Malini asked to borrow a lady diner's hat for a coin trick."

Knowing murmurs arose throughout the audience, and the magicians sitting in the front row nodded, to the last man.

"Yes, some of you know the trick I mean. Mr. Malini would spin a silver dollar, place the woman's hat over it, and ask her if it would come up lady or eagle—that is, heads or tails. She would guess, of course, but when he lifted the hat, there on the table would sit a solid block of ice that seemed too large to have been hidden beneath a lady's hat. The trick you will now see is an homage to Malini's ice block production."

Gilbert moved to stand at the edge of the parachute, facing the audience. He stared intently at the center of the fabric. Nothing seemed to happen for five seconds or so. Then, as with the eagle's shawl, the parachute began to rise, an irregular shape taking form beneath it. And, as with the eagle, there was stirring beneath the cloth. It swiftly reached about six feet in height and continued to grow, the topmost part swaying from side to side. The audience gasped in ragged unison as the parachute stopped growing only when it was over twice Gilbert's height.

Gilbert now walked around the outer edge of the parachute to the front of the stage. Once there, he announced, "Siegfried and Roy gave you the Magic of the White Tiger. I give you the Magic of the White Bear!"

He leaned over, grasped the edge of the parachute in both hands, and pulled it away with a grand flourish to reveal a gigantic, live polar bear, balanced on its hind legs. The bear was not chained, and it seemed to be looking directly into Gilbert's eyes. It was enormous, larger than any bear Jack had ever seen. He estimated it stood well over ten feet and surely must weigh close to a ton.

Jack felt every cell in his body go into flight mode, and divined a similar response from everyone around him. The audience drew back from the menace as a single entity, with cries and gasps of alarm. People in the front row slid lower in their chairs . . . or leapt up and looked for a path of escape.

But at a gesture from Gilbert, the bear dropped to all fours and made a friendly chuffing sound, as if to say, "What's all the fuss?"

"Have no concern," Gilbert said. "You are all perfectly safe." He motioned to the bear to approach him.

The bear lumbered over to nuzzle Gilbert's neck, then it stood passively as the little magician climbed onto its back and rode it around the stage, much as Siegfried and Roy used to ride their white tigers.

The audience burst into applause with cries of, "Bravo!" whistles, and foot stomping. Gilbert was obviously ecstatic, grinning from ear to ear and waving at his new fans. The spotlights followed him as he rode the bear over to the open cage and dismounted. At a gesture, the huge animal rambled up the ramp into the cage and sat down.

"Say good night," Gilbert commanded, and the bear opened its immense mouth and gave a loud roar.

Gilbert closed the cage door, hopped up on the rear of the wagon, and beckoned to the eagle, still on its perch. With two flaps of its mighty wings, the huge bird lifted itself to the roof of the wagon, whereupon Gilbert signaled the stagehands to roll it offstage. They obeyed immediately, stowing the ramp and hauling the cage—bear, magician, eagle, and all—off into the wings. Gilbert smiled and waved until he disappeared from sight.

The audience continued its applause, but clearly there was to be no encore. The house lights came up, signaling that the show was well and truly over.

Conversations started up all around Jack. People marveled, questioned the reality of what they'd just seen, stated their hope that they'd get a chance to see Gilbert the Great perform again, and soon. Jack ignored all of it. All he could think of was Gilbert. He was terrified, he realized, that the younger man had likely just committed suicide. He headed for the wings, leaving Joan to deal with Arnie Rosen, who'd appeared at the end of their aisle looking like he'd had a religious experience. Dodging people, Jack ran backstage and wove through the props, stage sets, and backstage staff to find the magician.

He was gone.

Jack stopped in consternation. Where would he go? Back to the Mirage? Or to the nearest restaurant?

"Are you Dr. Madison?"

Jack turned to find himself facing one of the stagehands who'd wrangled some of the props earlier.

"Yes, I'm Jack Madison."

"Mr. Gilbertson left a message for you." He handed Jack a folded piece of paper and went back to his duties without further comment.

Don't worry, Doctor, Gil had written. *And I know you will worry. I'm okay. But I need to reload. So, I'm off to find the biggest steak in town, drink a pitcher or two of water, then sleep for as long as it takes. I'll contact you when I wake up. Sincerely, Gilbert Gilbertson*

"Jack?" Joan came up beside him and laid a hand on his arm. "Is he—?"

He handed her the note, which she read swiftly. She looked up at him. "Rosen wants a meeting. Right now, while this is all fresh."

"What could we possibly have to meet about?" Jack asked ironically.

The corner of Joan's mouth twitched wryly. "I don't know, but aren't you just agog with curiosity?"

Chapter 24

Seeking Arnie Rosen, Jack and Joan were directed to a meeting room in the Rio's mezzanine-level event space. They walked into the middle of a verbal cage match. While Arnie Rosen and Devin Spader stood at the rear of the room looking disconcerted, a half dozen of the pro magicians who'd been present for Gil's performance went at it in the center aisle, flanked by chairs set up for the panels held earlier in the day. The group included Penn and Teller, David Copperfield, David Blaine, Criss Angel, and Lance Burton. A watchful Wil Benson stood on the periphery, apparently trying to run interference.

"I'm telling you," Penn Jillette was saying, "I was not—I repeat, *not*—part of a setup. Okay?"

"Yeah," argued Blaine, facing off against the taller man, "but you failed to pull his teeth. I mean normally, you'd just call him out and explain how he did it. You *let* him get away with—"

"I didn't *let* him get away with a damn thing!"

"Gentlemen!" Admiral Benson held up his hands in a placating gesture. "Please. Let's be civil."

Blaine ignored him. "If you didn't help him out, how did he 'read' your mind?"

"I don't fucking *know*! I admit, when I walked out there, I figured he was just doing a schmuck's con. I mean, c'mon. You know me well

333

enough; what else would be going through my mind? But he used the words 'asshole' and 'jack-off.' He didn't just go for generalities. He literally repeated back my exact thoughts. And he kept on doing it. When he mentioned my uncle, I almost crapped my pants. Honest, I did first think of Einstein, and my uncle, and Mom, and the dog. He was not only right about the components, but that was the order they came to mind. And I'll be damned if I can tell you how he knew that goddamn dog's name."

"And that doesn't explain the bill trick," said Copperfield quietly. "Or the levitation or," he added, looking pointedly at Blaine, "the croquet balls."

Jillette nodded. "The bill trick? Oh, *hell*, yeah. When he pulled out that old chestnut, I was suspecting a Himber wallet and a shill, but Blaine, you picked the guy out of the audience. And you saw me try and screw him up with the bill numbers, but he got it right anyway. This was real spooky shit."

"So, if you're not the shills, then who is?" demanded Criss Angel, turning a baleful gaze on Teller.

The famously speechless magician was now anything but. "I was absolutely determined not to say a word, and you guys know, as well as anyone, I'm pretty good at that after all these years. But when he told me that he could make me talk if he wished, I *knew* he could. I *felt* the words wanting to come out. If he had pushed me, I would have done it. Couldn't have helped myself."

Mac King chimed in from the last row of chairs: "For what it's worth, I know that rope trick he did with me may have looked like Bill Neff's routine, but it was nothing at all like it." He pulled the rope out of his jacket pocket and held it up so everyone could see it. It was still an endless loop of rope. "This is not magic store rope, guys. I really did get it at Home Depot." He turned his attention to Arnie Rosen. "By the way, I heard a rumor this magic clown has been screwing with the slots and keno. Is that true?"

Rosen blanched. "No comment, gentlemen. And I do not want to be quoted on even that statement. Not a fucking word spoken in this room leaves here. Okay?"

Jack thought this was a good a time as any to cut in. He moved away from the door. "What happens in Vegas stays in Vegas, Arnie?"

Rosen looked relieved. "Dr. Madison, could you please . . . ?" He made a broad gesture.

Jack inclined his head in assent, though he wasn't quite sure what the guy expected him to do. Rosen introduced him, giving a quick rundown of his credentials. It turned out that everyone in the room knew who he was and had at least seen him interviewed on TV. Penn Jillette and Ray Teller had actually read his books.

"Here's the thing," Jack said, moving up the aisle to lean against the panelists' table that was set up across the front of the meeting room. "You seem to be sweating the small stuff. Unless you're seriously thinking that Penn and Teller were willing shills, I think you need to let that go for now and move on. So, Gil did mind reading and something a bit more . . ."

"Sinister?" asked Criss Angel.

"More disturbing, certainly," agreed Jack. "What about the sleight of hand and the levitation?"

Angel snorted. "As far as I'm concerned—and I don't say this lightly—it was impossible. There were no loads and no tells. Unless those balls were holographic and he had one hell of a Foley artist . . ."

David Copperfield turned to look at Blaine. "David can tell us. I ask again, what about the croquet balls? What about the box? You checked them—carefully, I assume."

Blaine shifted uncomfortably in his chair. "Yeah. Both. There was nothing unusual about the box. It was just a plastic box, no back panels, nothing. And it was as deep as it looked. Plus those balls were solid wood. Wanna talk about your levitation?"

Copperfield shook his head. "I can't even begin to describe what that felt like. It was as if there was solid flooring under the chair . . . except that my feet dangled below it. So it was certainly not a clear plastic platform connected to an offstage device. And there were definitely no wires. It was eerie." He gave the barest hint of a smile. "And pretty damned exciting."

"Yeah," said Jillette wryly, "for us, too."

Lance Burton had dropped into a chair in the front row, listening. Now he leaned forward, elbows on knees, and looked up at Jack. "What about that bird? I kept thinking it must've been loaded in some way, but that leather sleeve was just that—a leather sheath thick enough to protect my arm from those talons." He shivered. "It was weird because the bird was heavy, but not as heavy as I would've expected something that big to be. Man, I'd pay a lot to know how he pulled off that routine."

"That," said Copperfield, "was more than a routine. All of his tricks were . . . extraordinary. And speaking as the subject of the levitation, I think this is something qualitatively different than we're used to seeing. In fact, if he starts a show here in Vegas, the rest of might as well become parking valets."

The Admiral spoke up. "You boys have given me a lot of shit about the Hindu rope trick. If my memory serves me correctly—and it does—several of you accused me of senile ramblings when I told you what we'd seen in Chicago. I've seen it twice now, and one of the things I come back to is how that weak little guy can climb up that rope. And what about that polar bear? Anybody ever see anything like that before?"

There was no response. Everyone knew the answer was no, but no one wanted to say it.

Finally Teller said, "Dr. Madison, is this more your bailiwick than ours? Is this something that needs to be debunked by a scientist instead of a bunch of professional tricksters?"

"I don't know if debunking is the appropriate response to what Gil does. Though I would love to study it scientifically. I can tell you one thing: I have seen a few polar bears in my life, and that bear is—if indeed it really is a bear—among the most tractable specimens I've ever seen."

Penn Jillette frowned. "What do you mean 'if it was indeed a bear'? It sure as hell wasn't a fucking camel. What I can't figure out is how on God's earth he ever got the thing into town. Where did he keep it?"

"You're right about it being tractable," said Burton. "A zoo animal, you think? Or maybe owned by a private party? We could do some sleuthing, find out if there are any animal rescue ranches close by."

There was a moment of silence into which Joan lobbed a question of her own. "Aren't you guys missing the obvious here?"

All eyes turned to her.

She spread her hands in apparent bemusement. "Gentlemen, does it matter how big the bear is or where it came from? It appeared from under a parachute on a solid stage."

"Well, not solid, exactly," admitted Jillette, scratching his cheek.

She gave him a droll look. "You boys got room under that stage for a twelve-foot-tall polar bear?"

"No, ma'am."

"So," Jack said, "no clues to how he did his act?"

Blaine wandered up the aisle to join Burton in the front row. "At one point, I was thinking some kind of holographic projections, sort of a portable version of Disney's Haunted Mansion, but that just couldn't be. As I said, those croquet balls were solid wood. And I know from experience that you need a medium to do holographics that solid looking. Smoke or mist. There was none."

"David's right," said Burton. "If he sticks around, we're going to have our hands full trying to keep up with him."

"I don't think you have to worry about that," Jack said softly. "I don't think you'll ever see this act again."

"What makes you say that?" Spader spoke for the first time. Jack had almost forgotten he was there.

"Gil made it clear that he intended to hang up his magic hat after this. This is a one-time thing. I really can't say more than that."

"Did anybody record this?" asked Blaine.

Rosen shook his head. "Nope. Part of the deal with Gilbertson was no video. Frankly, I'm just as glad we didn't record it. I just hope this fucker is happy now and goes away. I can only imagine the media tomorrow when word of this gets out. Here's what we all say: we saw a spectacular show, we are impressed by his work, and magicians never discuss how tricks are done. Period."

The expressions on the magicians' faces were eloquent with their disdain for that proposal. Jack met Joan's eyes and knew she'd caught that too. He doubted anyone could stop these guys from discussing this as much as they bloody well pleased.

A knock sounded on the door, and Menkin, the director of the venue, poked his head in and beckoned Rosen over to him. They spoke for a few seconds, then Menkin handed Rosen a piece of paper.

Rosen scanned it, then turned to the assembled group. "Well, what do you think of this? The eagle and the bear are gone. They were in the cages, a trainer was backstage with them, and they just disappeared. Nobody knows where they are. The trainers said the cage doors were still firmly locked. Gilbertson apparently left Dr. Madison a note." He looked at Jack. "Care to share, Doc?"

Jack shrugged, taking the note out of his pocket to glance at it. "Gil said he was exhausted and ravenous and intended to eat and sleep, in that order, and would contact me when he was ready to be seen again." He had to admit, he rather admired the way the seemingly meek Gilbert managed to call the shots for even people as allegedly powerful as Arnie Rosen and Chief Spader.

During the brief lull, the magicians had gone back to dissecting Gil's performance, and Spader moved to peer over Jack's shoulder at the note.

"Have I got a polar bear loose in this city, Doctor?" he asked.

"Captain, I believe I can state with a ninety-nine percent certainty that the bear is gone."

"Gone?"

"Yes, Captain, gone. As in, not wandering loose in Las Vegas."

Spader screwed his face into a mask of disdain. "If that bear causes any problems . . . Tell you what, regardless, I'm going to scour this place for any signs of it."

"Hey, if that makes you feel more at ease," Jack replied, shrugging. "I'd hate to see you develop a facial tick . . . like Father Lyons."

Spader's eyes narrowed, and he rather hurriedly let himself out of
the room.

"Why did you let Spader know that you knew about that meeting
with Lyons and Gilbert?" Joan asked when they were in the secure
confines of her car and headed back to her place.

Jack stared out the window of the car, barely seeing the brilliant
lights of Las Vegas. "I wanted Spader to know that we're not blind to
his connections. Maybe get him to think about where his loyalties lie.
He's supposed to be a secular law enforcement officer. Right now, it
seems to me that his relationship with Powell—whatever it is—might
be challenging to his objectivity."

"Do you really think the bear is gone?"

"Yeah, I do. I'll know for sure when I talk with your buddy Roscoe
and see if he got anything on video. But I'm starting to put the pieces
together."

"That was taking quite a chance, you know, Jack. Having Roscoe
record him. Even from where he was sitting on the catwalk, Gil
might've made him."

"I don't think so. Gil seemed quite happy with the whole affair. He's
never met Roscoe, doesn't know the . . . the texture of his thoughts."

"Hmm. Well, I'll be interested to see what Roscoe got. It's a sure
thing those pros haven't the faintest idea of how he did what he did
tonight. He made quite the impression."

Jack sighed, feeling sudden discontent, even sorrow. "Yeah, but he
won't be here to remind people. Three months from now, he'll just be
a shiny memory, or people will have talked themselves into believing
they didn't see what they actually saw. And those that do believe . .

. well, he'll be something guys talk about late at night when they're sitting around in their cups. Historically, there have always been tricks that no one has any clue about how they were done. People either exaggerate or explain them away. Then, as the years go by, they forget that they were ever . . . all that, if I may use that expression."

"Like the Hindu rope trick."

"Exactly."

"But that trick is legendary, Jack. So maybe Gil will be a legend, too. And isn't that all he's ever really wanted?"

She had a point. "Yeah."

She was silent for a quarter mile or so, then said, "You know, I kind of wish you hadn't said what you did to Captain Spader. If he's in too deep with the Society, you may have just thrown a can of gas on a fire."

Jack swallowed. She had a point there, too. "Probably shouldn't have, but can't take it back. And who knows, maybe it'll flush out Lyons and his cronies."

"Oh, I'll just bet it'll flush them out, Jack. I'm just worried about what they'll do when flushed."

"Aren't you just the little bluebird of doom," he said with mock severity, turning his head to admire her profile.

She didn't laugh. She gave him a severe look from the corner of her eye, with nothing mock about it and said, "First thing in the morning, Doc, you're calling the cardinal."

"Yes, ma'am. Can I at least have my coffee first?"

Finally, she laughed.

Chapter 25

"We have been terribly misguided, my brothers. Gilbertson is not a gift from God to mankind and to our holy cause. He is the opposite—an agent and weapon of the Devil."

Father Michael Lyons turned from the window of Bishop Powell's residential office to face the other men in the room—Brothers Matthew and Humility, the bishop himself, and Chief of Detectives Spader. His face was drawn into a rictus of loathing; his fists were clenched at his sides.

"But tonight," Spader interjected, "the things he did—"

"What he did tonight only proves my point. This was not a magic show, this was supernatural intervention—but not by God. It was perpetrated by the Great Dragon, Satan, through his agent. Every magician in that auditorium tonight was fooled. *I* was not fooled. An eagle. A bear. The trickster lacked only a leopard and a lion to seal his mockery of scripture. He read one man's mind, made objects appear, levitated a man, and brought forth impossible animals from the fires of Hell! He defied the laws of the universe, just as prophesied."

"'For there shall arise false Christs and false prophets,'" quoted Brother Humility in a hushed and awe-filled voice, 'and shall shew great signs and wonders, insomuch as to deceive (if possible) even the elect.'"

Lyons cringed as if about to go into a seizure. A tic twitched at the corner of his right eye. "Only a day ago, that man caused me to act as if I were demon possessed by the sheer power of his will—or the will of the one who gives him power."

Devin Spader bowed his head and studied the grain of Bishop Powell's hardwood floor. One minute Gilbertson had been their saint-in-waiting, and now he was the beast of prophecy? Perhaps churchmen knew more of these things than he did, but what Lyons was saying hardly made sense to him.

"But you once believed him sent from God," he said, barely able to keep the exasperation out of his voice.

"Before I knew of *that!*" Lyons gestured at the prints of Gilbertson's MRIs that lay scattered atop the bishop's desk. "What a fool I was to have been so nearly taken in! It is time to take things into our own hands, my friends. It is the will of God that we act."

Captain Spader shifted uneasily. "Hold on a minute, Father. My faith is the heart of my life, but using our religious beliefs as an excuse to break the law and cause others harm is hardly a demonstration of faith. I'm trying to be true to my God, but what you're saying . . . we can't act on your interpretation of a few lines of scripture."

Lyons's face flushed, making his pale eyes stand out in glittering contrast. "I assure you, brother, it is far more than a few lines of scripture, and I am guided in my interpretation—"

"The same way you were guided to think Gilbertson was an angel or a prophet or something? Let me tell you all, right now, that we cannot take the law into our own hands. Period. Full stop. No one is going to do anything illegal here. Not on my watch!"

"Captain, what would you say if I told you that I believe Gilbert Gilbertson could well be the Antichrist?"

"I'd say I have heard enough of your particular interpretation of scripture. I think it's time for you and your brothers, here, to go back to Los Angeles. If you're not gone by tomorrow morning, I will personally see you out of town. I don't like Jack Madison any better than you do, but I cannot believe that inoffensive little mouse of a magician is a biblical horror."

Lyons opened his mouth, most likely to utter more verses of scripture, but Spader shut him down. "Don't cite chapter and verse to me, Father. St. John says there is a spirit of antichrist, and I've been around Gil Gilbertson long enough to know that he doesn't have it. Neither, for all his atheistic twaddle, does Jack Madison. He may be an arrogant ass, but he's not evil." He turned to shoot Bishop Powell a narrow look. "Excellency, I don't know how you got me into this mess, and frankly, I don't know how deep into it you are yourself, but you had better rethink your involvement with these men if you think they will really do violence to anyone. That is neither right nor righteous. And you know it, sir."

Powell said nothing. He seemed flustered, and his face was nearly as pale as his cassock. Spader shook his head, gave the three clergymen a parting glance, and headed for the door.

Lyons spoke from behind him. "God's will shall prevail."

Spader turned at the door and looked back, spearing the priest with a glance. "I sure hope so. I'll let myself out."

Chapter 26

On Tuesday morning, Joan lay awake watching the sunlight creep across the bed to light Jack's face. He was a stunningly attractive man at any age, and she had a random, fleeting wish that she'd met him before Carolyn had. It was an unworthy thought, and she apologized to God immediately for having had it.

"I dreamed about you last night," Jack said. His eyes were still closed, for which she was glad.

"Really?" She tried to sound skeptical.

"Really. We were in a cave with a waterfall, lit like one of those tourist spots—all froth and crystal—and you were wearing a flowing silver gown. Looked like you were wearing the water. You were like a goddess or something. You fed me and gave me wine and made love to me and sang me songs."

"That was no dream, you silly man. That was last night, don't you remember? And I was covered in froth and water in a hot tub." She leaned in and kissed his forehead. "But I do like the goddess part. Who was I, Aphrodite? Athena? Diana, goddess of the hunt?"

He opened his eyes and reached up, pushing her hair back from her face. "Definitely Athena. You are a genuine wise woman. You see right through things, people . . . me."

"That's why I'm good at my job."

"Yeah. Which makes me wonder if you really want to give it up. Are you sure?"

"Sure as sure can be. I told you before all this: I'm ready to move on. Complete my degree and live somewhere besides this place I got stuck in all those years back. What about you? Are you sure you want Chicago to be the place I live?"

"Well, it will make our marriage more manageable."

Joan felt as if she'd been dropped into the eye of a storm. In here was quiet, stillness. Along the periphery was a chaotic whirlwind of emotion. She did not want to respond while in the grip of that storm. She needed to stay in the eye.

"Are you sure that's what you want, Jack? Marriage?"

He rolled up on one elbow and studied her face. "I don't know if it's being a doctor and having seen all of the bad that can happen to people, or losing Carolyn the way I did, or being alone for almost two years. Whatever it is, it's forced me to have to know myself. You've helped with that self-knowledge more than I can say. Helped me understand what I want—who I want to be. So, I know what I want. And what I want is you. And I know who I want to be. I want to be Jack Madison, Joan Firestone's partner in life. It's not that I can't imagine my life without you—I don't have to imagine it; I lived it. I don't *want* to imagine my life without you."

"Well, that's a kissing line, if I ever heard one." She started to kiss him, but he held her at bay.

"Marry me, Joan Firestone?"

"Will you call me Athena, goddess of wisdom?"

He sighed. "From now on I'm going to keep my dreams to myself."

"Yes," she said. "Yes, I will marry you. If your daughters approve."

Jack snorted. "Are you kidding? Irene was egging me on, and Katy was cheerleading."

"I think I'm going to like your daughters."

They lingered over breakfast in the sunny nook overlooking Joan's backyard. Afterward, over coffee, Jack checked his phone messages. He had a call from Bill Pittman at the Neurological Institute, which he returned immediately.

"Jack," said Bill when he came on the line, "is what I'm hearing about the magic show last night true?"

Well, that was unexpected. "Depends on what you're hearing. How did you find out about it already?"

"Are you kidding me? It's all over town. My wife wants me to have you get us tickets for the next show!"

Deep breath. "Bill, I think you and I know that there's not going to be a next show."

Pittman sighed. "Yeah, I've spoken to two neurosurgeons—one at Stanford and another at Johns Hopkins—and they both say that, based on the MRI, the growth is inoperable. You'd be effectively cutting out half of his brain. I even called Pittsburgh and asked about whether the Gamma Knife might work, and they said there wasn't a chance. Frankly, Jack, I doubt even if we had the tech, there'd be enough time . . ."

Exhale. "Yeah, that's what I thought too. Look, Bill, I've got one more rabbit left in my hat. Well, probably more of a wild hare, but . . ."

"I'm listening. What've you got?"

A ping from his phone told Jack another call was waiting. He checked the caller ID; it was Tom O'Connor. "Hey, Bill. I've got another call I need to take. I'll get back to you on the wild hare."

"Sure thing. Later."

Jack switched to the incoming call. "Tom."

"How'd Gilbert do last night? Is he . . . okay?" The cardinal's voice sounded unusually tentative.

"No. And there's not a damn thing I or anyone else can do about it at this point, I'm afraid. Every time he stresses himself as he did last night, that mass grows. He's a menace to his own health and well-being." He briefly described Gilbert's spectacular *tour de force* the prior evening, then said, "Speaking of menaces, your erstwhile sidekick is definitely here in Las Vegas. He showed up with Rosen and Spader at a meeting with Gilbert—was pretty rude to him as it happens."

Jack could almost hear Tom's forehead wrinkling in a frown. "That's not good. But not unexpected. Lyons has always thought of himself as a Bible scholar. When you told me about Gilbert's brain lesion, I connected it with the prophecies in the apocalypse of St. John almost immediately. I imagine he's done the same. That would explain his reaction to Gilbert. He's gone from righteous miracle worker to beast."

"So, what does Lyons imagine he can do about the fulfillment of prophecy?"

"Prevent it from happening. The prophecy requires that the beast's head be healed of its grievous wound. This is pure speculation on my part, but I'd think that the Society would like to keep that healing from occurring."

Jack shook his head in frustration. "I read those prophecies after you brought them to my attention. Gil is completely innocent of many of the components of the typical antichrist legend. He's not a charismatic leader, has no Middle East ties—"

"But he *is* charismatic, Jack. Look at the effect you say he has on his audiences. On other magicians. Even on you. You and Joan want to protect him, fight for him."

"Yeah, but not because he's lordly and powerful. It's because despite all his abilities, he's vulnerable."

"I assure you. All those things will go over Lyons's head if he's convinced himself that Gil Gilbertson is a minion of the Devil."

"Minion, my ass," growled Jack. "He's a babe in the woods."

"Yes, in your world. In Michael Lyons's world, that seeming vulnerability only makes Gil seem more dangerous."

"Camouflage."

"In a word, yes. And, of course, the fact that this is all happening in the modern-day Sodom and Gomorrah doesn't help things."

"That's about the craziest thing I've ever heard, Tom. And I have heard a great many crazy things. Besides, Gilbert is not going to be around for much longer without a curative operation. One that is not going to happen, according to all the experts we've consulted. Even if it were possible, Gilbert is adamant that he'll never have another diagnostic or therapeutic procedure. Without it, odds of him living another few months are pretty slim."

There was a moment of leaden silence, then Tom said, "It's not really Gilbertson I'm worried about Jack; it's you. These people saw you as the enemy before Gilbert raised a new blip on their radar. Now they think you're the one who's helped Gilbert acquire a following, the one who might heal him."

Jack glanced across the table at Joan. She was ostensibly reading the news on her iPad, but he knew she was listening to his side of the conversation. "They're rank amateurs, Tom," he said casually. "They haven't even bothered to barrage me with threatening tweets or hate mail. They'll have to get in line."

"Jack, I have been on the phone since four this morning with some personal contacts who know a great deal about this radical group. With Coughlin gone, Lyons is the ringleader, and believe me, I'm not blowing smoke. These guys are every bit as deranged as any Islamist or neo-Nazi. I wouldn't put anything past them. Look . . . I'm going to fly out to Las Vegas later today. I think it's time I had a long talk with Bishop Powell—and Lyons, if I can. Maybe I can find out the truth about Powell's history with Gil and Ruth, and put the fear of the Lord into Lyons. In the meantime, you and Joan be very careful. I'll see you late this afternoon."

Joan was watching Jack like a hawk when he hung up the burner phone. He felt as if she were looking right through him into his innermost thoughts. It was disconcerting.

"He's worried about you," she said.

"Damn, how do you do that?"

She rose from the table and gathered up her dishes. "Don't dodge. I'm going to put a security detail on Gilbert . . . and you, too."

"Let's hold off on that, okay? I'm really not all that concerned. Sure Lyons and his bunch are radical, but for God's sake, he's a priest."

She set the dishes down again. "Jack, are you forgetting that Father Lyons is in league with those terrorists that burn down abortion clinics?"

"All right, look, call up your security detail if you insist. But have them concentrate on Gilbert. In fact, I'm going to call him right now." He suited action to word and called the Mirage, asking for Gilbert's room. After four or five rings Gil answered. He sounded groggy.

"I'm sorry, Gilbert. Sounds like I woke you up."

"No. I've been 'wake fer a while, but I'vn't been able t' get up. Feel awful, Doc, jus' awful. Pain in my head is worst it's e'er been. Med'cine's not working. You come over?"

Jack didn't have to convince Joan this was an occasion to use her roof light and siren. The slurred speech and grogginess told Jack all he needed to know about Gilbert's condition. Joan called the dispatcher and requested an ambulance to meet them at the hotel. They got to the Mirage in record time, the paramedics arriving only moments after. Joan had the foresight to request that hotel security accompany them to Gil's room. This proved to be prescient; Gil did not answer their knock, and the security officer had to let them in.

Inside the room, they found Gilbert still in bed in his pajamas. His eyes drooped half open; his right pupil was enlarged.

"He's beginning to hemorrhage," said Jack. "I'm going to call Pittman, have him meet us at the university medical center." *And ask if he knows any neurosurgeons who can pull rabbits out of their hats.*

The paramedics swung into action immediately, starting an IV and moving Gil from the bed to a gurney. Models of efficiency and care, they had him out of the room and downstairs on the way to the waiting ambulance in roughly five minutes. Jack and Joan followed, crossing beneath the portico in the wake of the EMTs, heading for Joan's car.

That was when Jack saw Chief Spader coming toward them along the front of the hotel to their right. Spader raised a hand, not to wave, but to gesture urgently past them toward the road. Frowning, Jack turned in the direction Spader indicated. He saw three men in priestly garb and recognized Lyons as the priest lifted an arm to point at him.

Someone shouted, "Get down! Get down! Get down!"

"Jack!" Joan snarled just before she threw herself against him, pushing him toward a parked car.

There was a loud *pop!* and Jack felt a searing pain in his back below his left shoulder. He fell then, the ground rushing up to meet him. The popping sounds and shouting continued, growing louder before they faded away.

Fireworks, he thought. Someone was setting off fireworks in the middle of the day.

Chapter 27

Jack woke in an ICU bed with an endotracheal tube in his windpipe. If that were not unpleasant enough, his left side hurt like hell in a dull, all-consuming throb . . . until he breathed, then the pain seared like a hot knife. He tried to talk, though he knew the futility of that with the tube in place. Fortunately, his nurse saw that he was awake and hurried to his bedside.

"Easy, Dr. Madison. You're doing fine. Try to relax and we'll get that tube out as soon as we've checked your oxygen saturation levels." She bent slightly and pressed a lighted button on the monitor rack at the head of the bed, then straightened again, smiling. "I imagine you're wondering what happened. You've been shot, Doctor. You had emergency surgery the day before yesterday. A complete success; you're going to be just fine. You've got two drainage tubes in your left side that should be coming out in the next few days. Both of your daughters are here and a friend. As soon as we get that trach tube out, I'll let them come in and see you."

She bustled off then, leaving Jack to flog his gray cells into unwilling activity. He could tell it was night, and he struggled to remember how he had been shot—Tuesday! He remembered the scene beneath the hotel portico as if it were from a TV show. Watching Gilbert being delivered to the ambulance, seeing Spader . . .

Had Spader shot him?

No, Spader had tried to warn him about Lyons, who'd raised an accusing hand. Lyons had shot him. Joan had tried to push him out of the way.

Joan. Where was Joan? She wasn't among those the nurse had announced were in the waiting room. Unless she was the friend mentioned. She was a police detective after all, so perhaps that didn't qualify her as friend or family. She was probably asleep or down at HQ filling out papers.

Jack tried to take a deep breath and almost choked on the trach tube as pain lanced through his rib cage. He had never been here before. Never been the still form on the stretcher. Never been the helpless human in the ICU bed. He had been helpless at Carolyn's deathbed, but he could at least pretend to have some control in that role. Here, he had not even pretense. He could only lie here and wait for the nurse to return.

She did that a few minutes later to remove the endotracheal tube. He coughed a lot and it hurt, but that was swiftly overtaken by the sheer relief of having it out. True to her word, after he had sipped some water and tested his voice, the nurse brought Katy and Irene in. The friend turned out to be Tom O'Connor.

Irene came through the door first, her expressive face going from concern to relief. "Daddy! Thank God you're okay. You've been out of it for almost two days."

Katy was right behind her. She said only, "Oh, Daddy!" and rushed to kiss his forehead and hold his hand.

Cardinal Tom was dressed unassumingly in street clothes with a clerical collar tucked into the lapels of his shirt. He stood inside the door, letting the girls assuage their anxiety over their father's condition.

Irene moved to put an arm around her younger sister's shoulders. "So, now you think you're James Bond, do you?" she asked Jack with severity that was only half-feigned. "Damn it, Daddy, you're a doctor, not an FBI agent."

"Bond was MI-Five," Jack objected. "They told you what happened, I take it."

"Yes. You were shot. By a fanatical priest, apparently."

"Gilbert?" Jack looked past his girls to Tom.

"The police think Gilbert was shielded by the ambulance. You presented Lyons with a better target."

"But is Gilbert okay?"

"He wasn't hit, but his condition isn't good. The lesion is killing him, Jack. As you feared it would."

Jack spoke the name that no one else had spoken. He tried to speak it without dread: "Joan. Where's Joan?"

Both girls looked down, and Tom's lips compressed. Dread raced through Jack's mind and body.

"Jack," said Tom, "Joan threw herself between you and the shooter. She was shot in the abdomen and has had extensive surgery."

"Then she's in the ICU too." Jack felt an urgent need to get up out of his bed but knew that to be impossible.

Tom nodded. "I won't lie to you, Jack. Her condition is poor."

Jack entertained any number of responses to that and settled on denial. Joan was a fighter; she would fight to live. She'd pull through.

"Daddy," Irene said, "I called Greg Wilson as soon as I understood the situation. He flew out with us. He's with Joan now."

Greg Wilson was chief of trauma surgery at MSM in Chicago, and a close friend of the Madison family. It was typical Irene to have gone to him so immediately. Jack found himself overwhelmed by contradictory feelings of impotence and safety. He was helpless, but his family—especially take-charge Irene—had his back. Did Joan have that same sense as she battled for survival?

As if divining the tenor of his thoughts, Irene said, "Joan's mother is here too; we've spent a lot of time with her."

"Does Joan know she's here?"

The girls exchanged glances, then Katy said, "She's still unconscious, Daddy. Your operation was over by the time we got here from Chicago," she rushed on. "Greg consulted with your surgeon, though. He said the bullet went through your lung and caused a lot of bleeding, but they were able to save it. You needed several blood transfusions."

Jack understood that asking the girls or Tom about Joan wasn't profitable. He'd have to wait to talk to Greg. He decided to ask the other questions that were pressing to come out.

"What happened at the hotel? I mean, what happened with Lyons? Did they arrest him?"

Tom answered. "He's dead. He refused to stand down, and Chief Spader shot him. His companions were unarmed and claim ignorance of any planned violence; they're both in jail. Spader . . . Spader is in absolute shock. He clearly meant no harm to anyone and is devastated that he was part of this whole mess. In fact, he confessed to me—not in the Church sense—that he had told Lyons to leave town before there was any trouble. Right now, he believes this is all his fault."

"Has Bill Pittman seen Gilbert?"

Tom nodded. "He came in yesterday and got him stabilized and stopped by again today as well. Gilbert's in good hands, Jack. As is Joan. Dr. Wilson told us her surgical team was fantastic and that she would have died but for them."

Jack met his old friend's eyes and got the unspoken message: Joan wasn't doing well. He felt a cold lump form in the pit of his stomach.

Irene, in her role as cheerleader, seemed to take the sudden change in Jack's demeanor as a cue to herd her charges out of the room. He was barely aware of their leaving. Suddenly, they were gone and the nurse was back to administer some pain meds. Jack hoped it wouldn't make him dozy; he was too afraid to sleep, afraid that when he woke up, Joan would be gone. But sleep he did, and awakened to find sun pouring through the window blinds.

He came fully awake on a surge of freezing adrenaline and called the nurse. She insisted that his drains needed to be removed before she would do anything else, but ten minutes after that, he was face-to-face with Greg Wilson, demanding an update on Joan's condition.

Greg sat down in a visitor's chair, pulled off his glasses, and rubbed the bridge of his nose. "Jack, it was pretty bad. Two shots in the upper right quadrant of her abdomen. Tore up her liver real bad, nicked her inferior *vena cava* and right diaphragm. She was lucky to get out of the OR. They had to remove about three-fourths of her liver but were able to repair her vena cava and diaphragm. The surgeons were amazing! She's still on a ventilator and will be for a while. Big problem is maintaining liver function with all of that trauma. She is developing jaundice and getting some associated kidney insufficiency."

Jack swallowed. "I know that the human liver is able to regenerate. Is that a possibility?"

"Liver regeneration can take months, Jack. Best case scenario: what remains of her liver will be enough to buy her the needed time for that to happen."

"Greg, I need to see her."

Greg opened his mouth to discourage the idea, but apparently the look on Jack's face changed his mind. He grumbled a bit as he managed to get Jack into a wheelchair and took him down the hall to Joan's room in the ICU.

"I'll be back for you in a bit," he told Jack. "I have to check in with my office in Chicago."

He slipped out of the room, but Joan had already claimed all of Jack's attention. She looked horrible; her face was puffy and her skin sallow with developing jaundice. Jack got as close to her bed as the wheelchair would allow and called her name. Her eyelids fluttered, but there was no other response. Jack took her hand.

"Joan, honey. Joan, listen to me. I need you to come through this, okay? I just barely found you, and I am no way willing to let you go without a fight. If I have to play Orpheus to your Eurydice, I swear to God, I'll do it. He'll send you back just to make me stop singing." He tried to laugh and couldn't, so he pressed her hand to his forehead, wishing he could hold her, wishing she would open her glorious eyes and look right through him the way she did and see to the bottom of his soul. "I love you, Joan. I need your love, your wisdom, your humor, and your voice. Don't let go, all right? Don't."

Her fingers flexed in his. Not much, but enough that he was certain she'd heard him. Certain she knew he was there. That wasn't enough.

"I'm so sorry, Joan. I should have listened to you about the security detail. If I had . . ."

She squeezed his hand again, harder this time. He stifled a groan and kissed her fingers.

"You must be Jack."

Jack turned to see a lovely black woman who looked younger than the sixty-plus he knew she had, standing inside the door. She came toward him with her hand extended.

"Joanie has been telling me so much about you. What a shame that we have to meet like this. I'm her mother, Rachel Firestone."

He took her hand. It was warm and reassuring like her daughter's. He tried to speak but couldn't.

"Your daughters and Cardinal O'Connor have been so kind to me," Rachel told him. "I'm here with my sister, and they have treated us like we're part of your family."

Jack found his voice. "As far as I'm concerned, you *are* part of my family. I—I asked Joan to marry me. I don't know if she'd had time to tell you."

"She didn't, but I'm so happy to hear it. I've been hoping my Joan would meet someone who would appreciate her as more than just a good detective or a good student. Someone who wasn't threatened by her strength." She tilted her head to one side and Jack realized where Joan had gotten the gesture. "It takes a rare man not to be threatened by a woman like my Joan."

"We've had our moments. Trying to decide who gets to lead in the dance." Jack tried to smile. "I get waltzes. She gets fox trot. Tango, we split the difference."

Rachel Firestone's smile was quite as blinding as her daughter's. "Sounds like a good arrangement."

Jack had much more he wanted to talk with Rachel about, but Greg appeared in the doorway to demand he go back to bed. He didn't want to, of course. He clung to the superstitious absurdity that if he kept his eyes on Joan, she couldn't die. But the nurse and Greg both insisted. So Jack went back to his room and prayed for the first time since he was twelve. Then, he asked to see Dr. Pittman the next time he was on the floor.

"How's Gilbert doing, Bill?" were the first words out of Jack's mouth when the neuroradiologist appeared in his room.

"When he arrived here, he was almost in a complete coma. I knew the AVM must have started leaking, so they decompressed his brain with a shunt and he's improved a bit. He's awake and alert, but it's only a matter of time. I put your wild hare idea to my friend at Stanford, Jack. He thinks there's a paper-thin chance that forcing the AVM to thrombose could work—that if the thing were cut off from its supply of blood, it might shrink enough that it could be safely removed."

"Would he be willing to perform the surgery himself?"

"Willing? He volunteered. He's ready to fly out here on a moment's notice. You know neurosurgeons—half of them are crazy and all of them are half crazy. The major task would be getting Gilbert to go for it. He's still upset about the shunt. He told me he doesn't want surgery. If you can't persuade him . . ." He shook his head. "He doesn't have much time, Jack, even if he never does another magic trick."

"Can you arrange it so I can talk to him?"

"Well, I don't know what harm it can do. Sure, I'll go get him. Right now, I think he's more travel ready than you are."

Bill Pittman left only to return twenty minutes later with Gilbert in a wheelchair. He obligingly left them alone but warned that he'd be back in fifteen minutes to get Gilbert back to bed.

Gilbert looked bad, very weak and pale. He didn't know all of the details regarding the shootings, so Jack gave him a terse recounting. His brow furrowed as Jack spoke, and when Jack had finished, he looked up and asked, "Detective Firestone is dying. Is that what you're saying?"

"No, I . . ." That was denial talking. Time for honesty. "I don't know, Gil. I'm afraid she might be. But I didn't bring you here for that. Dr. Pittman consulted a highly respected neurosurgeon, and he believes there might be a chance to circumvent that thing in your head—without surgically removing it—and maybe kill it."

"You speak as if it's a malevolent intelligence," Gilbert said, still frowning.

"I don't mean to. I just think I might know a way to save your life."

"I see." Gilbert stared blankly at the wall for a moment, then said, "What do you mean—circumvent?"

"The surgeon would simply cut off the blood supply to the lesion. If we starve the AVM of blood, theoretically it should shrink."

"I see," Gilbert said again. "And if it did shrink, what would happen to my . . . my magic."

"I don't know. Your brain would theoretically rewire itself. It's done that already to a great extent to work around the AVM."

"You think my magic might go away."

Jack nodded. "That is one possibility."

"What about the detective? Can't these doctors save her?"

"Gilbert, Joan is dying. Her liver and her kidneys are failing. If she had the time to regrow some of her liver, she might make it, but her doctor isn't sure there's enough time. There's no way for them to grow her a new liver."

Gilbert nodded solemnly, then said, "Could I go see her?"

When Pittman returned, Jack managed to wheedle his permission to have both men taken up to Joan's room. It was late in the evening by now, and the hospital was quiet. Dr. Pittman and Jack's nurse delivered them to Joan's room, then left them alone with her.

"Just for a few minutes," warned the nurse severely, but Jack could tell that there was a warm heart beneath the gruff exterior and suspected that they'd get more than a few minutes if they wanted.

Gilbert wheeled himself to the side of Joan's bed and took her hand, just as Jack had done earlier. He sat for a few minutes watching her, then put his head down on their clasped hands. He began to murmur words that Jack couldn't quite make out. Was he praying? Or . . .

Jack's head came up. "Gil?"

The younger man behaved as if he hadn't heard him. He continued to speak in a soft, almost musical voice. It was like chanting. Then the sound stopped and Gilbert sat up and let go of Joan's hand. He turned to look at Jack with bleary eyes.

"I'm sorry, Doctor. I don't know if it's enough, but that's all that I can do."

"Do?" Jack repeated, feeling his heart ice over. "What did you do?"

Gilbert only shook his head and said, "I'm so weak, and my head is really starting to throb something horrible. Feels like it is going to explode." He put both hands up to his head and pressed at his temples.

"Gilbert . . . ," Jack said, pushing his wheelchair toward him.

"Okay, that's quite enough of that." Bill Pittman strode into the room, gesturing into the hall behind him. He grasped the handles of Gilbert's wheelchair firmly. "Gilbert, you and Dr. Madison are both going right back to bed. And that's the last time we try any of this stuff. Neither of you is up to this right now. You both look like shit."

That night, as Jack lay in his hospital bed, wondering if he'd have a chance to ask Gil what he'd done, he decided to give some sort of nonhypocritical prayer a shot. It was not a comfortable conversation.

"Don't know who or what is out there, if anyone, and I feel like a perfect hypocrite, waiting until now to wonder. If you're there, you know that Joan believes you're there. I hope that counts for something. You know I could do the whole 'save my beloved and I'll believe you exist' cliché, but you also know that I'm not big on clichés. But if you are there and hearing what I have to say, I sure hope you are the God that Tom O'Connor and Joan and my daughters believe you to be. I know I don't follow all of the rules, but you have to admit they're sometimes confusing, depending on who you listen to. But I've always been pretty good to other people, maybe not for the right reasons, but it's impossible for me to believe that doing it because it's in the Bible or some other book is important, or if it really matters at all."

He hesitated, struck by how hard this was, wondering how important the words were. He felt self-conscious asking for favors when he'd been so snarky about religion—sometimes even when someone he loved brought the subject up. He tried on a different attitude.

"Thanks for all the breaks I've gotten in life. I guess I'm asking you for one more. For Joan to live. She is a wonderful woman who is dying because of some people who have a horribly misguided view of you and your messages. I don't believe you're responsible for that, given that they pretty much had to disown your stated preferences to do what they did. But all Joan did was her job . . . no, she did more than her job. She sacrificed her life to save mine. If anything I've read in scripture is halfway accurate, that counts for a lot with you. I won't insult you with any promises of what I will do in the future, except to tell you that I will keep trying, in my own way, to lead an honorable life and do as much good as I am able."

He didn't feel an *amen* was right, so he just said, "Thanks." He was tired, and depressed, and still terrified of sleeping. He slept in fits the rest of the night, waking from dreams of Joan when fear overpowered his medication. He dreamed of Carolyn, too—a strange, half-awake dream in which she seemed to be sitting on the foot of his hospital bed watching him.

"Look at you, Jack," she said, smiling. "You've bitten off more than you can chew, haven't you? How like you. I'm pulling for Joan, you know. I think you need someone like that in your life to balance out that adolescent risk-taking you like to do." She shook her head. "And I thought plummeting down mountainsides on skis was the worst you could do to yourself. You're a crusader, you know. That's not a bad thing, but I think you need some balance in your life. God bless," she added, and vanished.

Suddenly, it was morning and Greg Wilson was yanking open his window shades.

"Good, you're awake," Greg said, appearing at his bedside. "I have to go back to Chicago, Jack. I have a surgery scheduled that I cannot miss. I'm going to check on Joan one more time before I leave and advise the attending surgeon as best I can. I've done all I can for her. Now it's just wait and see."

Jack took in the words and nodded. "You've been great, Greg. I don't have words to thank you for dropping everything and flying out here on no notice."

"Nothing you wouldn't have done if the shoe were on the other foot." Greg squeezed Jack's shoulder and left the room.

He was back not ten minutes later, his face wearing a tense expression that Jack couldn't interpret. He tried to sit up but couldn't.

"What?" he said, knowing that Joan must be in crisis. He'd have Greg take him to her.

"What, I can tell you. How is a mystery. Joan's kidneys have started functioning; she's peeing like crazy—good urine. The attending says it started right around midnight. Her bilirubin is down fifty percent since yesterday. Her blood gases are normal, and they're actually thinking about extubating her if she continues to improve." He paused to smile. "Jack, she's awake and asking for you."

Jack was momentarily unable to assimilate what his friend was saying. "But . . . her liver . . ."

"It's like she just got a liver transplant. Ultrasound an hour ago shows unprecedented growth. Most incredible thing I've ever seen. I think she'll recover. Yesterday, I was sure she wouldn't last two more days."

Jack felt tears sliding down his cheeks and did nothing to stop them or wipe them away. "Take me down there. Please."

That first visit was brief. She was awake, yes, but dopey as hell. Jack could only sit by her bed, hold her hand, and grin like a kid who'd just gotten an entire set of Guardians of the Galaxy action figures for his birthday.

The next day Joan had all her tubes out and was sitting up in her bed when he rolled in. After the litany of assurances and kisses applied to the back of her hand (which was all he could reach), Jack asked the question that had been nagging at him since Greg had visited him the previous day.

"Joan, do you remember Gilbert coming into your room?"

"Sort of. I mean, I thought I'd just dreamed it at first. What I remember most is that when you and he were with me, and while he was holding my hand, I felt this gentle warmth come over me. Not like a fever, but like warm fluid running through me. It seemed to start in my head and flow down through my body. It was as if I could suddenly feel my blood pulsing through my veins. I thought maybe I was dying. I mean, really dying—letting go. But the next thing I knew, I was opening my eyes." She smiled. "You shoulda seen the look on my nurse's face. I thought he was going to faint."

"You remember the shooting?"

She nodded. "In vivid detail. I was terrified he'd gotten you."

"Well, he sort of did get me."

She slapped his hand. "You know what I mean. Devin came in this morning and gave me the rundown on what happened. I took the opportunity to tender my resignation."

"I bet he didn't take that well."

"He was disappointed, but I've been up front with him about my plans to move on, get my music degree, teach. Besides, it didn't escape his notice that you were staying with me. He read those tea leaves accurately. Now tell me, Doctor. How's our man, Gilbert?"

Jack was appalled to realize he had not even asked. He had been so focused on Joan that he had not followed up on Gilbert's condition. He did so now. The news was not good. That morning—the morning after they'd gone to see Joan—Gilbert had suffered a massive intracerebral hemorrhage and slipped into a coma.

Five days later, Jack was allowed to get out of bed and walk, though they insisted he use a walker. He swallowed his pride and hobbled to Gilbert's room. The younger man looked as if he were merely sleeping; his face was relaxed, serene. He looked younger than his thirty years—almost boyish. Jack stood at Gilbert's bedside and found himself praying again. Apologizing for not realizing what Gil had done.

Sacrifice. Joan had sacrificed her well-being for Jack's; Gil had sacrificed his for Joan. *What've I done?* Jack asked, not sure whether he was speaking to God or to himself or to the cosmos. *Who have I sacrificed for?*

Jack watched as a nurse bustled into the room to check Gilbert's vitals and IVs, to peek into his eyes and make notes on her iPad.

He did something instinctive then, not caring whether the nurse saw him or not. He took Gilbert's hand in his own and said, "Thank you, Gilbert. You're greater than any magician I've ever known."

The nurse smiled. She was halfway out of the room when Gil's vitals simply dropped. The heart monitor let out a plaintive wail and the nurse wheeled around and rushed back to Gilbert's side. In seconds, the crash cart appeared and Jack, his own heart thudding, backed out of the way so they could work. He moved toward the window, through which spring sunlight poured, throwing his shadow against the wall above Gil's bed. At least he thought it was his shadow until it moved independently of his head and shoulders—a quick flicker of movement.

He froze, holding his breath. It was the shadow of the great bird— Ruth and Gil's Guardian—thrown exactly as if that being were perched on the foot of Gilbert's bed. In a heartbeat, the head turned, and Jack saw the silhouette of a hooked beak. He could almost imagine the eagle gazing at him over its shoulder. He shivered, and in a flash of shadowy wings, the guardian wraith shot upward, leaving behind Jack's human silhouette.

He shook his head; his shadow moved in unison. The sound of raised voices brought his attention back to the code team. He could tell them that nothing they did would revive their patient. He didn't, though; he simply slipped from the room and went to see Joan.

Gilbert had left a living will so that his kidneys, liver, lungs, and heart would be available for transplantation. He willed his brain to science with directions that, after he died, there should be a full autopsy on his brain and that Doctors Madison and Pittman be made aware of the results. And he left a sealed letter personally addressed to Jack. His nurse said he wrote it after he got back from his visit with Joan, only hours before his lesion ruptured and put him into a terminal coma.

Jack read the letter sitting in Joan's hospital room while she went through a battery of tests of the sort he subjected patients to all the time. The letter read:

Dear Doctor Madison;

Thank you for all that you tried to do for me. You are a good man and it was an honor for me to meet you. I believe I may now call you "friend." Now I know why my mother always thought so highly of you.

I hope I did not cause you too much grief by refusing to have an operation. I just knew it was not my path. Don't know why, but I have always been sure that once this started, there would be a quick ending.

As for Monday, that was the best night of my whole life. Thank you for that, too. Also, for the record, I knew some guy named Roscoe was recording a video on Monday night—but that he was doing it for you. I'm not sure what it's going to show, but I think you will find it interesting. It's okay for you and Ms. Firestone and people you trust to see it, but I don't want it to be public. Not for a while. I'd like to ask that you put it in a vault or safe deposit box for at least 25 years.

I was so sorry you and Detective Firestone were hurt trying to protect me. I could have told you I didn't need your protection, that something much more elemental was protecting me. I could have told you, but I suspect you wouldn't have understood or believed me. I'm glad you took me to see the detective. I was happy to have been able to help. I think she is going to be fine and that the two of you will be very happy together.

If you ever get a chance, please tell the folks at St Mary's in Springfield that I really loved working there and was always grateful for how nice they treated me—even though my magic stunk in those days.

Good luck in your future from your friend,
Gilbert
PS: A goddess is real easy to heal.

Chapter 28

Joan was released the day after Gilbert's death. Her healing was nothing short of miraculous: her liver was back to near normal size, her scars looked as if they were months, not days old. She was a phenom; her doctors were perplexed.

"She heals faster than any person I have ever seen, Dr. Madison," her attending physician told Jack the day she was discharged. "I'm at a loss to understand why. I assume it must be genetics."

Jack smiled. "Maybe it was a miracle," he said without mentioning Gilbert's visit to Joan's bedside the evening of her sudden recovery.

"I'd call it that," the doctor agreed. "Or maybe she's an alien."

Jack laughed—which hurt. "Or a goddess."

"Goddess it is. Let me just put that in her discharge papers."

Jack was released several days later, his ribs sore, his iron depleted. Joan was well enough to drive him back to her place. He had a follow-up appointment with his attending physician the next week and only then *might* be allowed to fly back to Chicago.

Joan installed Jack in one of her two spare bedrooms; her mother had stayed in town and now roosted in the other. Irene had had to go home briefly to put out a fire at work, but Katy had arranged to do her college assignments online; she stayed. Both women hovered over the couple, fed them well, and got to know each other. Irene came back to Vegas the day after Jack's release, intending to spell Katy, but Katy refused to leave until their dad did. After a day or two, it became obvious to Jack that Irene had come as much to be with Joan and her mother as to see him.

Far from disconcerting him, it warmed the cockles of his heart. What he found disconcerting was the way Joan's mother and his daughters joked about the sleeping arrangements and the potential of catching him trying to sneak into Joan's room in the middle of the night.

Then there was the video of Gilbert's act at the Cavalcade of Magic. Roscoe Smith had burned it to a DVD, which he brought to Joan's house. The first part, the rope trick and the mind reading exercise, showed exactly what the live audience had seen: Gilbert magicking a garden variety rope into an impossible loop, reading Penn Jillette's mind, and coming that close to getting Teller to speak. After that, the experience became surreal. For the entire rest of his act, all that the camera caught was Gilbert, standing at center stage in the auditorium. He spoke at all of the appropriate times, but whenever he was supposedly doing manipulations, sleight of hand, levitations, the Hindu rope trick, or the production of either the eagle or bear, the video showed nothing of the sort. He simply stood and spoke, an expression of rapt concentration on his face.

When he called people to the stage, they would mount the ramp, move to stand beside him, fold their arms, close their eyes, and simply recite lines in response to his. The entire physical part of the act was just Gilbert, standing and sometimes holding the sides of his head while his lips moved slowly. He climbed onto the large animal wagon all by himself at the end of the show. The trainers did nothing but move the empty wagon and other props in and out. Whatever the audience was reacting to with cheers, applause, and awful silences, the camera failed to capture.

When the video was done and the screen had gone dark, the three people watching it sat in silence for several minutes before Roscoe asked, "What did we just see?"

Jack let out a pent-up breath. "Reality. Gilbert the Great was never a magician. He was something completely other."

"What?"

"I don't know. A miracle. An angel. I'm not sure it matters. He's gone now, and there are no surviving members of his family to study."

There was only the autopsy.

Bill Pittman brought Jack the report the day after Roscoe's visit. It showed a massive arteriovenous malformation that occupied the entire right side of the magician's brain. Its rupture had killed him.

Jack read the clinical notes with growing fascination.

Interposed with the vessels of the AV malformation is a mass of embryonic-appearing nerve tissue: axons that seem to be traveling in non-directed fashion, and a large number of unrelated glial cells. There is a general absence of laminin throughout. Electron microscopy demonstrates, within this mass of what can only be described as very primitive neural tissue, islands of highly developed synapses. Biochemical analysis shows high concentrations of calcium, and a variety of neurotransmitter components and neuroproteins. Most significant and unusual are the high concentrations of netrins—at levels two to three times higher than that seen in the earliest embryonic tissue of any known animal.

In short, Gilbert's AV malformation contained some of the most primitive and angry-appearing nerve tissue that anyone in Bill's staff had ever seen. All agreed that it must have caused a high degree of neuro-electrical activity. Jack wasn't sure what to think of that. He uploaded the data to his laptop and promised himself—and Bill—that he'd do some serious analysis when he was more fully recovered.

Jack and Joan were both surprised and wary at finding Arnie Rosen in their visitor's queue . . . repeatedly. He came to visit several times and was effusive in the gratitude he and his associates felt for all that they'd done. He was profusely apologetic about his prior attitude, though Jack suspected he was secretly relieved that Gilbert was out of the picture. He never once asked how Jack thought Gilbert had accomplished his great feats of magic, and Jack felt no duty to tell him. He and the Casino Owner's Association came up with an additional $500,000 in recognition of his services to them—not without reminding him of his confidentiality agreement.

He asked Jack if he thought anyone like Gilbert was still "out there somewhere."

Jack toyed with the idea of proclaiming that anyone with an AVM like Gil's *might* be able to replicate his results, but he opted to be more honest.

"I think," he said, "that the odds are overwhelming that Gilbert was vanishingly rare."

"Yeah? What kind of odds?"

You shouldn't have asked. "Greater than the odds of one person winning the Megabucks grand jackpot twice in his lifetime."

Rosen gave him a wry look. "That's been done three times, Doc."

"Wow," said Jack. "Imagine that. I guess I just hope it doesn't happen again before you retire."

The last of the Vegas shoes to drop was Captain Spader, who came to report on the law enforcement aspects of the case. Like Arnie Rosen, he apologized for his earlier behavior.

"I had no right to conceal what I knew about the SPCD and Lyons. I told myself I was doing it because their motives were pure and they meant no harm—that their involvement didn't intersect with your concerns for Gilbert. It wasn't until the evening before the shooting that I realized they were willing to do anything for their cause. They weren't about protecting the Church; they were trying to promote a zealot's view of the world. Trying to shape history to their own ends—as if God wasn't capable of working His will in the world without their help."

He paused and shook his head. "But that's all wrong. What I, or anybody else for that matter, believes concerning the overall direction of the Church, it should never result in violence against another person. When we use the Enemy's tactics, we become the Enemy."

They were sitting in Joan's living room over coffee and something Irene called hamantaschen but Jack had always thought of as tri-corner tarts. Joan leaned forward in her chair and placed a hand over her chief's.

"You didn't do violence to anyone, Dev. You were misled."

"I was slow on the uptake, Joan. And even when I realized the error I'd made, I didn't do what I *should* have done—called you and told you what Lyons was thinking. I just told him to get out of Dodge, as if that was going to make him go away. That trick never works with zealots."

"So what are you going to do?" asked Joan.

"I'm going to tell Cardinal O'Connor everything I know about the Society, for one thing. After that, well, I'm eligible for retirement. I may just do that. I let my religious beliefs interfere with the way I did my job. That's hard to forgive myself for. As is my attitude toward you, Jack. Lyons got it into my head that you were Satan's yappy little dog. I came to realize that you're more Christian than someone like Lyons, who spouts scripture but doesn't actually understand a word of it."

Jack had to smile. "Satan's yappy little dog, huh? I don't get to be a Rottweiler? At least Benedict got to be God's Rottweiler. Look, believe it or not, I know how you feel. I have made more than my share of mistakes over the years and, in my business, as in yours, a mistake can cost someone their life."

Jack regretted the words almost as soon as he'd said them. He had reminded Spader of his own predicament: he'd not only fired his service weapon in the course of duty but had killed a man with it. That meant he was, himself, under investigation by Internal Affairs.

"So," said Joan, no doubt reading Jack's mind, "what's going to happen to Lyons's two buddies?"

"They've pleaded guilty to accessory to attempted manslaughter two. They'll get five to eight years, which I suspect will be a good message to their colleagues in the Society—which, by the way, has gone so deep underground, I can't raise any of them."

"And Powell?" Jack asked, finding even saying the name unpleasant.

Spader looked down at his coffee cup. "It seems Bishop Powell has been unexpectedly transferred to a post in Los Angeles, as an auxiliary bishop of the archdiocese under Cardinal Munoz. It was a polite demotion." The corner of Spader's mouth twitched upward. "Losing his diocese is probably worse than the wool scapula the Society monks wear."

Jack did not give voice to his suspicion that the transfer was a way of keeping Powell away from children . . . and punishing him for the sin of prejudice by making Cardinal Munoz his boss.

"We can't find anything that will hold water against any of the ones who stayed in LA," Spader continued. "They all insist that they were completely unaware of any ill intentions against any of you, and we have no proof otherwise. They're a legitimately odd group, but there's no law against being odd."

"He's okay," Jack told Joan when Spader had left.

Joan nodded, her eyes fixed on some point near the front door Devin Spader had just walked through. "Yes. Yes, he is. I kind of hope he gets through this without losing his career over it. I think police work is in his blood in a way it isn't in mine. I wish him well."

A few weeks later, Joan and Jack flew to Maui for a two-week vacation. They stayed in a fancy hotel, all courtesy of Arnie Rosen and the Casino Association, and even used Rosen's private jet for the round trip. They made a lazy and sensuous time of it, spending many hours talking, getting to know all about one another, discussing the past and what the future might hold for a mixed-race couple. Their families were on board; what other people thought was irrelevant to both of them.

Sitting on the ocean-facing terrace outside their room, Jack broached the idea of getting married in Maui, but Joan was having none of it.

"Jack Madison, have you no sense of kismet? Cardinal O'Connor is going to marry us in the church gardens, I think, with your family and mine there. No white wedding dress or big party; but I want the important people in our lives to witness our vows."

"Does Tom know this?"

"I've already discussed it with him."

"I see. How about your mother and/or my daughters? Have you discussed it with them, too?"

"What do you think? Of course I have. We talked about it while you were recuperating, and we chat online almost every day while you're out catching all those rays and getting rid of that starving artist look you've got going on there. They've already got their dresses."

They married in a side chapel of Holy Name Cathedral as the garden was being soaked by a late summer rain. The ceremony was followed by a small reception for family and friends. That included the Admiral, who spoke for thirty minutes, doing a combination of stories, jokes, and magic tricks, which Cardinal Tom seemed to enjoy as much as anyone. Even the statue of the Holy Virgin seemed to be smiling on the old man. Her smile stayed firmly in place, Jack noted, even when Wilfred told a joke about a sideshow magician who married a female contortionist. It brought down the house; Jack was red with embarrassment. Joan's mom and Tom almost fell off their chairs laughing.

Joan got her degree in music and won a teaching post at DePaul University in Chicago. She loved it, and her students loved her. She and Jack bought a house in Evanston near his daughters. There, one night at a family dinner, Joan announced that Irene and Katy were going to have to share their dad with a much younger sibling. Jack was stunned speechless; Irene and Katy couldn't stop talking; Joan couldn't stop grinning.

"So much," she said, "for the ticking of the biological clock."

At five months, she had an amniocentesis—being, at forty-two, hers was a geriatric pregnancy. Irene and Katy were having a perfectly normal little brother.

Partly in response to this new facet of his life, Jack cut back his consulting hours to concentrate on teaching. But also because it had become important to him to make sure that the young doctors coming up were steeped in the need for cool deliberation and empirical facts, learned to have flexible minds, and were willing to be surprised. Willing, as science fiction writer Phillip K. Dick put it, to "be content with the mysterious."

He had another book in him, too, but he knew it would not be like his previous publications. He'd had most of the snark knocked out of him and all of the certainty that the miraculous was always some form of scam. In some ways, he realized, he was going to give the SPCD and perhaps the entire Catholic Church (if not people of all faiths everywhere) exactly what they wanted: an unblinking admission that he did not always know how things worked. That there might well be explanations for phenomena that were yet beyond the sure comprehension of even a Chicago neurologist and knowledge junkie like Jack Madison.

Until he was ready to write that book, he declined media appearances and, in graduation speeches, told his audience only to keep an open mind, to apply Ockham's razor to every proposition, and to never assume that knowledge could be discarded based solely on its source; not understanding how or why something worked did not mean it wasn't valid or real.

In general, Jack Madison kept a low profile, wondering how long it would be before he stopped seeing the shadow of an eagle from the corner of his eye. And once a month, he went to church with Joan.

Epilogue

On a cool spring evening that marked the anniversary of Gilbert the Great's memorable Las Vegas debut, Cardinal Tom held another dinner to which he invited Joan and Jack, his two daughters, and the Admiral. After several glasses of wine, from which Joan abstained, the group recalled the magical events of the previous year (with many asides from the Admiral).

At length, Tom asked Jack how he put Gilbert's abilities together with his medical condition and with what was on the video, which they had all seen, before Jack had consigned it to a safe deposit box in his bank.

"Even Joan has said you weren't surprised by what was on the Cavalcade video," Tom observed. "That you already suspected there was an element of hypnosis or mass hysteria involved. How did you come to that conclusion?"

Jack shrugged. "What were the options? One: that Gilbert's condition granted him the power to bend the laws of physics even further than most human beings do. Or two: that his condition created a sort of . . . field, I guess you'd say, that allowed him to manipulate the electromagnetic impulses of other minds. Off the record—at least for now—I am firmly convinced that Gilbert had some most unusual cerebral powers. First of all, I think he had literal extrasensory perception. Not stage magic, but the real deal. I think the mass in his brain may have given him the ability to gather electrical signals from other people's brains the way the eye gathers photons or the ears gather sound waves. On occasion, he could send signals back into those other brains. He could give the guy in the Burger King momentary paralysis or give Lyons a facial tic. His mother must have exercised the same ability when she caused those three boys to go blind. In both cases, I think the AVM was an expensive proposition in terms of energy. Poor Gil was always ravenous and thirsty after he'd performed his magic or a healing, and he'd sleep for a day or more to compensate."

"What about the machines, Daddy?" asked Irene. "You said the casino owners were afraid of him manipulating their machines."

Jack spread his hands. "Electrical signals, again. Machines—like slot machines, and the keno random number generators—generate electrical impulses, so—"

Irene snapped her fingers. "Like the way electromagnetic and radio frequencies interact and interfere with sound equipment or radio broadcasts."

Jack nodded, gratified that his daughter hadn't turned her surmise into a question the way so many women her age did. "I'm convinced it's not only possible, but that that's exactly how he did it. Gil once told me he kept his face off of the digital photos—which of course are all electronic—as a clue to me about how he was doing what he was doing."

"Which begs the question," said Joan, "if he could affect a digital video, why didn't he? Why does the video show him doing virtually nothing?"

Katy grinned. "Maybe the video is the lie and what the audience saw was real."

The entire group groaned in close harmony.

"Don't even go there," said Jack. "Hurts my head to even think about it."

"There's one thing I don't get," said Joan. "What you're saying explains the mind-reading, but what explains that first rope trick he did? I got a close look at that rope—which I expect Mac King will never part with. There wasn't a break or patch or seam in it anywhere. It looked as if it had been made that way. According to Roscoe's video, that was real."

They digested that in silence for a moment, then Jack smiled crookedly. "It's a mystery. And I'm content with that."

"Even if none of his magical acts actually happened," said Tom, "even if they were all RF or EMI interference with the visual cortex, that's still amazing. How did he figure out how to do it?"

"From what I gather it was instinct and trial and error. How does a goose know when to fly home to Canada, which direction to go, and when they've gotten there? They have an innate sense of direction. I think Gilbert had an innate sense of how to manipulate electromagnetic fields."

"It's too bad we don't all have that sense," sighed Katy. "Wouldn't it be great if people could just do stuff like that?"

"Would it?" Jack asked. "Gilbert said something to me once about being afraid of his ability to cause other people to do or experience what he wanted. I think that was one of the reasons he was resigned to his fate. He didn't want to abuse his ability. Gilbert," he added, "was an exceptionally gentle soul. Not all human beings are that . . . benign."

"That's a miracle all by itself," said Joan. "Especially after what that poor kid went through."

Tom let out an audible breath. "You think his . . . experiences with Powell triggered all of this?"

Jack nodded, noting Tom's neglect of using the clergyman's title. "I know that both Ruth and Gil interacted with Powell right before they began to manifest these abilities. That doesn't prove causality, but it's highly suggestive of it."

"I wonder," said Joan. "What did all this look like from Gilbert's point of view? I mean, when he was doing his magic act, did he know he was manipulating people's minds or did he think he was really doing it?"

Jack shook his head. "That's a mixed bag. Given the clues he left—the blurry face, his comment about wondering what Roscoe's camera would record—I think he knew. But I also think he let himself dream. That he bought into his own illusion. That it was real to him on some level because it was real to his audience."

"But how, Daddy?" asked Irene. "How does he get *other* people to buy into *his* illusion?"

"I think it's the same principle that works with machinery—the excitation of electromagnetic fields. It's also possible that's the mechanism for the healing as well. I'm not entirely sure how it works. Possibly he was able to cause the release of some sort of embryonic growth hormone or primitive stem cells or something else that triggers what I can only describe as rapid remodeling. That might account for how he could treat a burn or stimulate a liver to regrow but not be able to do anything about cancer."

Katy looked disappointed. "So, not miracles after all, then."

"Who says?" Jack asked. "Isn't it miraculous when someone—not necessarily a Moses or a Christ or a Buddha or some other holy man—learns or knows how to manipulate reality in ways the rest of us don't understand?"

Tom O'Connor shook his head and laughed. "Well, I'll be dipped in chocolate. Dr. Jack Madison is admitting there just might be more to this whole experience than we mere mortals can measure by our feeble attempts at science. I think it's time we all had another drink."

Jack refilled their glasses and proposed a toast.

"Long after we are gone, may there still be tales told of that early spring in the twenty-first century that witnessed true miracles and the greatest magic show ever seen, all performed by Gilbert the Great: King of Cards, Rajah of Ropes, and Master of Mystery."

Notes

1. This is my first novel. I have spent most of my life in scientific writing; fiction is far more difficult.
2. The book would never have been worthy of publication without the professional talent and creativity of Maya Bohnhoff.
3. The views concerning religious topics and ESP expressed in the novel should not be considered as mine.
4. One thing I have learned for sure in my life as a physician and surgeon is that what we are convinced is absolute truth has a funny way of changing. Knowledge of how our bodies and minds work remains embryonic. Read any fifty-year-old medical journal.
5. I believe there is a strong and primitive connection between our minds and the basics of medicine, mythology, religion, spirituality, and magic. Ask any shaman.
6. I have been interested in magic since I was seven or eight years old (seventy-plus years!). I hung around magic stores (Stoner's in Fort Wayne), bought and read books, and spent hours of practice. Magic taught me how to think on my feet, to speak to an audience, to recover from failure, and increase my dexterity (which helped me as a surgeon). Later in life I became more interested in the history of magic and magicians.

7. The book is dedicated to Bill Hall, a prominent Fort Wayne businessman and father of a close friend. Bill had eclectic knowledge and taught me a lot about card magic (still my favorite), showing me some tricks that I still use today. Bill introduced me to J. Elder Blackledge, the famous society magician of the 30s and 40s who performed on many occasions in FDR's White House and at fine hotels, supper clubs, and private homes from Chicago to NYC. J.E. let me hang around his magic workshop in Leland, Michigan, where he told me stories of some of his friends, including Okito, Blackstone, Dunninger, Dante, and Bert Allerton—who I saw do the Pump Room Phantasy in Chicago when I was about fifteen. When Blackledge died, he left Bill his collection of magical ephemera, including his collection of playing cards and his original set of Chinese Linking Rings. After Bill's death, his widow, Sally Hall, gave them all to me.

8. Unlike #4 above, the basics of magic are slow to change. Read any fifty-year-old magic book/journal and you are likely to find tricks that are still fooling people today.

9. Magic is making a wonderful comeback, as it seems to do every few generations. A lot of that is due to the great magicians who have headlined in Las Vegas in the last fifteen or so years. I mention some of these artists in the novel; however, I have never met anyone mentioned, and the interaction of them with Gilbert and other characters is simply how I imagined they might respond in this fantasy situation. Go see them; sit back and just be entertained. Don't try to figure things out, just enjoy them. Great magicians offer a wonderful escape from our day-to-day routines and worries.

About the Author

Lawrence Michaelis is a retired cardiac surgeon and hospital/medical administrator. He has been an amateur magician for seventy years.

Made in the USA
Las Vegas, NV
14 October 2021